carrington cove: book two

SOMEONE YOU *deserve*

HARLOW JAMES

Copyright © 2024 by Harlow James

All rights reserved.

No part of this publication may be reproduced, distributed, or transmitted in any form or by any means, including photocopying, recording, or other electronic or mechanical methods, without the prior written permission of the publisher, except as permitted by U.S. copyright law. For permission requests, contact [include publisher/author contact info].

The story, all names, characters, and incidents portrayed in this production are fictitious. No identification with actual persons (living or deceased), places, buildings, and products is intended or should be inferred.

Book Cover by Abigail Davies

Edited by Jenny Ayers (Swift Red Pen)

ISBN: 9798336491814

Contents

Dedication	V
Epigraph	VI
Prologue	1
1. Chapter 1	6
2. Chapter 2	21
3. Chapter 3	21
4. Chapter 4	21
5. Chapter 5	21
6. Chapter 6	21
7. Chapter 7	21
8. Chapter 8	21
9. Chapter 9	21
10. Chapter 10	21
11. Chapter 11	21
12. Chapter 12	21
13. Chapter 13	21
14. Chapter 14	21

15.	Chapter 15	21
16.	Chapter 16	21
17.	Chapter 17	21
18.	Chapter 18	21
19.	Chapter 19	21
20.	Chapter 20	21
21.	Chapter 21	21
22.	Chapter 22	21
	Also By Harlow James	21
	Acknowledgements	21
	Connect with Harlow James	21

To those that have built up walls to keep themselves safe...

I hope you find someone you can trust to help break them down.

You deserve to be loved for exactly who you are, and that means telling the truth about what you want. Don't live your life to make others happy. Find your happiness within yourself.

The most confused we ever get is when we try to convince our heads of something our hearts know is a lie.

Unknown

Prologue

Astrid

Five Years Ago

I lick the frosting from my lips and a satisfied moan escapes me, barely audible over the noise Bentley and Lilly are making in the living room. "Yup. I think those are my best yet." Placing each of the cupcakes carefully in the container for the bake sale tomorrow, I admire my handywork, wondering if I'll ever be able to turn it into something more than a hobby.

It's not always easy to create something sweet and delicious uninterrupted, especially during the day when the kids are home. But when they find a new movie to fixate on, I use that as my opportunity to experiment in the kitchen, creating the perfect mixtures of flavors and textures, eager to see if I can top what I created last.

And I think these lemon raspberry cupcakes with white chocolate frosting and extra slivers of white chocolate on top are one of my best creations yet.

"Are they watching Moana again?" My husband, Brandon, walks through the front door, surveying the chaos of the house before his eyes land on our kids who are glued to the television.

"Uh huh. It's the third time today. I'm pretty sure I have the soundtrack memorized by now."

He drops his bag by the door, kicks off his shoes right beside it, and then heads for the couch, plopping himself down in his usual spot. "Can you grab me a beer, Astrid?"

No "*Please.*"

No "*How was your day?*"

No kiss hello.

I can't even remember the last time he bothered.

Sighing, I close my eyes, take a deep breath, and then reply, "You can get it yourself."

His head whips in my direction. "What?"

"I said you can get it yourself, Brandon."

He eyes me curiously. "Jesus. What crawled up your ass today?"

My jaw tightens as indignation courses through me. "Excuse me?"

He stands from the couch, crossing the living room to meet me on the other side of the island in the kitchen. "I just walked in the door and you already have an attitude."

"I'm sorry. I didn't realize that me telling my husband who's a grown ass adult to get his own damn beer is me having an attitude." I roll my eyes sarcastically. "Forgive me."

The look on his face is one of uncertainty until he casts his gaze over the mess on the counter I've yet to clean up. "So this is why the house is a mess and the kids are being babysat by the tv? You're baking again?"

Irritation bubbles up inside of me like lava ready to erupt from a volcano. "Is that a problem?" I ask instead, wondering where the conversation will go this time.

It's usually one of two avenues, and if he decides to go down the path of self-destruction, I'm not going to hold back tonight.

"Well, I mean, I know the women at the elementary school appreciate your baking, but aren't there more important things you could be doing?"

Yup. Looks like he chose violence.

Slamming the spatula into the bowl and throwing the measuring cups in on top of them, I glare at my husband and say, "You know what? No, Brandon. There aren't more important things for me to be doing because no matter how much I do, none of it is appreciated by you anyhow."

He rolls his eyes as he moves to the fridge. "Oh, great. Here we go again..."

I watch him take out a beer, close the fridge, and then turn back to me. "Is it unacceptable for me to have this one passion that makes me happy?" I hold up my index finger. "One thing that is only for me, and every time I get a chance to spend time on that, you demean it?"

His eyes dart to the cupcakes and then back to me, his brow furrowed. "I don't understand how cupcakes make you happy. It's not like you're going to be on The Next Greatest Baker or something."

Tossing my hands up in the air, I raise my voice now. "And that's the problem! You don't get me at all!"

He lifts his hands in the air as well. "What do you want from me, Astrid? I swear, you're like a different person lately. I go to work every day, make money so we can pay our fucking bills, leave our life for months at a time, and when I come home, you're pissed off at me the second I walk through the door!"

For the past three years, ever since Lilly was born, we've done nothing but drift apart. Each deployment should have made the heart grow fonder, but all they've done is drive a bigger wedge between us. I've never admitted it out loud, but when he's gone, I feel relieved. I feel like I can do what I want when I want without judgment from him.

Brandon has never been controlling or abusive. But he also has never paid attention to my needs—an issue I didn't realize was so glaring until after we had kids.

I guess it's easier when you don't have other people to care for, when all of your attention can be directed at your spouse. And when you've been together as long as we have—since the tender age of seventeen—it's easy to become complacent.

But lately, all I keep asking myself is 'is this it?' Is this how the rest of my life is going to be? Sitting at home, raising our kids and putting my dreams on hold so he can uphold the promise he made to his country? Wondering what version of him I'm going to get when he returns from his next deployment? If our marriage will get better, or just progressively keep getting worse?

I knew what I was signing up for when I married him. I knew this life meant long stretches apart and sacrifices we would both have to make. But when does it stop? When do I get to start living *my* life and chasing after *my* dreams?

I love my kids…but being a mom is not enough.

I want more.

I need more.

And I'm tired of being made to feel like desiring more is unrealistic.

Staring at the man I married, the only man I've ever been with, my first and only love, I relent to my turmoil.

"I'm not happy, Brandon."

He scoffs. "Yeah, I think we've established that."

"No. I mean…I'm not happy with *us*, where we're at." His eyes lock onto mine as I muster up the courage to finally say, "I think…I want a divorce."

Uttering those words feels like letting a bird out of a cage that has been trapped for far too long. They've been in the back of my mind, on the tip of my tongue, but I've never given them life. Not until tonight.

His mouth falls open just slightly. "What?"

"You heard me," I reply. "I can't do this anymore. The fighting, the animosity. I feel like we're always angry with each other and I'm sick of it. I'm sick of feeling invisible."

Our eyes drift over to the kids in the living room, oblivious to the shift in their lives that's happening just in the next room.

"You don't mean it," he whispers.

And even though I can physically feel my heart break, I say, "Yes, I do."

Chapter One

Penn

Present Day

"To Astrid!" My older brother, Dallas, raises his glass and the rest of the crew follows his lead, echoing his sentiment as they do.

"Thank you, Dallas." The apples of Astrid's cheeks turn pink, but I know it's because all the attention is on her. She's not a fan of that, but I also know that in this moment, she fucking deserves it.

"Seriously," he continues, "I'm pissed I'm losing my top waitress, but I'm also so damn happy for you." He pulls his girlfriend, Willow, to his side as she nods her head in agreement. If it weren't for Willow, we wouldn't even be celebrating Astrid tonight. Her arrival in Carrington Cove has done more than just improve my brother's mood over the past two months.

Catch & Release, my brother's restaurant and bar, is packed with employees and friends, closed to the public for Astrid's going away party. As of last week, she is now the proud new owner of the Sunshine Bakery, a Carrington Cove icon. Greg and Jenny, the former owners, opened the doors to the bakery over forty years ago and have made a name for themselves with the townsfolk and tourists. Astrid started working part-time for them about four years ago, just after her husband—and one of my best friends—Brandon died.

That's the thing about living in a small town: everyone knows everyone, and we all show up for each other.

Dallas continues his speech. "Everyone here has been lucky enough to sample your talent each time you brought in your latest creation for us to try. Those days when there were cupcakes in the breakroom, you would have thought there were the winning lotto numbers scratched onto a paper for someone to find." The room fills with laughter and several heads nod. "And now, the entire town of Carrington Cove will be blessed to partake in your treats and talent any time they want. We will miss your smile and energy around here, but now is your time to shine."

Astrid's eyes fill with tears as she mouths, "Thank you."

"To prosperity and good fortune! May your business flourish and the headaches of business ownership be mild!" Dallas calls out once more as the entire bar erupts in cheers and everyone takes a drink of their beverage in hand.

"I told you he was going to make you cry," Willow says as she walks up to Astrid and pulls her in for a hug.

"I swear, I feel like I've cried more in the past week than I have in years." Astrid wipes away a tear from under her eye. "But seriously, Willow. None of this would be happening without your generosity."

"That's not true. You'd make it happen."

"Not likely—unless I had won the lottery."

Willow Marshall is a self-made millionaire and my brother's new girlfriend. A little over two months ago, she unexpectedly inherited a century-old beach house on the coast that had been vacant for years, and she recruited me to do the renovations on it in order to sell it. Well, things got complicated when my brother tried to convince her to sell it to him since he's wanted to buy the place since we were teenagers.

In a twist that further complicated their dynamic, it turned out that the house was actually left to Willow by our father in an attempt to make amends for the past. After a brief battle of wills, Willow and Dallas's intense feelings toward one another blossomed into love and now she's here to stay, which worked out well for Astrid since their friendship also blossomed, and Willow volunteered to be the bakery's silent investor. Brandon's death benefit paid off their house, but on her income and less than stellar credit, she didn't qualify for the business loan on her own.

"Doesn't matter. Now, you have the ability to make it exactly what you want. Have you thought any more about what changes you want to make?" Willow asks, taking a sip from her martini.

Astrid's eyes drift over to me for the first time in a while. And just like every other time our eyes meet, I wait with bated breath for what she's going to say. "Actually, I have some ideas. And I wanted to talk to *you* about them." She points at me playfully with one eye closed.

"Me?"

The corner of her mouth lifts. "Yeah. Word on the street is you're still the resident handyman around town. Or did that change in the last day or so?"

That's right. I'm the guy everyone calls when something needs to be fixed or built.

Penn Sheppard, the Carrington Cove handyman.

The guy who helps everyone when they need it.

I guess I took after my father in that regard. And my specialty is helping Astrid, especially since Brandon died.

"Not that I'm aware of," I reply, watching Astrid's shoulders fall but her lips lift up.

Willow grasps her arm. "I'm going to let you two talk. I'll catch up with you in a bit."

"Okay." Astrid watches Willow walk away and then she turns back to me. "Do you want a refill?" She gestures to the nearly empty glass of beer in my hand.

"Yeah, but I can get it. Remember, you're not a waitress anymore."

She chuckles, tucking a strand on her long, chestnut hair behind her ear. It's such a simple move, but it still unnerves me every time. "Old habits die hard."

"You'll get used to it." I stand from my stool, round the bar, pull the tap on the lager I've been drinking, and fill my glass before rejoining her on the other side of the bar again. "So, what's on your mind?"

She blows out a breath and says, "I want to do some renovations at the bakery."

I nod, taking a big drink of my beer. "I figured."

"I know the place is a landmark, but it's in desperate need of a face lift. New paint, new floors, new décor, and a new display case in the front, for starters."

"You might have to shut the doors for a few days to get that done, but if I do stuff at night we could possibly avoid it."

She nods. "I'm aware, but I know it will be worth it. I can still fill orders for the Cove Inn and other offices around town from the kitchen, but I want a clean slate. I want a fresh start so the place feels more like mine."

"It is yours, Astrid."

Her smile is slow and soft but completely breathtaking. And with a crinkle in her nose, she whispers, "It is, isn't it?"

I can't help but smile back at her. "It is."

"What are you two grinning about?" Dallas strides up to us, taking a sip from his own beer.

"Penn is gonna help me renovate the bakery," Astrid answers, glancing up at him now.

"Like there's anyone better for the job." Dallas huffs out a laugh.

"I know, but it's going to be a lot of work."

Dallas leans toward Astrid. "You do realize he just renovated an entire house for Willow, right?"

"Yes, I'm aware. But I also know he's busy…"

"I'm never too busy to help you, Astrid," I say, cutting her off.

"I just hate to ask you for *another* favor…"

"It's not a favor. I want to help," I declare adamantly. "You know I'd do anything for you."

She reaches over and grabs my hand, squeezing it. "Yeah, I do. I can always depend on you, Penn. You're such a good friend and I'm so lucky to have you in my life."

Do you see that knife she just plunged into my chest? Yeah, doesn't feel so good.

"You're such a good friend."

That's me.

Mr. Dependable.

The king of the friend zone—a place I never wanted to be but reluctantly found myself the president of after one drunken night three years ago. I was just a *friend* before *that* night. But before then, that word didn't hold the same type of meaning.

It's just as well though. The last thing I need is to draw attention to myself by pursuing the widow of my best friend, an issue I never would have predicted having.

Astrid was Brandon's wife. They had been together since we were teenagers. We all grew up together and were as thick as thieves. I stood as the best man in their wedding, I'm the godfather to their kids, and I've been there through every milestone and crisis.

The two of them were so in love, the quintessential family that everyone strives for. Brandon would brag about his life every chance he got, especially to me. And I always envied the life he had with Astrid, one of the most amazing women I've ever known and someone I'm lucky enough to call my friend, too.

And I never thought about her otherwise until a few months before *that* night—the night that everything changed.

"Proud to wear the title," I mutter, trying to hide the irritation that word evokes in me. But my brother catches it, smirking in my direction.

"Great. Well, maybe when you come over this week for game night, we can talk about it more?" She blinks a few times, tilting her head at me as she waits for me to respond.

Every week I spend one evening over at her house playing games with the kids. Bentley is eleven now, and Lilly is seven. It's a tradition I started with them after Brandon died. My entire family grew up playing board games together, and I wanted to help them have that same sense of togetherness. After losing my dad this year, I understand the absence that creates even more now.

"Sounds like a plan."

"Astrid!" Brian, the other manager of the restaurant, calls out to her. "Get your ass over here! We're taking shots!"

"Ugh. I really don't want to be hungover tomorrow," she whispers.

"One won't kill you," Dallas chimes in. "After that, use the vodka bottle full of water under the bar and pour your own if they keep pressuring you to take more." He winks at her.

Dallas learned from the previous owner to keep a dummy bottle of alcohol for those patrons that just didn't know when to stop. Pouring them shots of water never gets old, especially when they act like it tastes bad or burns going down.

Fucking funny as hell.

Grinning, she stands from her stool and smooths down her light pink top, the one that offers the perfect sliver of her cleavage. It's a favorite of mine. "Perfect. See you boys later."

The two of us watch her walk away before Dallas slides onto the stool she just vacated. "You're such a good *friend*," he says in a feminine voice, imitating Astrid from before.

Glaring at him, I bark out, "Shut the fuck up."

"I can't. It's in the older brother by-laws that I must give you shit about your unrequited crush every hour, on the hour. And getting a front row seat to your misery is just icing on the cake."

"You're a dick."

"Yes, I can be." Dallas grows serious now, slipping into his concerned, big brother role. "But I also just hate seeing you hung up on her like this."

I shrug. "It is what it is."

"It doesn't have to be, man."

I pin him with my eyes. "Yes, it does. I'm tired of having this fucking argument with you. Just drop it."

He holds his palms up. "Fine. I'll drop it, especially since this is her night and I don't want to ruin it. But I hate seeing you waste time not going after what you want. It's been four years, Penn…"

"You think I don't fucking know that?" I cut him off, tired of having this same conversation with him over and over again.

For the past year especially, Dallas has made it a mission to give me shit about my feelings for Astrid. I guess I thought I was better at hiding it than I was, and then a few weeks ago, I made the mistake of telling him that I had my shot with her three years ago and she said no. Now he really won't let it go.

"Just because you're happy and in love now doesn't mean you have the responsibility to help other people get there, okay?"

He studies me over the rim of his glass as he takes a drink of his beer and grows serious, the teasing lilt in his voice gone. "No, but if the past couple of months have taught me anything, it's that life's fucking short and ruminating on shit that we have no control over doesn't solve anything. All it does is force us to waste time we could spend being happy."

Our father died eight months ago now, and his death hit my older brother the hardest. Their relationship was tumultuous at best since my father, a retired Marine, never approved of my brother enlisting in the Marines himself. He wanted to save him from the guilt and horror that serving could wreak on his mind, but Dallas didn't listen. Even up until our dad died, he and Dallas had animosity between them. It wasn't until Willow entered Dallas's life and he was forced to face the truth behind our dad's strong opinions that he finally found some peace.

I'm relieved he has because, as much as I hate that he's hell-bent on being so involved in my life, I do it right back to him. It was time he started letting go of the anger and guilt he carried around. And Willow finally helped him do that.

But facing my own demons?

Yeah…I don't have time for that shit.

"Things between us work. There's no sense in messing with that," I counter, feeling like I'm defending my friendship with Astrid like always.

Dallas scoffs. "Yeah, I thought things were working in my life, too. And then Willow stormed in and showed me what I've been missing."

"You talkin' about me?" The woman in question slides in next to my brother as his arm wraps around her waist.

He stares up at her from the stool, lovesick and fucking beaming. It's sickening, really. "Maybe, Goose," he replies, using the nickname he gave her shortly after she arrived in town and established a war with the geese that were out to get her.

"Good things?"

"Just how you've managed to make rainbows shoot out of his ass," I answer before he can.

Willow snorts. "Oh, Jesus. I take it Dallas has pissed you off already this evening?"

"Naturally."

"Penn is just sulking like normal. He's mad because I keep telling him to make a move with…"

"That's enough." I cut him off, standing from my chair and draining the rest of my beer. My phone vibrates in my pocket, and when I take it out to see who's calling, my pulse spikes. "Fuck, I've got to take this."

"Secret girlfriend?" Willow teases.

"Like I have time for that," I grate out, sending the call to voicemail so I can call back in a minute.

"Nope, all of his free time is held for Astrid, remember?" Dallas croons, drawing Willow closer to his chest.

Willow swats at him. "Oh, stop. Penn, don't listen to your brother. I get it."

"Get what?" I ask, eyeing her skeptically.

"Why you don't cross the line."

"Cross the line?" Dallas interjects. "He's so far away from the line that he can't even *see* the line. Hell, the line is a dot to him."

Willow arches her brow at him. "Was that your attempt at a *Friends* reference, babe?"

Dallas grins. "Yeah, Goose. How'd I do?"

"Well, you didn't quite use it in the right context, but I appreciate the effort." Willow kisses his lips and then turns back to me. "We've been bingeing the series together because I make references to it and your brother has no idea what I'm saying."

"Sounds exciting," I say sarcastically.

Willow rolls her eyes at me. "It's the best show ever, and just because you can't appreciate it, doesn't mean you should yuck someone else's yum, Penn." I chuckle silently as her gaze softens. "Astrid has been through a lot, and she's about to take on an entirely new level of responsibility of owning a business," she says, returning to the topic from before, even though I was hoping she would leave it alone. Looks like I'm not that lucky. "Just continue to be there for her the way you've always been. She appreciates you, you know."

Sighing, I nod. "Yeah, I know. Look, I've got to go. Make sure she gets home all right?" I say to Willow, standing from my stool.

"I will."

With a parting jut of my chin, I head for the front door, but get stopped by Mrs. Hansen before I can leave.

"Penn!" she calls after me.

I spin around to face her. "What's up, Mrs. Hansen?"

"I was wondering if you could stay later at the hardware store tomorrow?" she asks, batting her eyelashes at me. Elizabeth Hansen is older than my mother, so when she does this, I just get creeped out. But she's my boss, so I hold in my reaction.

"Well, I have plans on Tuesdays..."

"I know, but Harold has a doctor's appointment and he can't drive himself afterward. He has to get his eyes dilated."

Sighing, I agree. After all, it's not like she can help that. And this is what I do. I help people when they need something. "Sure, Mrs. Hansen. I can stay late."

"Thank you, Penn. Also, there's a new load of lumber that's coming in tomorrow that I'm going to need your help with too."

"What about Vince?" I ask, referring to another employee who usually handles the outdoor area of the store.

"He hurt his back. Won't be in for a few days."

Shit. Between him and me, we usually handle the heavy lifting around the store, but without him, that means I'll be the one that will take the brunt of the physical labor.

Nothing I can't handle, but still.

"Okay. We'll get it done. But you might want to think about hiring someone new," I tell her.

"Oh. Yeah. I know." She turns away from me, avoiding my eyes. "I'll see you tomorrow morning, Penn," she says before walking away, back to Astrid's party.

With one last parting glance, I push through the door of the restaurant and head straight out to my truck before I can get stopped again. The sun is almost past the horizon in the distance, leading to nightfall. Carrington Cove sits right on the coast in North Carolina, and the view of the ocean I've seen for my entire life never gets old. Turquoise and dark blue waves crash onto the white sandy beaches, the last remaining daylight reflecting off the water in the distance. Streetlights and neon signs begin illuminating the coast, and the Ferris wheel on the pier shines brightly against the purple and navy sky.

And as I drive, I hope that I don't run out of daylight before I can arrive at the place that may be my own little venture in the near future.

***

"They accepted your offer, Penn." Pam from Cove Real Estate smiles at me as I walk through the house.

"I can't believe it." I don't think the reality has hit me yet, but as I walk around the space and make a mental list of everything that needs to be fixed, I'm sure it will feel real the second I start pouring money into the place. It's a good thing they took twenty thousand less than the asking price.

"Well, money isn't everyone's top priority. Tom and his wife knew you'd take care of the house, and I may have put in a good word for you as well."

I spin to face her. "You didn't have to do that, Pam."

She lays her hand on my shoulder, our height difference making the gesture difficult. At six foot five, I'm taller than most everybody, so I'm used to it. "I know I didn't, but you deserve this."

Hearing those words from her only feeds into the anxiety brewing in my chest. For years, I've had this idea of flipping houses and turning them into vacation rentals for tourists in our town. The Cove Inn only has so many rooms, which means many out-of-towners end up staying in the handful of rentals in town or finding accommodations in nearby towns instead. It robs Carrington Cove of more revenue, and that's revenue that I saw as an opportunity for a business, especially since I know just about everything about maintaining and owning a home. And now that this house is in escrow, it seems like I finally have a chance to make something of that beyond my reputation as the local hardware store handyman.

But the threat of failure is still lurking under the surface.

"Thanks, Pam."

"Not a problem. Since we opted for a fast escrow, the keys will be yours by Friday. Tom was eager to get out from under the mortgage."

"Damn. This is really happening, isn't it?" I mutter mostly to myself. Friday is only five days away.

"It is. How long do you think it will be before the place is ready? You know I have clients that I can send your way." Pam owns the real estate office in town, and she also runs the travel agency with her husband. When I told her about my plan, she was the first one to encourage me to go after it and introduced me to Tom and his wife before they even listed the house on the market.

"Well, I'm doing the bulk of the work myself, so I'm not sure, honestly. Between working at the restaurant and hardware store, and now helping Astrid renovate the bakery…" My eyes cast over the house again. "Maybe a couple of months as long as the weather cooperates?"

She nods, happy with my answer. "That sounds reasonable. It's the off-season anyway. Winter is coming, so take your time. But if you could have it ready to go by March, that would be ideal so we can book for the spring break crowd."

"I should be able to make that happen." *That is if I don't go bankrupt first.*

One day at a time, Penn. That's what you promised yourself, remember?

She pats me on the shoulder once more. "Well, I'll call you when I can officially hand over the keys, but I wanted to bring you by in person so you could get an idea of what you're working with."

I've driven by this house for most of my life, but I'd never seen the inside. Pam showed me pictures when she called with the information of the listing, and I put in an offer without seeing the place in person. I couldn't pass on the opportunity and the price was right.

All these years I'd been putting off pulling the trigger on this venture, worried about timing, not having enough money, and what people might think. So, even though I'm finally taking a chance, I'm keeping this piece of information close to the vest right now. I don't need anyone's input and pressure to make this work. I don't want people inserting themselves into my business. And if worst comes to worst and things don't pan out the way I want them to, I could totally live in this place. It would beat the two-bedroom house I snatched up years ago and have called home ever since—a place that I could rent out right now for income if I needed to while I worked on this one. I don't mind living in a construction zone. I've done it before.

"I appreciate that. And, as we discussed, please keep this to yourself, okay?"

She eyes me curiously. "I will, but you should be proud, Penn. You've made a sound investment. That should be celebrated."

"It will be, but now's not the right time. I want to make sure everything is perfect before I let people know what I'm up to."

She huffs out a laugh. "News flash, honey. Owning a business is a lot like having a kid. No one is ever really ready, but you just have to have faith that you'll figure it out as you go. And you know how this town can be. Secrets don't stay secrets for long."

Faith.

That's the one thing that's been missing, the reason why I've been waiting until now.

Do I have faith in myself to make this business successful? I want to believe that I do.

But being a leader? Being a pioneer or the one in charge? That was always more of Dallas's role.

And what would my dad think? He was always the one that was about helping others, donating his time volunteering at the Veteran's Center in town after he was honorably discharged from the Marines when I was a kid. I swear, any Marine in or near our town knew who he was. While my brother was traveling around the world serving his country, my dad taught me to be someone others could depend on, a man who stood by his word because that would be what I was judged upon someday.

But I liked blending into the background.

Even Parker, my younger brother, shot for the stars, academically inclined and steadfast about pursuing a career as a veterinarian.

Hazel, my younger sister, took her passion for photography and turned it into a business.

I'm the Sheppard sibling that always blended into the background. Hence why I help out at Dallas's restaurant, and at the hardware store with Mrs. Hansen, and anywhere else around town where I'm needed.

It's just been easier that way—less responsibility, less pressure, less to answer for when something goes wrong, but I could be there for people the way my father taught me to be.

I was rarely the one in trouble at home, unless I fed into one of Dallas's not-so-bright ideas. My parents didn't hover over me like the others, and I realized early on that if I didn't do much to garner attention, it stayed that way.

But now? Sitting on the sidelines doesn't hold the same appeal. Losing my father eight months ago was a wake-up call that I need to start living my life.

Except there's no one else to blame if this goes south.

But it's time for me to put my neck on the line—for myself, and my future.

I've always wanted more, and even though I'd never admit it to him, Dallas is right.

The time is now.

So I'm taking my chance.

Too bad I don't have the guts to do that in other aspects of my life.

Chapter Two

Astrid

"I'm home! I'm home! Sorry I'm late." Scrambling through the front door, I drop my purse right in the entry way and rush toward the kitchen.

"Calm down. Everything is fine." My mother brushes her hair over her shoulder as she takes dinner out of the oven. "I was running behind on dinner anyway."

Sighing, I take a moment to catch my breath and then pour myself a glass of water from the fridge, draining it quickly. "I lost track of time and then started panicking when I saw the clock."

"You had a good day then?"

"I did," I say, just as my mother turns to me. "I think I've narrowed down the menu."

"Well, that's amazing, Astrid." She turns off the oven and reaches for plates from the cupboard. "I hope you kept the lemon raspberry cupcake on there. You know that's my favorite."

Smiling, I move to gather utensils and set the table. "I did. I knew you'd disown me if I didn't, and I kind of need your help with my children still."

She chuckles. "Good to know that I have the ability to sway your menu selections. I'll keep that in mind for later." Then she calls over her shoulder, "Bentley! Lilly! Mom's home!"

Lilly comes barreling down the hallway, slamming into my legs. "Mommy!"

"Hi, sweet girl." I kiss the top of her head. "How was your day?"

"Ugh. Addison told me my dress was ugly, so I told her that her hair was stupid."

Rolling my eyes, I reply, "You shouldn't say that to her."

"Why? She started it."

"Yes, but you saying something back to her like that only makes you as mean as she is."

"Addison deserves it. She's a spoiled, rotten brat." Bentley enters the room with much less enthusiasm than his little sister. And even though I don't condone my kids calling other kids names, it's nice to know that he stands up for his sister when it counts.

"Hey, bud." I pull him forward and kiss the top of his head as well, but he moves away from me as quickly as he can. "How was your day?"

"It was fine."

Yup. That's all I get. If eleven is any indication of what the teen years are going to be like, I hope God helps us all.

"Did Grandma make enchiladas?" Bentley asks, peering over the counter at the pan on the stove.

"I sure did."

"Heck yes!"

"I hate enchiladas!" Lilly whines right on schedule. It wouldn't be dinnertime without one kid liking what is being served, and the other one hating it.

"I made you a quesadilla, Lilly Bear," my mother croons, feeding into her demands. "But you know the rule. You must try at least one bite of what I made."

"I don't want to..."

"Lilly. That's enough," I scold, moving toward the table with plates full of food. "You'll try a bite and that is that."

I swear, I don't know what I would do without my mother, especially during these past four years. Before Brandon died, I was basically running a household by myself anyway, but when I had to start working two jobs just so we could survive, she helped fill in where she could. As a recently retired nurse, she says she's happy to spend the time with the kids and keep herself busy, but sometimes I wonder if I ask too much of her.

Still, when I told her I wanted to buy the bakery, she was the first person who encouraged me to do it.

"You deserve this, Astrid. As a mother, it's important to have something just for you, something that feeds your soul separate from your children. They grow up to be their own human beings, and you need to have a life to live that's outside of them when they do. I wish I could have done more of that when you and Grady were younger, but you have the chance now, so you'd better take it."

"Fine," Lilly relents as we all sit down and begin eating.

"You need to make sure that you eat a good dinner because Uncle Penn will be here soon for game night, and you know he always brings candy."

That makes her eyes light up again. "Yay!"

"Aw, man. I was going to play my video game again after dinner," Bentley whines.

"Well, your game can wait."

My mother eyes me across the table. "Do you know what game you'll be playing tonight?" she asks me.

"Uno!" Lilly shouts. "Can we please play Uno?"

"Ugh, that game is for babies." Bentley drops his fork to his plate in protest.

"It is not! It's fun!"

I pinch the bridge of my nose. "Please stop, you two. I just got home and the last thing I want to do is listen to the two of you fight."

"I swear, they save it for you," my mother says, grinning in her chair as she holds her glass of water in front of her.

"Of course they do."

On the nights when I come home late from work, my mother picks up the kids from school and cooks dinner for us. She always eats with us before heading back to her quiet house. My father left when I was little, so it was just her, me, and Grady, my older brother, growing up. She's dated here and there, but no man ever really stuck. I think she had a hard time letting another man in after my dad left her all alone with two small children.

But selfishly, I'm glad I have her to relate to all the tribulations of being a single mom because she knows what it's like firsthand.

The doorbell rings, and Lilly bolts from her chair and runs to the door, swinging it open. "Uncle Penn!" She lunges for him as soon as he crosses the threshold.

"Hey, Lilly Bear." He scoops her up in his arms, lifting her as if she weighs nothing. With the way his muscles bulge under the sleeves of his shirt, I can see why it's so easy for him.

Ugh. Stop looking at his muscles, Astrid.

"You ready to play a game?"

"Can we play Uno? Please?"

He bops her on the nose before setting her back down. "I think that's a great idea."

"Yay!" She runs back to the table and stands right next to Bentley, leaning into his space. "We're gonna play Uno, Bentley. Ha, ha!"

"Lilly!" I admonish. "Don't start trouble. Now go get in the shower first before we play the game. You know the rules."

She races to the bathroom, granting me a moment to gather my sanity again before I stand and greet Penn. "Hey, there."

One of his hands is holding a bag filled with something, but he shoves his free hand in his jeans. "Hey."

God, he's so tall. Seriously, it never fails to amaze me just how big of a man he is—and strong, dependable, stoic, but not afraid to speak up when it counts.

Jesus, you're doing it again, Astrid. Stop ogling him in front of your mother, for crying out loud.

My mom chooses that moment to clear her throat. "Hi, Penn. Good to see you."

"Hey, Melissa. Did you make enchiladas?" Penn sniffs the air dramatically.

My mother chuckles. "I sure did, and there are plenty left over. Help yourself."

"Awesome. I didn't eat yet."

"You know there's always a spot reserved for you here," I say because it's the truth. If there's one other person on this planet that helps keep my world spinning besides my mom, it's this man right here.

He's the rock I never had, and the one I can't afford to lose.

"Today was crazy, and I didn't want to be late getting over here." My mother fixes him a hefty plate as he takes a seat at the table. "Thanks."

"Bentley, go get ready to get in the shower after your sister," I say, glancing at the clock. Our game night won't be a long one tonight since it's already after seven.

"Fine." He clears his plate and then scurries down the hall.

"Well, I'm gonna get out of your hair," my mother declares as Penn scarfs down his food and I start cleaning up the kitchen.

"Thanks, Mom. I'll see you tomorrow?" Once I get a solid schedule down at the bakery, I probably will only need my mom early in the mornings. Owning a bakery means rising before the sun most days so the baked goods are ready by six as people stop by on their way to work.

"Yup." She kisses me on the cheek. "Have a good night, sweetie. And you too, Penn."

Penn waves at her until he finishes chewing. "Thanks for dinner, Melissa."

She winks at him. "My pleasure."

After the door shuts behind her, I sigh as I make my way back over to the kitchen, turning the faucet on to wash the sink full of dishes. When my mother cooks, I clean. It's the least I can do.

"So, busy day?"

Penn nods as he shovels his last bite in his mouth. "Extremely. I had to help Dallas at the restaurant during the lunch rush, and then I headed out to a project I just started working on."

"What kind of project?" I ask, eyeing him over my shoulder.

He shrugs, avoiding my eyes. "It's nothing. Just something to pay the bills."

As I place the last clean dish in the rack on the counter, I say, "Well, I've got another project we need to discuss, too."

Penn grins. "I'm ready." He wipes the corner of his mouth, brings his plate to the sink, and takes the sponge from my hands, cleaning his own dish before placing it into the rack with the others.

God, he washes his own dishes. Why is that so freaking hot?

Once he's done, he brushes past me, our arms touching as he walks by, and takes a notepad from the bag that he brought with him, along with a pen. "Oh, but before I forget." He takes out a brand-new bag of Hershey Kisses, heads over to the glass vase on the small table by the front door, rips open the plastic, and pours in the candy until the vase is full once more.

"Penn...you don't have to keep doing that," I say, watching him as he empties the contents, careful not to spill them all over the floor.

"Yes, I do, Astrid."

"Bentley already knows that you fill it up. Lilly will realize soon too, you know…"

He lifts his head and his eyes meet mine. "Well, until she does, I'm going to keep that smile on her face for as long as I can."

If I didn't already have feelings for this man, that would have sealed it right there.

I know what you're thinking.

"Your husband is dead, and you're lusting after his best friend? That's some daytime soap opera shit right there."

But in my defense, these feelings weren't always there. In fact, I never felt like this about Penn until *after* my husband died, and almost a year later at that.

And did I do anything about it? Absolutely not. I stopped it from going anywhere, and with good reason.

But sometimes I wonder what would have happened *that* night if I hadn't stopped it.

The truth is that back then, my head was a mess. It had only been a year since I lost my husband, I was a single mom, and I was still trying to find our new normal.

And it's Penn.

He's...my *friend*. Has been since we were kids.

But that was three years ago, and even though I hoped those glimmers of feelings would go away, they never did. Actually, they've only amplified over time. And lately, I feel like this thin thread between us is only one tug away from snapping.

But when he does things like this? Fill up the "Kisses from Daddy" vase that I started during Brandon's first deployment after Bentley was born—it makes it harder to argue with both my body and my heart.

"Now." Penn walks back over to the table, grabs his pen and notepad, and takes the same seat as before. "Tell me what you were thinking."

"I want something fresh and clean. White and pink. I know the place is called the Sunshine Bakery, but I'm over all the yellow. A little is okay, but it needs to be dialed down for sure."

He scribbles notes. "Okay. Do you want to change the name too, then?"

I nod. "Yes, but I haven't landed on the winner yet."

"Let me know when you do, and we'll get a sign made for you too. As for the floors, we could bring in gray and white checkered floors for contrast, but I can work with pink and white. Chrome details on the case then?"

I ponder his suggestion. "I think so. The case is so old, so it needs to be brought up to modern times."

"I agree. What about the back of the house? The kitchen?"

"Greg and Jenny just replaced a few of the pieces of equipment, so I should be good there. But the storage area could use a makeover, something more organized. Maybe some more shelves?"

He nods, scratching down more notes. "Got it."

"How long do you think it will take?"

"A couple of weeks, but I can replace the floor and things like that at night so you don't have to close the front doors the entire time. I was thinking about that today actually."

"You're willing to work at night?" I say, surprised by the suggestion.

"Yeah, it'd be easier since I wouldn't have to worry about moving around you or any of the other employees." My staff consists of me and three other employees, so it's not like there's a soccer team to dance around.

"But when will you sleep?" I tease him.

"Sleep is overrated. Besides, I don't mind missing some shuteye for something like this."

I reach over and place my hand on top of his, the heat of our skin touching traveling all the way up my arm. "You're the best, Penn. You know that, right?"

His eyes drop to my hand. "So I've been told."

"Mommy!" Lilly exclaims as she enters the room. I retract my hand from Penn's as if we'd just been caught doing something we shouldn't—which is preposterous—and then twist to find my beautiful daughter with soaking wet hair, dressed in her pajamas.

"What's up, baby?"

"Can I have kisses from Daddy now before we play our game?"

I nod, swallowing down the lump in my throat that forms each time she asks for the chocolate so innocently. I hate that her memories of Brandon are so few. I think she loves the idea of him more than the actual time she can remember spending with him. He was gone on deployment almost half of her life up until he died.

"I love chocolate," she mumbles around the first piece as she climbs into her chair, resting on her knees so she can reach the table.

Penn replies, "Just like your mom. In fact, I brought a special chocolate to share with her tonight."

"Really?" I say, arching my brow at Penn.

He returns the gesture. "Yup." Reaching into his bag, he takes out two Ferrero Rocher, the individually wrapped ones, and hands me one like he's making a drug deal. And in a way, he might as well be. Penn knows these are my favorite decadent treat.

"Oh, you know me so well." I take the chocolate from him, unwrap it, and pop it into my mouth.

Staring intently at me with eye contact that is borderline unnerving, he says, "I do, Astrid."

Our eyes remain locked on one another, until Lilly breaks the moment. "I wanna play Uno!"

Snapping myself out of the electrically charged eye contact, I turn to her and smile. "Okay. Let's play, baby." I call over my shoulder, "Bentley! Get out here!"

Once we're all settled, the blood bath begins. Call me unorthodox, but I take pride in the fact that both of my children are turning out to be highly competitive. We're still working on graciously losing, but for the most part, their competitive nature is alive and well. They're learning to be strategic, think ahead, and problem solve. It's one of the best side effects of our game nights.

The ultimate repercussion though is the time we spend together, and the time that Penn gives us.

After Lilly calls Uno, Penn slaps her with a reverse card. "Aw, man!"

Penn chuckles as the order moves backward around the table. "Should have seen that coming, Lilly Bear."

Bentley laughs and changes the color, which works out perfectly for me as I lay down another reverse card, skipping Lilly for a second time.

"That's not fair, Mommy!"

Laughing, I say, "Life isn't fair, baby girl. Better you learn that now."

Penn and I successfully reverse the order two more times as Lilly grows beet red with frustration, then he slaps her with a draw four and you'd think the world was ending.

"Hey." I place my hand on her arm, signaling her to breathe. "It's just a game."

"But I want to win!" Her bottom lip trembles and her eyes fill with tears.

"Sometimes you have to play a few rounds before you can win, Lilly Bear," Penn says as he lays down his card, eyeing me across the table, his words feeling like they have a double meaning.

Lilly huffs and rearranges her cards in her tiny hands.

"I bet she still wins," Bentley grumbles as the game continues, and in less than five minutes, Lilly is crowned the winner.

"I won! I won!" She fist pumps the air as she does laps around the living room, making Penn and me laugh and Bentley roll his eyes, a reluctant smile on his face.

"Yes, you won. Now, it's time to get ready for bed." I glance at the clock on the microwave.

"Aw, man," Lilly grumbles as she and Bentley head toward the bathroom to brush their teeth.

"That one is going to be a force to be reckoned with," Penn says, standing from his chair and stretching his arms above his head, giving me a glimpse of the sliver of skin between his shirt and the top of his jeans. That little happy trail I've seen a time or two always makes my thighs clench together.

God, it's been too long since I've had sex.

"You don't have to remind me."

"She's gonna be strong and fiery, just like her mother." He glances at me over his shoulder as he begins cleaning up the cards.

"Ha. I don't know about that. She's got more moxie in that little body than I'll ever have."

Penn drops the cards on the table, turns, and closes the distance between us so fast I nearly fall over as he grips my chin, lifting my face so our eyes can connect. I can hear my heart in my ears and suddenly breathing feels like a monumental task. "You have no idea how strong you are, Astrid. That little girl couldn't ask for a better example of a mom. You've turned a shitty hand of cards into something incredible—without any reverse cards in the pile." He gives me a reassuring grin as his eyes bounce back and forth between mine, and I have to remind myself to breathe. "Don't doubt your strength for a second. You hear me?" All I can manage is a nod. "Good. Now, I'm beat, and I have a bakery to tear apart tomorrow." The corner of his mouth lifts as he releases my chin and steps away, robbing me of his warmth and the confidence he instills in me with his words.

I've never felt that from a man. My father left when I was so little, I don't even remember him. And with Brandon, the only man I've ever been with, I felt so alone, blending into the background, a trophy for him to have on his arm, not a partner he was proud of.

Penn makes me feel like I'm front and center stage.

It's unnerving and relentless, and it makes me want things I know I can't have.

"You want to start tomorrow?" I ask, pulling my thoughts back to our conversation.

"If that's okay, yeah. The sooner the better. I can work there during the day until I do the floors and that leaves me the afternoon to work on my other projects."

"How are you gonna manage this all? The restaurant, the hardware store, the bakery, and your top-secret project." He grins. "Seriously, you're never this cryptic. Why won't you tell me what you're working on?"

His smile fades and then he moves back to the table, gathering his things and shoving them into the bag. "It's nothing."

"Doesn't seem like it."

"I said it's nothing, Astrid. Okay?" His words are clipped and final.

His tone honestly takes me aback for a moment, but I nod and say softly, "Okay. I'm—I'm sorry."

He pinches the bridge of his nose. "No, I'm sorry. It's just...I just don't want to talk about it yet, okay? I'll tell you when it's the right time. I promise."

I nod again. "Okay."

"Uncle Penn, will you tuck me in?" Lilly calls from her bed, offering a reprieve from the tension building between us in the dining room.

Penn draws in a deep breath and calls back, "Yeah, Lilly Bear. Be right there." His eyes meet mine once more. "Duty calls."

"You don't have to do that, you know."

"I know, but it's what Brandon would have done. And since he can't, it's the least I can do."

As I watch him walk down the hall, my heart twists in my chest again. If only Penn knew how little Brandon really helped around here. He merely kissed the kids good night from his seat on the couch most nights while I made sure they had their favorite blankets, their nightlights were plugged in, and their sound machines were turned on. I'm the one that assured them there were no monsters under their beds or in their closets. And I'm the one that got all of the "I love you's" right before they drifted off to sleep.

Penn might think he's doing what Brandon would have done.

But the truth is, he's always done more.

And that's something I don't ever want him to know.

That's why I never crossed that line, and why I pushed him away when I could have taken what we both wanted—because the man Penn has been in our lives is more than we've ever had, and the last thing I want is for the three of us to lose him forever too.

***

Three Years Ago

"I can't believe it's been a year," Penn slurs, reaching for the bottle of tequila again, pouring two shots and handing me one.

"You've already said that."

"But it's true. One fucking year, Astrid. One year that my best friend hasn't been on this earth." His eyes are bloodshot as he stares at me. "I still can't fucking believe it."

I think this is our fifth shot, but honestly, I haven't been keeping track.

Tears well in my eyes again as I toss the shot of alcohol back and wince as it goes down. "One year of my kids not having their dad."

I think that's the part that cuts the deepest—all the things they'll miss out on because he's not here.

Of course I'm sad. I lost my husband. But the truth is, I lost him long before he ever left this world.

It wasn't supposed to be like this. He was supposed to come home. We were supposed to go through with the divorce and co-parent. He still would have been here for soccer games and dance recitals. He still would have seen them on Christmas and their birthdays.

Selfishly, I was looking forward to the time for myself, the ability to focus on my dreams and aspirations without him mocking me about it and me having to listen to him. I had planned trips I wanted to take by myself, work I would have time to do on my thoughts, and just finally having space to breathe.

Our relationship may have been over, but his relationship with his kids was still supposed to survive. In fact, I was hoping it would get stronger since his limited time with them would be even more precious.

But we never got the chance to make that work.

"I'll be there for them, Astrid. I promise." Penn grabs my hand, bringing it to his lips and kissing the back of it. It may just be the tequila, but his touch and the softness of his lips warm my entire body from head to toe, the strongest heat pooling between my legs.

That's been happening more lately—each time we touch, each time he hugs me or holds me while I cry—my body has the most visceral reaction to it.

The night that he came over and cooked us dinner and forced me to take an hour-long bath after I'd had a horrible week was the night I started to see him differently—and I think it was because he showed up for *me* and took care of *me* in a way that no one else ever had.

"I know you will," I whisper.

"And I'll be there for you too." He kisses my hand again, and then places another one on my wrist. "Whatever you need."

My body instinctively starts to lean forward. "You already have been." He shakes his head, pulling me into his chest and wrapping his arm around me now. I feel safe, protected, and dare I say...treasured. "I wouldn't have survived the last year without you, Penn."

"Yes, you would have because you're incredible, Astrid. Strong, resilient, and brave. But I'm glad I could be here for you and the kids. It makes me feel like I'm at least doing *something* when honestly, I just feel fucking helpless. I can't take away your pain. I can't bring him back..."

Breathing him in, I clutch his flannel and bury my face in his neck. He smells of sandalwood and pine, with a hint of sweat that only enhances his natural scent. He smells like a man, and my body is aching for more.

But it's Penn. I can't go there. It's wrong—so very wrong.

But god, I bet it would feel so right.

It's just the alcohol talking, Astrid. Tequila makes people want to take their clothes off, remember? There's even a song that says so.

I lift my head so our eyes can meet. "You've done more than I can ever thank you for." Brushing his hair from his face, I swear I hear him take in a sharp breath of air, and then his grip on my waist tightens. "When the roof had that leak, you fixed it the next day. When the air went low on my tires, you took them to the garage to fill them up. On the days when I left Catch & Release utterly exhausted, you brought pizza for dinner and entertained the kids because you knew I just didn't have the energy to do so." My eyes dip down to his lips. "You've done more for me than anyone ever has."

I watch his gaze drop to my mouth now just as his tongue darts out to wet his bottom lip. "I wanted to. I *had* to. I couldn't stand the thought of you being alone, or feeling like you have to do this on your own."

"I'm never alone when you're here."

"Astrid," he whispers, his eyes bouncing between my mouth and my eyes. "Do you ever feel..." He pauses. "Do you ever think about..."

"What?" I breathe out, my heart hammering wildly.

Penn reaches up and strokes the side of my face, a pinch in his brow hinting at the battle he's fighting in his mind.

I can feel his breath on my lips, smell the tequila on both of us, and feel the effects of it all over my body.

But then I concentrate on the way his finger traces my skin, the flecks of gold in his otherwise brown eyes, and the stubble that dusts his jaw so perfectly.

Penn is rugged but still put together. He's handsome but doesn't flaunt it. He's noble and loyal and so utterly dependable that you'd think he could be a superhero in another life. But he also has an edge to him, a thin line of control that I have a feeling could snap under the right pressure.

"Feel what?" I practically moan as his head dips closer to mine.

"This." He takes my hand and places it over his heart where I feel the organ in his chest thrash against his sternum. "Does yours do this too when we're around each other?"

I pause for a moment, debating how honest I should be with him. But the alcohol decides for me. "Yes."

Time stands still as we stare at one another, and then before I can say a word, Penn mutters, "Fuck it," and his lips crash into mine.

An inferno rages through my body the second our lips touch. I push myself into his chest and straddle his hips, burying my hands in his hair. Penn frames my jaw in his hands and tilts my head to the side, swiping his tongue across my lips to make me open up for him. And as soon as our tongues tangle, I let out an embarrassing moan.

My hips start moving, rolling over his lap slowly, finding him hard beneath me. *So very hard*.

God, I want him inside of me.

I miss sex.

I'm tired of my hand and feeling so alone.

"Jesus, Astrid," he mumbles against my lips, kissing me deeply again, over and over, stealing the breath from my lungs.

But then reality slams into me.

His voice brings me back to the reality of what it is we're doing.

I'm kissing Penn—my dead husband's best friend.

Oh my God. What am I doing?

"Shit," I curse, launching myself from Penn's lap and the couch, creating as much space between us as possible as I hold my fingers to my lips, where I can still feel his mouth on mine.

Penn's eyes are wild and wide, staring up at me. "Astrid..."

"This was a mistake. I'm—I'm sorry."

"Don't apologize. I made the first move. I just..." He moves to stand, but I put my hand up to stop him.

"No. Don't. I—I don't know what we were thinking."

"Well..." he starts, but I cut him off again.

"No. This can't happen, Penn."

A flicker of irritation crosses his face. "Okay..."

"This was a mistake," I repeat.

"No, it wasn't." He stands now and makes his way over to me. I'm holding my breath, warring with myself over wanting to push him away or pull him close again and pick up where we left off.

But then I hiccup loudly, and my eyes dart to the bottle of tequila on the coffee table. "We're drunk. That's all this is."

Blame it on the alcohol. Yes. There's a reason Jamie Foxx coined that phrase and put it with music.

"I'm not that drunk, Astrid." He stands right in front of me now so I have to crane my neck back to see his eyes.

"Well, I am. I'm sorry. Let's just forget this ever happened."

"What if I don't want to?" he counters, making my breath hitch.

"I'm—I'm not ready, Penn." It's not a total lie, but honestly, the reality that I just kissed another man who wasn't my husband is making me want to puke.

A man who is also his best friend and completely off limits.

"But..."

"No," I interrupt. "This is wrong. On so many levels." I turn away and head for the hall closet, pulling out a spare blanket and pillow. I return and toss them on the couch. "You should stay here tonight."

His brows are drawn together fiercely, and his voice accepts no argument when he says, "Astrid, we need to talk about this."

I shake my head, trembling all over. The nerves, the reality of what I've done, the shame and guilt and longing that's racing through me—I need to be alone right now before I fall apart. "I can't, Penn. I'm begging you, just...please pretend this never happened. Tomorrow, everything goes back to normal. I'm just emotional." I shrug. "It's the anniversary of Brandon's death, and you're here and you're such a good friend, and I..."

He hangs his head, closing his eyes and breathing harshly through his nose. He stays like that for so long that I almost think he's fallen asleep, until he finally mutters, "Okay."

Silence hangs in the air between us as I wrap my arms tighter around my body. "Thank you. I—I'll see you in the morning."

Turning his back to me, he arranges the pillow and blanket on the couch and then slides in. "Yeah. See ya."

Fighting back tears as I stare at the man who has been the strongest constant in my life recently, I cover my mouth to stifle my sobs and then head back to my room, shutting the door before sliding under the blankets and burying my head in my pillow to cry.

And because Penn is the best man on the planet, he honored my request and never mentioned that night again. He acted as if it never happened.

But we both know it did.

Now, three years later, I think it's safe to say that that night wasn't just a drunken mistake. It was real. At least, those feelings were real for me. And they've only grown since then.

Too bad I can never do anything about them.

Chapter Three

Penn

"You thirsty?"

I glance down from the ladder I'm standing on to find my mother holding out a glass of water to me. "Yeah, thanks." Taking the glass from her, I drain the entire thing.

"Thank you again for getting to the gutters today," she says as I hand her the empty glass.

"No problem, Mom. You know I'm here to help."

"I can always count on you, Penn. I don't know what I would do without you and your siblings most days," she says, a solemn tone to her voice.

Since Dad died, she has good and bad days. Today, she is dealing with a lot of feelings. I can see it in her eyes.

"Well, we will always be here," I reply, reaching up and clearing out the last bit of leaves from the gutter and tossing them to the ground.

It's fall in Carrington Cove, bringing a chill in the air and a cascade of leaves falling from the trees. I had plans to get my oil changed this morning, but when my mom called, I rearranged my schedule so I could help with her gutters as soon as possible. Grady told me to stop by the garage whenever and he'd fit me in.

"Lately it seems like you're the only one I see." My mother shields her eyes from the sun as she looks up at me. It's early in the morning, but the sun is already bright.

"That's because I'm the best one."

She scoffs, but she's smiling, which makes me feel like I have magical powers. "Don't go getting a big head now, Penn. It's unbecoming of you."

I laugh as I begin climbing down the ladder. "I'm already the tallest one, so why not add biggest head to the mix?"

She stands to the side as I grab the trash bag and start gathering the leaves with a rake, scooping them inside. "That's not who you are, Penn."

I glance up at her. "Who am I then, Mom?"

"My boy who always wants to help." *See? Even my mom knows my role.* "Just like your father." Tears well in her eyes now.

I drop the rake and peel off my gloves, tossing them to the ground. I walk over and wrap my arms around her, dropping my chin to rest on her head. "Today's a bad day, huh?"

She sniffles against my chest. "Yeah. The holidays are coming, and it just reminds me that he won't be here."

It's the end of October and my mother has always made a big deal about Thanksgiving and Christmas. Last year we knew were the last holidays we'd have with Dad because the cancer had progressed so fast there was nothing else to be done. But it still doesn't make his absence sting any less.

"I know. But your kids will be here, and we still need to eat."

She chuckles now, wiping the tears from under her eyes as she leans back to look up at me. "Always thinking about your stomach."

"I'm a growing boy, what can I say?"

She elbows me in the ribs. "You definitely ate more than any of your other siblings. That must be why you turned out to be so tall."

"Still don't know how that happened, huh?"

"All the work on our family tree, and now one else was as tall as you." My mother is a retired teacher, so now in her spare time she's been working in her garden, volunteering around town to keep herself busy, and spent some time this past summer digging into our family's lineage.

I wish I had time to do that kind of shit some days, but then I also know that keeping busy is what fuels me. I've never known anything else.

When she steps back, she brushes her hair from her face. "What else do you have planned today?"

I move back to the leaves, putting my gloves on once more. "Getting the oil changed on my truck at Grady's, then I'm headed to the bakery to start renovating for Astrid."

"I'm so proud of that girl. She was beaming the other night at her going away party."

My mother and Astrid's have been close friends since we were kids, so my mom is fully aware of what Astrid's gone through the past four years.

"She was." I feel the corner of my mouth lift as I echo her sentiment.

"Well, she deserves it. Going after something you really want is a gamble, but the payoff can be life-changing." She pauses, giving me a pointed look. "Are you ever gonna take that gamble yourself, Penn?"

I meet her gaze, feeling a mixture of nerves and excitement. And even though I hadn't planned to tell anyone about my recent leap of faith, I know I can trust my mother to keep it to herself. "Actually, I just bought a house, Mom."

"What?" She places her hand over her heart. "You're selling your place?"

Shaking my head, I explain, "Nope. I'm gonna fix it up and start a rental business, turn houses into vacation homes."

"I'm not sure I believe what I'm hearing. What sparked that idea?"

I brush the sweat from my temples with my forearm. "I've been thinking about it for a while. I enjoy what I do now, but I want more. I want to be my own boss, finally create my own contracting business and the rental houses will create passive income once they're ready." I stare off to the side of the yard now. "I'm taking a risk, but..."

Stepping closer, she cups my face in her hands. "There is no reward without risks, honey. And you deserve your reward, Penn. You help others achieve their dreams all the time. It's finally time for you to chase your own."

"I get the keys this afternoon, but I won't be able to do much until I finish up some other jobs."

She drops her hand and wraps her sweater around her body tighter, warding off the chill in the air. "Just promise me that you'll make time for your own projects, Penn. This is a big step. I'm proud of you."

"Thanks, Mom."

She flashes me a sad smile. "I'm so proud of all of my kids, but you're the one I always worried about the most."

"Why?"

"Because you're always so up in your head." She stares at me with a pinch in her brow. "You're the quiet, observant one. My cautious child that always stood back and watched because you wanted to know what to expect. I guess a part of me is relieved to see you finally taking risks."

Jesus. Is this how everyone sees me? Penn, the safe, cautious one?

"I just wanted to make sure Dallas wasn't going to break a bone doing something before I tried it, you know?" I joke, trying to bring some levity to the conversation.

My mother rolls her eyes. "You know what I mean."

Blowing out a breath, I pull her into my chest again. "I know, Mom. This is a lot of responsibility, though."

"You have nothing to be nervous about Penn. You're one of the hardest working people I know. I swear, I don't know where you got that work ethic from, but it's ingrained in you. At the end of the day, the determination to never quit is what determines success, not intelligence or money. I used to tell my students that all the time."

Grief slams into me because I know exactly where I got my work ethic from.

"Dad made me this way," I say softly as her eyes lift to find mine. "Dad taught me the importance of helping others, Mom."

Tears well in her eyes again. "Then that makes my heart happy."

I kiss the top of her head and release her. "I need to get this finished so I can get everything done today that I need to."

She nods and takes a few steps back. "Okay. When you see Astrid, tell her that I'll be by tomorrow for the order for the gardening club. I'm in charge of bringing the muffins this week."

"I will. Although, something tells me she already knows."

"That girl makes the best blueberry muffins this side of the Mississippi."

"Yeah, she does."

I turn back to the leaves, but don't miss my mother's final comment. "That's not all that she's good at, though. She has a lot to offer to the world...I just hope she finds someone who can see that."

***

Grady slams the hood on my truck, wiping the sweat from his brow. "There. You're good to go."

"Thanks, man. I appreciate you fitting me in this morning."

"No problem. If you'd have waited any longer though, your engine would have been smoking."

My truck was way past due for an oil change, but I've been so damn busy that I've kept putting it off. "Pays to know the owner of the garage then, doesn't it?"

Grady is Astrid's older brother, so I've known him just as long as Astrid and Brandon. When Grady was drafted to an MLB team in California right after high school, we still kept in contact even though his schedule was sporadic and crazy. But when an injury ended his career, he moved back home to Carrington Cove and took over the automotive repair garage from the previous owner whom he worked for throughout high school. Grady's Garage, as it's named now, is his pride and joy after he lost the first love of his life, baseball.

But I know there are still days when he misses it.

"It does." Grady wipes his hands on the towel he pulls from his back pocket. "So, what's on the agenda for the rest of the day?"

"I'm headed to the bakery, actually. Astrid wants me to do some renovations and give the place a face lift."

"I heard you two talking about it last weekend at her going away party."

"She seems to be excited about it."

Grady scoffs. "Dude, you have no idea. She's waited years for this. It wasn't exactly an option for her when Brandon was still alive."

That little tidbit of information has my brows lifting. "What do you mean?"

He shakes his head, drifting his gaze to another part of the garage as his thoughts consume him. It takes a minute before he finally replies, "Nothing. I'm just happy for her."

"Yeah, me too." I want to press further about his comment, but he dodges the topic.

"But renovating sounds like a good business move. It will make the place feel new and more like hers."

"Yeah, and I'm gonna help out by cutting her some slack on labor costs."

He scowls at me. "You don't have to do that, Penn. You deserve to be paid for your work."

"I know, but I don't want her sinking herself in debt even more right in the beginning, you know?"

"Overhead costs are part of owning a business, man." He pats me on the shoulder. "Although, I suppose that isn't something you'd have any experience with, is it?"

His words cut deep, and the smirk on his face tells me he knows exactly what button he just pushed.

While Dallas likes to give me shit about my personal life, Grady is the king of pushing me in my professional life. When he came home three years ago and saw that I was still picking up odd jobs around town, he wanted to know why I didn't establish my own contracting business and do that full time. I told him that owning my own company wasn't what I wanted because that was easier than admitting the truth—I was scared.

In a small town like ours, there's a limit to how much success you can have. Sure, Dallas's restaurant can thrive on tourism, and hell, even Hazel benefits from visiting families for her photography business. Parker is the vet, so there's never a shortage of animals that need tending to. But fixing someone's deck? Unclogging a pipe or cleaning out gutters? Building a chicken coop or mending fences? There's only so many people in Carrington Cove to help with those things. Most people here would rather take care of those projects themselves.

Plus, the last thing I want to do is fail and make a mockery of myself. That's why I always blend into the background. I don't like the fucking attention. I've seen what that's been like for my siblings, and nope. I'm good.

But lately, I just want more for my life. I guess death has a funny way of making you question how you're living.

My mood instantly sours. "It sounds like you're wanting to piss me off already this morning, Grady."

Chuckling, he says, "No, just checking on you."

"And why is that?"

"Well, for starters, my sister just took a leap of faith on a new business, your brother is doing well, Parker mentioned trying to buy the practice from Dr. O'Neil, and you're still…"

"Just the local fix-it guy?"

He tips his head to the side and shrugs. "Yeah. And you could have so much more, man."

Staring at the sky, I momentarily debate telling him about the house I'm in escrow on right now. But until those keys are in my hand later today, I don't want to jinx it. Confiding in my mom is one thing, but telling others isn't something I want to deal with just yet. And the look on his face when he finds out later will be worth the wait. "Look, I appreciate you worrying about me, but maybe the real issue is that you need to get a life so you're not so fixated on mine."

"I have a life."

"Really? What do you do after work? Or on the weekends?"

"Work on rebuilding the Nova," he says, gesturing to the '73 Nova he's had under a sheet in this garage since he bought the place.

"Really? Looks like it's going really well."

Grady laughs again and holds his hands up. "All right, I can take a hint. Just wanted to see where your head was at this morning."

"My head is fucking fine."

"All you do is work, Penn—and for other people. If you're not careful, you'll burn yourself out with nothing to show for it."

Reaching for the handle on the door to my truck, I say, "I like being busy. Gives me less time to think."

With a tip of his chin, he says, "Can't say you're wrong about that. Catch you this weekend?"

"Are you coming to Bentley's soccer game?"

"Most likely. I was gonna have Chet manage the place that morning so I could take a break. You think you guys will make it to the championship in a few weeks?"

"If we keep playing like we have been, then yeah."

"Cool. Then I'll see you there."

After I settle into the driver's seat and crank the engine, I take off for the boardwalk, hoping Astrid is ready for me to start tearing her bakery apart.

Nestled right by our town's namesake cove, the bakery and my sister's photography studio are in a prime location. Just across the street, the tranquil waters of the cove are right at your toes. Dallas's restaurant is a short walk up the boardwalk, too, so it makes it easy for me to shuffle around between work and helping out where I'm needed.

Well, because...that's what I do.

The bell above the front door chimes as I walk in, and the sweet smell of sugar and cinnamon fills the air. I take a moment to look around, taking note of the same walls, tables, and chairs that have been here since I was a kid and Dallas and I used to ride our bikes to the bakery to get donuts on Saturday mornings. I guess I never really paid attention to the inside because I was more fixated on getting two or three donuts in my mouth, but Astrid is right. The place desperately needs some life brought back to it.

"Hey! Sorry about that, I had to put a batch of blueberry muffins in the oven," Astrid says as she emerges from the back of the bakery, a light pink apron tied around her waist and her hair tossed up in a clip. A few pieces have fallen out, framing her face, but it's the flour on the tip of her nose that really catches my attention.

"No problem. I just got here," I reply, looking around at the aged paint and furniture. "Just taking a look at what we're working with."

"I can't wait until you work your magic, Penn. But do you mind coming back to the kitchen while we talk so I can multitask?"

"Of course."

Watching her ass sway in her jeans as she walks away from me, I'm grateful that her back is to me so she can't see how transfixed I am by her curves. Astrid has always been a beautiful girl, but after she became a mom, and more importantly, in the years since she's been a single mom, there's something about her that sets her apart. Maybe it's that she's so busy, she barely bothers with makeup, which she doesn't fucking need anyway. Maybe it's that she makes a simple t-shirt and pair of jeans look like they were made for her perfect fucking body.

Or maybe it's the fact she has no idea just how sexy she is by just being her.

God, I'm hopeless and pathetic.

When she finally stops moving, I reach out and wipe the flour from her nose, showing it to her on the tip of my finger.

She rolls her eyes and groans. "Flour practically seeps from my pores these days."

I lean in and take a whiff of her, which catches her off guard. "What are you doing?"

"Seeing if that's true."

She grins at me curiously but then I see her shudder as I get closer. "Well?"

I inhale deeply once more and then lock my eyes onto hers when I say, "Nope. You smell like fucking sugar."

Her throat bobs and she smiles nervously. "Well, there are worse things, right?"

"Definitely." Standing tall again, I cast my eyes over the kitchen and remember why I'm here instead of imagining tasting her sweetness as well. "Okay, so I figured I'd start in the back, work on those shelves for the pantry for you since that will leave the front untouched for a day or so. Then those tables..."

"They're hideous, right?"

"Nothing some sanding and a new coat of paint can't fix."

"Perfect." She reaches for a big metal bowl and starts scooping in cups of flour.

"The display case is going to be the most expensive change."

She sighs, leveling out sugar and adding that to the bowl. "I know."

"I did some research on them last night and the ones that had the best reviews were about $2500 apiece."

She freezes and looks up at me. "You researched them last night? After you left my house?" I nod, but she looks at me like I'm a fucking alien. "God, Penn. When do you sleep?"

The truth is that I don't, not for long anyway. If I can manage a solid five hours, then I consider that a good night. But by two or three in the morning, I'm usually wide awake and my mind is racing with everything that needs to be done.

Or how I'm stuck in the same place in my life that I've been in for years.

Well, as of this afternoon, that won't be true anymore, for better or for worse.

"I manage. So, do you want me to order those, or would you like to research some on your own?"

She shakes her head. "I don't have time for that. I trust you."

"All right. I'll place the order today." I take out my notepad I keep in my pocket, jot down my to-do list for the day, and then shove it back in my jeans just as the chime above the front door rings out again, and Astrid groans.

"I keep getting interrupted. I need to get these cupcakes going or I'm going to be behind filling an order."

"Where's Tanya?" I ask. Tanya is a recent high school graduate who worked for the previous owners. She's eager to be a pastry chef, so when Astrid took over she agreed to stay on, promising she wouldn't leave her high and dry. In fact, she was more than excited to be working for her and Astrid promised to teach her everything she knows.

"She had a doctor's appointment this morning, so I gave her the morning off."

"And what about Vanessa and Anthony?"

"They won't be here until nine."

"Then I'll handle the customer."

"No, Penn. You don't have to…"

But it's too late. I head for the front of the store, pushing through the swinging door that separates the kitchen area from the storefront and come face to face with Richard Cockwell.

Yes, his name is really Dick Cockwell.

We had a field day giving him shit in high school, but he took it in stride. You almost have to with a name like that.

But now's he a teacher at our alma matter, so I can only imagine the creativity his students have with butchering his name.

"Hey, Dick. How's it going?"

He rolls his eyes. "Nice to see that some of us haven't matured since high school." But then his smile turns placating as he shoves his hands in the pockets of his khaki trousers. "Does Astrid have you icing cupcakes back there, Penn?" His grin grows. "You really are a jack of all trades, aren't you?"

I flash him a tight-lipped smile, sensing some sarcasm in his tone. But now's not the time to get in a verbal spar, especially since he's a paying customer of Astrid's.

Dick teaches science at Carrington Cove High School, so while he may have fancy degrees and a pension, I'd bet he's more familiar with books and beakers than a set of tools.

"Actually, I'm here because Astrid hired me to do the renovations on the bakery. I'm just taking some measurements and then I've got to stop by the hardware store. You have heard of it, right?"

His eyes narrow at me across the counter. I knew he always thought he was better than Dallas and me, but the smarmy tone he's taking with me just confirms it. "Yes, Penn. I have lived in Carrington Cove my entire life, just like you."

"Just making sure." I straighten my spine. "So, what can I do for you?"

"Well, I wanted to bring some baked goods into the school today for the office staff." He peeks around me, trying to get a look in the back. "Is, uh, Astrid here?"

"She's busy," I say just as she barrels through the door.

"Richard?"

He perks up like a fucking puppy as he looks at her. "Hey, Astrid! How's it going?"

Astrid casts a quick glance at me before standing across from Richard, the case a buffer between them. "It's going. Busy." She brushes her hair from her face and pastes a smile on her lips. "How can I help you?"

"I'm here for my usual Friday order. The office staff always go nuts for your muffins and Danishes."

"Oh, well, I'm happy to hear that!" She grabs a box from behind her, folds it together and then starts grabbing items from the bakery case with tongs.

"How is running the bakery going? I can't wait to sample that new menu."

I feel like I'm watching a teenage boy try to get the nerve to ask out the girl he has always had a crush on. It's oddly unsettling. Now I understand the term second-hand embarrassment.

"How did you know about that?" Astrid asks, eyebrows raised in surprise.

"I ran into your mom at the grocery store earlier this week. She says you've been working on it." Then he leans over the counter, getting closer to her as he says, "Just so you know, I have a weakness for cupcakes."

A snort escapes my lips, drawing both of their attention. "Sorry," I say as Astrid narrows her eyes at me.

But really? A weakness for cupcakes? What a fucking twatwaffle.

I mean, I would eat anything Astrid makes, so maybe I have that weakness too. But I'd never say it out loud.

"Well, then you'll be a happy customer. I've been so excited to unveil the new menu, but I might wait until after the renovations are done. Kind of like a grand re-opening, you know?"

Dick nods as I pull out my phone, checking my text messages and trying to make it less obvious that I'm listening to every word of their conversation.

"Makes sense." Dick clears his throat as he meets Astrid at the register, handing her his card. "So, I know this may seem out of left field, but...I actually came in here this morning with the intention of asking you something."

Astrid hands him his receipt. "Okay..." she slowly draws out with an uncertain smile.

"I know you're busy, taking over the bakery and everything. But I've wanted to ask you out for a while now, and I figured, there's no time like the present."

Astrid drops his card from her hand just as my head pops up so fast I nearly give myself whiplash.

"What?" she asks for clarification, clearly stunned by his admission.

Yeah, me fucking too.

"Yeah, uh." Dick rubs the back of his neck. "I think you're great. Beautiful. And it's been four years, so I figured..." He shrugs. "Maybe you might be ready to start dating again?"

My stomach feels like someone is squeezing it in their palm, and fury crawls up my chest.

Dick is asking Astrid out?

But I think the more important question is, what is she going to say?

"Oh, uh. Well, thank you." She picks up his card, handing it to him once more before tucking a strand of her hair behind her ear, her hands visibly shaking. "I'm sorry," she laughs. "I guess you just caught me off guard."

I can feel him wanting to dart his eyes over to me, but I've got to hand it to him, he doesn't. He keeps his gaze on her. "Look, you don't have to give me an answer now." Reaching for the box of baked goods, he tucks it under his arm and takes a step back. "Think about it this week and when I come in next Friday, just let me know."

Astrid licks her lips and then nods. "I—I can do that."

"Great. Well, I hope you have an amazing rest of your day." He turns to me again now, nodding his head once. "Penn. Good to see you."

"Yeah. Pleasure." I watch him walk out and then the sound of Astrid blowing out a breath pulls my attention back to her. "So, uh...that was interesting."

Astrid shakes her head and moves right toward the back of the bakery again. "Yeah."

I follow her, watching her move right back to making cupcakes. "So..."

She flicks her eyes up to me. "So, what?"

I look around the room as if someone else might be wondering the same thing I am. "Uh...are you going to go out with him?"

Astrid shrugs as she starts cracking eggs into the bowl. "I don't know. Maybe?"

My blood starts to boil in my veins.

I know I have no claim to this woman, but for the past four years I've stood by her, helping her in every way she's needed.

And no, I didn't do it just to get her in bed. But I figured that one day, if she felt like she was ready to move on, I'd be the one she'd move on with.

You mean you were still holding out hope after she rejected you three years ago?

Oh, poor Penn. You're a little stupid, aren't you?

Fuck.

I point to the front of the store and try to reign in my frustration. "Really? Him?"

That causes her to stop and turn to me. "What's wrong with Richard?"

Nothing. Nothing is wrong with Dick. He's got a good job, owns his own home, and no one has anything bad to say about him really.

But he's not me.

He doesn't see Astrid for how utterly spectacular she is.

"I just think you can do better."

She scoffs. "Yeah, okay. Tell me where all the men are who want to date the widowed single mom of two kids who works all the time, Penn. Please."

I stare at her, wondering if she is just that clueless.

Has all the tension between us been in my imagination?

Am I really the only one who has felt anything over the past three years?

I feel like my entire world just shifted in one conversation.

I've buried my feelings all this time, intent on letting things be. I was happier having Astrid in my life as a friend then not at all. And in less than ten minutes, this surge of possessiveness has kicked in that I've tried to keep buried and I don't know what to fucking do about it.

Needing space to process what I'm feeling, I shake my head and turn away from her, heading for the door. "You know what? Just forget it."

"Penn!" she calls after me.

I glance at her over my shoulder.

"You're coming back to start on the shelves, right?" she asks me timidly, a look of uncertainty in her eyes.

Fuck. That's right. I can't just run away from her right now. I have a job to do, one I promised her that I would.

And I always keep my promises.

"Yeah, I'll be back."

Her smile is unsure, but she grants me one nonetheless. "Okay. See you later."

"Yeah, see you later, Astrid."

Walking out to my truck, my skin feels itchy. My chest feels tight. My mind is at war with all of these thoughts and feelings bubbling up to the surface.

Maybe I can't have Astrid the way I want.

But I sure as fuck don't want Dick Cockwell to have her.

Jesus Christ. How did I get myself into this mess?

And more importantly, how the fuck do I get out of it?

Chapter Four

Astrid

"I swear, I could hear that noise from down the boardwalk." Hazel Sheppard walks through the door of the bakery, her voice barely carrying over the sounds of Penn working out back.

The sound of the sanding machine outside is so loud that I've had to wear earplugs for the past few days, but I know the makeover Penn is giving the old table and chairs will make the racket worth it.

Plucking the ear plugs from my ears, I wait for a break in the clamor to respond. "I know. He's almost done though." Like we planned, Penn came by and started on the shelves last Friday, but he left early for another project—the same one he's being very cryptic about. And normally I would push him to open up to me, but I've been so stressed with the renovations, keeping up with incoming orders, and finalizing the details for the grand reopening in three weeks, all while trying to keep up with my kids and running a household, that I have no energy left to give to that matter.

"Thank God." Hazel laughs as she brushes her long, dark hair over her shoulder and saunters up to me.

"So, what brings you in today?" This girl feels like my unofficial younger sister since I've watched her grow up. I can't believe she's twenty-five—it makes me feel older than I am.

"Well, a little birdie told me you're going to start offering custom wedding cakes." Her eyebrows bounce up and down. "And, since I photograph weddings, I was wondering if you'd like to give me some business cards so I can pass them along to my clients. Maybe we can agree on a discount if they book with both of us?"

"Damn. Look at you, you little businesswoman," I tease her as I reach under the counter and hand her a stack of cards. "And would this little birdie happen to be my mother? I'm going to need to have a conversation with her later about her telling people my business plans."

First Richard and now Hazel? I wonder who else she's told.

"Don't get mad at her. I'm the one that asked. We ran into each other at the nail salon and I kind of pulled it out of her."

"Well, she's not wrong, but I haven't advertised it yet. I'm waiting until everything is done here for the re-opening. Plus, I'm thinking of changing the name of the place, so these cards might be out of date by then."

"No biggie. I've always kept some in my studio for clients, and Greg and Jenny did the same for me." The former owners ran this place more like a quick-stop people could pop in for donuts and muffins. My goal is to expand what we offer, converting the store to a full-service bakery—cakes, cookies, bread, pies, and other sweet treats. The possibilities are endless. As long as I have the manpower to do it, that is.

"I appreciate the support no matter what," I say just as Penn walks into the store.

"Is that my little sister?" He slides his safety goggles up his face, resting them on the top of his head. His shirt and jeans are covered in dust, but it's the sheen on his forearms that is truly garnering my attention.

Sexy, strong, glistening forearms.

Lord have mercy.

"It is. God, you're a mess." Her eyes move up and down his body. "Please tell me you're almost done, by the way. The noise is just awful."

Penn scratches the back of his head. "Yeah, I didn't really think about the noise bothering folks."

Hazel rolls her eyes. "Doesn't surprise me."

"Hey, I'll remember that the next time you want me to build a set for a photo shoot." He arches a brow at her.

She crosses her arms over her chest and returns the look. "Well, I guess now isn't the right time to ask you for one for Christmas photo sessions then, is it?"

Penn rolls his eyes and sighs. "When do you need it by?"

Batting her eyelashes, she clasps her hands in front of her. "Thanksgiving, if you can?"

"Yeah, I can make that work." He takes out his notepad, writes something on it, and then shoves it back in his pocket. "Now, if you're done whining, I actually came in to tell Astrid that one of the chairs is done, but I wanted her opinion on the final product before I start the rest."

I turn back to Hazel and smile. "Duty calls."

"No problem. But, before I leave, I also wanted to extend an invite to you for this passion party that I'm having."

"What the fuck is a passion party?" Penn asks, wrinkling his nose.

"It's a sex toy party," Hazel tells her brother, and I watch as Penn shifts from confusion to disgust.

"Jesus Christ, Hazel."

"Newsflash, Penn. I'm twenty-five. I'm a grown woman and I've had…"

"La, la, la!" He plugs his ears like a petulant child, which makes both Hazel and me laugh. Shaking his head, he heads to the back of the bakery again. "I'm just going to pretend I never heard those words come out of your mouth. Astrid, I'll meet you out back when you're done."

Hazel and I watch him retreat, and then I turn to her. "You probably just scarred him for life."

She shrugs. "Serves him right. I'll just think of it as payback for every time he chased me with a lizard."

Laughter bubbles out of me. "So, a passion party?"

"Yeah. It's the Saturday after Thanksgiving. One of my girlfriends is throwing them for some side money and she'll be home for the holiday. I told her I would invite everyone I know, so…"

"I get an invite too."

"Obviously. And I'm sure you could use a few new toys. I mean…" She bites her lip. "I don't want to be presumptuous, but you're still a woman, Astrid. And you have needs, right?"

God, if she only knew just how true that statement has been lately.

"Yes, but…"

She cuts me off. "No buts. You're coming. I'll even buy you something."

Mortified, I say, "Oh, God. You don't have to do that."

"Nonsense. I insist…especially because I was wondering if we could have the party at your place?" She bites her lip again, this time in anticipation of my answer.

"You want to have the party at my house?"

"If you don't mind. It's just that my apartment is way too small, and I refuse to ask my mother." We both start laughing again. "I promise, it will only be for a few hours."

Looking at the ceiling, I consider if I could make that work. I mean, I'm sure my mother would watch the kids or take them to her house for the night if I asked her to.

"Okay," I relent. "Send me the date and I'll make it happen." I have a feeling I'm going to regret this later, but making decisions in the moment is what I do. It's necessary when your life is as chaotic as mine.

Hazel claps her hands together. "Gah, thank you! It's going to be a blast. A true girl's night. I've invited Willow too!"

"Joy," I say sarcastically, even though part of me is interested to see what kind of new toys are out there now. I've had the same vibrator since before Brandon died. Only recently did I actually feel like my libido has returned. It may be because I'm in my thirties now, or maybe it's all the mental images watching Penn working around the bakery has evoked.

Yeah, I definitely need something to take the edge off.

"Don't stress. I'll handle everything." Hazel glances at the clock on the wall. "Okay, I've got to get going. I have a full day of editing ahead and then a session at sunset tonight. It's a surprise engagement, and I'm already crying." She fans her face.

"You're just a hopeless romantic, aren't you?"

She shrugs. "I can't help it. I love love."

I smile and shake my head. "Text me later."

"I will. Bye!" She waves as she exits the store and I sigh heavily, remembering when I was younger and had that same outlook. Just another reminder that we're all getting older, even though sometimes it doesn't feel that way. I'm thirty-two and most days I still feel like I'm fifteen with no idea what I'm doing with my life still.

I find Penn out back standing over a table, drilling metal legs into the bottom of the chairs. But as soon as he sees me, he stops what he's doing, reaches into his tool bag, and hands me a Ferrero Rocher.

"You just carry these around in your tool bag now?"

"When I know I'm going to see you, yeah." He nods toward the candy. "Go ahead. You look like you could use a little pick-me-up."

I unwrap the chocolate and pop it in my mouth, closing my eyes and moaning at how the flavors meld together. I swear, I could survive on these little morsels of heaven alone. When I open my eyes, I find Penn staring down at me intensely. But I choose to focus back on the reason I came out here. "Thank you. That did help calm me. So, what are you doing?"

"Giving these chairs new life like we agreed."

"But what happened to the legs that were on them?"

"I found these online for cheap and thought they give them a more feminine, romantic feel to match the new décor's theme." He flips the finished chair over and sets it on the ground. The dark nickel brushed legs are modern, but still have a classic feel. The wood of the chair itself is painted in the light gray we agreed on, and he sanded them after painting them to make them look a bit more rustic. I couldn't have asked for a better realization of my vision if I'd done it myself.

"Penn, these are beautiful." I stare at the chair in awe and then look up at him. "Thank you."

He nods curtly. "Glad you like them."

"No, I love them. Seriously. They're perfect." Circling the chair, I admire all the details. "God, I can't wait to see it all come together. You're—you're making my dreams come true."

Penn swallows roughly as I look up at him again. "Just doing my job, Astrid."

Resting my hand on his chest, I stare up into his eyes. "I seriously don't know what I would do without you. I hope you know that."

A pinch in his brow forms before he sighs. "Well, good thing you won't ever find out, huh?"

"I hope not."

"So, you're seriously considering going out with Dick, then?" he says, catching me off guard because why would he bring this up again?

We stare at each other, time nearly standing still before Tanya comes out of the back door of the bakery. "Uh, Astrid?"

Retracting my hand as if Penn's chest just burned me, I turn to her, brushing my hair from my face and pulling my shirt back in place. "Yeah?"

"We just got an order for six dozen blueberry muffins for tomorrow."

Penn clears his throat. "I'll let you get back to it. I'll bring the finished chairs inside before I leave for the day."

"Working on your super-secret project again?"

He sighs. "I wish. Not enough time before soccer practice."

"Thank God there's only a few weeks left of the season, right?"

"You have no idea. I'll be happy to get that time back, but I'll miss it a little, too. It's been awesome seeing the kids improve and come together as a team this season." He flips his safety glasses back over his eyes. "Now get back to work, boss. I'll see you later."

A little thrill races down my spine at the name. "Thanks again, Penn."

"My pleasure, Astrid."

And then I walk away, back to my new responsibilities. But I swear I can feel Penn's eyes on my ass the entire time.

***

"And what are we doodling this evening?"

Sitting in my chair, I glance up to find Grady peering at my notebook over my shoulder. It's just after six and Bentley's soccer practice is underway. Lilly is running around with one of the siblings of another boy on the team, and I'm head down in my notebook, sketching ideas for my new logo and making notes of what I need to do this week. I swear, I have so many lists now that I'm not sure which is the most current one.

"Oh, just sketching some ideas for a new logo. Typically, you'd have these things sorted out sooner when you're opening a business, but I guess I'm keen on doing things backwards. It's kind of my specialty."

My brother takes a seat on the grass beside me, folding his knees up to rest his hands on them as he stares at the field, watching as the team listens to Penn and Dallas explain their next drill. "There's nothing wrong with doing things backwards, sis. Just as long as you accomplish what you set out to do."

"I'm working on it."

He smiles at me proudly. "I know you are."

"What are you doing out here tonight? You don't usually come to practices." Grady is great about attending the games on Saturdays and taking Lilly to her dance classes if I need him to, but during the week I barely see him. It's still a huge improvement from when he was playing baseball professionally and we saw him maybe five times a year. Even though I know he wishes he could still play, I'm selfishly grateful that he's back home.

He shoots me a look over his shoulder, his lips contorted in disgust. "Would you judge me if I said I was bored?"

Chuckling, I reply, "Bored?"

He runs a hand through his hair and shrugs, stretching out his legs in front of him now. "I'm waiting on parts for the Nova, so until those arrive, I don't have much to do. The shop closes at five and sometimes, the last thing I want to do is work on any more side projects, you know?"

"I get it. The idea of going home and cooking after I've been baking all day doesn't appeal to me at all."

"Exactly." His eyes drift back out toward the field. "I don't know, Astrid. Sometimes I just feel like there's got to be more to life than this..."

"Getting philosophical on me tonight?" I tease him.

His face is contemplative. "No, just...restless."

God, I understand that feeling more than he knows. "What about dating? Have you given that any thought?"

His gaze turns to a glare. "Uh, no thanks."

"Why not?"

He twists slightly to face me. "Do you know how many single women come into the garage with car trouble on a day-to-day basis?" I fold in my lips to hide my smile. He glares at me harder. "I feel like I'm fighting them off left and right these days. I mean, I haven't played baseball in years, and they still act like I'm a fucking celebrity."

"You were one of the best pitchers of your time, Grady."

He shakes his head, picking at the grass, the lines of his face deepening as he frowns. "I wasn't fucking done playing, Astrid."

"I know." I hate seeing my brother like this. I can't imagine what losing baseball was like for him, but that's partly because he never talks about it. Anytime his career comes up, he shuts down the conversation. Then again, I do the same about Brandon, especially lately. Those seven stages of grief are real, and I don't think they ever really end. In fact, I think they go on a loop, and anger seems to be where I'm stuck the most recently.

Remembering him will always be important because of the kids, but knowing that I've been hiding the truth of our marriage from everyone makes me avoid the topic if I can. I just hope I don't collapse under the weight of this secret.

Guilt slams into me.

I'm the worst widow on the face of the planet.

"Well, *I'm* going on a date," I say, changing the subject for him as his head pops up so he can look at me. If I'm already feeling shitty, might as well place a cherry on top of the shit sundae.

"Seriously?"

"Well, I mean, I haven't exactly said yes yet, but I'm thinking about it."

"Who with?"

"Richard Cockwell."

Grady's lip curls in disgust. "Dick Cockwell? Really, Astrid?"

I swat at him, but he dodges it. "Don't call him that."

"Oh come on. Everyone called him that in high school. What kind of parents do that to their kid? Give them a name like that?"

Rolling my eyes, I continue. "Anyway, he asked me out last Friday and told me to think about it, and I think…I think I might go."

Grady's face softens, but there's still some disapproval there. "Well, I mean, that's good, I guess. If that's what you want."

Is that what I want?

Well, it's definitely not *who* I want.

"It's time to move on," I say, leaving my torturous thoughts to myself as my eyes drift over to Penn, hunched over as he watches the boys execute their drill, his ball cap on backwards. I clench my thighs together as I sit here staring.

What is it about a backwards ball cap that just makes a man ten times sexier?

"Moving on is overrated," he grunts.

"Yeah, but so is staying in the same freaking spot, or letting guilt and shame rest in your chest." I lean forward and lower my voice. "Buying the bakery was my first step in moving on, Grady. If I can do it, you can too."

His face softens just a bit. "And I'm proud of you for doing that finally, Astrid. But I have moved on. To my garage."

"You said yourself that it feels like something's missing from your life."

He shakes his head. "Dating sounds awful, Astrid."

"What sounds awful?" Penn startles us both as he appears right next to Grady's spot on the grass, grabbing his water bottle and taking a long swig from it, and then bringing the hem of his shirt up to wipe his mouth, granting me a glimpse of his abs—all one-hundred of them.

"I was telling Grady that he should try dating." I shield my mouth from my brother as I whisper to Penn, "He says he's bored."

Penn shakes his head. "Sorry, Astrid. I agree with Grady. That sounds fucking horrible."

"What? Why?"

"You do realize that we know all of the single women in town, right?" Grady chimes in.

"Is there a list or something?" I glance between the two of them.

"No, but it's a small town, sis. Plus, this is the time of year when people start coming back around because of the holidays, visiting family and crap. It's like a high school reunion every weekend."

Penn nods in agreement. "Again, your brother is speaking the truth."

"Is that why you don't date either?" I stare up at Penn, the man who's starred in one too many of my fantasies.

Penn stays quiet for a while before he finally answers, looking out over the field. "I'm just not interested in a relationship right now. I'm too busy."

Grady juts his thumb over his shoulder at me. "Astrid's not, apparently. She's already got a date lined up."

Penn's eyes dart to mine. "So you *are* going out with Dick?" His jaw clenches and he looks away from me again.

I shoot my brother a glare as I search for the right thing to say. I've been avoiding bringing this up to Penn after his reaction to Richard the other day.

"Penn! Come on, man!" Dallas waves for his brother to join him back on the field.

"I've got to go." Penn saunters off without another word, leaving Grady and me alone again.

A few moments of silence go by as my heart races with nerves. But why am I nervous?

Is it the idea of actually going on a date again?

Or is it the way Penn just reacted?

Was it just me, or did he seem angry? Am I creating his reaction in my mind, or was that real?

Jesus. Get a grip, Astrid.

And it's not like I can ask my brother if he sensed it without inviting a whole new line of questioning.

"See? I told you. Dating is a waste of time in a town like Carrington Cove," Grady finally says just as Lilly comes running up to us.

"Mommy! I'm hungry!" She juts out her bottom lip and then turns to my brother, instantly distracted. "Uncle Grady!"

"Hey, sweet pea." He kisses her on the head and then pulls her into his lap, tickling her until she's screaming.

"Stop, Uncle Grady! Stop!"

"Not until you tell me I'm your favorite uncle," he growls exuberantly.

"You're my favorite! I promise!"

He lets go of her as she scrambles to get away, both of them trying to catch their breath. "Good. Just want to make sure I'm still number one."

"Uncle Penn is number one too though," she says, squealing when he reaches for her again, but she escapes his grasp.

"You can't have two in first place, Lilly."

"But I can't choose. I love you both. Uncle Penn plays Uno with me and reads me bedtime stories and when Mommy's not looking, he gives me some of the chocolates he brings her."

My eyebrows shoot up. "Is that so?"

"Yup!" Lilly runs away from us again, finding the other little girl she was playing with, completely forgetting about how hungry she was just moments ago.

"Looks like I'm going to have a discussion with Penn about the candy," I say, scanning the field and finding him crouched next to one of Bentley's teammates, giving him pointers.

"And looks like I'm going to have to up my game to reach favorite uncle status."

"It's not a competition, Grady. Penn has just been around more. That's not your fault."

"Yeah, but I could be around more now."

I place a hand on his shoulder and squeeze. "Then come around more. Like tonight. It was nice catching up with you."

"Yeah, sis. It was nice catching up with you too. But do me a favor?"

"Okay..."

"Don't marry Dick, okay?"

I snort. "All right."

"I just can't get behind your last name being Cockwell."

And even though I don't say it, I don't think I could get behind that idea either. But going out with the man can't hurt, right? It might be nice to eat a meal I didn't have to cook and enjoy some adult company for the evening. Getting dressed up and having a man's full attention sounds nice too.

"I'll let you know if it gets to that point."

"I doubt it will. Besides, you deserve better than that. Brandon wouldn't approve of him either."

Yeah, something tells me that Brandon *really* wouldn't approve of the man I actually want.

Chapter Five

Penn

"Here you go, Mrs. Owens." I hand her the receipt from the register and watch her shove it in her purse. "Do you want help out to your car?"

"Yes, that would be lovely, Penn." She smiles warmly at me as I come around the counter to grab her cart. Mrs. Owens is in her seventies and the last thing I want to do is watch her hurt herself on my watch. I push the cart with one hand and hold her up with the other, leading her out the front door of the store and to her car.

"Where's Baron today?" I ask as I load the bags into her trunk. Harriet Owens is married to Baron, one of the old men who play darts at Catch & Release every Friday night.

"Oh, he's supposed to be cleaning out his side of the closet so you can start on those shelves next week for us." She waggles her finger in the air. "And if he's not, he's going to be in for an ass kicking when I get home."

My eyes drop to her cane and I find myself wondering if it's just a prop she uses to keep her husband in line. If so, I'm impressed. "Should I text him and let him know you're on your way?"

She swats at me with the cane. "Don't you dare!"

I hold my hands up in surrender. "Don't worry. I know who's in charge."

"That's right. I'm the one that writes the checks too, Penn. Don't forget that." Laughing, I help her settle into the driver's seat. "So, when are you gonna find a woman to boss you around?"

"Oh, I don't know..."

"What about Astrid? I assume you two have been bumping uglies this entire time, but..." She shrugs and I nearly choke on my tongue.

"Bumping uglies?"

"I don't know what you young people call it these days, but you're always together."

"Yeah, well, in case you forgot, she was married to my best friend," I say, lowering my voice.

Harriet shrugs. "So what? Life's short, Penn. I met Baron through Harold, who was both his best friend and my boyfriend at the time," she admits, surprising me even further. Harold is one of Baron's darts buddies. I know they were all in the Marines together, but this piece of information is news to me.

"Really?"

"Yep. And Janet and I were friends before that," she says, referring to Harold's wife. "Love can be messy sometimes, but it's worth it. When you find the right person, you figure it out together and it all just becomes part of your story."

I nod in response, processing what she said.

She pulls her door shut and starts backing out of her parking space. "See you next week, Penn!" she calls through the open window and takes off like she didn't just spill some sixty-year-old drama to me, leaving me standing there reeling.

When I make my way back inside the hardware store, I find Elizabeth Hansen, my boss, behind the counter, emptying the drawer next to the register that's filled with boxes of screws. "Hey, you're back."

"Yeah, what are you up to?"

"These need to be stocked on the shelves, but they're all mixed up." Dumping box on top of box, she scatters the screws all over the counter, making an even bigger mess than they were.

"I can see that," I say through gritted teeth.

"Can you organize these and put them where they go, please?" she asks before walking away. And as much as I want to just throw them all in the trash, I do what's asked of me while reminding myself that I only have to follow someone else's orders for a little while longer.

***

"Damn it!" I shout as the whipped cream smashes into my face.

Tonight, Bentley got to choose the game for game night, and he chose Pie Face. That little bastard.

Astrid hands me a wet washcloth with a delighted smirk on her lips.

"I hate this game," I grumble, wiping the sticky, sugary goop from my face.

"Me too," Lilly whines. She's already been pied three times, so she's done for the night. But her brother is still sitting across the table, beaming from ear to ear with a perfectly clean face. That's about to change here in a minute, and Astrid probably isn't going to be happy with me when it does.

"We've played this before when you wanted to, Lilly," Astrid reminds her. Lilly's arms are folded across her chest as I slide the plastic catapult in front of Astrid for her last turn. When she makes it through unscathed, cranking the knob but avoiding the cream being thrown into her face, we all let out a sigh of relief.

"You sure you don't want some whipped cream, Bentley?" I pick up the bottle and shake it up before squirting it into my mouth.

"I want some!" Lilly shouts, pushing herself up in her chair to her knees. I lean over and give her a quick shot in her mouth.

"Astrid?" I arch a brow at her.

"Why not?" She licks her lips and opens her mouth, her perfect pink lips glistening. When she darts her tongue out to catch the whipped cream, I feel my dick twitch in my jeans. There are so many scenarios I've envisioned of her, me, and a can of whipped cream...

Fuck, maybe this was a bad idea.

Quickly giving her a shot of the sugary substance, I watch her throat bob as she swallows it down and all I can think about is how I wish it were my cock between her lips instead.

Yup, I'm going to hell.

"Fine, I'll take some," Bentley declares, reaching for the can, but I swipe it away before he can take it.

"Nope. I'll do the honors for you too."

He rolls his eyes but opens his mouth, trusting me far too easily. And before he can think otherwise, I shoot the whipped cream all over his face and everywhere *but* his mouth. He jumps up in surprise, whipped cream flying. "Uncle Penn! What the heck?" he shouts.

Lilly cackles and Astrid laughs until she realizes that I'm not stopping. "Oh my God, Penn! That's enough!"

I stand and shoot the can in her direction now, getting whipped cream all over the table and her upper body. Lilly jumps to scoop it up and put it in her mouth, but not before I douse her with some and then spray it all over the three of them, laughter and screaming carrying over the chaos.

When the can finally empties, all four of us are breathless and then we break out in laughter again.

"You're cleaning this up!" Astrid yells at me, even though there's a smile on her lips.

"That was the best game ever!" Lilly shouts, licking her arms and fingers.

"Penn isn't allowed to be in charge of the whipped cream ever again." Bentley glares at me. "But that was kind of fun," he admits before heading down the hall toward the bathroom, slamming the door shut behind him.

Astrid points to the table. "Start cleaning this up while I hose Lilly down." She grabs Lilly under her arms and carries her down the hall. "We'll rinse off together, baby."

After surveying the mess I made, I head for the laundry room, grab a few cleaning cloths, and get to work wiping down the table, chairs, and floor, and running the steam mop over the floor for good measure. After about twenty minutes, the mess is gone and Bentley and Lilly are changed and ready for bed. I sneak into both of their rooms to say goodnight, and when I enter the kitchen again, Astrid is standing at the sink washing a few dishes in her pajamas with her wet hair thrown up in a hair clip. The short blue shorts she has on hit just below her butt cheeks, showcasing her long, lean legs that I can't help but imagine wrapped around my waist. She has a matching tank top on that is lightweight and loose fitting too, but I can still see the outline of her chest under the fabric.

God, she's so fucking gorgeous and has no idea what she does to me every time I see her this way.

Why does she have to be off limits?

When she hears me, she glances at me over her shoulder before focusing back on her task. "That was a bit extreme, don't you think?"

"Oh, come on. The kids thought it was fun."

"And did you enjoy cleaning up your mess?" She grins at me over her shoulder this time.

"Immensely."

When she turns the faucet off, she reaches for a dish towel and dries her hands off. "The kids definitely had fun."

"Good. That's what these nights are all about, right?"

She showcases her brilliant smile as she stares at me, crossing her arms over her stomach. "Yeah." But then her smile drops.

"What?"

"I don't know. It's not that I don't enjoy these nights. I do. But life has been so crazy lately that I feel like my mind is always spinning. There's so much going on and so many decisions to make sometimes I wish I could just have one night off with no practice and no errands to run, and…"

"Go on a date?" I finish for her causing her head to pop up so our gazes meet.

"What?" She places her hand over her heart.

"You told Grady that you were going out with Dick. I'm guessing that's the kind of break you need?"

This isn't how I wanted to broach this topic with her, but ever since Monday night when I overheard the conversation between her and her brother, I haven't been able to stop thinking about her going out with Dick Cockwell. I mean, it was bad enough witnessing him putting his neck on the line, which is more than I can say for myself. But then hearing her confirm that she wanted to accept his offer made a migraine manifest in record time.

My stomach has been in knots every time I realize we're one day closer to Friday when he's supposed to pop into the bakery and ask for her answer.

Her brow is furrowed as she debates her response. "I mean, not necessarily, but I think it might be good for me."

"A date with Dick? How so?" Spreading my legs apart further, I cross my arms over my chest and steel my spine.

"Why are you acting this way?" she fires back at me.

"What way?"

"Like an older brother who doesn't approve of me going out with a boy." She mimics my stance. "Newsflash, Penn. I already have a protective older brother. I don't need another."

"Trust me, I have no desire to be your brother, Astrid. But I just don't understand where your head is at. Dick is the last guy on Earth you should be going out with."

She rolls her eyes. "Jesus, you and Grady must have talked."

We did, but she doesn't need to know that. "He's not good enough for you," I say instead—because it's the fucking truth.

"I'm not going to marry the man, Penn. It's just dinner." Then she straightens her spine and steels her gaze. "And you know what? It felt nice to be wanted. It's been a long time since I've felt that way."

If she only knew how badly I want her, how much I fucking crave her.

Does she not think about that night as much as I do?

Tell her, Penn. Tell her and remind her what that kiss felt like three years ago. Show her how she makes you feel, how she makes your body come alive—how being with her feels like breathing.

"Astrid, I..." *I fucking want you.*

"Mommy?" Lilly comes down the hall, rubbing her eyes.

Fuck.

It's just as well. Letting the truth run from my lips would only do more harm than good.

Astrid instantly softens and approaches her daughter. "What's up, baby?"

"I had a bad dream." Her bottom lip trembles.

"You were barely asleep so I'm not sure that's possible." Astrid rubs Lilly's back and rolls her eyes at me. "Let's go back to bed and twirl your dream catcher, okay?"

She nods, her eyes half closed already. "Okay."

Rubbing the back of my neck as Astrid walks away, I say, "I think I'm gonna take off."

She nods hesitantly, a crease between her brows still, but her shoulders fall. "Okay. See you at the bakery in the morning?"

"Yeah, I'll be there."

"Good night, Penn."

"Good night, Astrid."

I watch the girls walk down the hallway and then I head for the door. I can feel her eyes on my back for a moment, and I almost turn back around. But what would I do?

It's not like I can change her mind. It's not like I can tell her that the thought of her going out with Dick or any man that isn't me makes me want to vomit and explode at the same time.

And even though I live for our game nights, part of me feels like it's just another thing that keeps me firmly planted in the friend zone.

But that's where you chose to live, Penn, and that's where you have to stay.

Astrid belonged to Brandon first and she always will on some level.

And now she may belong to Dick Cockwell.

Lava is boiling inside of me, and I feel like it's only a matter of time before I erupt. I just hope I don't create a crack in our friendship that is beyond repair when I do.

Because hurting my relationship with Astrid isn't an option. It's why I'm still on the outside of this wall between us, knowing that everything will change once it's torn down.

***

"Penn. Are you listening to me?" Dallas snaps his fingers in front of my face, pulling me out of my head.

"Sorry. What?"

"Jesus, what is going on with you tonight?" He hands me the tray of drinks. "Take these to table seven, please."

"Yeah. Got it."

I trudge away, trying to shake off the image that's been on repeat in my brain since eight o'clock this morning.

"So, did you give any more thought to my question from last week?" Dick rocks back and forth on his heels, his hands in his khaki dress pants as he waits for Astrid to answer him.

She tucks her hair behind her ear as her cheeks pink up. And even though I'm hiding behind the swinging door that separates the front and back of the bakery, I can still see the change in the color of her skin. "I did." Dick doesn't say anything, just waits for her to continue. "I think...I'd really like to go out with you sometime."

If she wasn't standing right in front of him, I bet he'd fist pump the air. Instead, his smile becomes blinding. "That's great, Astrid."

"My schedule is kind of crazy though, so..."

"I'll be free whenever you are," he says, cutting her off. "Why don't we exchange numbers and try to set something up for next week?"

She nods, but it's not confident, and her hands are shaking as she reaches for her phone.

Meanwhile, I'm clenching my jaw so tight that I might just crack a fucking tooth.

After they exchange numbers, Dick grabs his box of baked goods and leaves the store.

And I have the strangest desire to go out after him and break every one of his fucking fingers so he can't touch her—ever.

Once I drop off the drinks at the table and clean the one right next to it, I toss the empty drink tray on the counter behind the bar and blow out a long breath.

"All right. What's got your balls all twisted up?" Dallas leans over to me as we rest our backs on the counter behind us, watching the restaurant run around us.

"That's a visual I never needed to conjure up."

"Well, that's how you're acting." He raises one brow in my direction. "You're scaring my customers."

"I am not," I argue.

"Sure. You didn't see the looks on the faces of the two women at table eight as you stomped away after delivering those drinks to table seven."

I turn my attention to the elderly women sitting there as one looks in my direction, assessing me with wide eyes.

"I'm just tired."

Dallas shakes his head at me. "Nope. Not buying it."

"Hey, gentlemen." Of all the fucking people to come into Catch & Release tonight, it had to be this fucking guy.

Dick Cockwell stands on the other side of the bar, grinning like a fucking fool, like he had the best fucking day of his life, and you know what? He probably did since Astrid agreed to go out with him.

I know I'd feel the same way.

"Richard. Good to see you," Dallas greets him as he pushes off the counter behind us and reaches out to shake his hand.

"Same to you. I was craving the fish and chips, so I stopped to grab some on the way home."

"Did you call your order in?"

Dick nods. "Sure did. Although, it was weird hearing someone other than Astrid answer the phone."

Dallas eyes him curiously. "Yeah, we really miss her around here."

"Her baking skills are being put to better use now though, aren't they?" Dick turns his eyes to me, a cocky grin on his lips. "How's it going, Penn?"

I glare at him, debating how many bones I could break in his body with one punch. "It's going."

"Still doing work on Astrid's shop?"

"Yup."

"Did she tell you she agreed to go out with me next week?" he says, and Dallas's head twists in my direction so fast that I'm surprised he doesn't topple over.

"Was she supposed to?" I counter as my blood pressure rises.

Dick shrugs as Dallas blows out a breath and intercepts Dick's order from one of the other waitresses that just finished packaging it up from the kitchen. "I just thought you two were friends and you were there when I asked her out, so..."

"Richard, let me ring you up at the register," my brother interrupts, and in that moment, I'm grateful that he did. Otherwise, the tension in my jaw was about to crack my skull in two.

"Thanks. See ya around, Penn." Dick fucking waves at me as he walks away. I close my eyes, take a deep breath, and then head toward the back of the restaurant, slamming the swinging door against the wall as I walk through it.

I run my hands through my hair and fucking seethe, looking for something to punch but knowing that won't fucking help. And besides, Dallas's restaurant doesn't deserve to be the victim of my anger.

A few minutes pass by as I pace and then I hear Dallas come up behind me. "So, I think I figured out why you're in a pissy mood."

I glare at him over my shoulder. "Fuck off."

"Hey, you have every right to be pissed off, Penn." I eye him skeptically. "I guess my question for you is, what are you going to do about it?"

"What am I supposed to do, Dallas?"

"I mean, are you just going to stand by and do nothing? Or are you going to fight for her?"

Dropping my hands to my sides, I stare at him. "I can't fucking do anything, Dallas. And you know that."

Dallas scoffs. "God, you're so fucking stubborn." Then he shakes his head. "You know what? No, stubborn is giving you too much credit. You're a fucking coward!"

My desire to punch Dick just instantly shifted to my brother. "I'm not a fucking coward!"

"Yes, you are." He pokes me in the chest, but I don't budge as he gets right in my face. "You've been pining after Astrid for years, and now she's about to slip through your fucking fingers, and you're going to just watch it happen?" I stay silent, meeting his glare with my own. "I thought more of you, Penn. I really thought that eventually you'd get over this hero complex, stop putting Brandon on a fucking pedestal, and finally go after what you want. But I guess you're just too scared."

His words sting because deep down, I know he's right.

I am scared. I'm fucking terrified.

It's why I never pulled the trigger on my business idea.

And it's definitely why I never said anything else to Astrid after that night—because the reality is, she could turn me down again—and she probably would.

"If you don't fucking say anything, you're never going to know, Penn. And she will move on eventually, but not with you. That's the truth you need to face."

Keeping my composure but vibrating with adrenaline, I say, "What if it fucking ruins everything, Dallas? What if she turns me down again, or it makes things weird between us? I can't lose having those kids in my life."

He crosses his arms over his chest and takes a step back. "Well, seeing as how you never told me what happened between you two, I can't give you my honest opinion. Regardless, that was a long time ago. You've both changed since then. And bottom line, living with regrets fucking sucks, Penn. At least trust me on that one."

My chest starts to ache because regret has been a close comfort lately, especially in the last week.

"When I took my chance with Willow, despite the complicated situation between us, you were the one that told me to make a decision, and I did. And it was the best fucking decision of my life."

"This is different."

"It's taking a chance, Penn. There's always excuses you can make to talk yourself out of what you want, but if you never try, you'll never know. That's the harsh truth of it." He rests a hand on my shoulder now, making me tense up even more. "Take off the rest of the night. Me and the crew can handle the rush. Figure out what the fuck you want to do and do it quickly because the last thing I want is for you to look back later and realize this was the moment that your entire life changed for the worse because you didn't take a chance on getting the life you wanted—the life you fucking deserve."

Dallas walks away from me, back out to the main part of the restaurant, and I stand there for a few moments, getting my thoughts together. Once I feel composed enough to drive, I find my keys in the office, exit through the back of the building, and hop into my truck, headed straight for my rental property where I can process everything.

With my safety glasses on and rock music blaring from my portable speaker, I take a sledgehammer and go to town on the kitchen counters, breaking up the old tiles and smashing the cabinets to pieces. Every swing helps me channel the anger that's been building in my body. Every crash of ceramic on the floor makes me feel lighter. And every chunk of wood I get to toss into the pile building in the dining room helps me sort through the chaos in my mind.

Astrid is everything I've ever wanted in a woman, which is why I've never felt this way about anyone else. Even the handful of relationships I've had over the years never lasted and never ignited emotions like this. No one else has made me want to better myself either.

Honestly, I wonder if she's been the perfect woman in my mind for far longer than the past three years. She's the standard I've compared every other woman to.

She's strong, resilient, kind, genuine, and sexy. She loves hard, is an incredible mother, and is gracious to the people in her life. She befriended Willow without a second thought and took a leap of faith buying the bakery from the previous owners.

If I'm being honest, a part of me knows that going after my business idea is in part so I feel like I fucking deserve her.

She did it. She went after her dreams after years of waiting. And she ought to have a man who is brave enough to do the same thing.

And that's when Dallas's words come back to me.

I *am* being a coward by holding back, by not being truthful with her, by letting Dick have his chance when I know I deserve mine.

As I toss the last scrap of debris into the pile, and look at the gutted kitchen, I make peace with myself.

This could end in disaster, or it could be the beginning of everything I've wanted for the past three years. Either way, my life isn't going to be the same after today—because this is either the moment I lose Astrid forever, or the moment we start something new together. And it might get messy, but I'm finally ready to take that risk.

Chapter Six

Astrid

"Sorry I'm late."

Grady is smiling from ear to ear as he watches Lilly dance around in front of the mirror in the dance studio. The parents have to watch from a separate waiting area because it prevents distractions for the girls, but you can still see what they're learning through the glass.

"The class isn't over yet. You're fine." He pulls me into his chest as we watch Lilly spin and smile. "She's a natural, Astrid."

"I know. I'm glad she enjoys it. Bentley has soccer and she has dance—something to keep them both busy."

"And if the boys win tomorrow, they play in the championship game next week, right?"

I blow out a breath just thinking about how busy life is right now. "Right."

Bentley comes up behind me and wraps his arm around my waist on my free side. "Hey, Mom."

"Hi, kiddo." I welcome this rare initiation of affection. "How was your day?"

He shrugs. "I hate school."

"What happened?"

Pushing himself from me, he heads back to his chair with no reply. Great.

"He's been in a mood since I picked him up from Mom," Grady mutters in my ear.

"I wonder what happened?"

"He'll talk to you about it when he's ready," Grady says nonchalantly as the dance class ends. Easy for him to say as the uncle and not the default parent, the one who worries at all hours of the day that I'm not present enough to know what's going on with my kid. We wait for Lilly to grab her things, listen to her teacher remind us for the hundredth time about the Christmas recital in December, and then head out to the parking lot together.

"Grady! Grady!" A female voice calls out to us just before we arrive at our cars.

My brother turns around and winces when he sees who's trying to get his attention. "Oh. Hello, Miranda."

Miranda Thorn brushes her long, blonde hair from her shoulder, which exposes her cleavage even more. She's recently divorced, and it looks like she's trying to let everyone in the vicinity know that she's available. "I wanted to catch you before you left."

"Well, here I am." Grady waves awkwardly as I usher the kids into the car. Thank God they can buckle themselves in now so I don't have to miss this.

"I feel like it's been forever since I've seen you," she croons, twirling her finger around her hair. I cover my mouth to keep myself from laughing out loud. This must be what he was talking about earlier this week—the blatant flirting.

"Funny because it was just yesterday when you came by so I could put air in your tires."

"Huh. Well, it feels like forever."

Grady takes a step back. "Well, it was good to see you…"

"Are you seeing anyone?" she asks blatantly, surprising us both.

"Uh…"

"Because I would love to go out with you sometime." She bites her bottom lip and bounces her eyebrows. "I think we could have a lot of fun. Talk about baseball, how you used to be famous…"

I can't help it. I snort. "Sorry," I say as I turn my back to them.

"Uh, I actually am seeing someone, Miranda, so…" *Liar, liar, pants on fire, big brother.*

"Oh." Her smile drops but she recovers nicely as I turn back around. "No worries. Say, do you know if Penn Sheppard is seeing anyone, then?"

My amusement from before instantly disappears. Grady looks over at me. "Uh…"

"Why do you ask?" I say, entering the conversation for the first time. I was enjoying being the spectator there for a minute, but now I feel the need to be involved.

"Come on, Astrid. You know how handsome the man is, and I'm a single woman"—she covers the side of her mouth and says with a wink—"with needs."

I never understood the term cat fight until right now because I instantly want to claw this woman's eyes out. "Actually, he just told me the other day that he doesn't have time for a relationship, so…"

"That's what all men say until they find the right woman."

"Mom, I'm hungry!" Miranda's daughter calls out to her from the window of her SUV, interrupting the conversation and it's probably for the best.

"I'll be right there!" Turning back to us, she looks me up and down, sizing up the competition I'm sure. "Penn just doesn't realize what he needs yet."

Grady grabs my arm, leading us back to our cars. "Have a good night, Miranda."

She waves her fingers at us before spinning around, her hair flying through the air as she does. "Yeah. You too."

When she gets far enough away, Grady lets out the breath he was holding. "Jesus Christ."

I jut my thumb over my shoulder. "Is that what you deal with?"

He points to where Miranda went. "Yes. That's exactly what I'm talking about. See? Dating is a lost cause."

I instantly think of my upcoming date with Dick and my stomach twists. "Yeah, I can see why."

"Well, needless to say, I'm beat." Grady leans down and kisses my cheek. "Have a good night, sis."

"Yeah, you too. Thanks again for taking Lilly to dance."

"Anytime."

As I drive us home, eager for my dinner date with Willow later, I can't get Miranda's words out of my head.

"That's what all men say until they find the right woman."

Was she implying that she's that woman for Penn?

And worse than that—what happens when Penn does find that woman?

Because I know that it can't be me.

***

"God, I needed this." I lift my wine glass to my lips and take a big drink, savoring the crisp Chardonnay before gulping it down.

"Well, I'm glad you could make time for us to catch up." Willow smiles at me from the other end of the couch. It's Friday night, we just got home from Lilly's dance class, and my feet are throbbing, but at least I finally get a chance to relax after this crazy week. When Willow texted me earlier today asking what I was up to tonight, I immediately invited her over for wine and pizza since I know Dallas is working at the restaurant and she'd be alone. The kids are in their rooms entertaining themselves now so we can have some adult conversation.

"I know. I've been a horrible friend, but between the bakery and the kids, I don't have much time for a social life right now. It's been a long, busy week and I'm ready for the weekend to get a bit of a break and catch up with laundry. Tanya agreed to open the bakery on Saturday mornings so I can enjoy the day and go to Bentley's soccer games without guilt."

Willow reaches for my foot and squeezes. "Oh, Astrid. I know. I was only joking with you, but I'm glad you're learning to find balance already. It won't always be this crazy, but in the beginning, your life will center around your business. That's just the way it is."

"It's exhausting but exhilarating at the same time." I can't help but smile. "I'm more tired than I've ever been, but I love knowing that the store is mine, that I get to make the decisions on what we sell, what it looks like, and everything in between. I will say, though, that the adrenaline is definitely the only thing keeping me going right now."

"I can't wait to see it when it's all done. Did Penn say when he'd be finished?"

Just the mention of Penn makes my pulse spike. "Well, the new display cases just came in today, and he plans on installing them on

Sunday since the bakery is closed that day. Then he plans on painting sometime this week and installing the new flooring next Friday night."

"I can't believe it's almost done. And when's the grand reopening?"

"I'm thinking in two weeks, just in time for the holidays."

Willow perks up in her spot. "Oh, that reminds me. I sort of have a business opportunity for you."

"Okay…" I take another sip of my wine, waiting for her to continue.

"So, one of my clients, Morgan Hotels, just opened a new hotel in Raleigh earlier this year. They throw a benefit every year to raise money for charity, and Wes Morgan, the owner, asked if I knew anyone who specialized in catering desserts in the area since they want to throw the event at their newest location." My heart starts to beat more rapidly. "I know that catering isn't in the spectrum of your business right now, but I thought this could be a great way to get more eyes on the bakery and hopefully bring people into town." She shrugs as a million questions fill my mind.

"Would it just be dessert?"

"Yes. The dinner is always served at the hotel anyway, but they wanted some kind of sweet treat that was on brand that they could give as party favors to the guests, and a table filled with options for people to sample."

"How many people?"

"Around five hundred."

My eyes bug out. "Five hundred?"

Willow winces. "I know it's a lot, especially right now. But again, I was just thinking about the advertising opportunity. I can't help it. That's immediately where my mind goes."

Willow owns her own advertising firm back in D.C. where she's from. She recently stepped down as acting CEO when she moved to Carrington Cove full time about a month ago, trying to enjoy other aspects of her life and find a work-life balance. But she's still involved in many aspects of the company and she's an investor in my bakery, so it doesn't surprise me that she saw this opportunity and wanted to share it.

I just don't know if I can handle this.

"You can't do that on your own, Astrid. No way."

A memory of Brandon flashes through my mind as soon as that self-doubt resurrects itself.

I start thinking about how crazy the next few months will be as the holidays approach, but determination rushes through me. November and December were always the busiest time of year when Greg and Jenny owned the bakery, so I know what to expect at least a little bit, and November is already underway. But knowing that Willow believes in me and I've already proven to myself that I'm capable of achieving my dreams, I straighten my spine and say, "I'm definitely interested."

Willow beams. "Really? Again, you can say no."

"I'm sure. You're right. It would be great exposure since a lot of tourists come from that area."

"They wanted to throw the party the second week in December. Would that work?"

I pull out my phone and look at my calendar. Soccer season will be over by then and Lilly's dance recital is the weekend after, so I know I'm free, and I'd be a fool to let this opportunity slip by. "Yes, I can make that work."

Willow shrieks this time, kicking up her feet. "Yes! This is going to be amazing, and of course, I'll help with whatever I can."

"I'm going to hold you to that because I might have to hire everyone I know to help frost cookies and cupcakes on the days leading up to the event."

Willow tosses her hair over her shoulder. "Hand me an apron and I'm there."

Once I put the event on my calendar, I put my phone back down and reach for my glass, draining what's left. "There's more of this, right?"

Willow laughs as she stands from the couch and heads to the kitchen, grabbing the already open bottle and a slice of pizza, taking a bite of it on her way back to the couch. As she sits, she hands me the bottle and I refill my glass. "So, what else has been going on? How are the kids?"

"Bentley is definitely hitting his pre-teen years. The attitude, the talking back. There are days where I think this can't get any worse, and then I remember he's only eleven and I have a long way to go." Willow chuckles. "But thankfully he has soccer to keep him grounded. And he's doing well in school, which is all I can ask for. Although today he said that he hates school, so I know something must have happened. And Lilly just has so much energy. I wish I could syphon it from her little body and use some for myself."

"She is a rambunctious girl, but so sweet."

I sigh wistfully. "She is. I know she's going to keep me on my toes, but I love watching her grow into her own person. She's loving her dance classes, is reading so well on her own now, and loves going to school, which I'm so grateful for because Bentley had separation issues when he was younger." I sigh and admit, "I just hope I don't mess the two of them up somehow, you know?"

Willow moves her eyes down to her lap as she fiddles with the bottom of her sweater. "Astrid, trust me. My parents died when I was two and they still messed me up. I don't think there's a way to get around that."

I close my eyes and sigh. "Shit. I'm sorry, Willow. I didn't even think about that..."

"Don't apologize, hon." She lifts her eyes back to mine. "I'm just saying, there's no telling the future. The only thing you can do is love them with everything you have, and make sure you take care of yourself too. You are a remarkable mother, Astrid, and I don't say that lightly. I'm in awe of you and want you to know that."

Trying not to cry, I croak out, "Thank you."

A few weeks ago, Willow sat down with me and told me the entire story of how she ended up in Carrington Cove, inheriting a house from a mystery benefactor who had known her parents. She shared her childhood with me, how she grew up with her godparents, and how she met her best friend Shauna in college. When she unveiled who the man was that left her the house, I couldn't hide my shock. After we shared several tears, she vowed not to hide anymore secrets from me, even though I didn't fault her for being cautious about sharing personal details. I happen to have a little bit of experience with that as well. But it felt good to really get to know the woman sitting across from me, a friend that feels like she was destined to be in my life.

And it's that realization that has me preparing to admit my recent life development before I explode. I take a big sip of wine before I blurt, "I'm going on a date next week."

Willow's eyes snap back over to me. "Oh my God! Who's the lucky guy?"

"Richard Cockwell." At that, she lets out a surprised laugh that she tries to cover with a fake cough. Ignoring her, I add, "He's a regular at the bakery who asked me on a date out of the blue last week. We went to high school together, and now he's a teacher there."

"Well...that's great!" she finally says, far too cheerily. "Do you like him?"

"I mean, yeah. He's a nice guy."

Willow narrows her eyes at me. "Just nice? He's your first date in four years and you're settling for *nice*?"

I throw my free hand up in the air. "What's wrong with nice? There aren't exactly a lot of single men in this town. He asked me out and it felt good to be pursued. Yeah, I'm nervous, but how bad can it be?"

Willow shrugs. "Well, my dating experience is pretty minimal, but I don't know…I feel like you should be more excited about your first date in years. It's a big deal!"

Chewing on my bottom lip, I say, "I think I'm more excited about not having to cook a meal and getting to talk to another adult for the night rather than the date part."

Willow smirks. "Can't say that I disagree with you there. I guess I just figured if you went out with anyone…it would be Penn."

My stomach instantly knots and I tilt my head at her. "Why would you think that?"

She folds in her lips and then it's her turn to take a big gulp of wine. "No reason," she murmurs, avoiding my eyes.

"Willow Marshall, what aren't you telling me?" I purse my lips as she squirms on the other end of the couch. Our eyes lock, and her silence speaks volumes.

"I mean…you don't see it?"

"See what?" I ask, leaning forward slightly in my seat.

"The way he looks at you, Astrid."

That sends a chill straight down my spine. The reality is, I've been so concerned with not showing how *I* felt about *him* that I haven't really considered how *he* feels about *me*. And so much time has passed since that night when our lips touched and my life was forever changed. The truth is, I put him in the friend zone after that just so I could be around him and have some semblance of control.

But I've seen it.

Hell, I've *felt* it.

And I've fantasized about what it would be like to give myself permission to kiss him again.

"I haven't noticed," I lie.

Willow arches a brow. "You haven't noticed, or you haven't *let* yourself see it?" I take a swig of my wine, avoiding answering. "That's what I thought."

"It's complicated, Willow."

"Then explain it to me." She situates herself into the cushion, tucking her legs up under her. "Because I know I haven't been here very long, but it only took a couple of encounters with you two to see the affection there. And I'm pretty sure you feel the same way about Penn as he feels about you."

I remove the clip from my hair and toss it onto the coffee table. "Of course there's affection there. It's Penn. I've known him for most of my life. Even when Brandon and I were stationed in Yuma for a few years, Penn would come out to visit us. He was the best man in our wedding, waited in the hospital when both kids were born, and has been there whenever I've needed him since Brandon died."

"Sounds like a pretty great guy, like a man you can count on. Way better than *nice*." Willow looks at me knowingly.

"That's the thing, Willow...I *do* count on Penn."

"So you're saying you wouldn't consider crossing that line?"

I take another drink of my wine. "Do you want me to admit that I've thought about it?"

"Uh, yeah." She laughs.

"Fine. I *have* thought about it, more than I probably should."

Her face softens. "And he's never said anything to you?"

I stare off into space across the living room. "No, he has...but I shut it down." I chug down the rest of my wine after that admission.

Willow's eyes bug out. "What? When did this happen?"

"A little over three years ago," I tell her. "It was the anniversary of Brandon's death. There were copious amounts of tequila involved, and we kissed."

"Holy shit!" Willow shrieks before covering her mouth and lowering her voice. "Sorry."

"But that was it," I continue quickly. "It was a momentary lapse in judgment."

"And nothing ever happened after that?"

"Nope." I shake my head and reach for the bottle of wine. "And I imagine he's moved on by now..."

She scoffs. "Uh, doubtful. But would you even be willing to go there again?"

I turn my face to meet her gaze. "I can't."

"Why not?"

"Because I can't risk losing him. And he was Brandon's best friend—people would have opinions," I answer honestly.

Willow gives me a sad smile. "I get that. I do. I mean, hell...my relationship with Dallas had its complications too. But nothing worth having comes easily. And excuse my French, but fuck people and their opinions. They're not the ones living your life, so they don't get to dictate your happiness."

I fluff the pillow behind me, more to stall than anything. "I'd rather have Penn as a friend than risk losing him."

Willow sighs. "That's too bad, because I know he must feel the same about you."

I give her my attention again. "What makes you say that?"

"Because I've watched him, Astrid. And don't get me wrong, my experience with men is negligible, but I've never seen a man show up for a woman like he does for you. Well, excluding Dallas, of course." She winks. "Throughout the months when he was working on my house, I got to know him. He's definitely the strong, silent type, but he's loyal, hardworking, and selfless. He's always helping others and pays attention to details. I just wonder if you're both so worried about jeopardizing your friendship that you tiptoe around what you both really want, which could be something even better."

Everything she said about Penn is true and why I value having him in my life.. "He was right there when Richard asked me out, Willow. Other than being an overprotective friend, he hasn't made any move to stop me from going on that date." My heart thrashes wildly as I finally voice that concern.

"Did you think he would?" Willow asks. "I don't know him as well as you, but I get the feeling that storming in and claiming you isn't really Penn's style."

Maybe it should be—because that would have been really hot.

But stuff like that is only hot in romance novels.

Yeah, I probably would have yelled at him for acting like he owned me.

"So you're saying..." I continue, pulling myself from my thoughts.

"I don't know what I'm saying. I just know that I'm proud of you for taking some action in your love life, but I don't think Richard Cockwell is the man you really want." She taps her chin with her finger. "And while we're on the topic, I just have to point out that his name is hideous."

I can't help it. I let out a loud laugh that fills the room. "Grady told me I'm not allowed to marry him because of his name alone."

"I second that."

"So what do I do? Do I cancel the date?"

Willow ponders her response. "No, I say you go. See if there's something there, and like you said, at least get a free meal and evening out of it. Plus, I think it will be a good way to see what you really feel for Penn."

"What do you mean?"

"Well, if you're comparing Richard to Penn all night, that's a huge red flag."

"I wouldn't do that."

Willow smirks. "Okay, if you say so."

How does she know that I've already done that so many times in my mind? Penn is much taller than Richard, although Penn is so much taller than most people. Penn has dark hair, which I favor more than Richard's dirty blonde. Penn isn't afraid to get his hands dirty while Richard's hands are so pristine he probably gets regular manicures.

But more than anything, the idea of Richard doesn't get my blood pumping like thinking about Penn does.

Willow snapping her fingers in front of my face pulls me from my thoughts once more. "Hello? Astrid, are you in there?"

"Yeah, sorry."

"Daydreaming about Penn and his muscles?" she teases.

I roll my eyes and stand from the couch. "No."

"Liar." Willow follows me into the kitchen as Lilly comes around the corner, sliding across the tile in her socks.

"Mommy!"

"What's up, baby girl?"

"Can I have kisses from Daddy, please?" She juts out her bottom lip, turning her nightly ask into a spectacle when she doesn't really have to.

"Yes, baby. But only two. You're going to go to bed soon."

She nods and races over to the vase. "Okay."

"The vase just guts me every time I see it," Willow says as she enters the kitchen.

Willow and I watch as Lilly unwraps each kiss and plops them in her mouth, leaving the foil wrappers on the table. Normally I remind her to throw them in the trash, but I'm too transfixed as I watch her. "I know."

"And who is the one who fills up the vase again?"

"Penn," I say without pause.

"Hmmm."

I twist to face Willow again, noticing the smirk on her lips. "What?"

"I'm just saying...a man that takes responsibility of a sentimental gesture like that?" She shakes her head slowly. "That's the type of man you keep for yourself, Astrid."

"Subtle."

She chuckles. "I wasn't trying to be, but that brings me to my next question. If you're not willing to act on your feelings, what happens when Penn meets someone else?"

My stomach drops and reminders of my interaction with Miranda Thorn earlier tonight replay in my head. "What do you mean?"

"Well, I mean, he won't be single forever, right? Eventually some woman is going to catch his attention, value him for everything that he is. He won't be in your life the same way he is now, that's for sure."

"Oh, well..." Sweat starts to build at my temples. "Penn's allowed to live his life..." My pulse is racing and I'm sure my concern is written all over my face.

She pats my shoulder and then walks back to the couch. "I think my work here is done."

I curse her as I have a mild panic attack in the kitchen after she Jedi-ninjaed my mind.

What *if* Penn starts seeing someone?

I doubt it would be Miranda, but still.

What if she doesn't want him spending time with me and the kids anymore?

Would he still come over for game night?

Would he still coach Bentley's soccer team?

Would he still pick up the phone if I needed him?

I could scream from all the questions Willow's mind game just plagued me with. But ultimately, there's only one question that needs answering: What am I going to do about it?

Chapter Seven

Penn

"What's for dinner tonight?" I peek over my mother's shoulder as she stirs something on the stove.

"Chicken bog," she says, swatting me away. "Now get out of here so I can finish cooking."

"We haven't had that in a while." The rice, chicken, and beef sausage are boiling in the broth in the pot, infiltrating the air around the kitchen, making my mouth water.

"I know. I had a craving for it, so for once, I'm making what *I* want to eat," my mother replies. It's Sunday, which means family dinner night. We don't always make it each week, but the weeks we can, my brothers and sister and I gather at our childhood home and Mom cooks us a meal like she did when we still lived here. Even before Dad died, this was a tradition. But now that he's gone, it's even more important to all come together.

"You know we'll eat whatever you make, Mom." I kiss her on the cheek and then head to the fridge, grabbing a beer for me and Dallas. My brother and Willow are currently outside on my parents' deck, watching the sun set in the distance. His arm is wrapped around her, and as I watch them, envy courses through me.

I want to have that with Astrid.

As much as I hate to admit it, my brother gave me the clarity I needed Friday night. My anxiety is at an all-time high, but that's because I'm making risky moves in my life for the first time. It's fucking terrifying, but I don't want to live with regrets.

As I open the back door, Dallas glances over Willow's head to meet my eyes. "What's up, dickhead?"

Willow elbows him in the ribs. "Don't call him that."

"It's okay. You may not understand it, but it's actually a term of endearment between us." I hand my brother his beer.

Willow shakes her head. "I'll never understand men in that regard, I guess."

"It's the brotherly thing too," Dallas adds. "Just wait until Parker gets here. He'll probably refer to us in the same way."

"You realize I've seen the three of you interact, right? I'm aware that you call each other names. I just don't understand it," Willow says.

This isn't her first family dinner that she's attended, but now that she's a part of our lives, she's becoming accustomed to the way we talk to one another.

If Astrid were here, she'd already know too.

Dallas kisses her temple, pulling her in closer to his body. "Just let it be, babe. It is what it is." Then my brother meets my eyes again. "You doing better than you were Friday night?"

I nod, popping the top on my beer and taking a sip. "Yeah. Thanks for letting me leave. I needed to demolish some shit."

Willow squints at me. "What happened Friday night?"

Dallas turns Willow in his arms so they're both facing me now. "Penn was on the verge of a meltdown at the restaurant. I had to let him go early before he punched Dick Cockwell in the face."

Willow's eyes go wide. "The guy Astrid is going on a date with?" She practically shoves Dallas off her as she stands and steps closer to me. "What happened?"

"Jesus, do you tell her everything?" I ask my brother.

"He didn't have to. Astrid did," Willow answers for him.

I drop my eyes to hers. "She told you about her date?"

"I went over to her house Friday night to hang out, and yeah...she told me." And then it dawns on her. "Oh my god! You're jealous, huh?"

I close my eyes and huff out a breath. "Jesus, I'm not jealous."

"Yes, you are," Dallas says matter-of-factly.

Willow practically vibrates with excitement. "Oh my god. Does this mean you're finally going to do something about your feelings for her?"

Pinching the bridge of my nose, I mutter, "Nothing is a secret in this family, I swear."

Willow shoves my shoulder. "It's not a secret when everyone can see it, Penn. Like I told you at her going away party, I get why you don't cross that line. But if she goes out with Richard, you're going to kick yourself for letting her slip away."

"That's what I told him," Dallas interjects.

"I know, all right? I fucking know." I drain half of my beer before continuing. "Look, I'm going to talk to her, okay? I've made the fucking decision and I'm tired of us tiptoeing around each other, but I can't just ambush her. I need to do this right."

Willow folds in her lips to hide her smile and bounces on her feet. "Oh my god! I'm so fucking excited!"

Dallas laughs at her. "Don't get ahead of yourself, Goose. He has to actually go through with it."

"You think I won't?"

Dallas shrugs. "I think you overthink shit too much."

"Well, what if I told you that I'm quitting the restaurant and the hardware store?"

Both of their eyes snap to mine. "What?" Dallas asks. "Are you serious?"

"Yeah, I am. Not yet, but soon. I was going to wait to tell you, but since you're being a dick, now seemed like a good time." I flip him the bird.

Dallas furrows his brow. "Why are you quitting?"

I take a deep breath and finally utter the words out loud. "I'm starting my own business."

Willow's eyes bug out. "Penn! That's amazing! Do you need an investor?" She grabs my bicep with both of her hands.

Chuckling, I say, "Not right now, but I appreciate the offer, Willow. Especially since you have no idea what I'm doing yet."

"Doesn't matter. I would invest in you in a heartbeat. I know how hardworking you are, and I know you won't fail."

I pull her in for a hug, wishing I had the same confidence in myself that she does. "That means a lot. Thanks." It's crazy to me that I've only known this woman for a few months, but she already feels like my sister-in-law, like a part of our family that was missing. And the fact that she believes in me without question boosts my confidence that I'm making the right decision.

"So what are you going to do?" Dallas asks.

"I'm going to buy houses and turn them into rentals for tourists and maybe residents of the town. I want to offer more lodging for people visiting mostly. The Cove Inn can only accommodate so many people, you know? I'll still do contract work on the side. I'm just ready to be my own boss."

Dallas smirks. "It's about fucking time."

I roll my eyes. "Yeah, I know."

Willow squeezes my arm. "This is amazing, Penn. What made you decide to go for it?"

"Pam contacted me about a house for sale that I couldn't pass up. But honestly..." I stare out across the yard. "It was Astrid."

They both look at me knowingly, so I'm guessing I don't need to explain why.

"So, what about Dick?" Dallas asks.

"I don't know. I haven't figured that out yet."

"Well, you should. Clock's ticking," he says.

Willow grabs my forearm now to get my attention. "She doesn't really want to go out with him, you know."

"Why do you say that?"

"Because she told me. Well, not in those words exactly, but the message was clear under the surface. I think you should talk to her, Penn. Like, soon." She widens her eyes to the point that she almost looks scary.

"Why are you looking at me like that?" I move away from her, slightly concerned.

"She may have some insider knowledge," Dallas mutters against the lip of his beer can.

Confused, I look back at Willow. "What the fuck is he talking about?"

Willow smirks. "Let's just say I think Astrid would drop Dick in a heartbeat if you gave her a reason to, Penn," she whispers, leaning back into my brother's chest. The two of them are acting like teenagers, giddy because their friends are crushing on each other and they're in on it.

Jesus, is this what this situation has come to?

"As much as I appreciate the two of you trying to be matchmakers, just stay out of it, okay? I'll act when the time is right."

Dallas mumbles in Willow's ear. "That means we'll be waiting another year."

"Fuck you."

Dallas laughs and Willow chastises him just as Parker exits the house and joins us outside. "Hey, it's the hometown hero! Save any kittens from trees today?" Dallas says to our younger brother.

"I'm not a firefighter, moron," Parker replies, flipping Dallas off as he lifts a beer to his lips.

See? This is how we tell each other we care. It's our own love language.

"Too bad. Firefighters are hot," Willow chimes in. "I recently read a book about a firefighter who marries a girl he's been crushing on to help her in a custody battle. And believe me, he definitely set those pages and my loins on fire."

The three of us just stare at her.

Willow rolls her eyes and begins to walk back to the house. "If there were another girl out here, they totally would have appreciated that."

The door shuts behind her and then Parker and I turn to Dallas. "Did you know she reads books like that?"

Dallas smirks as he lifts his beer to his lips. "Who do you think helps her live out the scenes when they get her all worked up?" He waggles his eyebrows as Parker and I groan.

"Didn't need to know that," Parker grumbles.

"You're just jealous because I'm getting laid regularly. *Very* regularly. So regularly it's probably considered irregular."

I just roll my eyes, but Parker replies, "Not that it's any of your business, but I got some action not too long ago."

I pat my brother on his shoulder. "By someone other than your hand? Good for you." I know it's ironic that I'm giving him shit for the same circumstance I'm in—a dry spell by choice—but this is just what we do to each other.

He pushes my hand away. "Fuck you. It was at the conference I went to last month. I met this girl on the plane and she was gorgeous. One night, no names." He blows out a breath. "It was hot."

"Nice to see someone is breaking their dry spell," Dallas says, eyeing me from the side. "But I gotta say, having the same woman in your bed every night is so much better."

Even though it's been years since I've been with a woman, I have to agree. Knowing someone under the surface and learning their body makes that physical connection so much more intense.

I can only imagine how mind-blowing it would be with Astrid.

Fuck. She just might ruin me if that's the case.

Like she hasn't already owned you for the past three years?

"Well, I had the same woman every night and we all know how that ended," Parker says, reminding us of his bad luck in love. But the fact that he's even bringing it up is surprising. "So a hot night with no strings attached was exactly what I needed, and it delivered." He pushes his glasses up his nose.

"Then I'm happy for you." Dallas clinks his beer with Parker's.

"Boys, it's time to eat!" Our little sister, Hazel, peeks her head out of the back door.

"Hey, look who decided to show up finally!" Dallas teases her. "You'll be late to your own funeral, won't you, Hazelnut?"

She flips him off this time, further solidifying just how bizarre sibling relationships can be.

We settle in around the table, and Willow lets out an audible moan when she gets her first taste of the food. "Oh my god. How have I never had this before?"

"Chicken bog is a Southern staple, Willow," my mother replies. "And any Paula Deen recipe is bound to be good just based on the amount of butter used in it."

Willow nods her head with her mouth full and then replies once she's finished chewing. "I don't even care."

"You will when you have to unbutton your pants afterward," Hazel replies.

"I've already had that issue from Astrid's blueberry muffins." Willow reaches for her glass of water. "I had to put myself on a limit because the addiction was real."

"It's just so amazing that the bakery is now hers," my mother chimes in.

"I'm so proud of her. And I got her to agree to a huge event next month that will bring her even more business," Willow says.

Curious, I ask, "What event?"

"It's for Morgan Hotels. She's going to cater the desserts for their charity event at their newest location in Raleigh. There will be over five hundred guests. Wesley Morgan is a client of mine, so I couldn't pass up offering her the opportunity to advertise to that many people."

"Sounds great. She didn't mention it this morning, though," I say, trying to hide the surprise in my voice.

Willow shrugs, but her eyes flit around nervously. "She probably just hasn't wrapped her head around it yet. I only spoke to her about it Friday night."

Seems a lot of things went down Friday.

I went to the bakery this morning to install the new display cases, but our conversation was very surface level. We talked about the championship soccer game coming up next week since we won our final season game. She asked me more about the flooring and painting I'm doing this week.

But that was it.

Granted there were people all around us, so it wasn't the best time. But even I could sense that the tension was high.

"Besides, she kept telling me that once the soccer season is over, she'll have more time to focus on the bakery. I think she's secretly looking forward to it even though she loves watching Bentley play."

Dallas chimes in. "As much as I love the season too, I'm ready for the break."

"Yeah, same," I say, moving my newfound knowledge to the back of my mind for the moment. But the extra time will be necessary as I focus on my rental property.

"So that means you'll have time to build the Christmas backdrop for me then, huh?" Hazel asks, batting her eyelashes at me just like she did when she asked me the other day.

"Yes, Hazelnut. I've got you. It'll get done." Not sure when, but I'll make it happen. I always do.

She blows me a kiss. "Best big brother ever."

"Hey!" Parker and Dallas interject at the same time.

"It's about time I claim the title," I mock them, but my mother puts an end to the battle, addressing our plans for Thanksgiving before the bickering gets out of hand.

And as I sit there, listening to the usual conversation that happens at our family dinners, I wonder how much different the next one might be if I actually get the chance to talk to Astrid about so many things.

Here's hoping I take the opportunity when it arises.

***

"You're in here early today," Dallas says as I walk toward the bar he's standing behind in Catch & Release. It's Thursday, which is when Grady, Parker, and I all come in for lunch each week. Dallas doesn't open until four in the afternoon on weekdays, so the place is dead and it allows us all to catch up.

I flip my ball cap around and take a seat on my usual stool. "I needed to get out of the hardware store. Mrs. Hansen was driving me nuts."

"Did she make you sort screws again?" An amused grin spreads across his lips.

"Fuck you. You have no idea what a nightmare that was."

He taps on the metal bar where the food is placed as it's cooked, signaling to Jerry in the kitchen that I'm here. One of the cooks always comes in earlier in the day to prep a few things before the doors open to the restaurant. "Oh, no I'm sure it was horrible, which is why it baffles me that you're still working for the woman."

"Believe me, I'm questioning that myself." I take a stack of papers from my pocket and lay them on the bar in front of me. "But I finally filed for my LLC with the town, so the wheels are in motion to get out for good."

Dallas picks up the paperwork and nods approvingly. "Nice, Penn."

"Thanks."

"You should just quit then. I know it's not about the money for you since you pick up every penny you find on the street." My brother is right. I'm about as frugal as they come, and my savings is stacked because if I don't need something, I don't buy it. I also have some money in the stock market, so it's not like I'm struggling, but I think we both know my reservations go deeper than that.

"Sometimes it's not always about money, Dallas. It's about loyalty."

"Yeah, but sometimes you've got to put yourself first."

I lean back in my chair. "So are you saying you're ready for me to quit the restaurant?"

He shrugs and then crosses his arms over his chest. "If that's what you need to do, then yeah."

I can't say the next step of quitting my two jobs hasn't been on my mind, but I wanted to be further along with my new venture before I cut all ties. And I'm not one to leave anyone high and dry either. I'd like to make sure that Mrs. Hansen has someone to replace me before I leave the hardware store completely.

But maybe Dallas is right. That needs to be sooner rather than later, especially because the craziest time of the year is about to commence. I could use the extra time.

"I'll let you know when I'm ready," I say, just as Jerry slides my burger onto the counter. Dallas grabs the plate, a bottle of ketchup, some extra napkins, and a Coke from the fountain, dropping everything off in front of me.

"Don't keep pushing it off though, Penn. Time's a-wasting. Speaking of which, have you talked to Astrid yet?"

I knew that was fucking coming. "Not yet," I mumble around a bite of my burger.

"Willow's getting anxious. Every time the phone rings, she thinks it's going to be Astrid calling to tell her that you've confessed your feelings to her. I swear, she's going to have a damn heart attack."

"Maybe Willow needs to go back to work since she has too much time on her hands to worry about my and Astrid's lives."

Dallas glares at me. "Hey, watch it. That's my girl you're talking about."

The corner of my mouth lifts along with one of my shoulders. "I said I'll talk to her. I didn't say when."

My brother leans over the counter in front of me. "A little birdie also told me that her date with Dick is tonight."

Fury erupts in my veins. "Is that so?" I grate out.

Dallas smirks at me. "Yup. Still think you want to wait to have that conversation now?"

I glare at my brother before going back to eating my burger, wishing I never would have come in here for lunch now.

***

My phone vibrates in my pocket for the third time. Shutting off the table saw, I set my safety goggles to the side, turn down the music blaring from my speaker, and dig my phone out of my pocket. But when I see the number for Bentley and Lilly's elementary school, my stomach plummets.

"Hello?"

"Hello. I'm looking for Penn Sheppard?" the female voice on the other end of the line says. And it's not like I don't know who it is, but I assume Alaina Bell must act professionally even though everyone knows she's the principal of Carrington Cove Elementary.

"This is Penn."

"Yes, well, sorry to bother you today Mr. Sheppard, but I have Bentley here in my office and was wondering if you'd be able to come pick him up?"

I reach for my keys on the side table and immediately lock up the front door before heading out to my truck. "Is something wrong?"

"I'm afraid Bentley was in a fight today. He'll be suspended for the rest of today and tomorrow, so someone needs to take him home."

"A fight? Bentley? Are you sure?"

"Yes, Mr. Sheppard."

"Shit. Does Astrid know?"

Alaina clears her throat. "I wasn't able to get ahold of her, Mr. Sheppard. Or her mother. Hence why I'm calling you. You're the next person on the emergency contact list."

Why the fuck wouldn't Astrid be answering her phone?

Before I go down the rabbit hole of what could have happened to her, I give my attention back to the phone call. "I'll be there as soon as I can, Alaina."

She exhales and relaxes her voice, the professionalism drifting away. "Thanks, Penn. See ya in a bit."

This afternoon was supposed to be *my* time to work on *my* rental house. After having lunch with Dallas and the boys, I was eager to come here and let off some steam. I just started cutting the tiles for the shower when Alaina called.

Bentley in a fight?

I mean, I know I wasn't an innocent eleven-year-old boy, but the only time I got in a fight was in high school and it was on the football field. The testosterone was running rampant and it was a rivalry game. Other than wrestling with Dallas and Parker, I kept my fists to myself.

Something must have triggered him. Bentley isn't that kind of kid.

On the way to the school, I try calling Astrid myself, but the call goes straight to her voicemail. I try calling Melissa, but she doesn't pick up either. And what about Grady? Was he after me on the emergency contact list?

Something about that makes me both proud and concerned at the same time.

I race into the parking lot of the school, shoving my truck in park and leaping from the vehicle, headed toward the front office. It's at that moment I realize that I'm covered in dust and there's a hole in the black shirt that I'm wearing, but this is as good as it's going to get with no notice.

"I'm here for Bentley Cooper," I tell Janet at the front desk when I walk into the office.

"Penn Sheppard?" Janet peers up at me over the rim of her glasses, her gray hair tied up in a bun.

"Hey, Janet."

Her eyes drop down my body. "You look like you were in the middle of something."

"What gave me away?"

She chuckles. "Well, whoever it's for made a sound decision. That deck you built for us is still standing strong."

Janet Connely is married to Harold, one of the three old men that play darts at Catch & Release every Friday night. They've lived in Carrington Cove since before any of my siblings and I were born, and last summer, I replaced and extended the deck off the back of their house for them. It was some of my best work, if I do say so myself.

"Glad to hear it. Now, about Bentley…"

Janet pushes a button under her desk, unlocking the half door beside her, letting me past the barricade. "He's in Ms. Bell's office. I have to say I was surprised to hear he was involved in an altercation."

Sighing, I step past her desk. "Yeah, me too."

I head down the hall that is lined with offices on either side, and finally arrive at Alaina's office on the left, knocking to signal my arrival.

"Come in."

I step into the room where Alaina sits behind her desk with Bentley occupying one of the chairs across from it.

"Hey, kiddo."

Bentley doesn't look up from his lap, but the redness on his cheek tells me he's either been crying or he took a punch in this fight. Secretly, I hope it's the first option.

Nothing's a shot to your pride quite like getting caught off guard and taking a sucker punch.

"Thanks for coming, Penn. I've tried calling Astrid and Melissa again, and still no luck."

Alaina looks up at me from her chair, her blonde hair pulled back away from her face and her blue eyes full of remorse. She's always been a pretty girl, and we even went out a few times right after high school, but agreed we were better off as friends. The romantic chemistry just wasn't there.

"Yeah, I tried on the way over here too. I'm sure there's a logical explanation for why they're not answering."

Alaina directs her attention to Bentley. "Bentley, I hope you take some time during your suspension to think about how you could have handled the situation differently, okay?"

Grabbing his backpack from the ground, he heaves it over his shoulder and mutters as he walks past me. "Whatever."

I pinch the bridge of my nose before meeting Alaina's eyes. "Do we know what started the fight?"

Alaina shakes her head. "Neither one of them wanted to talk about it. When they return from suspension, we'll do a conflict resolution between the two of them, but it was nasty, Penn. Bentley had Marcus pinned to the ground and was wailing on him before the teacher on duty aw and finally broke them up."

Well, at least Bentley didn't lose.

"I'll see if I can get it out of him before his mother finds out. I'm sure it will probably go over better if she understands why he acted this way."

She smiles. "Good luck."

Bentley is leaning against the wall just outside Alaina's door, waiting for me as I step out. "Come on. Let's go."

I don't look behind me to make sure that he's following me, but I sense it. At least we know he's not stupid enough to wait around for his mother to pick him up once she realizes she has a dozen missed phone calls from the school.

After we situate ourselves in my truck and take off for Astrid's house, I wait a few minutes before finally breaking the silence. "You know, this will be a lot easier to understand if we know what happened, Bentley." He stays silent, twisting his head to stare out the passenger side window. "I get being so angry with someone that you want to hit them. Trust me, I do." My mind wanders back to Dick Cockwell and the audacity he possessed asking Astrid out in front of me, and then gloating about it at the restaurant, and now taking her on a date tonight. *Fucker.* "But putting your hands on someone else is never okay."

"He freaking deserved it," Bentley finally says, his jaw clenched and his eyes rimmed with tears.

"What did he do?"

All I get is a shake of his head.

"Did he piss you off?"

Bentley nods, still avoiding my eyes.

Sighing, I stare out the windshield as we come to a stoplight. I know that taking him home to Astrid would be the right thing to do, but something tells me this kid needs a different kind of therapy at the moment.

As soon as the light turns green, I gun it, speeding past a few cars so I can change lanes and make the turn that I need to.

Bentley grips the handle on the door, bracing himself with his other hand on the seat. "What the heck, Uncle Penn?"

"We're taking a detour."

"Where are we going? The fire station?"

I look at him, bewildered. "Why on earth would I be going to the fire station?"

"Travis said you can abandon kids at the fire station."

Kids are the fucking worst. I swear, I don't remember ever being that clueless when I was his age.

Instead of calling Travis a fucking dumbass, I roll my eyes and take the next turn to lead me back to my project house. "You can only do that with babies, Bentley."

"Oh. Then where are we going?"

"Somewhere to help you let out your anger in a healthier way."

***

Bentley stares at me like I'm crazy as I place a hard hat on his head. "You want me to hit the wall with this sledgehammer?" He asks, struggling to lift the tool in question. I grab it myself and demonstrate how to hold it.

"Yup. As hard as you can."

He still looks skeptical, so I show him what I mean. Nudging him to the side, I get in my stance and swing hard, punching a hole through the drywall and sending dust flying everywhere.

"Whoa." He stares open-mouthed at the hole, motionless.

Placing the tool back on the ground, I smile and pat him on the back. "It helps, I promise."

I gave him the smallest sledgehammer I have, so I know he can lift it. But I really think a few swings and some destruction will be enough to get this kid talking.

Anger always needs an outlet before reason can come through.

"Okay..." Bentley grabs the tool, hoists it over his shoulder, and swings, making a dent right next to the hole I punched.

"Nice! Do it again."

"You really don't care how much damage I do?"

"Nope. I'm tearing down this wall to make the entire living area open."

The wall wasn't on my agenda for the day, but neither was picking up my godson from school because he got suspended for fighting. Today, I'm literally rolling with the punches.

The corner of his mouth picks up just a bit as he swings the sledgehammer again. And this time, he makes an even bigger dent. "Yeah! That was a good one. Keep going."

Bentley gets serious now, preparing his body with each swing, making a mess of the wall in front of me. And I'm not going to lie, watching him focus and partake in this unorthodox form of therapy makes me proud.

But then my phone vibrates in my pocket and brings me back to reality.

"Hey, Bentley? It's your mom."

He freezes. "Is she coming to get me?"

I stare at the screen as the call ends, debating what I should do. But then her name flashes across the screen again. Deciding to do what's best for Bentley right now, I step toward the front door and tell him, "No. I'll take you home when we're done here. But just know that she's not going to be happy."

He hangs his head. "Yeah, I know."

I pat him on the shoulder reassuringly. "Just keep at it." I step outside, close the door behind me, and answer the call before it goes to voicemail again.

"I have him, Astrid." I say into the phone reassuringly, watching through the window as Bentley gears up to take another swing at the wall.

"Oh, thank God!" I can hear her exhale in relief. "I started freaking out when I saw how many voicemails I had from the school and you."

"I bet. Why weren't you answering your phone? They couldn't reach your mom either."

"My phone died and I meant to plug it into the charger, but then I got distracted and forgot. And my mom was in a movie with one of her friends, so her phone was on silent."

"Well, they went down the list and called me. I was at a job site, but I rushed over and picked him up."

"What the hell happened? Ms. Bell said he was in a fight?" I hear something metal hit the ground in the background. "Ugh! Stupid bowl!"

"Calm down, Astrid. He's okay." If I were there right now, I'd shove a Ferrero Rocher in her mouth.

"I cannot calm down, Penn! My son was in a fight, neither my mom nor I were there for him, and I have a date tonight for the first time in over four years. I am anything but calm!"

Fuck. So she really is going out with Dick tonight.

My concern quickly morphs into frustration. "I don't know what the fight was about yet, okay?" I say, trying to keep the focus on what's important here, not how worried I am that I'm too late to stop this thing between her and Dick.

Now's not the time to discuss *us*, but shit. The timing fucking sucks, as always.

"Whatever it was about, fighting is inexcusable, Penn."

"Sometimes that's how boys solve their problems," I argue, even though I know it's weak.

"Not my son. He needs to talk, and he's going to talk right now! Put him on the phone."

A loud crash echoes from inside. I glance through the window to make sure he's okay. Bentley's chest is heaving, his face is flushed, and sweat is beading at his temples as his anger rises to the surface.

Now we're getting somewhere.

"That's not a good idea right now."

"What?"

"I'm handling it, Astrid, okay?"

"What do you mean 'handling it'?"

"I'm trying a different approach to get him to talk to me."

Astrid groans. "Oh, God. Penn! My son hit another boy…"

"Listen," I cut her off. "I know you're upset, but there's a reason Bentley hit another kid, Astrid, and it has to be a good one because we both know he normally wouldn't hurt a fly."

I can hear her sigh and after a few seconds she finally relents. "You're right."

"So, let me see what I can get out of him, and I'll bring him home later. You can lay into him then."

"I was so scared, Penn." Emotion clogs her throat. "I didn't know what to think. So many scenarios went through my mind when I saw my phone…"

"I know, but he's safe. I've got him, Astrid. I'm doing what I can for our boy, okay?"

She grows quiet and then I hear her sniffle. "Okay. I'll see you later. And Penn?"

"Yeah?"

"Thank you."

"Of course, Astrid."

When I hang up the call, a scream pierces the air. Heart racing, I rush inside to find the sledgehammer on the ground and Bentley attacking the wall with his bare hands, ripping at the broken pieces of drywall. I run over and grab him by his shoulders, yanking him back before he hurts himself.

"What the hell, Bentley?" I shout and take a step back, chest heaving.

Red-faced with tears welling in his eyes, Bentley yanks the hard hat off and throws it to the ground. Clenching his fists at his sides, he shouts, "It's not fair!"

Trying to steady my breathing, I soften my tone. "What's not fair, buddy?"

He shakes his head. "It's just not fair!"

"What's going on, Bentley? What did that kid do?"

"He deserved to be punched. He deserved a lot more for what he said!"

I close the distance between us and pull him into my chest. "What did he say, Bentley? You can talk to me."

He buries his face in my shirt, gripping the fabric tightly. "He said my dad isn't here because he couldn't stand to have me as a son!" he shouts into my chest and then the tears flow freely.

I'm holding him close as my body vibrates with anger. "What the fuck?"

He sobs uncontrollably and all I can do is rub his back while I contemplate how to get revenge on an eleven-year-old boy. "Shhh. It's okay. I'm right here."

"It's not okay!" Bentley yells.

"I know, buddy. I know it sucks."

"Everyone else has a dad but me," he cries on a broken whimper. He wipes under his nose with the back of his hand and looks up at me. "And some days I can barely remember him. I feel like I've already forgotten who he is..."

Is this what a broken heart feels like? The pain of a child, so deep and raw that you can't soothe it away. Even though every fiber of your being aches to protect them from this hurt.

"I know that feeling," I finally say, trying to comfort him but not sure if it will work.

His head pops up and he stares at me through the mess on his face. "What?"

"My dad isn't here anymore either."

Bentley nods once. "Oh yeah."

"Granted, he was in my life much longer than yours was, but even now I'm afraid of forgetting him." Memories slam into me as we sit there. "I can't hear his laugh anymore, or the sound of his shoes on the hardwood when he'd walk through the house. But his presence—that will always live on in here." I pound a fist on my chest, warring with my own emotions. "Tell me what you remember about him."

Bentley wipes under his nose. "I remember when he coached my soccer team when I was five."

The corner of my mouth lifts. "I was there. He would scream louder than your mom sometimes. He loved watching you play when he could, Bentley. We talked about it all the time."

"You played soccer together, didn't you?"

"We did. Your dad and I were an unbeatable team on and off the field." The pang of loss hits my chest hard.

Bentley sniffles. "I remember that he always put his bag on the floor by the door when he'd get home from the base."

I nod. "What else?"

Bentley wipes his nose on his sleeve again. "I remember trying to walk in his boots. I was really little, but I swear I can still see him holding my hands as he helped me walk."

"That's a great memory." Then I pinch his chin between two of my fingers, direct his face to mine, and say, "And that's something that no one, not even that little shit Marcus, can take away from you, do you hear me?"

He nods, tears sliding down his face.

"That kid has no say on the relationship you had with your dad, Bentley. And your father died protecting and fighting for his country. There is no more noble way to go. He loved you and always will. He's with you every day in here." I tap his chest. "And I will always be here for you too. Any way I can."

Bentley doesn't say anything as he rests his head back on my shoulder, but his breathing has started to slow and the red blotches on his face are fading.

"Uncle Penn?"

"Yeah, bud?"

His fists tighten in my shirt. "I'm really glad you're still here."

My heart swells with emotion and a tear slides down my cheek. "Me too, Bentley. Me too."

And I will be here for these kids no matter what. But if Astrid and I become more, would they accept my new role in their lives? Would I want my role to be different?

And then I think about Brandon and my dad. *Once a Marine, always a Marine*, as my dad would always say. The two of them had a relationship of their own. Would my father be angry with me for acting on my feelings toward another Marine's wife? I mean, Brandon's not coming back, but still—there's an unspoken code there.

The resolve I had earlier about moving forward with her is dwindling the longer I sit here with Bentley in my arms, considering everything at stake.

Squeezing him into me, I breathe him in from the top of his head and focus on what I can control.

At this rate, I may never have children of my own, but I could die happy with that reality because these kids—Bentley and Lilly—they feel like mine in my heart. And that will never change.

***

"Oh, thank God!" Astrid rushes down the porch as Bentley and I exit my truck. As soon as she reaches her son, she encases him in her arms and kisses the top of his head.

"I'm okay, Mom," Bentley grumbles, glancing up at me, silently asking for assistance. But now that he's in Astrid's hands, he's on his own.

"You may be okay on the outside, but we clearly need to talk about what's going on in here." She lays her hand over his heart, her eyes scanning his face. "Have you been crying?"

"A little sawdust got in his eye," I chime in, winking down at Bentley.

Astrid arches a brow at me. "Is that so?"

"Yeah. Speaking of, Bentley, why don't you go inside and take a shower? You're filthy."

He rolls his eyes, but walks toward the house, leaving me and Astrid alone. She watches him walk away and then turns back to me. "So you *handling it* was getting him all dirty?"

Crossing my arms over my chest, I stare down at her. "Look, he needed to release some anger, all right? So I took him to a job site and let him swing a sledgehammer into a wall a few times."

Her eyes go wide. "You did what?"

"Haven't you ever wanted to go to one of those rage rooms so you can take out all of your aggression on a bunch of shit and fucking destroy it?"

She casts her eyes to the side and nods. "More than you'd probably think. Did it work?"

I clear my throat, trying not to get emotional just thinking about watching that little boy fall apart in front of me again. Taking a deep breath, I nod. "He broke down and talked to me."

"And?"

"That other kid said some shit about Brandon and how he died because he didn't want Bentley as his son." Her shoulders drop and her lips part slightly. "I'll let him fill you in on all of the rest."

She covers her mouth now with her hand. "Oh, God." Closing her eyes, she shakes her head, hanging it low.

Reaching out for her, I place my hand on her shoulder until she looks back up at me. "He's going to be okay, Astrid."

Her eyes fill with tears. "I—I can't protect him from that, Penn."

"I know."

"Why do kids have to be so cruel?"

"I wish I knew the answer to that fucking question, believe me. As it is, I'm trying to think of a way to fuck with the kid that isn't illegal so he knows not to mess with our boy again."

Her brow furrows. "You said *our* boy..."

I freeze. "And?"

"You said it earlier on the phone, too."

My heart starts to beat fast because I'm not sure where she's headed with this. "Well, I mean...we are both responsible for him, aren't we?"

Her gaze is so analytical that I'm having the hardest time reading her. Normally with Astrid, I can gauge what she's thinking, whether she's happy, stressed, or emotional. But right now, she's looking at me like I'm a freaking math problem that she doesn't know how to solve.

"Mommy?" Lilly calls from the front door, breaking our eye contact.

"Yes, baby?"

"Grandma says it's time for dinner."

"Okay, I'll be right there!" Astrid calls over her shoulder.

Lilly waves at me enthusiastically from the door. "Hi, Uncle Penn!"

"Hey, Lilly Bear."

"Bentley said you let him smash walls at your house! I wanna do that too!"

Chuckling, I reply, "Next time I'll make sure you get to come."

"Yay!" And as quickly as she came, she disappears back into the house.

"What were we talking about?" Astrid says as she turns back to me.

"Fuck if I know."

She laughs, and the sight of her smiling instantly calms me. But then I remember that she's supposed to be going on her date tonight and the peace I just felt gets replaced with rage.

"I'd better get going. Don't want you to be late for your date."

Her face falls. "Oh, uh...that won't be a problem."

"Why not?"

"Because I canceled it."

Relief floods my chest, but I don't get too comfortable with the feeling until I know more. "Why?"

"Because my son needs me tonight. Dick can wait."

I internally smile at the fact that she called him Dick, but not before I do the running man in my head, celebrating that she's not going out with him after all. Maybe Willow talked some more sense into her too.

"I think that's the noble choice."

She rolls her eyes at me. "I can tell you're *so* disappointed for me."

"Look, despite how I feel about Dick, your kids will always come first, Astrid. Any man worthy of your time will understand that. And if he doesn't, then he doesn't fucking deserve you."

"And what about you, Penn? You say you don't have time for a relationship, but you don't have a family or a business keeping you from having a life. From finding someone worthy of *your* time. So what's your excuse?"

This is it, Penn.

Now's the time to tell her.

Lay it all on the line and take the risk.

Find out if your feelings are one-sided.

But then I think about what's transpired today—Bentley's fight, his breakdown, Astrid's stress over not being there when she needed to—and I think twice.

It's not the right time.

When I tell Astrid what I'm feeling, I don't want it to be a rushed confession on her front lawn, made in desperation.

I don't want it to be when she's being pulled in ten different directions, her mind a muddled mess.

When I tell her what I'm feeling, I want her undivided attention—her energy, her focus, and those eyes locked on mine so she knows that I'm serious. So she can't hide behind her responsibilities.

"Timing," I finally answer.

She huffs out a laugh. "Well, I understand that one."

"Timing is everything. And lately, I just think it's been...off."

"Mom! Dinner!" Lilly shouts from the door again.

"I'll be right there!" Astrid yells back.

I start to walk backward. "Go eat. Talk to Bentley and then pour yourself a glass of wine and relax." Then I toss her the chocolate I was holding in my hand. She catches it reflexively.

"I think I'll need a whole bottle and about a dozen more of these after today." She rubs her temples. "Mother of the year over here."

"Don't think for a second you aren't exactly the mother that those kids need, Astrid."

Her eyes lift to mine, tears threatening to spill over. "Thank you. For everything."

"I didn't do anything."

She shakes her head. "You do so much, Penn. And today? You were there for Bentley in a way I never could be."

"And I always will be. No matter what." I take another step toward my truck. "Go eat."

"I'll see you tomorrow night at the bakery for the floors?"

"Yup, I'll be there."

"Good night, Penn."

"Good night, Astrid," I say as I hop in my truck. As I drive away and watch Astrid fade in my rearview mirror, I'm not really sure where I'm headed, but I'm content knowing I was able to be there for Bentley today when he needed me the most.

Chapter Eight

Astrid

"Thank you, Tanya." My assistant moves around me, sliding a brand-new tray of fresh muffins into the stunning new display cases that Penn installed last Sunday.

"No problem. I'm going to get back to filling the eclairs and then move on to the macarons."

"I'll be back there to help when I can." I hear her glide through the swinging door to the kitchen as I focus back on the inventory sheets on the iPad in my hands, making a note of our products and how much we're selling so I know what to order for next week from my supplier. This was my least favorite task when Greg and Jenny still owned the place, and even though I've simplified it by updating the system, it's more complicated in other ways now since I'm expanding the menu.

The only thing I have left to do is land on a name. The bakery will either be Cooper's Creations, paying homage to my married name even though my husband didn't support this "hobby" of mine or Whisk Me Away Bakery since baking always helped me escape when I was lonely and needed some time for myself. I'm not sold on either option, but I haven't come up with anything better.

"Good morning, Astrid!" The cheery voice of Pam from Cove Real Estate summons my attention as she walks through the door of the store.

"Hi, Pam. How are you?"

Brushing her gray bangs from her eyes, she pushes her glasses up the bridge of her nose and smiles as she walks over to the counter where I'm standing. "I'm fantastic, dear. How are you? How's it feel to be the boss?"

"Oh, it's something." We share a laugh. "Honestly, it's overwhelming and exhilarating and some days I still can't believe that it's real."

"Well, it is dear." Her eyes scan the shop. "And the improvements look just gorgeous! Seriously, this place looks completely different."

I track her eyes as she takes it all in.

Penn has done an amazing job repainting the walls a soft pink with white stripes. The display cases really pop against the pale color, and the new tables and chairs remind me of antique furniture you would see at a Victorian tea house—elegant, yet rustic. The only thing left to do is the floors, which he's working on tonight. I have to stay late just to let him in since I only have one key to the shop right now. Getting another is one more item on my very long to-do list.

"Thank you. Penn's done amazing work."

Pam smiles knowingly. "He's so talented. I can't wait to see what he does with Tom's old place."

"Tom Nelson?"

"That's right."

"Huh. I didn't know he got contracted for that."

"Oh, it isn't a contracting job. Penn bought the place! He's going to fix it up and turn it into a rental. Brilliant idea, if you ask me." The crease between my brows must be so harsh because Pam studies me and then says, "He didn't tell you about it?"

My mind is spinning. A rental? Is that where he took Bentley last night? When we were eating dinner, Lilly kept asking if she could go to Penn's house to smash stuff since Bentley got to. I thought it was a little weird that he would let Bentley destroy a wall at his place, so this makes a lot more sense.

But more importantly, why didn't Penn say anything?

Oh my God. His super-secret project is his own rental business?

"Uh, nope. He hasn't said anything."

She purses her lips. "Interesting. I mean, he told me not to say anything, but I assumed he'd have at least told you, as close as you two are. Hell, if I didn't know any better, I'd think you were involved." She shrugs and then begins scanning the display case for her purchase as my heart has palpitations that are rocking my entire body. "I'm sure he would have told you eventually."

Would he?

Penn and I normally tell each other everything. Why would he keep something this big from me?

Really, Astrid? You tell each other everything? *Then why haven't you told him about the dirty dream you had about him last night? Or the one the night before? Or about the Morgan Hotel event that is stressing you out while simultaneously making you giddy about the opportunity...*

Okay, subconscious. You've made your freaking point.

"Yeah, you're probably right," I say, agreeing because it's the polite thing to do and because it's easier than saying what's really on my mind right now—how that man frustrates me like no other. "Do you know what you'd like today?"

After I fill Pam's order, take her payment, and talk to her about her grandkids for a few minutes, she leaves and I pick up my iPad again, trying to focus on order numbers when all I want to do is call Penn and interrogate him about the house he bought.

Yet, as soon as I reach for my phone, the chime above the door rings and in walks Richard Cockwell, professionally dressed and smiling, despite the fact I had to cancel our date last night.

"Hello, Astrid."

"Um…Hi, Richard." I set my clipboard down and move closer to him. "Look, I'm so sorry about last night…"

He holds up a hand to stop me. "No apologies needed. I get it. You're a mom. Your kids will always come first."

A sigh of relief leaves my lips. "Thank you."

"I'm not going to lie and say that I wasn't disappointed, but I get it."

"I know. I'm sorry…again."

"It's okay, but I had to stop in this morning to fulfill my weekly order for the office ladies. Can't let a failed date get in the way of making sure my girls at work are taken care of."

The corner of my mouth lifts. "That's sweet of you."

"I'm a sweet guy." He winks and then rattles off his order. Once he pays, he tucks the box under his arm. "I don't suppose you might want to reschedule for tomorrow by any chance?"

"I would, but Bentley's soccer team has the championship game at three, and then his team party afterward."

Richard nods. "Gotcha."

"I'll text you Sunday though," I say, even though the idea of trying to reschedule our date is making me sweat. The truth is, I think I was more infatuated with the idea of going out than *who* I was going to go out with.

Nevertheless, his face lights up. "I'll be looking forward to it."

"Bye, Richard."

"Bye, Astrid."

I watch him leave and then pick up my phone again, but I don't call Penn like I planned. I call my mother to check on my son and see if I can get any more information out of him.

"Hello?" My mother answers, the volume of the television on full blast. She must be watching one of her talk shows.

"Mom, turn down the television, please."

"But Maddox Taylor is on the show right now." She goes silent for a moment. "I've never been one to watch football, but I would watch that man run around in tight pants any day of the week."

"Mom!"

"What? He's a handsome man. His wife is one very lucky lady."

I close my eyes and pinch the bridge of my nose. "Can you focus, please? I called for a reason."

"Okay, fine. But it's just on a commercial break, so you'd better hurry up."

"Nice, Mom. Is Bentley around?"

"He's still pulling the weeds out of the flower beds."

After I talked with my son last night, and cried myself to sleep over not being able to shield him from the pain of losing his father, I spoke to him this morning about how he's going to spend his time away from school. A few chores around the house needed to be done, and even though I don't blame him for hitting that kid for what he said, I can't condone that behavior as a means to solve his problems and deal with his emotions.

And then this morning, I added *find a therapist for Bentley* to my to-do list.

I really think he should talk to someone about everything he's feeling, especially as he's getting older. I was also a child that grew up without a dad and it's not easy. I know it's affected a lot of aspects of my life, but at least I can help my son process it sooner than I ever did.

"Can you put him on the phone, please?"

I hear rustling in the background, and then the creak of the back door opening. "Bentley, your mom wants to talk to you, sweetie!"

"About what?" he calls back.

"I don't know, honey. Just come grab the phone."

When I finally hear my son's voice, my shoulders sag with relief. "Hey, Mom."

"Hey, honey. How are you feeling today?"

"Besides being sweaty and dirty, I'm okay."

"Well, a little hard work won't kill you."

"I know, Mom. You and Uncle Penn tell me that all the time."

"Yeah, I know. Speaking of Uncle Penn, I have a question."

"Okay?"

"He mentioned that he let you demolish a wall last night?"

"Yeah..."

"Was it at his house?"

"No. It was some house I'd never been to before."

"Did Uncle Penn tell you who the house belongs to?"

"Uh, no. Not that I remember."

"Did you recognize the place, though?"

He thinks about it for a minute. "Maybe? I think it was in the neighborhood we trick-or-treat in. Yeah, it definitely was," he says confidently now.

"Okay. Anything else about it that stood out?"

"Why are you so curious about the house?"

"No reason. I just wanted to know where he took you, that's all."

"Honestly, I wasn't paying attention too much, Mom. I was angry and just kept swinging the sledgehammer. And then..." he trails off.

"I know, Bentley. It's okay."

He draws in a shaky breath. "Well, anyway, I'm almost done with the weeds and then I have to crush all the aluminum cans."

"Good work, honey. I'll see you later tonight. We'll make some popcorn and watch a movie and just relax before your big game tomorrow."

"Okay. Love you, Mom."

My heart instantly melts for the boy I'm still raising and the man he's slowly becoming. "Love you too, Bentley."

When I hang up the phone, clutching it to my chest, I take a moment to breathe deeply and remind myself of everything I have to be grateful for. My kids are healthy, I now have a business that I love, and a mother and brother that support me no matter what.

And then there's Penn.

The man I count on for everything the other people can't give me.

But do I really want more than that from him? And can that happen without jeopardizing everything else?

**

By the time I got back to the inventory sheets, I decided to wait to speak to Penn about his secret until he came by tonight to install the new floors. That way, I had plenty of time to decide on how I wanted to broach the topic with him. But the more I thought about it, the more it sank in that he kept something *that* significant from me, and the more hurt I felt.

And here's the thing—we're not in a relationship. Hell, I can't even tell you the last time the man went on a date. I technically have no right to be upset that he chose not to share his new venture with me.

But I am.

And he's going to hear how I feel about it before the night is over.

Maybe it's the stress of this week. Maybe I'm about to start my period.

Or maybe I'm so sexually and mentally frustrated by the man that I'm about to explode, but when he knocks on the back door to the bakery just after six, I swing the door open and glare at him while simultaneously fighting tears back.

"Uh. Is everything okay?" he asks, staring down at me timidly.

"No, Penn. Everything is not okay." I let the door go, not bothering to hold it open for him as I walk away, striding back to the kitchen where I still have an order of a few dozen cupcakes I need to put frosting on for a birthday party tomorrow.

The door slams shut and then I hear his tool bag hit the floor behind me, but I don't look back as I reach for the bag of frosting to start piping it onto cupcakes again. My chest feels like it's cracking into pieces, my jaw is clenched tight, and my hands are shaking from the adrenaline racing through me.

"Care to tell me what the hell is wrong then? Because if I'm reading the room correctly, it seems like you're pissed off at me."

Spinning around, I stare at him. "Maybe you're not a complete dumbass after all, then."

Penn's brows pinch together. "A dumbass?"

"Yeah, a dumbass. A big, tall, muscular dumbass."

One of his brows lifts and he eyes me cautiously. "Okay…"

"I can't believe you!" My voice cracks as I toss the bag full of frosting onto the metal counter and throw both of my hands in the air.

"What the fuck did I do, Astrid?" he asks, his voice uncertain. "I mean, shit. I just got here and you're already fucking pissed at me. Am I late?" He pulls his phone out of his pocket to check the time and then shakes his head. "By three minutes? Is that the problem? I'm fucking three minutes late?"

"No!" My hands cover the center of my chest. "The problem is you never told me!"

"Told you what?"

"About the house!"

"What house?"

"The one you bought to turn into a rental!" Realization dawns on his face as his features drop and his spine straightens.

Both of our chests are rising and falling with labored breaths as we stare at one another, the tension rising in the room.

After a few moments, he says in a low growl, "How did you find out about that?"

"Do you think I'm stupid? That I wouldn't find out? In this town?"

"Not at all." And then it hits him. "Bentley told you, huh?"

"No. It was Pam. *Bentley* didn't even know where you took him last night, Penn. I asked him and he said you never said anything about the house. But Pam came into the bakery today and mentioned it casually because she assumed you would have told me. Since we're so *close*." Shaking my head, I point a finger to my chest. "Me! The person you tell everything to!" Tears fill my eyes now. "But I guess you don't..."

Penn tilts his head at me, confused. "I was going to, Astrid. I was just waiting for the right time." He runs his hand through his hair in frustration and huffs out, "But it's never the right fucking time."

"The right time? Why? Why not just tell me when you bought it? Why wouldn't you let me celebrate that with you?"

He swallows roughly. "I..."

"I just can't believe you didn't trust me with this. What you're doing for yourself...it's huge, Penn. It's amazing and brave and..."

"Why are you so mad that I didn't tell you?" he asks, cutting me off. His question catches me off guard. "What?"

He moves a step closer. "Why are you so hurt? I know for a fact there are things you keep close to the vest, so why am *I* the bad guy?"

I stare up at him, watching his eyes bounce between mine. He smells fresh from the shower, which doesn't make sense because I know he's about to get dirty tearing up the floors of my bakery. But his scent—it's intoxicating—masculine, rugged, and drugging me, pulling me closer to him on instinct.

"I asked you a question, Astrid."

"I...I thought we were better friends than that, Penn," I manage to say through the emotion and arousal coursing through me simultaneously.

Penn huffs out a laugh. "Friends? That's why you're pissed? Because I'm your *friend* who didn't tell you that I bought a house to fix up and try to rent out? That I've had a business plan for rental properties and my own contracting business for years and have been too chicken shit to pull the trigger on it?" My mouth falls open slightly. "Or is it really because I'm your *friend,* but you and I both know there's something more between us that we're both too afraid to fucking do anything about?"

My heart and stomach plummet at the same time. "What are you talking about?" I whisper.

Penn stands so close to me now that I can feel his breath on my lips. He's so much taller than me, but he's leaning down so close to my face that I can see every eyelash framing his dark, hypnotizing eyes. "Tell me why you didn't go out with Dick last night."

His question stuns me for a moment. "Because Bentley needed me."

"No, that's an excuse. Tell me why you *never* wanted to go out with Dick in the first place."

"I..."

"Tell me that you've never wanted him because it's *me* you've wanted all this time."

The floor feels like it's falling out from underneath me. My brain is malfunctioning, tripping over itself because I'm having trouble processing that Penn is saying these words to me right now.

What the hell is happening?

"I'll tell you what you and I both know, Astrid." He swallows roughly and then bends his knees so our eyes are at the same level. "That kiss three years ago wasn't just a drunken mistake. It wasn't just a fluke." He shakes his head as his eyes dip down to my lips for a beat and then back up. "And I'm tired of pretending that it was."

"Penn..."

He inhales deeply, looks down at my lips again, and then mutters, "Fuck it."

And then his lips are on mine.

It's dizzying how intense the kiss is, especially since it's just our lips touching. But it's not just our mouths that are tripping my balance. It's Penn's calloused hands moving under my shirt and up my back as he pulls me into his chest. It's the way his arms feel wrapped around me.

And it's the way when our tongues do collide, every nerve ending in my body comes alive, a euphoric pleasure coursing through me that is unparalleled.

Penn lifts me up and sits me on the metal counter, shoving cupcakes and utensils to the side. Luckily nothing falls, but at this point, I wouldn't fucking care.

"Tell me that you want this," he growls against my lips. "Tell me that you've thought about this as much as I have."

"Yes," I reply instantly because the filter is gone. It left long before we ever got to this point and I'm tired of feeling like I'm wearing a muzzle.

My mind is telling me this is moving too fast, but then Penn lifts the hem of my shirt and pulls it over my head, revealing my chest to him. His fingers trace the edges of my bra, and I instantly wish I had on something sexier.

"I'm sorry. I wasn't expecting this...and my body..."

He presses a finger to my lips. "Don't you fucking dare." He licks his lips and then traces his fingers over every inch of my arms, chest, and even the soft flesh of my stomach that's covered in stretch marks while his eyes follow the path of his fingers. Then he buries his fingers in the hair at my neck, and he's pulling my head back, exposing my neck to him so he can lick, kiss, and tease the sensitive flesh there.

It never crossed my mind that Penn would be seeing me like this, even though I fantasized about it so many times. But now that it's happening for real, I'm suddenly very aware there's only one other man that's seen me naked.

But I don't want to think about that right now.

"You are so goddamn perfect, Astrid." He takes my hand and places it over the rock-hard erection in his jeans, shocking me but lighting my need for him on fire. "Do you feel this? This is what I've been fighting for years. I want you so fucking badly that I can barely think straight. But right now, the last thing we need to be doing is fucking thinking. I'm tired of it." He cups the side of my face. "And I'm tired of waiting for the right time. Tonight I'm going to take what I want."

My mind says we're crazy, but my body—she is so fucking ready to feel everything Penn has to offer.

"And I'm not going to stop unless you tell me to."

"Penn…"

"Do you want me to stop?" he asks, jutting his cock into my hands and drawing his fingers down the side of my neck simultaneously.

"No," I answer without hesitation because if he stops, I just might die.

The deep gravel of his voice vibrates down my spine as he says, "Thank fuck," and then he presses his lips to mine again, leaning over me as I wrap my legs around his waist and lie back against the cold metal table.

I shiver as I run my fingernails under his shirt, the chill of the metal biting into my skin. Penn breaks our lips apart and kisses a trail down my neck, along my collarbone, and over the swell of my breasts. "God, you always smell like fucking sugar."

"Perks of the job."

He lifts his head from my stomach and looks me in the eyes as he says, "I wonder if you taste just as sweet too."

He keeps his eyes locked on mine as he pops the button on my jeans and pulls the zipper down slowly.

I lean back and stare up at the ceiling, trying to control my breathing. "Oh God. This is really happening, isn't it?"

"You're only allowed to say four words to me right now," he says, ignoring my comment.

My head pops back up. "What?"

"Listen, Astrid, or I'm stopping until you agree." He prompts me to lift my hips as he pulls my jeans down my ass and legs, tossing them to the side.

"Oh, God. Okay…"

"Those four words are…" He licks his lips before he continues. "Faster, slower, harder, or softer."

I think I'm going to die from this. *Has anyone had a heart attack during sex because they were so turned on?* "Jesus..."

"Actually, let's add one more." He hooks his thumbs under the sides of my underwear at my hips and begins pulling them down as well. *Thank God I trimmed the other day.*

"Okay?"

He stares at me again as he dips his head down, pushing my knees open to expose me to him, and lining up his mouth to the juncture between my legs. When he lifts my feet and plants them on the counter on either side of his shoulders, he says, "*More.* You can tell me *more.* Do you understand me?"

"Yes."

"Good girl. Now let me know exactly how to make you come on my tongue."

With his eyes locked on mine, his tongue connects with my clit and I nearly come apart just from that simple touch. Soft circles, long licks, and short flicks—Penn works me over, figuring out what I like and taking his time.

I feel like I'm outside of my body, watching myself experience this carnal moment—a sexy man with his head buried between my legs, worshipping me. It's the kind of thing that happens in fantasies, not real life.

But this is as real as it gets.

"More," I finally manage to say, closing my eyes and burying my hands in his hair.

He circles my entrance with his finger and slowly inserts it all the way inside of me. "Is this what you want?"

God damn. "Yes."

Penn goes back to licking me softly, exploring my flesh, his touch so soft and slow that it's tortuous.

"Faster," I moan as his tongue circles my clit again, picking up speed. "Yes, Penn."

"Those weren't on the list, but I'll let it slide."

I chuckle, but it's cut short as Penn works his finger and tongue in tandem. My breathing becomes shallow, and I'm so entranced in this experience that I'm fairly certain I've forgotten how to breathe. One of Penn's hands reaches up and pulls down the cup of my bra, tweaking my nipple as he keeps eating me, licking me, and fucking me with his hand, adding another finger.

"Oh God. Harder."

"Fuck, you taste incredible, Astrid."

I pull on his hair harder as my climax builds. "Don't stop."

"Keep telling me what you need, baby."

"Faster, harder, more…. oh God, more!" I scream as my legs begin to shake. But Penn doesn't let up. He keeps the pace, building my orgasm and when it hits me, I thrash on the counter, squeeze his head between my legs, and cry out until the very last wave subsides.

Panting, I lie back again, struggling for air, throwing my hand over my face as I try to recover. "Oh my God. We just committed so many health code violations."

Penn laughs and then pulls me up to a sitting position. "Some rules were made to be broken, right?"

Staring at him, I think about the biggest rule we just broke—crossing from friends to more.

But that's exactly what I want.

Without thinking, I wrap my arms around his neck and pull him down to me until our mouths meet again, tasting me on his tongue.

It's erotic, primal, and has my body begging for more. Reaching for his jeans, I pop the button and drag the zipper down.

"Astrid, I don't have anything."

I reach inside and find his hard, hot, length. Velvet over steel—that's what Penn feels like all over. With my other hand, I lift the bottom of his shirt, suggesting that he remove it. And when he does, I lock onto the sight of his broad, muscular chest with the perfect smattering of chest hair across his pecs, and that happy trail that I can finally see the end of—and I have a feeling I'm going to be very happy when this is over.

"I have an IUD. I got it after Lilly." Brandon and I knew we were done having kids, and I just never had it removed. And as soon as those words leave my lips, I realize that we're really about to do this.

I'm about to have sex with Penn. There's no going back after this.

"Fuck, Astrid." When our lips connect again, he shoves his pants down and kicks them off, and then reaches behind me to pop the clasp on my bra, tossing it aside as well. "Stand up."

I step down to the floor from the metal counter and Penn spins me around, pushing my torso over the edge of it now. Bracing myself on my forearms, the cold surface bites into my skin, but then I feel Penn tracing my spine with his finger, and that's what truly inspires the goosebumps.

I wait with bated breath for him to bury himself inside me, but he continues to explore my body with his hands and then I feel his lips on my shoulders, moving up my neck to my ear. "Are you ready for this?" He reaches beside me, picking up the bag of frosting. I try to look over my shoulder to see what he's doing, but he pushes me flat against the counter and holds me down. When I feel the frosting hit my back, I gasp. It's cold, but the smell of the sugar hits my nostrils and makes me moan when I feel his fingers smear it into my skin.

Then I feel him move the bag to my ass as he draws something on one of my butt cheeks.

"Penn?"

"Shhh…" he commands, tossing the bag to the side and moving away from me. But before I can glance at him over my shoulder, I feel his mouth on my skin, licking up the trail of frosting, nipping at me, dragging his teeth across my flesh, and sucking my skin between his lips, marking me.

"Oh my God," I moan, lying flat on the counter as Penn's fingers slide inside of my core again and his mouth licks my ass free of the frosting.

"Fucking sugar. Every time I smell it, I think of you," he mumbles against my skin, making sure my ass is clean before he moves to the spot on my back.

"Penn." I reach behind me, pulling him closer as his fingers continue to slide slowly in and out of me. "Please."

"I'm not done eating my dessert."

"I need you…to fuck me."

He groans and stands up. "Fuck, Astrid. I need you too."

His fingers leave my core and then I feel him line up his cock to my entrance and push in slowly. We both moan as he works his way inside, stretching me around him.

And it's fucking perfect.

"Holy shit," I gasp as Penn pulls out before thrusting back in to the hilt.

"Jesus…" Penn lets out a guttural groan and then leans over my body, lining up his mouth to my ear again. "God, you make me crazy. I've thought about this so many times, Astrid. How you would feel, how you would sound."

"Fuck me, Penn. Please. Harder."

He picks up his pace, interlacing his fingers with mine as he gives me his weight on my back. He's so deep, so long and thick that it doesn't take long before I feel an orgasm start to bloom. The sound of his hips slapping against my ass echoes in the kitchen and the metal table rattles with each of his thrusts.

"Fuck, you feel too good. I'm not done with you yet, but you make me want to lose my fucking mind." Penn buries his face in my neck, grunting as he fucks me hard. But then he abruptly lifts off me and pulls me up from the table, hooking his arms under mine and holding me to his chest as he bends his knees, changing the angle and sliding out of me because of our height difference. When his hands cup my breasts, I twist my head to the side and find his lips, pressing our mouths together.

Penn spins me around and lifts me up so I can wrap my legs around his waist, holding me above the ground. He lines back up to my core and pulls me down on his cock, fucking me mid-air, guiding me up and down as if I weigh nothing.

But this isn't nothing.

This is everything.

His cock slides in and out of me as I push my pelvis against him, my arms wrapped around his neck for leverage. His hands lift me by the hips, pulling me up and down his length, building me toward an explosion I don't think I'm ready for.

Penn lays me back down on the counter and hovers over me, his hips never breaking their rhythm. "Touch yourself. Make yourself come, Astrid. I can't hold back much longer."

Reaching between us, my other arm wrapped around his neck for support, I find my clit and rush to meet him at the finish line. It doesn't take much since I'm already so close, and when I start to clench around him and moan incoherently, Penn pulls me to him harder and deeper, bringing us both over the edge together.

When we're spent, clutching one another so tightly, our bodies coated in a layer of sweat, the weight of what just happened hits me and it's as if I snap awake from a dream.

I slept with Penn.

Oh my God. What did we just do? Funny how our brains can think rationally again once the desire wears off.

Penn pushes off of me slowly and runs a hand through his hair. "Stay here." I watch his naked backside as he strolls away from me to grab a clean dish rag, runs it under water at the sink, and then he walks back over to me, lifts me off the table and spins me around, cleaning my skin where the frosting was earlier, his touch so delicate compared to the ferocity he displayed just moments ago.

Then we dress in silence, barely making eye contact.

I don't know what to do now. It's not like I have much experience with this.

But as the quiet between us grows, the more I fear we've made a huge mistake, especially because Penn isn't saying anything either. For a man who told me he was going to take what he wanted tonight, he suddenly is giving off a completely different energy.

Penn finally looks at me, his gaze unreadable. But as he closes the distance between us and peers down at me, I accept that things between us will never be the same. And now I'm not sure what happens next.

"Astrid," he says, reaching up to cup my jaw. But before he can get another word in, my phone rings in my pocket.

"Shoot." I scramble to take it out and see it's my mom calling, almost dropping the phone because my hands are shaking so badly. "Hello?"

"Hi, hon. Lilly is asking for you. She wants to make sure you'll be home to tuck her in for bed." Glancing at the screen, I notice the time and wince.

"Yeah, I'm on my way." My eyes find Penn's again as he takes a step back from me.

"Okay, see you soon. Be careful."

"Bye." When I hang up the phone, I sigh. "I need to get home," I say as I walk to my office to grab my purse. I half expect Penn to follow me, but he doesn't. Instead, when I come back out, he's still standing right where I left him. Still shaking and uneasy, I move to turn away from him, but he grabs my hand before I get too far, spinning me back around and into his chest.

And then his lips are on mine again.

It's electric the way he makes my body come alive, the way his touch makes all of the worries in my head drift away. But I know I need to get back to reality—even though it was incredible escaping it for a little while. All of my feelings are boiling beneath the surface right now, and I need to get some space from him before they run over—before I break apart and convince myself I regret what just happened.

Because the truth is, I don't.

I wanted it. I've wanted to be with Penn for so long.

But I honestly just don't know how to process everything right now.

"Good night, Astrid," he says simply.

"Good night, Penn," I whisper back as he releases me and then I leave the shop and walk out to my car to drive home, not remembering how I even got there because the only thing I keep replaying in my mind is the fact that I just had sex with Penn—and there's no going back to the ways things were after that.

Chapter Nine

Astrid

"No matter what happens today, just know that I'm proud of you." I lean down and kiss the top of Bentley's head, even though he's trying to pull away from me.

"Mom, stop," he groans, fixing his jersey.

"Just go out there and do your best. That's all you can do."

He shakes out his limbs and jumps up and down a few times. "I know, but I just really want to win."

"I know you do."

"Boys, time to warm up!" Dallas calls from his spot on the field, and the team rushes out to meet him.

"Be careful, please!" I yell at my son as he rolls his eyes and runs to where the other boys have all gathered.

It's the championship game for Bentley's soccer team, and I can't deny that my nerves are high. They are on a normal game day too, but today they're exacerbated by the fact that Penn and I had sex last night and we still haven't had the chance to talk about it.

Part of me expected a text or call from him this morning, but the only one I received was a picture of the floors that he finished early this morning. When I went into the bakery to fulfill the cupcake order that got ruined during our sexcapades last night, I couldn't believe how beautiful the store looked now that the renovations are all completed.

But as soon as I walked into the kitchen, all I could see and think about were our naked bodies and every surface they touched last night. And to make sure that the health department could never accuse me of being an irresponsible bakery owner, I disinfected the entire kitchen, especially the metal counter where we spent our time.

I figured Penn probably slept most of the day so he could be coherent enough to help Dallas coach the game this afternoon, so when I arrived and he greeted me as if nothing happened, my anxious thoughts started to spiral out of control.

Did he regret what we did? Did the time between last night and now give him clarity that we shouldn't have gone that far? What does this mean now? Are we going to chock it up to a one-time thing, or pretend like it never happened?

"God, you make me crazy. I've thought about this so many times, Astrid. How you would feel, how you would sound."

His words conveyed a strong message in the moment, but I honestly have no idea where his head is right now because I'm having a hard time getting my own under control.

"Hey, there!" Willow comes up beside me, startling me so badly that I jump.

"Jesus!" I place a hand over my chest, feeling my heart thrashing underneath. "I am already on the verge of a heart attack, so please tread carefully."

Willow rubs my shoulder, looking slightly concerned. "Sorry. Didn't mean to scare you."

"It's okay. It's just been a crazy morning and I'm really nervous about the game."

She wraps her arm around my shoulders. "Dallas is confident they can win this thing. They have a strong offense. He told me all about it this morning after we had sex on the kitchen counter."

I turn to face her slowly. "Didn't need to know that."

"Sorry. But it was amazing and I'm still thinking about it." She waggles her brows.

Yeah, I know the feeling.

In a matter of minutes, the game is underway, and I can't stay seated in my chair for longer than two seconds. My eyes keep bouncing between the game on the field and the man whose lips I can't stop feeling against my ass as he licked frosting off of it. I'm so on edge that I start biting my fingernails, a habit I kicked a long time ago, but somehow my nervous system hasn't forgotten about.

"Astrid, if you don't stop, you're not going to have a fingernail left." Willow pulls my hand from my mouth, holding it with her own instead.

"God, I hate this. Bentley wants this so much." I feel her stroke my arm, trying to offer me an ounce of comfort as we stare out at the field, watching the teams fight tooth and nail, each pass and missed goal amping up the anxiety on the sidelines.

"I know, hon. But losing is part of life too. He'll be fine either way."

I shake my hands out at my sides, releasing hers from my grasp. "I'm just so on edge."

Willow narrows her eyes at me from the side. "You are, more so than usual. Are you okay, girl?"

I dart my eyes over to hers quickly before returning right back to the field. "I'm—I'm fine."

"Uh, I don't believe you." She steps in front of me, snapping her fingers in my face, which forces my eyes to hers. "Astrid Marie, what are you not telling me?"

"That's not my middle name," I argue, wary of how she's staring at me right now.

"I don't care. There's something else going on here, and you'd better spill. We don't keep secrets from each other, remember?"

Staring back at her, I chew on my bottom lip. "Willow..."

Her face morphs from curiosity to concern. "Do you need an attorney? Did you do something illegal?"

"What? No!"

"Then what is it?"

This is the last place I should be talking about this, but I can't keep it to myself any longer. I look around us before leaning over and whispering, "I had sex with Penn."

"What?" she shouts, drawing anyone within thirty feet's attention to us. "Oh my God, I'm so sorry," she whispers now, even though it's too late.

"Jesus, Willow. Now everyone is going to know." Burying my head in my hands, I kick myself for saying anything. I should have just waited until we were alone.

She pulls my hands away and forces me to look at her, lowering her voice and leaning in closer to me. "No, they won't. All they heard me say was 'what.'" We both blow out a breath at the same time. "Now, tell me how this happened. And more importantly," she says, arching a brow at me, "was it good?"

I groan, closing my eyes and sighing. "It was incredible. So hot. There was frosting involved." Popping one I eye open, I gauge her reaction.

"Frosting?" she asks, surprise in her voice.

"Yes. It happened at the bakery last night, but, it can't happen again." I shake my head furiously as our team scores a goal, deciding in that moment that it's better to just move forward than stay in this limbo I'm currently suffering in.

We pause our conversation to celebrate the goal. As soon as the game starts back up, Willow turns her head toward me once more. "Why not? I thought that's what you wanted?"

Anguish makes my chest even heavier now. "I can't do it, Willow. It's Penn...he's my friend. *Was* my friend?" I draw my brows together, even more confused. "How do you stay friends with a man after you sleep with him?"

"Brandon has been gone for four years, Astrid. And it is *Penn*. You know him. He wouldn't let this come between you two..."

"I know, but..." I take a deep breath and say, "There's something that Penn doesn't know. And when he finds out, it's going to ruin our friendship if it isn't already."

Willow's mouth falls open as a whistle rings out on the field. But I don't turn to look at her because I can only imagine what she's thinking. And now is definitely not the time to have that conversation.

"What do you mean?" She leans into me again.

"Not here, okay?" I plead as Bentley comes running up to me, grabbing his water since it's halftime.

"We're winning, Mom!" Sweat slides down his temples even though the fall chill in the air makes me grateful I brought a jacket today.

"I know, hon. You're doing amazing!"

"I'm gonna try to score a goal for you, okay?" He lifts his water bottle and squirts a stream of liquid into his mouth.

"That's so sweet of you, baby, but not necessary. Just play your hardest."

"I am. We're ahead and we're gonna win this thing!" He tosses his water bottle to the ground and then races back out onto the field where the team is huddled around Penn and Dallas talking strategy.

"He seems to be doing better," Willow says as we stare at the boys.

"He is for now. I have an online appointment with a therapist for him this week. I think it's important for him to start talking to someone as these situations and feelings start to rise to the surface as he gets older."

"I think that's smart. I wish I had gone to therapy sooner," Willow agrees. "You're doing the right thing for him, Astrid."

"I hope so. But this is just another reason Penn and I shouldn't get involved. He's such a huge part of my kids' lives, Willow. If something happened and they lost him too…"

"What is it that you're keeping from him, Astrid?"

I shake my head and whisper, "Now isn't the time to discuss it, Willow."

"Okay… But regardless, I can't see why you two don't belong together. I mean, anyone with two eyes and two ears in this town can see how much you two care about each other."

"But is it worth the risk?" I say quietly, mostly to myself.

Willow picks up on it, of course. "I think so."

"You're just saying that because you're in love and it's new. Try throwing a couple kids in the mix along with a dead husband and his best friend. Then come talk to me."

Willow laughs. "Well, why don't you talk to me about it and I can help you see reason? I can come by tomorrow morning sometime. I'd suggest tonight, but the team party is after this, right?"

A whistle rings out on the field as the referee calls a foul on our team. "Yeah."

"Then it's a date."

"You mean like the one I never ended up going on?"

Willow bumps her shoulder against mine. "You and I both know you never wanted to go out with Dick."

"I know."

"So don't stress about it."

"He wants to reschedule, though."

"Well, if he tries to, just let him down gently. You're good at dealing with people, Astrid. I mean, hell...you got me to open up."

Her comment makes me chuckle, but the truth is I know she's right on some level. I am good with people. It's never been an issue for me.

But dealing with Penn after our choices last night? That is something I have absolutely no experience with whatsoever.

***

"To the under twelve champions!" Dallas shouts in Perky's Pizza, a local pizza joint that is always the hot spot for team get-togethers. I remember having my own team parties at this place when I was a kid. That's how long it's been around.

All the boys holler loudly, rattling the old walls.

"This season has been one of a kind," Penn says, echoing Dallas's sentiment. He's barely made eye contact with me all night, so I still haven't been able to get a read on him. "I think I speak for my brother too when I say that coaching this group of boys has been an honor and a privilege. And we know that none of this would be possible without the support of the parents. So let's give the parents a round of applause!" Penn claps his hands together loudly as the boys join in. Bentley claps his hands right in my face, making me laugh. And when I look up, Penn's eyes lock on mine and he winks.

A flash of heat travels all the way through my body.

From a wink.

God, I'm in trouble.

"I wish there was a way to keep this crew together every season, but we will always remember this team as champions. Now let's party!" Dallas pumps a fist in the air as the boys rush him and Penn for their free tokens—and when I say free, I mean the brothers bought tokens for all the boys to be able to play games.

Yet another reason why Penn is just simply irresistible—his generous heart.

"Mommy, can I have tokens too, please?" Lilly turns to me, bouncing in her chair.

"Yes, baby."

But before I can reach into my purse to grab cash, a large hand I would recognize anywhere slides right in front of my face and hands a stack of tokens to my daughter. "Here you go, Lilly Bear."

"Thanks, Uncle Penn!" Scrambling to keep the tokens in her tiny hands, she puts them all in her pockets and then scurries off. Penn stays standing behind my chair, not saying anything. But I feel him.

I always feel him.

"Having a good time?" he asks, his voice low but steady.

Too scared to face him, I look down at my hands and manage a shaky, "Yeah."

"Good."

"You?" I ask, wishing he'd give me any clues as to what he's been thinking.

"Absolutely. The boys did incredible today. I'm proud of how they played."

"You should be. You and Dallas are exceptional coaches, Penn."

"Thank you."

I reach for my water and take a sip, clearing my throat.

"We need to talk," Penn says quietly, leaning down so his mouth is right by my ear. When I slowly turn to the side, he places a hand on my shoulder and squeezes. "Not here."

"Okay," I whisper.

"Can I come over later?" he asks, his voice deep and gravely now.

"Probably shouldn't. My mom is supposed to come by to congratulate Bentley."

"Tomorrow night then?"

I swallow hard but then think the timing would be better. I'm supposed to talk to Willow tomorrow, right? Maybe she can help me make sense of everything that I'm feeling.

I know I told her earlier that this thing between Penn and me can't happen, but I'd be lying if I said I actually meant it. Hell, just a glance at my nipples could tell you I'm lying.

I should have worn a thicker bra today.

"Okay."

"Okay." His finger dances along the skin right above the neckline of my shirt. "Looking forward to it. See you then, Astrid." And then he walks away, acting like he didn't just wreak havoc on my nervous system.

I let out the breath I was holding and watch Penn saunter across the room, dodging kids running through the restaurant and pausing to talk to parents every time they stop him.

He looks like he's in control, and now I know from experience just how controlling he can be.

But he doesn't look how I feel on the inside. He doesn't look like his head is a mess or like he's so on edge the slightest noise could scare the shit out of him. And I'm not sure how that's possible given the huge boundary we crossed last night.

Before I can ponder things further, my phone vibrates on the table. The screen lights up and then I see a message from Dick—I mean, Richard. When I open it, my eyes read the words so fast that I have to read his text over again to make sure I read it right.

Richard: *Hey, Astrid. Hope you're having a great Saturday. Just texting to see when you might be available this week to reschedule our date. Let me know as soon as you can.*

Sighing, I debate how to respond. But then my eyes find Penn across the room, helping Lilly with the Skee-Ball game, rolling the balls with enough force that she can actually score points. They're smiling, laughing and giving each other a high-five, and right then I know what to do.

Me: *Hey, Richard. Listen, I really appreciate you asking me out. I was sincerely flattered. But the more I've been thinking about it, the more I think I'm just not ready to date yet. My life is crazy right now, and that wouldn't be fair to you. I don't have the time and attention to give to that part of my life right now. I hope you understand. I wish you the best of luck in finding someone, though.*

When I hit send, I turn my phone over so the screen is down and then another parent comes over to talk about the bakery.

Later that night as I go to bed, I realize Dick never responded, and I honestly think it's better that way. Now, all I have to worry about is what Penn is going to say to me tomorrow night when he comes over.

Chapter Ten

Astrid

"Was that my first birthday party?" Lilly asks me as I flip the page in the photo album, stroking the pages with my index fingers as the memories start blending together.

"Yup. As soon as you took one bite of your cake, you had to eat the entire thing, so you just buried your face in it." Chocolate cake crumbs cover her face completely so the only color you see is the white of her eyes.

Lilly giggles as I kiss the top of her head.

"Gosh, I was a fat baby," Bentley says from the other side of me.

"You were a chunk, that's for sure. You loved to eat. But look at you now." Pinching his ribs, I wait for him to start squirming and leap from the couch. My little boy isn't so little anymore.

"Where's Daddy in this picture?" Lilly asks, pointing to a photo of them opening Christmas presents. Lilly was two and Bentley was six.

"Your dad was in another part of the world at the time."

Lilly nods as her lips fall solemnly. "Kind of like he is now?"

"No, baby. Your daddy is in heaven now, sweetie. He's in the clouds watching over us."

"I wish you could visit the clouds," she says, her bottom lip sticking out.

"I know, sweetie. Me too."

Although, right now, I'm not sure what Brandon would have to say to me, and that's part of the turmoil I'm still facing in light of recent events. The doorbell rings, thankfully pulling me from my thoughts. "Bentley, can you answer that, please? It's Willow."

"Can I have kisses from Daddy?" Lilly asks, staring up at me. Normally I wouldn't let her have chocolate this early in the day, but I can tell she needs the comfort right now. Looking at these pictures brings up a lot of emotions for all of us.

"Sure, baby. But just one."

"Okay."

"Hey, Lilly," Willow says as she steps through the door and Bentley shuts it behind her.

"Hi, Willow!" Lilly takes a Hershey Kiss out of the vase and holds it out to Willow. "Want a kiss from Daddy?"

Willow glances at me and I nod slightly, encouraging her. "Sure, sweetie. Thank you."

"Chocolate makes everything better."

"You're only seven and if you already know that, life will be a little bit easier for you." Willow bops her nose playfully.

"Kids, Willow and I are gonna visit, okay? You wanna play in your rooms or outside?"

"Can I play video games now?" Bentley asks. He's been grounded from them since his fight.

"Yeah, I guess. You've done everything I asked of you this week."

"Yes!" He runs toward his room and Lilly follows him down the hall to hers. She'll be content playing with her dolls for hours.

"You want some coffee?" I ask as Willow follows me into the kitchen.

"No, thanks. I had my quota for the morning. Besides, we have things to discuss and you need to stop stalling."

"You just got here!" Reaching for the coffee pot, I top off my cup.

"And I'm ready to get down to business." She follows me back to the couch and grabs the photo album from the cushion where I left it. "Taking a trip down memory lane this morning?"

"Yeah."

"Out of guilt?" She casts a glance at me as she flips through the photos.

"Pretty much." As soon as I take a sip of the hot liquid, I wrap my hands around my mug and sigh. "I'm a horrible human being."

Willow's eyes snap to mine. "No, you're not. You're an amazing, hardworking mother who's allowed to have feelings, desires, and needs."

"But Penn shouldn't be the person I want to fulfill those things."

"Says who?"

"Society?"

"We've been through this, Astrid. Fuck what anyone else thinks. Now spill. You said there's something that Penn doesn't know and it could ruin your friendship. What's going on?"

I stare down at my mug and lower my voice so the kids can't hear me. "Well, you know that Penn and Brandon were close, but I'm pretty sure Penn never knew that we were on the verge of a divorce before he died."

Willow's brows pop up. "Oh my God."

"Yeah. Our marriage was over, Willow. We had so many issues and I told him I wanted a divorce a few weeks before he deployed. The timing was awful, but I couldn't keep denying what my heart already knew. He begged me to give it some time and wait until he got back to make the final decision, and I told him I would. But honestly, I was already done."

Tears well in my eyes. "We were so young when we got married. I was nineteen and he was twenty. We were kids ourselves and I got pregnant right away. We grew into two different people and I started resenting him, and vice versa." My eyes find the photo album, looking at a family picture from when Lilly was three, just before Brandon left on the deployment he never came home from. "Then he died, and I should have felt guilty, but I was angry. Angry I wouldn't get the chance to live the life I envisioned after we divorced, one that he would still be involved in for the kids. How horrible does that make me?" I choke out.

Willow scoots closer to me on the couch and rests her hand on my thigh. "You're not horrible, Astrid. You're human."

"My husband died, my kids lost their father, and all I kept thinking about was me. And then once I snapped out of that, I felt guilty for not loving him enough. I lost the man that was such a huge part of my life for so long. I grieved the relationship we used to have and the one that we could have had if I had tried harder. I felt horrible because he was upset with me before he died. Our last conversations weren't always pleasant. We put on a good show for the kids, but after they left the room and we could talk privately, the animosity and frustration came out. Brandon was angry that I wanted out, and I was angry that he couldn't see why." Shaking my head, I sigh. "I didn't feel like I had a partner. His job took him away, and I knew that was the sacrifice that we made, but I feel like it took *him* from *me*, too. He wasn't the same man I fell in love with, and he never supported me finding an outlet for myself."

"That's to be expected. Like you said, you guys were young when you got together."

"Yes, but I also felt like he didn't see me. I felt inconsequential, like he assumed I'd just always be there. I wanted more for myself, and every time I brought it up, he'd dismiss my dreams."

"Like the bakery?" she asks.

"Yes. Baking was just a stupid hobby according to him."

"I'm so sorry, Astrid. This *is* heavy. You've been carrying this around all this time?"

I nod. "Yes. The only person who truly knew what was going on was my mother, and I regret even telling her because it changed the way she saw him. That's part of the reason I never told anyone else. Not only did I not want people in our business, but then Brandon died and I didn't want his memory to be tainted by our marital problems." I stare down at the photo album. "He was a good man, a loving father, and the boy that I gave all my firsts. But he wasn't a great husband, and the last thing I wanted was for him to be remembered that way."

Willow twists to face me, tucking her legs up underneath her. "So why does Penn need to know this now? After all this time?"

I asked myself this same question last night as I lay in bed, but I kept coming back to one issue. "I've only been with one man in my life up until two days ago, and for the past three years, I've done nothing but compare Penn to Brandon—how Brandon fell short where Penn rises above. And I feel so guilty. Will I always compare Penn to Brandon, or vice versa?"

Willow hums in thought. "I think that's only natural given that they're the only two men you've been with, Astrid. Give yourself a break. This situation is complicated."

"Complicated is putting it mildly. I just slept with my dead husband's best friend after lusting after him for years. How does that make me look?"

"Like a woman who finally realized she deserves to be happy." Her words hit me square in the chest. "Who cares who it's with? All I can say is it took me thirty-four years to find a man worth taking that leap of faith with, and I'm glad that I waited because I know what's possible now with the right person. You already know what you want because you now know what you *don't* want. The question is, is Penn the person to give it to you?"

"He's such an amazing man, Willow. I think he could be everything I need and it's terrifying."

"I understand that all too well."

"But I'm so scared of what would happen if it didn't work out."

"There's no way to tell the future."

"Believe me, I know. I never imagined my husband would die. I knew it was a possibility, but I never thought it'd happen to me."

"What has Penn said about everything?"

I shake my head. "We haven't talked yet. Actually, he's supposed to come over tonight. I thought maybe you could help me figure out how to handle this before then."

"Well, what do you want, Astrid? Are you willing to take a risk and really see where this could go? Or do you want to keep things the way they are?"

I chew on my bottom lip. "I don't think I can go back. Not now that I know how it feels to be with him. And it's not just the sex. But something between us shifted last night, and I really do want to explore that."

"Then you know what you need to do. You need to talk to Penn and tell him what you're feeling. And when the time is right, open up to him about Brandon."

"I don't want him to remember his best friend in a harsh light, but how do I start a new relationship without thinking about the old one, without being truthful with a new man about what I didn't get from the last one?"

"I know it's tricky, but as the man of your future, he deserves to know the parts of your past you don't want to repeat."

Chapter Eleven

Penn

Age Sixteen

"Grab that hammer and come over here." My father motions to the tool with his free hand, and as soon as I retrieve it, he points to where he wants me to place the nail. "That's it. Secure right here too." He points to the next spot.

As soon as the nails are in place, he stands up again and brushes the sweat from his brow. "Well done, Penn."

"Thanks. It looks good," I reply, surveying our last few hours of work even though the last thing I wanted to do was come out here and help him with this today.

"Looks a hell of a lot better than it did before now, doesn't it?"

While most teenage boys are sleeping in on Saturdays, my father drug me out of bed to spend the last six hours repairing a wheelchair ramp to one of the buildings at the Carrington Cove Veteran's Center. Ever since my father was honorably discharged from the Marines when I was little, this has been his home away from home, the place he dedicates his time to and the job he works now to help pay our bills. And when he commissions my help, I spend a lot of time here too.

"Sheppard." Hank Lyle, one of the staff sergeants here, comes up to me and my father, shaking my dad's hand. "Thanks for getting this done on such short notice."

"It's the least we could do."

"Once a Marine, always a Marine, right?" Hank says.

My father nods, his face almost stoic. "Yes, sir."

"Now I know this is just about finished, but I have a few more projects that need some attention as well. Care to stop by my office before you leave so we can figure out a timeline to get those things done?"

"Of course. Penn and I just need to finish up here. We'll save the painting for tomorrow."

"Sounds good. See you in a bit." Hank saunters off and my father motions for me to start picking up our tools.

"I don't know about you, but I'm starving. Let's get this done, see what else Hank needs, and then grab some lunch. My treat."

A little over an hour later, I'm sitting across from my father at Deedee's Sandwich Shop, a local spot in town that always has a line out the door. "Are you going to make me get up at six again tomorrow?" I ask him, already dreading his answer.

"I need your help, Penn."

"Why can't Parker help, or one of the other guys at the center?" I groan as I toss a chip in my mouth.

My father takes a moment to consider this before responding. "Well, if Dallas were here, he'd be helping us. But your brother chose to leave, and that means that I need your help the most now, especially since Parker's not quite old enough yet."

Dallas left just a few months ago for basic training for the Marines. It's been weird without him at home, and for the first time in my life, I feel like most of the attention is on me, and I don't fucking like it.

"Why is it so important? What do you get out of helping around the center? Or helping Mrs. Hansen fix her pipes?" I shake my head. "I just don't get it."

My father leans back in his chair and stares at me. "Penn, not everything we do in life has to be about us." I watch his throat bob up and down as he swallows. "In fact, there's so much that we do that affects more people than just ourselves, son. Giving back, putting others before our own selfish needs, is one of the greatest energies you can put out in the world. Trust me on that."

"I guess."

He leans forward now. "Let me ask you something. If Brandon needed something from you, would you be there for him?"

His question catches me off guard. "Well, yeah. He's my best friend."

"Right. So if he asked you to help his mom, or sister, or his wife one day...would you hesitate?"

"Not at all."

"Because Brandon is your brother, Penn."

My brow furrows. "Uh, no he's not."

My father grins. "Not literally, Penn. But by choice. My Marines, the men I work with, the men that I've served with? They're my brothers too, and you should always honor and help your brothers when they need you, even when they're not around."

My mind starts to reel back over the years—how many times random guys would show up to the house to help our dad with a project, how often he would do the same, how many funerals my father attended for men that died while serving. I know all about the sacrifice that it is to give your life to your country. I mean, hell—Dallas wanted to do it, and my father tried to talk him out of it, which tells me he knows the possibility of what awaits him.

"Why are you telling me this?" I ask him, taking a drink from my soda.

"So that you have something to aspire to, Penn. Your brother wanted to serve, and I couldn't stop him, even though I tried. But you? You have the ability to serve without ever putting your life on the line. You can serve your brothers at home—be someone they can depend on, someone loyal and trustworthy. You honor your brothers, Penn, even the ones not related to you by blood. Trust is something you never want to lose between men. And always remember that those relationships are the ones you should never turn your back on because those are the people who will be there for you no matter what."

***

Present Day

I slam the tailgate shut on my truck, grab my tool bag from the ground, and head for the front door of the rental house. The chill in the air nips at my skin, and when I unlock the front door, a blast of cold air from inside the house hits me too. I'd turn on the heater, but once I start swinging a hammer and moving shit around, I'll warm right up.

Placing my tool bag on the ground, I reach up to pull down my beanie. My eyes land on the pile of rubble from the night I brought Bentley here. It feels like a lifetime ago, but in reality, it's only been four days.

Four days and everything has changed.

For the millionth time since Friday night, the memory of Astrid and I fucking in the bakery enters my mind. I can't stop seeing it, reminiscing about it, replaying it over and over in my head—not just because it was the most erotic sexual experience of my life, but because it blew every one of my fantasies out of the water.

I know she felt what I did too. She had to have. There's no way our chemistry was surface level. But I could tell that she was having trouble processing what it meant. The look in her eyes before she left the bakery told me everything that I needed to know—she's scared.

But tonight, I want to assure her that nothing's changed. In fact, I want her to see the possibility of what could be if we gave this a real shot. I just really need to know where her head is at so mine isn't still such a fucking mess, but that's hard given that we haven't talked about it yet because, again, timing hasn't been on our side.

I know what I want, despite what my head has told me for the past three years. I know that us dating will invite questions and opinions, but after experiencing that night with her, I know that she's worth all of the bullshit we might endure. She's worth the guilt.

She's worth everything.

The woman who has been my friend for nearly my entire life just may be the person I'm meant to be with. That reality makes my stomach churn and my heart have palpitations. There are other things to consider too—her brother, the kids, and how fast this could move given how close we already are. But the biggest issue to address is Brandon. I have to know where her head is at in regard to him because mine's been plaguing me with memories that won't let up—and I'm not sure what to do about it.

I have a full day ahead, though—a few hours working on this house, then a half shift at Hansen's Hardware. Every minute of every day in my life feels like it's packed with work and obligations, which normally I don't mind. But now I have something to look forward to beyond work, making resentment build in my chest since I have such limited time to focus on that.

A knock at the front door startles me from my thoughts. When I turn toward the sound, Grady barges in, not bothering to wait to be invited in.

Fuck. What the hell is he doing here?

Maybe he knows you fucked his sister the other night.

Jesus Christ. There's no way. Right?

Astrid wouldn't tell him that…would she?

"Hey, man." Grady steps into the house, surveying the mess, looking normal and not pissed off, so that's probably a good sign.

"What's up?"

"I saw your truck outside and I was on my way to the gym, so I just decided to stop by to say hello. We didn't get a chance to talk at the game."

Grady showed up during the second half of the soccer game yesterday and watched us clench the championship, but then he had to get back to the garage to work on a customer's car. I barely got to say two words to him the entire time he was there, but based on how casual he's being right now, I'm guessing he doesn't know what transpired between me and his sister.

"Well, I was kind of busy."

He nods. "I know, but I wanted to congratulate you in person. That was a hell of a game and season. I bet you're glad to have a break."

"Thanks, man. Unfortunately, work was still calling this morning, so not much of a break."

"Just more *time* to work now, right?" He casts his hands out to the side.

"Yeah, something like that."

"What are you doing here? I thought the Nelsons sold it."

Fuck. Here we go.

Just tell him. You can't keep this from everyone forever.

I mean, hell...Pam already told Astrid, who will eventually say something to Grady and then he'll be pissed he didn't hear it from you.

"This house is mine now."

Grady's eyebrows pop up. "You're moving?"

"No." I take a deep breath and say, "I'm gonna turn this place into a rental and start my own contracting business."

"Shut the fuck up." I roll my eyes. "You're serious?"

"Yeah. Is that so hard to believe?"

"No. I'm just surprised. I know you've talked about this here and there, but you're actually doing it? You're actually starting your business?"

"I couldn't pass up the price on this place." My eyes move around the room. "It's a mess now, and I still have a lot of money and time to put into it, but yeah. I'm doing it."

Grady closes the distance between us and reaches out to shake my hand. I meet him halfway. "Then congratulations, man. This is huge."

"It's not that big of deal," I say, turning away from him to grab some work gloves from my bag and sliding them over my fingers, feeling his eyes on me as I do.

"Yeah, it is. It's you moving forward, finally taking control. Hell, did Astrid put you up to this?"

Fuck. Just him mentioning her has my spine stiffening, among other things. "No. She didn't find out about it until the other night. Why do you ask?"

He shrugs. "I don't know. You know how she can be pushy about things."

"Pretty sure you're the one that's been pushy with me about this topic."

He grins. "True, but hey, you finally did something about it, didn't you?"

The timing was serendipitous for me, much like her, but part of me doing this is so I have something for myself, *and* something to offer her. She deserves a hardworking man who can take initiative.

She deserves a man like her husband.

"I never told her about this plan."

"Really?"

"Yeah. Why is that a surprise?"

Grady eyes me wearily. "Uh, because you two spend every waking minute together and I assumed she'd know."

"Well, she didn't."

"Grumpy today, huh?" He grins at me. "Shouldn't you be in a better mood after your championship win?" Then he snaps his fingers and I have a feeling I'm not going to like what comes out of his mouth next. "I know what it is. You need to get laid, don't you?"

I nearly choke on my own saliva.

If you only knew, Grady. If you only knew.

"My sex life is none of your concern," I reply, wanting him to drop this topic before it gets really awkward, really fast. I know I'm going to have to talk to him eventually about how I feel about his sister, but now is not the time, especially since Astrid and I haven't even defined our relationship yet.

Fuck. Are we in a relationship now?

"I'm just looking out for you. I mean, maybe Astrid was right." He takes his beanie off his head, runs his hand through his hair, and then replaces it, sighing out loud. "Maybe we should start dating."

I eye him wearily. "Each other?"

He flips me off and I laugh. "You know what I mean."

"If that's what you feel like *you* need to do, then by all means, do it. But I'm not interested."

"Yeah, I guess you do have your hands full with this place now, huh?"

"Exactly."

"Does this mean you're quitting the hardware store and the restaurant?"

"Not yet."

"Why not? You're telling me that you're going to continue working at the hardware store, helping out at the restaurant, chasing my sister around, *and* renovate a rental property?" Grady shakes his head.

"Yeah, I am. I can handle it." I choose to ignore the comment about his sister.

He blows out a breath. "You're fucking crazy, man."

"Well, this is the only option I have right now." It's the only option that's going to keep me from flipping out entirely over the risk I'm taking, that is. Can I keep up with it all? Is this how my life will always be? Chaos wrapped up in duty? The feeling of having to be there for everyone else because that's what I've always done—what my father taught me to do?

I just wish I felt more secure, more confident that the choices I'm making won't come back and bite me in the ass. My anxiety is through the roof and my adrenaline is fueling me because otherwise I'd probably collapse from the exhaustion of it all. Life *has* been crazy—coaching soccer, renovating Astrid's bakery, balancing two jobs and now this place, plus trying to start something with the woman I want more than anything.

Will being selfish for once ruin the relationships I've made in my life and the reputation I've built for myself? Will going after what I want actually make me happy? Or will the foundation of my comfortable life shatter completely and leave me standing on nothing but fragments of who I was and what I wanted?

"I'm gonna get out of here. The gym gets too crowded if I get there after nine," Grady announces, pulling me from my thoughts.

"Have fun. My workout is here." I motion to the mess beside me.

Grady laughs. "I can't wait to see the place when it's done."

"Let's just hope I can find some tourists to book it."

"In Carrington Cove? That shouldn't be a problem at all. But I'll wish you luck, nonetheless." Grady shakes my hand and leaves, granting me silence again. But the silence only makes my thoughts spin more, so I turn on my music, strip my coat off, slide my safety goggles on, and get to work, trying not to think too hard about what I'm going to say to Astrid later tonight, but eager to see her nonetheless.

***

"I'm fairly certain this is where my childhood anxiety came from," Astrid says as she slowly lowers the tweezers to the Operation game board, trying to extract the wishbone, which is the hardest one to grab, in my opinion.

"It was either from this or Perfection," I reply, watching her jump as soon as the buzzer goes off because the tweezers touched the board.

She tosses the tweezers down and slides the game to Lilly. "That one definitely added to it."

While I was working on my house earlier, I envisioned our reunion going a lot differently than this. She'd open the door, our eyes would lock, I'd slam my lips to hers, and pin her up against the wall, showing her how much I want her so she doesn't question whether this was a one-time thing or not.

But scenarios like that don't happen in real life when kids are involved, especially given that Lilly and Bentley have absolutely no idea anything is going on between us. I mean, fuck. We haven't had a chance to say two words to each other since I walked through the door and Lilly shoved Operation in my face.

Our Thursday night game ritual was interrupted last week because of Bentley's fight and Astrid's date with Dick that never happened, and if there's one thing I've learned about little seven-year-old girls, they don't forget a damn thing that you promise them.

Lilly screams as the buzzer goes off, making us all laugh. "This game is scary!"

"You're the one that chose it," Bentley says.

Lilly glares at him before sliding the game over to me. We're down to two pieces, the Adam's apple and the wishbone, and with my big ass fingers, I already know I'm going to lose. Sure enough, it only takes a few seconds and the game fucking buzzes. "Shit," I mutter.

"Ooooo, Uncle Penn said a bad word!" Lilly giggles.

Astrid motions for Lilly to sit down in her chair since the kid is practically lying on the table right now. "Lilly, Uncle Penn is an adult. He's allowed to."

"Can I have kisses from Daddy again?" she asks, changing the subject. But just like she did earlier, Astrid meets my eyes as soon as Brandon is mentioned.

Fuck, these kids need to go to bed. *Now.*

"No, sweetie. You already had three."

Lilly leans back in her chair and crosses her arms over her chest, pouting. "Not fair. You've had more than three chocolates."

I brought over Ferrero Rocher for Astrid like I always do, and she's practically eaten the entire package, which means she's nervous. She always eats when she's got a lot on her mind, and the image of her licking her lips while eating said chocolate has been on my mind all evening as well.

Lucky for us, Bentley finishes up the game on his turn and then, because it's Sunday and the kids have school tomorrow, they go to bed early. As soon as Astrid comes back from the hallway to say good night to them, our eyes lock across the living room.

"Hey," I say as I hear my heart beating in my ears.

"Hey," she replies softly.

And then I move toward her, grabbing her hand and leading her into the kitchen, out of sight in case one of the kids comes out of their rooms. Spinning her around, I press her back to the pantry door, pin her hands above her head, and slam my lips to hers just like I wanted to, immediately feeling her melt beneath my touch.

Kissing now. Talking later. That's what my dick decided about ten minutes ago.

Astrid pushes her hips against mine as we kiss, so I reach down, hoist one of her legs up to wrap around my waist, and push my cock into her, letting her know how much I want her, how much I fucking need her.

"Penn..."

"Astrid..."

Our tongues tangle again and she lets out a soft moan. I release her arms and lift her up, wrapping both of her legs around my waist and pushing her against the door. She digs her nails into the hair on the back of my head, rubbing her pussy against my stomach, searching out friction.

We're supposed to be talking, using our words like adults. But it looks like we're desperate to talk with our bodies instead.

I rear back and take a moment to look at her. Her lips are wet and plump from the assault I just gave her mouth. Her hair is falling from her clip, framing her face. And her eyes—they're more golden than their usual green.

God, she's so fucking gorgeous.

I rest my forehead on hers and take a few deep breaths, trying to calm my dick. "Fuck, Astrid. God, I want you so much…"

She leans forward and kisses me again, deeply, intensely, before breaking our kiss and whispering, "I guess we could talk later then."

"I like the way you think." Smiling against her mouth, I hoist her up and carry her down the hallway to her room.

I lower her to the ground and shut the door softly, locking it for good measure. But that's when it hits me—I'm in her room, her room that she shared with Brandon. My eyes scour the space, taking in every detail that's hers and not finding much of my best friend anywhere.

"Penn?"

I look back over at Astrid, concern etched on her face. And then I wonder what my face must look like right now. "Sorry, I just…"

"I know." She fiddles with the bottom of her shirt but keeps her eyes locked on mine. "We can stop…"

"Fuck no," I declare, closing the distance between us and framing her face in my hands before kissing her again.

We might have our ghosts, but there's also the spirit of something new, something meant to be, something that we've been fighting for so long that it's finally developing into an energy that is overwhelming us both.

I lift Astrid's shirt from her body, finding her in a pink lace bra, the fabric so sheer I can see her nipples through it.

"I found something a little sexier than last time," she says, a shy smile on her face.

"You wore this for me?" She nods, chewing on her bottom lip. "Fuck. You know you don't need this, right? That I think you're so fucking sexy in anything…"

She runs her fingernails through the hair at my nape. "I know that *now*."

I back us up to the bed and then reach down to untie the drawstring on her pants, watching them fall to the ground to reveal matching pink lace underwear.

Jesus Christ. She's stunning. Perfect.

And right now, she's all fucking mine.

Astrid reaches for the bottom of my shirt, sliding it up my torso so I can pull it off. And then she leans forward and presses her mouth to my stomach, kissing my abs, licking between the muscles.

"Fuck, baby."

"I love your body, Penn."

I pull her up to look into her eyes. "Not as much as I love yours."

Our lips meet again, and Astrid pops the button on my jeans, shoving them down so I can step out of them. And then we tumble to the bed, taking our time exploring each other with our hands since we didn't get to do much of that the other night.

When she dips her hand below the waistband of my boxer briefs and wraps her fingers around my cock, I nearly come apart.

"Fuck, Astrid."

"I want you inside of me. Now."

I lean down and press a kiss to each of her breasts still covered by the lace, reaching behind her to unhook the clasp before peeling the bra from her body and tossing it to the floor. She slides her underwear down her legs as I do the same and then I rest my body between her legs, cupping her face with my hand.

"You're so fucking beautiful. For years, I've just wanted you to know that, to be able to say that to you."

Her eyes bounce back and forth between mine as she draws in a shaky breath. "Fuck me, Penn. Please." She pulls me down to her and claws at my back, shifting the tender moment between us to a carnal one in an instant. I can feel her desperation. Hell, I've felt the same way. I haven't been with a woman since we kissed three years ago. It's like my heart and body knew she was it for me in that moment.

And now I know for certain that it's true.

I run the tip of my cock through her slit, coating myself in her arousal. She's fucking drenched already, needy and desperate for me. In one smooth motion, I slide in.

"Oh God!" she moans a little too loudly. "Shit. God, you feel so good."

"Shhh. You don't want to wake the kids," I whisper in her ear as I start moving my hips.

"I know, but..."

I cover her mouth with mine, swallowing her moans as I thrust harder and deeper, shaking the bed and showing her how much I fucking want her, how crazy she makes me, how now that we've crossed this line, there's no way I'm going back.

When I release my mouth from hers, she sucks in a breath. "Oh God..." Her eyes are closed and her head is turned to the side, but she looks so fucking perfect—coming apart at the seams because of me. I drop my mouth to her exposed neck, kissing and licking her there, feeling her shudder in my arms.

"Yes, Penn. Yes..."

"Fuck, Astrid." I set a relentless pace, pinning her to the mattress with my hand on her hip as I thrust deep inside of her over and over, fucking her like I want to—like I *need* to—like I'm never going to stop.

Reaching between us, I find her clit and move my fingers in soft circles. She tightens around me, digs her nails into my back, and takes in labored breaths until I feel the flutter of her cunt grip me. "Oh, God! I'm gonna come..." And then she sucks in a breath and shudders beneath me, clenching my cock with her pussy, nearly pulling me over the edge with her, but I hold off and watch her ride out her orgasm, completely enraptured by the sight.

Jesus. I've never seen something so fucking exquisite.

"Shit," she breathes out as she comes down from the high, but my hips are still moving, still thrusting inside of her.

"I love seeing you like this," I whisper in her ear, turning us on our sides and wrapping her leg over my hip so I can stay rooted inside of her.

Her eyes pop open and meet mine, staring at me as if she can see right through me. "I can't believe you're inside of me right now."

I lean my forehead against hers again and shift her legs so they're folded up against my chest, her knees in line with my shoulders, changing the angle to make her feel good. And fuck, like this, her curled up against me, she feels so fucking tight and wet. I'm not going to last much longer.

"We could have been doing this for a while now if you weren't so stubborn."

"Are you seriously lecturing me during sex?"

I slam my hips against her ass, penetrating her deeper. "I am. Now stop talking and let me make you come again."

Her eyes roll in the back of her head as I swivel my hips, circling them around before thrusting deeper again. "Oh God, Penn…"

I reach up and cover her mouth with my hand. "I love hearing you, but if Lilly comes to that door, she's going to be scarred for life."

Astrid smiles beneath my hand and then I gently lift it off and replace it with my mouth. As my pace quickens, I can feel her tightening around me again and that familiar tingle at my spine builds. With our foreheads pressed together, my hands cradling her head, eyes locked on one another, her knees and legs still pressed against my chest, I bring us closer to the edge together.

"I'm there, Astrid." She nods. "Are you gonna come for me again?"

"Yes. Oh God. Right there..." she whispers and then gasps as her orgasm slams into her.

And then I let mine go as well. "Fuck. *Fuck*..." I feel like my soul leaves my body for a moment as my release fills her, my hips pulsing and slamming into her until she has every last drop.

Our bodies unclench and Astrid rolls to the side as I fall flat on my stomach, catching my breath. We lie there, still and frozen with our eyes locked on one another. And then her brows draw together right before she stands from the bed and heads to the bathroom to clean up.

When she returns, she has a robe wrapped around her body as she sits down on the bed, staring off into a corner.

"What are you doing?" I ask, propping my head up on my arm as I lay on my side, still naked.

"What do you mean?"

"Why do you have clothes on?"

She glances down at her robe. "Uh..."

"Take that thing off and get under the covers with me. We need to talk still."

"Penn..." She bites her bottom lip, still not looking at me.

I launch myself from the bed and round the bottom of the mattress, grabbing my briefs from the floor and sliding them on as I make my way to her. I take a knee in front of her and her eyes go wide. I shake my head, grab her hands in mine and bring them to my lips to kiss softly, trying to comfort her. "Talk to me."

"So...we just had sex. Again," she says shakily.

"Yes, we did."

"It was...great."

I arch a brow at her. "Just great?"

Her gaze turns icy. "Is there something wrong with great?"

"I mean, I feel like there are better adjectives you could use. Stupendous, transcendent, mind-blowing..."

"I'm sorry. Did I hurt your fragile male ego?" She scoffs. "Forgive me, please."

I find her ribs beneath her robe and tickle her, making her squeal. "Stop!"

"Shhh. You're so loud."

"Ha! That's funny. You didn't seem to be complaining when you were inside me."

I press a finger over her lips, rise to sit on the bed next to her now, and stare down into her eyes. "I loved every minute of it, every noise and every time you said my name, Astrid." She relaxes. "But I really wanna know where your head is at right now."

When I lift my finger from her mouth, she stares up at me. "I...I don't know."

"You've got to give me more than that, sweetheart."

"I mean...we had sex, Penn. You said things the other night..."

"Like what?"

"That you've wanted me for a long time, that you wondered how it would be when we were together..."

"Did you think I was just saying that in the heat of the moment?"

"No, but it was a lot. And I haven't really heard much from you since..."

I take her hand and place it on my chest, holding it there. "I meant every word of what I said, Astrid. That night three years ago wasn't just the tequila talking. My feelings for you are real. They always have been. And I'm tired of pretending like this isn't something that we both fucking want."

"There are so many reasons why we shouldn't though, Penn."

"But do you want me?"

God, please say yes. Please don't leave this magic between us to die.

Her eyes bounce back and forth between mine. "Yes, I want you. I did that night too…"

"Then let us explore this. I can't go back, Astrid." I lean down and give her a soft kiss. "And I don't want to. Everything is different now and I know what I want."

Chewing on her bottom lip, she says, "I'm scared of what people may think."

"About us?"

"Yeah. And not because I'm ashamed of you, but because of Brandon, and now the bakery." Her throat bobs as she swallows roughly. "I'm starting a business and I don't want to tarnish my reputation."

"So what are you saying?"

She brushes a hand through my hair, pushing it away from my face. "I'm saying, if we do this, I think we should keep it quiet for a while."

My gut instantly protests the idea. I want to claim her in front of everyone, show her affection in public, take her out and spoil her the way she deserves. But I also get where she's coming from, and as someone who's also starting a new business, it might be smart for us to lie low for a while.

"I understand."

"Not forever, obviously. But just until our lives smooth out a bit."

"Do you think that will ever happen, babe?"

The corner of her mouth lifts. "You called me babe."

"Is that a problem?"

"No. Not at all. It's just going to take some getting used to." She reaches down and strokes my cock with her hand. I've been half-hard throughout this conversation, but her touch is bringing me to full mast in seconds. "Like this. Touching you like this is…"

"Fucking perfect," I finish for her, twisting us so she's flat on her back again, staring up at me.

"Yeah, it is." Our lips meet and then we languidly kiss, exploring each other's bodies. Part of me wants to take her again, but I don't want to push her. And I don't want this to just be about sex.

When we finally come up for air, I get dressed, knowing that staying the night is out of the question with the kids. I quietly unlock and open her bedroom door, and then Astrid follows me back out to the kitchen where I left my keys.

"So when do we tell them?" I jerk my chin in the direction of the hallway, keeping my voice low as we talk.

"I can't give you a timeline, Penn." She takes in a shaky breath. "I just know that I need some time to wrap my head around this."

Pulling her into my chest, I rest my forehead on hers. "I know. And I'm here, okay? I'm not going anywhere."

"I'm so nervous about this changing our friendship."

"It won't. If anything, I think it's going to make it stronger."

"Aren't you scared? That something will happen…"

I lean back and stare at her, feeling like pieces of my heart are snapping into place, the fragments that have been floating around lost all finally coming together because all I've wanted for years is to be with this woman.

I can sense that she has doubts, that she's terrified of this shift in our relationship. But all I can do is show up for her and keep proving to her that it only means good things for us. I can't push for too much right now. I just have to accept that at least where we're at is a far cry from where we were.

"The only thing I'm scared of is going back to a life where I don't get to hold you like this," I say, pressing a soft kiss to her lips. "And kiss you like this," I continue, kissing her more deeply this time. "And tell you that you're gorgeous, incredible, and the only woman that I want."

Her eyes widen. "Wow."

"Just give this a chance, Astrid. Please?" My heart is thrashing because I can sense how uncertain she still is. And I wonder if I'm the only one that's truly worried about being hurt in this situation.

What *if* this doesn't work out?

I don't even want to entertain that thought.

"Okay." Her voice is unsteady, but she inhales deeply and then pulls my mouth to hers again.

When we part, I grab my keys from the counter and notice a few pieces of paper strewn about. "What's this?" I ask, lifting the papers from the counter to get a better look.

"Oh, sketches for the new name. I'm not sold on either option, though."

"Cooper's Creations or Whisk Me Away Bakery?" I wrinkle my nose. "Neither of these fits you."

"I know, but I haven't been able to come up with anything else."

When our eyes meet, the same sweet smell I take in every time I'm around this woman hits my nose. And then I grin over at her. "Smells Like Sugar," I say.

"What?"

I drop the papers to the counter and pull her into my chest again, dropping my nose to her neck and dragging it up the column until I get to her ear, watching how her skin pebbles right before my eyes. "Smells Like Sugar. That's what you should name the bakery."

She gasps as I lick and nibble on her skin. "Penn…"

"It's perfect." My voice is gravelly as I hold back, trying not to pounce on her before I leave. But my dick isn't getting the memo.

When I pull back, she's staring at me with wonder in her eyes. "Smells Like Sugar…" she echoes as her smile grows wider.

"I think it's the obvious choice." I press one more kiss to her lips and then head for the door.

"Good night, Penn."

"Good night, babe," I say as I leave and then head back to my own home, wishing I could spend the night wrapped up with this woman instead. But all in good time. Good things come to those who wait, right? And I've waited a long fucking time, but God—is she worth it.

Now I just need to get her to see that we're worth all the shit we still have to face together, including the memories and guilt that continue to haunt me at night.

Chapter Twelve

Astrid

"Mommy, why were you talking to God last night?" Lilly asks as she eats her cereal for breakfast.

I nearly spit my coffee all over the kitchen floor. Stuttering, I say, "What?"

"I heard you yelling, 'Oh God! Oh God!'" She furrows her brow at me. "If you were praying, Mommy, I think you could be a little quieter next time."

This is what mortification must feel like in its purest form.

It's Monday morning and Tanya is opening the bakery today, so I didn't have to be there as early as usual. But it's the morning after Penn and I finally discussed what is happening between us, and I'm already in a situation I am totally unequipped to handle.

"Uh. I'm sorry," I reply, still in shock. "I'll try to keep it down next time."

"It's okay, Mommy. I pray sometimes too."

"Really, baby? What do you pray for?"

"To see Daddy again."

And there's the knife slicing straight through my chest. My eyes travel across the room to a family picture on the wall, staring at the face of the man I should want to see again too.

My brain instantly wonders what he would think about this development between me and Penn.

Yes, I wish Brandon was here for my kids. But in my heart, I know it's time to let him go so I can move on. If he were still alive, I probably would have moved on a long time ago, and I can't keep living my life in fear of what other people might think.

Easier said than done, of course.

"I wish you could see Daddy again too, baby. But remember," I say, walking over to her to press my palm to her heart, "he's always in here."

"I don't want to go to school," she says suddenly, changing the subject out of nowhere.

"Well, I'm sorry. But if you don't go to school, then Mommy goes to jail. And we don't want that."

She tilts her head at me, considering this scenario. "If you go to jail, will we live with Uncle Penn?"

"What?" I ask her, surprised.

"I think it would be fun to live with Uncle Penn. He always has candy and games for us to play, and he kisses my boo-boos when I get hurt."

Maybe getting Lilly on board with the idea of Penn and me dating won't be a challenge after all. Convincing Bentley, on the other hand... Something tells me that's not going to be quite as easy.

"Are there anymore waffles?" Bentley asks as he stumbles into the kitchen, his dark hair still a mess from his sleep, but at least he's dressed.

"There should be some in the freezer," I tell him.

He moves to the freezer and pulls it open. "Are they chocolate chip?"

"Yes."

"I don't want chocolate chip. I want blueberry."

"Well, we eat what we have."

He slams the door shut and heads back toward his room. "Ugh. I just won't eat then."

Taking a deep breath, I blow out my frustration and remind myself that he's just a kid, even though sometimes my children can feel like mental terrorists, eager to see just how far they can push me until I snap. And as I wait for my mother to arrive to take them to school, I wonder whether things might be easier if I had someone by my side to help handle it all, someone who's been there through everything anyway and knows what this life is like. Someone like Penn.

***

"What are you doing in here?" The chime above the front door of the shop rings just as Willow steps inside.

"What? Am I not allowed to come visit you?" Her voice is almost an octave higher than normal, so I know she has an ulterior motive. We may not have been friends for very long, but I'd say I already have a pretty good read on Willow.

"You are, but it's Monday, and I usually see you on Saturdays for your weekend supply of blueberry muffins." I move toward the case, ready to fill a box for her, but she stops me.

"Fine. I'm not here for muffins. I'm here to see how it went with Penn last night."

"Willow!" My eyes dart over to the customers sitting at the table in the corner. I don't recognize them, so I'm pretty sure they're tourists, but I don't want to take any chances. "Don't say stuff like that out loud," I chastise through a whisper.

"Why?"

I wave her behind the counter and motion for her to follow me back to my office. Tanya and Anthony are frosting a cake for a special order, and Vanessa is washing dishes. "Vanessa, can you please watch the front for a few minutes? I'm going to talk to Willow really quick in my office."

"Sure, Astrid. No problem." She wipes her hands dry and then heads out to the front of the shop.

When Willow and I are securely behind my office door, she turns to me, her arms crossed over her chest. "What's going on?"

I look up at the ceiling in contemplation. "I just don't want to talk about Penn around other people."

"Why not?" And then her eyes widen. "Oh, God. Did things not go well?"

I fight back my smile. "No, they did. But we're keeping things quiet for now." And avoiding talking about the elephant in the room, but I can't go there just yet.

Willow claps her hands together. "Oh my God!"

"Shhh! I don't want Anthony and Tanya to hear you."

"Sorry, but can I just tell you how excited Dallas and I are?"

My smile falls. "What? Dallas knows?"

"Yeah." Willow stares at me with a pinch in her brow. "Did Penn not tell you?"

"Tell me what?" My pulse is wild as I wait for her to continue.

"Dallas was the one that told him to, in his terms, 'shit or get off the pot' where it concerns you. Penn was about to punch Richard Cockwell in the face when he came into the restaurant one night, and that's when Dallas told him he'd better do something about his feelings for you before he lost you."

My hand comes up to my mouth. "Oh my God."

"I told you, Astrid...we all saw it. We knew how he felt about you, which is why I thought it was so crazy that you didn't."

"I didn't allow myself to see it," I admit in a whisper.

"Now you do though, right?"

"Yes..."

"And you two are going to see where it goes?"

"Yeah." I swallow hard, still not resolute in how I feel. I know what my heart and body want, but my head is having a hard time catching up. "But like I said, we're keeping it under wraps for right now. With the grand reopening next week and Penn starting his new business, we don't want our personal lives to interfere with our business and reputations. You know how people can talk in this town."

Willow huffs out a laugh. "Um, yeah. I'm aware. The longer I live here, the more I learn about myself from other people."

"Really? What are they saying?"

"That Dallas knocked me up and that's why I'm staying. That I'm on the run from the law and I'm hiding out in Carrington Cove. Or my favorite...that I'm actually one of those undercover bosses and I'm here to shut down Dallas's restaurant, but I decided to date him first."

Laughing, I say, "Where the hell do people come up with this stuff?"

"The hell if I know, girl." Willow shrugs. "Whatever. The important thing is to not let people's opinions dictate your happiness."

"I'm not," I say, moving my attention to some papers on my desk. But Willow stops me and forces me to look at her.

"Astrid..."

"I just need some time, Willow." I can feel the tears building but I blink them away. "I'm crazy about Penn. In fact, I didn't know what I was missing. Being with him is…"

"Life-changing," she finishes for me.

"Yes. But it's also terrifying. And I need to decide how to talk to him about everything that I'm feeling. I don't want to mess that up."

She nods. "Then take your time, but promise me that you'll be honest with him eventually."

There was so much I wanted to say last night, so many concerns and thoughts that have been plaguing me. But as soon as he kissed me, the words left my brain. Only after we had sex was I reminded of everything we have to face, but then he told me how long he's wanted this, how much he cares about me.

I didn't want to dampen the moment. I didn't want to ruin the high.

So I kept it all in, letting my anxiety fester yet again. But the orgasms definitely helped me sleep, so there is an upside to all of this.

"I will," I say, coming back to our conversation.

"Then in the meantime, enjoy all the sex." She bounces her eyebrows up and down, releasing her hand from my arm.

Giggling, I say, "Oh, believe me. I don't think that will be a problem."

She smiles brightly. "I'm so happy for you. Now I bet you can't wait for Hazel's passion party, huh?"

I slap my palm to my forehead. "Shit. That's next Saturday, right?"

"Yup. And then the benefit is two weeks after that."

"Ugh. And the grand reopening is one week from today, then it's Thanksgiving. I can't keep anything straight right now."

Penn has not only scrambled my emotions, but my sense of time as well.

She reaches out to rub my arm again. "It will be fine. Focus on the reopening right now, and the rest can wait. Is there anything I can do to help?"

"Yeah. Do you know someone that can do some printing for me in less than a week?" I say, knowing I need new menus, business cards, and other marketing materials for the reopening with the new name of the bakery.

She takes out her cell phone, her thumbs poised over the screen. "Absolutely. Just tell me what you want and your wish is my command."

"You're like my own personal genie."

"Damn straight. And you don't even have to rub me the right way to get what you need."

***

Penn lets out another yawn as he slides his card in front of Lilly. It's game night and we're playing Kids Create Absurdity. It's basically Cards Against Humanity, but a kid-friendly version.

"You okay over there?"

He nods. "Yeah. I'm fine. Why?"

I tilt my head at him. "Because you can't stop yawning."

He covers up his mouth as another yawn escapes. "It's just been a long week."

I want to press him further, but Lilly starts reading off the cards in front of her and chooses Bentley's card, crowning him as the winner. "Aw, man!"

Bentley stands up from his chair and does a celebratory dance. "Heck yeah! It's all about knowing your audience," he explains to the three of us.

"I don't like this game," Lilly whines.

"You don't like any game when you lose," Bentley replies.

"Hey, hey. That's enough. Go get ready for bed, please." The kids head toward their rooms, leaving Penn and me alone. I stand from my chair and circle the table, standing over him, studying his face. "You sure you're okay?"

His lazy smile spreads and then his eyes bounce all over my body as he lifts his arm and wraps it around my waist. "I'm good, Astrid. Better now that we're alone."

"In about ten minutes we'll be even more alone." I push his hair from his forehead.

"Can't wait."

Lilly comes down the hallway and back into the dining room, so I jump away from Penn before she notices. "Uncle Penn? Can you tuck me in tonight?"

Penn stands from his chair, groaning as he stretches his body. "Of course, Lilly Bear."

When both kids are tucked in their beds, Penn meets me in my room, shutting the door softly behind him. He takes a few steps over to where I'm standing, cups my face in his hands, and presses his lips to mine reverently, so slowly and softly that my entire body melts.

"Fuck. I missed these lips." He cups me between my legs. "And this pussy. I need to fucking taste you."

A whimper escapes my lips. "Why are you so tired?" I mumble against his mouth.

"Work," he answers between nips of my lips, unbuttoning my pants and pushing them down along with my underwear. I step out of them and reach for the bottom of his shirt, pushing it up as he reaches behind his head and rips it from his body.

"Does this have anything to do with the house you bought?"

His head pops up now, our mouths fully detached. "Uh. Yeah."

"We need to talk about that," I tell him, not sure if bringing this up now is the best option, but the longer I watched him tonight, the more worried I became that he has way too much on his plate.

"I bought a house," he says bluntly.

Rolling my eyes, I say, "I know that. And your business plan is incredible, Penn. But are you sure you're not taking on too much? I've never seen you this exhausted." Sure, I've seen him tired before, but this level of fatigue can't be healthy.

Sighing, he releases my face and moves over to the bed, sitting on the edge and then tossing his entire body back, covering his face with his arm. "I'm handling it."

I take a seat next to him, dragging my nails across his stomach, tracing each of his abs. "Are you sure you can't cut back some?"

"Yes, Astrid. There are people counting on me, and I can't let them down. It won't be like this forever." He lifts his arm from his eyes and pulls me down to him before he twists me on my back. "But I don't want to talk about work. I need to fucking taste you. I've been thinking about it all week." His mouth meets mine and I let our conversation go because each time we touch, my brain shuts off—which is surprising because I never feel like it does.

Penn drags his mouth down my body, pushing up my shirt to play with my breasts through my bra before kissing my pussy and pushing my legs open wide. When his tongue drags through me, I moan and then cover my mouth with my hand. If I have to explain my bedroom noises to my daughter again, I just might die.

"So fucking wet," Penn mumbles against my core, spearing me with his tongue, lapping up every ounce of my arousal.

I bury my hands in his hair and gasp when his tongue touches my clit. "Oh fuck."

He doesn't let up, circling my clit with measured strokes, pushing two fingers inside of me, filling and stretching me so perfectly. And when he curls those fingers and strokes me deep inside, my orgasm slams into me so fast I can barely take in a breath.

"Oh God, oh God!" I whisper-shout, my chest heaving, my legs trembling from the pleasure rolling through my body. When I release his hair from my fingers, Penn crawls up my body, kissing my skin as he makes his way to my mouth. And then I taste myself on his tongue.

"Fuck, Astrid."

I stroke him through his jeans, hard and straining against the denim while our eyes remain locked on one another. Before he says another word, I push him back on the bed, crawl over his legs, and pop the button on his pants, shoving them down his hips along with his briefs so his cock bobs up, long and proud.

God, I love his cock.

As I get in position, Penn lifts his head from the bed and watches me. "Astrid..." he groans when my tongue circles the head of his dick. "Fuck. So good, baby." I take him in deeper and he lets out a groan that makes goosebumps spread over my body. "So fucking good."

My mouth slides down his length as far as I can go. I suck, lick, and stroke him while listening for his cues. Heavy breathing fills the room as he buries his hand in my hair. "Jesus. Yeah, keep doing that," he says when I flick the underside of his head with my tongue over and over and then take him in my mouth again. "Ah, fuck. I'm almost there." He taps on my cheek. "Astrid, I'm gonna..."

Nodding, I give him permission to lose it. I've never swallowed in my life, but with Penn, I want to. I want to watch him fall apart for me and feel it for myself.

"Shit. I'm coming," he says, and with our eyes locked, his cum fills my mouth. I swallow it as fast as I can, making sure he rides out his release.

When he's done, I swallow and then crawl up his body, resting my head on his chest as his hands stroke my back. "Jesus, Astrid. I think I blacked out there for a minute."

A giggle escapes my lips but then he pulls me up further and kisses me softly, turning me to my back again. After a few moments, we dress again—me in my pajamas this time—and I lie next to him and curl into his chest, breathing him in, enjoying the warmth of his body.

It's been so long since I've had someone in bed with me, holding me, cherishing me. And the fact that it's Penn takes the entire experience to another level. With our arms wrapped around each other, we lie there in silence and within minutes, I hear Penn's breathing grow steadier. I lift my head and look down at him, finding him fast asleep.

I should wake him. He can't stay the night, but he obviously needs rest. So I lie back down, watch him sleep, stroke his chest with my hand, and curl into his warmth, vowing to wake him up in an hour.

Only an hour turns into seven, and the sound of my daughter's voice wakes us both up in a panic.

"Uncle Penn?"

My eyes shoot open, and then my body follows as I launch myself up from the bed. Penn stirs next to me, but I put my hand on his stomach to keep him flat on the mattress.

"Lilly? What are you doing up?"

"The sky's awake," she says, quoting Frozen. "Why is Uncle Penn in your bed?"

Sweat instantly builds and slides down my spine. *Oh my God. How do I handle this?*

"I had a sleepover," Penn says groggily as he slowly sits up and rubs the sleep from his eyes. Thank God he put his shirt back on last night. "Your mommy knew I was too tired to drive, so she let me stay the night."

She tilts her head at us in contemplation, and I know it's only a matter of seconds before she calls bullshit. But she stuns us both and says, "Can I have breakfast?"

I let out the breath I was holding. "Yeah, baby. I'll be in the kitchen in a minute."

"Okay. Next time, Uncle Penn, you should bring your pajamas if we're gonna have a sleepover." And then she races out to the living room to partake in her morning ritual of watching cartoons.

I turn to Penn and he's smirking. "This is not funny."

"It's a little funny," he says through a chuckle.

"No. It could have been so much worse. What if we had been naked?"

He places his hand against my cheek. "But we weren't."

"I didn't mean to fall asleep against you. I was just going to let you rest a minute and then I was going to wake you up. But..."

"But?" His brow arches.

I lean forward and press my lips to his. "You were so warm and it felt good to have you next to me."

He nuzzles my neck with his nose. "I agree. Perhaps we can plan another sleepover that doesn't involve clothes."

I groan and stand up from the bed. "Not with how crazy my life is right now. I just need to get through the next couple of weeks."

"I know the feeling." When Penn stands, he stretches his hands above his head and then to the side, granting me the perfect view of his abs and happy trail. My vagina instantly wakes up and remembers what we did last night, requesting a replay. "I need to get going. Mrs. Hansen is going to wonder where I am if I don't get to the hardware store soon."

"You sure you're okay, Penn? That you don't have too much on your plate?"

Penn clears his throat and moves around me, avoiding my eyes. "I'm fine, Astrid."

"Okay." I want to believe him, but I know this man. He's too stubborn to ask for help and you can't tell him what he needs until he figures it out on his own.

I follow him out to the kitchen where he left his keys on the counter. Lilly is sitting there with a bowl and spoon ready for cereal, and when I glance at the clock, I realize I have thirty minutes to shower and get ready to head for the bakery. My mother should arrive any moment, and the last thing I need is for her to see Penn still here. I haven't discussed the shift in our dynamic with her yet. Not until I'm more secure in it myself.

"I wanna have a sleepover with Ryan," Lilly says, catching me and Penn both off guard.

"What? Why?"

"He's my friend," she answers dryly.

"But he's a boy," I counter.

"Uncle Penn is a boy and he slept over..."

Bentley chooses to enter the kitchen at this moment, confusion on his face as soon as he sees Penn. "Uncle Penn? What are you doing here?"

"Uncle Penn had a sleepover last night," Lilly answers him. "That must be why Mommy wasn't praying so loud again." She shoots a look over at Penn. "She was talking to God the other night and she was really loud."

Penn starts coughing. "Oh shit."

I shove his back, pushing him toward the door. "You should really be going."

Bentley looks around the kitchen, his brows drawn together. "Why is everyone acting so weird this morning?"

When Penn turns around, the grin on his lips is lethal. God, he's so handsome. I want to kiss him, jump into his arms and let him make me talk to God again, but...kids.

"I'll call you later," he says, winking at me for good measure. "P.S. I told you not to be so loud the other night."

"Go to work." I open the door and push him outside as he laughs.

"Have a good day, Astrid." He drags his eyes up and down my body and then he smirks at me before jumping in his truck and driving away.

And as I watch him go, I wonder if this is what it would be like every morning if I just gave us a shot to be together out in the open, if I could find the courage to bridge that gap between friendship and something more—because choosing to be more than friends is something different than what we've been so far. This time both of our hearts are on the line, and I'm not sure that I'm ready for the chance to be hurt again.

***

"It is with great honor as the mayor of Carrington Cove that I get to celebrate the grand reopening of a landmark in our town." Tyler Lexington, our longtime mayor, stands right beside me on the small stage right outside of my shop. Tons of people from the town are gathered outside, making my grand reopening a much larger spectacle than I anticipated.

When I glance over at Willow standing proudly in Dallas's arms, I have a feeling I know who to thank for that.

"The Sunshine Bakery fed the stomachs and hearts of our citizens for over forty years, but now it's time for a new legacy to take shape. Smells Like Sugar is officially a new staple in our town, and Astrid Cooper has shown us all what hard work and a dream can get you."

The crowd breaks out into applause as the mayor hands me a giant pair of scissors. He motions for me to cut the pink ribbon stretched across the entrance to the shop. When the metal slices through the fabric, the crowd goes wild and I feel my cheeks grow hot. "Congratulations, Astrid. I wish you an abundance of success."

Tyler shakes my hand, his eyes beaming with genuine excitement for me. Then, I find Penn in the crowd, clapping enthusiastically with those giant hands. We lock eyes, and the fierce look of pride in his expression sends my heart soaring. And in this moment, I allow myself to be proud too.

Brandon never supported this.

But Penn *does*. He always did. He encourages me to explore who I truly am.

God, why does this have to feel so good and awful at the same time?

As the crowd begins to thin out, many head to the bakery and form a line out the door. When I slip inside, I am instantly bombarded with people coming up to congratulate me, commenting on how much they love the new look of the place and the new menu items.

Willow came through for me with fresh marketing materials and my employees can't hand them out fast enough. The tables are full, boxes are being filled to the brim with new cupcake flavors and muffins, and the fancy new cappuccino machine I bought is getting put to good use.

"Are you happy with the turnout?" Willow asks, stepping up to my side once I finish talking with a customer.

"This is insane. I'm going to sell out before noon."

She nudges me playfully. "That's not a bad thing."

"I know." I take in a deep breath and smile. "This is just so wild."

"You deserve this, Astrid," she says, just as Penn and Dallas walk up to us. "And you deserve him too."

I smack her arm. "Shhh."

"Still keeping things under wraps?" she whispers as Dallas pulls her into his chest.

"The place looks amazing, Astrid. Congratulations," my former boss says, halting our conversation.

"Thank you. But it was all Penn."

The man in question steps up beside me and I nearly gasp when I feel his hand on the small of my back.

Did I imagine that? He knows we're trying to be discreet, so why on earth would he make a move like that in public?

"It was your vision, Astrid," Penn says.

I glance over to see how Tanya, Anthony, and Vanessa are managing the crowd, but the distinct pressure of Penn's fingers on my spine makes me jump.

"Uh, yeah. But you did the work." I take a step away from him and brush my hair from my face. "I need to go help out. I'll catch up with you guys later, okay?" But I don't wait for them to answer before scurrying behind the counter, checking the display cases and making note of what we need more of.

I'm in the kitchen, grabbing an oven mitt to take a tray out of the warmer, when I feel someone behind me. And by the way my body responds, I know exactly who it is. Penn wraps his arms around my waist from behind, inhaling against my neck. "I'm so fucking proud of you."

I take the tray out and set it on one of the metal counters behind me with him still attached to me. "Thank you, but this is not the place for you to be so affectionate"

He steps back, his brow pinched, and gestures to the empty room. "We're all alone, Astrid."

"Yes, but there are eyes everywhere and one of my employees could come in here any minute."

Hurt flashes across his eyes, but I can't worry about that right now. My body is on high alert. This day, this moment was years in the making, and I can't risk ruining it with a scandal that tarnishes my reputation.

Not today.

"We talked about this, Penn," I say when he continues to stare at me. "This needs to stay between us for now. Bentley is finally getting back to normal, Lilly hasn't asked any more questions, thank God, but I don't want her to get more suspicious. Today is a huge day for the bakery *and* I have that benefit to worry about. The last thing I need is added stress."

I can see him struggle with wanting to fight me on this, but thankfully, he surrenders. Smart man. "Fine. Just promise me you'll take out your stress on my dick when you need to." I roll my eyes as he steps up to me again, gripping my waist once more and leaning his head close to mine. "And while we're on the topic, when were you going to tell me about this benefit, huh? I had to find out about it from Willow."

I scowl at him. "I'm sorry, but when was I supposed to talk to you about that? While we were fucking?"

The smirk he gives me makes me wet instantly. I'm annoyed, but I love that even though our relationship has shifted, we're still not afraid to call each other on our shit.

"You could have told me that between all of the 'oh my God's,' for sure."

I push against his chest, but he just pulls me in closer. "Stop it."

"I can't. I love hearing you scream for me. It's become my new favorite sound."

I draw in a deep breath and let out a moan as he dips his head down and kisses my neck. "We can't do this here, Penn. Please…"

"Fine. But tonight, you're mine. Make time, call your mom. Hell, I'll tell my mom to go over and watch the kids. But I need to taste you again. I need to hear you scream." He lifts his head and looks me straight in the eyes. "I need a reminder that this is real."

Oh, this is so real.

"I'll try," I whisper before he lunges for my mouth, tangling his tongue with mine.

"Don't try, Astrid. Make it happen. I know you can make shit happen when you set your mind to it. I mean, hell…we are making out in the kitchen of *your* bakery, aren't we?"

"Shut up."

He huffs out a laugh. "I can't. In fact, I have many more words to say to you that I think you'll love."

"Like what?" I ask breathlessly.

"You'll just have to wait to find out." When Penn lets go of me, I turn to grab the tray of Danishes, and that's when I lock eyes with Richard Cockwell through the small window of the kitchen door.

Oh God. He must have seen us.

My stomach drops and the tray in my hands nearly does too. I scramble to steady it, narrowly avoiding a dessert disaster. I look back at the window and Richard is gone.

"I'll see you later," I tell Penn, and before he can respond, I hurriedly carry the tray out to the front, my heart pounding violently.

Richard steps up to the counter and I swallow hard. Before he can call me out on what he saw, I speak first. "Hi, Richard! It's so good to see you!" My voice is about three octaves too high and my smile must look deranged, but I'm going to fake it till I make it.

"Congratulations, Astrid. You've done a great job with the place." He returns my smile, giving me hope that maybe he didn't see anything incriminating after all. But I'm still on my guard.

"Thank you. And thank you for coming."

"You know I had to come in to sample the new cupcakes…and get a look around." He winks at me, and a shiver runs down my spine. He rattles off what flavors he wants as I start filling his box. "How have things been?"

"Crazy to say the least, and I don't expect things to slow down until we get through the holiday season." I move to the register and he follows me.

"Well, I wish you all the success. You deserve it." Just then, Penn returns from the back of the bakery, glancing in our direction. Richard and I are both watching him as he heads back outside to join Dallas and Willow. I clear my throat, but Richard speaks. "You know, I'm still disappointed we never got that date."

"I know…"

He hands me his card and looks me dead in the eye. "But at least now I know the real reason why."

A lump lodges itself in my throat. "I'm sorry…I didn't plan this," I croak out, my voice low so other people don't hear me.

"Your business is your own, Astrid. I guess I should just be glad I found out sooner rather than later. I mean, part of me always wondered about you and…" He shrugs. "Whatever makes you happy, I guess. Wasn't Penn your late husband's best friend, though?" he asks pointedly, rubbing salt in the wound.

I shakily hand his card back to him and slide the box across the counter. "Yes, but—"

"Sounds messy," he interjects, cutting me off. "But good luck." With a nod, he grabs his box and heads for the door, leaving me standing there in shock, wondering how I was truly naïve enough to believe that Penn and I could stay a secret, and what the fallout's going to be.

Chapter Thirteen

Penn

Work is the best distraction. When there's people to help at the hardware store and orders to fill at the restaurant, my mind has no choice but to focus on the task at hand, which means there's less time for me to wallow in my guilt over craving my best friend's widow.

God, just thinking those words makes my stomach roll.

It's part of why I'm so tired, part of why I am working myself to the bone. I know I should quit the hardware store and restaurant. Hell, I'm only working at each place three days a week now because I need time to work on my rental house and finish the paperwork to establish my business, but I need to stay busy so then at night, when I bury myself in Astrid, I don't feel the shame.

I can't wonder about what Brandon would think anymore. Every time I do, it kills me. And then I think about my dad—the disappointment in his eyes I'd be sure to see.

"You honor your brothers, Penn, even the ones not related to you by blood. Trust is something you never want to lose between men."

I shake off the memory of his voice and slather the wood in paint again, finishing up the Christmas backdrop that my little sister asked for so I can bring it to her tomorrow at Thanksgiving. She has sessions already booked for this weekend, and I'm already pushing the deadline she set for me pretty tightly. But again, I've been so busy and trying to keep Astrid close so she doesn't overthink our new dynamic and freak out that my responsibilities have gotten away from me.

After I finish the last coat of paint, I hop in the shower and race to Catch & Release for my shift. Dallas greets me as I slide up next to him at the bar.

"Do you realize you have paint in your hair?" he asks, glancing at me from the side.

"I tried to get it out, but honestly, it's easier once it dries."

"True." I can feel his eyes on me as I pour the tequila into a shot glass, making a margarita. "You okay?"

"I'm fine," I grate out, growing tired of being asked this fucking question.

"You don't seem fine." He leans closer to me and drops his voice. "Is everything going all right with Astrid?"

"It's fine."

"Jesus, you sound like a woman right now. You and I both know that *fine* doesn't actually mean everything is fine."

I shove him away and shake the tumbler before pouring the drink into a glass. "What do you want me to say?"

"I don't know. You finally went after the woman that you've wanted for years and you're not acting like a man should."

"And how is that?"

"Like a fucking peacock," he says, making me arch a brow at him. "Puffing your chest out, fanning your tail…" He trails off and then recognition dawns on his face. "Ah, fuck. You two haven't done much talking yet, have you?"

"Are you the fucking relationship guru now?" I retort.

"Hey, my relationship may be new, but I learned my lesson about not saying what's on my mind. Talking about shit sucks, but you can't read her mind and she can't read yours. Plus, you two are bringing another person into this relationship, and you can't pretend like that's not the case."

"I fucking know," I mumble, lowering my voice as I place the drink on the server tray waiting on the counter. "But we haven't exactly had the chance to dive into that topic yet and I don't want to rush that conversation."

"True. I don't know, though…" He scratches his chin. "I feel like you guys need to make time for that."

"And when the fuck would that be?"

He takes a step toward me and looks me dead in the eye. "You fucking make time, Penn—because when something's important to you, that's what you fucking do."

***

"God, it smells good in here." I inhale the aroma of turkey and whatever else my mom has cooking already right as I step into the house. Call me weird, but I love Thanksgiving food. I wore a worn pair of jeans today that have a little extra give just so I can gorge and not feel completely miserable. But that after-dinner nap is really what I'm looking forward to after the past few weeks.

When I round the corner and step into the kitchen, I'm greeted by the sight of my sister and my mother standing side by side, mixing food together in bowls with pans strewn all over the counters. I'm the first of my brothers to arrive, which actually pleases me since there's less shit talking I have to participate in. My mind and body can't handle too much thinking right now.

"Put on an apron and help," my sister says with a grin on her lips.

I take a seat at one of the stools on the other side of the kitchen counter instead. "I don't want to get in your way. You two look like you have a system going and the last thing I want to be accused of is disrupting it."

My mom grins at me knowingly. "Well played, son."

I tip my chin at her, smirking right back at her. "I thought so." Then I turn my gaze back to my sister. "By the way, your backdrop is in the bed of my truck."

Hazel does a little shimmy. "I'm so excited to see it! Thank you, big brother." She blows me a kiss and then goes back to mixing the stuffing together.

"You're welcome. I hope it looks okay. I was half asleep while I was building it."

"Using power tools while not fully conscious probably isn't a good idea, son." My mother shifts dishes around on the counter.

Hazel studies my face. "Yeah, now that you mention it, you look like shit." She points to my eyes. "You've got bags, big brother. You may want to consider using a night cream."

"Shut up, Hazel."

"I mean, you're not getting any younger, Penn." She giggles as she keeps stirring the contents of the bowl.

"Is it too early to start drinking?" I ask, moving to the fridge, but my mother blocks me.

"Yes. Now sit your butt down and relax. Your brothers will be here soon and you three can all gorge and drink until your heart's content once they arrive."

I head for the couch. "Sounds like a plan."

By the time Willow, Dallas, and Parker arrive, I'm itching to take off the edge of irritation and fatigue I've been riding all morning. My brothers and I turn on football and relax while the girls dance around each other in the kitchen.

Mom always serves dinner around two on Thanksgiving so we can eat and then eat again later if we want. I sit back in my chair at our family dining room table and feast on turkey, mashed potatoes and gravy, stuffing, green bean casserole, cornbread casserole, and cranberry sauce. My mom's cooking just gets better and better as time goes on, but I watch her glance over to my father's empty chair over and over again, and I can tell she's struggling today.

Even though all her children are here, we will never be enough to fill that missing piece in her heart.

After everyone eats, I notice my mom walk back to her room, so I quietly follow her.

"Mom?" I call out to her as I open the door and see the bathroom light on through the crack in the door.

"I'll be out in just a second." I wait for her to shut the light off and open the door, and when she comes out, I can tell she's been crying. "Penn? You're still in here?"

"Did you think I'd leave you alone?" I motion for her to move toward me so I can hug her. "I'm sorry I can't take away your pain, Mom."

"Thank you. It's just rough. The first holiday without him, and I..." She sniffles and sighs. "He was the love of my life, Penn. Words can't express how much it hurts to lose that."

The love of her life.

And is Astrid mine? I'm afraid that I already know the answer to that question.

"I'm sorry. I miss him too…Although I'm not so sure that he'd be happy with me right now."

She rears back, looking up at me with confusion. "Why would you think that?"

Sighing, I motion for us to sit on the bed, side by side. "I kind of did something and I'm fairly certain Dad wouldn't approve."

"What did you do, Penn?" She grabs my hand, looking up at me nervously.

I look my mom dead in the eye and say, "I went after Astrid."

Her eyes go wide. "Oh my goodness." But then she smiles and the light in her eyes returns. "I have to say, I always wondered if you felt that way about her."

"I did. I have for a long time, but I shouldn't, Mom." I hang my head and blow out a breath.

She places her hand on my knee. "Why not?"

"Isn't it obvious?"

"I mean, I can see why you might think that, but Brandon isn't here, Penn. Have you two talked about it?"

"Not really. We've been…doing other things," I say cautiously as my mother smirks. "But talking isn't really one of them. I'm afraid to push her to talk to me about him, but I know that we need to. I feel like I need to." I pound my fist on my chest, wishing the force would unwind the tightness there. "Life has just been crazy, and I'm not sure how to broach the topic with her. I want her to know that I'm serious about her, that I wouldn't have acted on these feelings if I weren't, but I also know that there are so many distractions and reasons we could use as reasons not to be together. How…" I take a deep breath and continue, "How do I get her to actually talk to me?" My mother hums. "We don't exactly get a lot of alone time to talk either," I add. "There's always a kid, or a job, or…"

My mother squeezes my hand. "You take her away."

"What?"

"Out of town, away from Carrington Cove so it's just the two of you with no one else around."

I brush a hand through my hair. "It's only been a few weeks and I'm already sick and tired of sneaking around, Mom."

"Then all the more reason to do this. Show her what it would be like if you two were a real couple."

"I mean..."

"Have you had *that* conversation?" my mother asks.

I lift one of my brows. "What did you not understand about the fact that we haven't really talked?"

"No need to get testy with me, young man. You're the one that came to me for advice, so watch your tone." My mother points a finger at me with narrowed eyes.

"Sorry." I sigh and run a hand through my hair. "But do you really think taking her on a trip is the solution?"

My mother nods. "Speaking from experience, the times when your father and I could get away, just the two of us...those were the times that kept our relationship alive. That's when we could actually *talk* and we weren't being interrupted by real life and kids around every corner. It was just him and me," she says, emotion clogging her throat now. "Those trips reminded us of why we chose each other all those years ago and why we loved each other." She tilts her head at me. "Getting away from reality can actually help you get a handle on reality, as backwards as that sounds. And you two need the space to figure out exactly what you want."

"What about Brandon?" I ask. "She was his *wife* and that won't change."

"He would want her and the kids to be happy and loved in his absence."

"But he was my best friend. It feels like betrayal. And Dad was always so adamant about loyalty, brotherhood..."

"Let me ask you this. Do you think your father wouldn't want me to be happy and move on if I had the chance?" my mother asks, catching me off guard—not only because that's something I hadn't considered, but also because I can't imagine my mother with someone else.

"I—I don't know."

She narrows her eyes at me. "Yes, you do, but let's try it this way. What if you had been Astrid's husband first?" My heart starts to race. "What if you were the one that died and Astrid fell in love with Brandon? Would you not want her to be happy if she had to live a life without you?"

Fuck. I never thought of it that way.

"I—I don't know how to answer that because how I feel about it is irrelevant. I'm not him."

My mother arches her brow. "Exactly. How Brandon would feel is irrelevant too— because he's not here, Penn. But you and Astrid are. And I swear," she says, clenching her teeth, "if you mess this up with her, I'll never forgive you."

"Are you threatening me?"

She nods, but her smile is playful. "You'd be a fool to let her slip through your fingers." Her eyes dance with emotion. "Don't be mad at me, but I always wished she had fallen for you instead of him."

"Mom..."

She holds a hand up. "I know things happen for a reason, but now you have a chance. Take her away, show her the man that you are, the man you can be for her. Make her talk to you and fight for what you want. I'll take Bentley and Lilly if need be, but you need to do this. Trust me."

"I don't know if she'll ever fully let me in, Mom," I say, voicing my biggest fear out loud.

"Then this is your chance to show her you can be who she needs. That she's safe with you."

I pull her into my chest and kiss the top of her head, breathing in the smell of garlic, rosemary, and spices on her. "Thank you."

"Anything for you, Penn. And please don't worry about letting down your father." She sits up again and looks me in the eyes. "I think you'd be surprised to know that your father was quite the hopeless romantic."

"Really?"

"Yes. In fact, I think that's where Hazel gets it from—that desire for love, that need to feel wanted. When he was struggling with depression, I reminded him of everything he had to live for, and it was his undying love for his family that pulled him out of that dark place. He could never be disappointed in you for going after what you want, especially if it's for love."

The corner of my mouth lifts up and emotion swells in my chest. "I think I needed to hear that."

"I wish he could have told you himself, but..."

"He's here with us today, Mom. I know he is." My throat grows tight, but only because I hope for both of our sakes that he is here and he knows that we miss him.

I miss him terribly.

And I hope to God he's not disappointed in me.

"I hope so."

With one last hug, I release her and stand from the bed. "I guess I need to talk to Astrid now."

"Make sure you do it in person, that way she can see the sincerity in your eyes. And she can't hide. Remember that our bodies can say just as much, if not more than words do."

If that's the case, then I'm pretty sure Astrid already knows how I feel. Now it's time for her to hear it, and for me to get over the guilt of wanting her once and for all.

Chapter Fourteen

Astrid

"Do you think I brought enough snacks?" Hazel asks as she, Willow, and I stare at the smorgasbord on my kitchen counter.

"Um, I think you could feed an army with this feast," I say. "Seriously, how many people are you expecting?"

Hazel bites her lip and winces. "I honestly don't know."

My head snaps in her direction. "Come again?"

"I literally texted everyone that I could think of because we never get to have get-togethers like this," she argues.

Willow's gaze bounces between the two of us. "Um, I know I'm new here, but is this something you guys do often, or...?"

"Willow, I assure you, we have never thrown a passion party together. This is definitely a first for me and Hazel."

Hazel huffs out a breath. "Well, we *should* be doing this more. I mean, why is it always the boys that get to hang out together? Always bro-ing out in their man caves." Then she looks at Willow. "Well, until you came along, that is."

Willow points a finger to her chest. "Me? What did I do?"

Hazel shakes her head. "Nothing. In fact, I'm so glad you're here because now Dallas is far less grumpy than he was before. But he's definitely not hanging out with the guys as much now."

"He has access to regular sex now, so I'm sure that takes priority." Willow winks.

"And that's also probably why he's far less grumpy," I add, making Hazel gag.

"Don't remind me that you're banging my brother, okay?"

"You brought it up," Willow reminds her.

"I know. I guess I just wanted something to look forward to, you know? It's not like there's a man in my life or *any* action for that matter, if you catch my drift."

Willow and I stare around the house at all of the penis décor and phallic-shaped foods. "I couldn't tell," I say, teasing her as she rolls her eyes.

"I'm happy for you, Willow. Really, especially after everything that brought you and my brother together."

"Thank you, but don't give up hope, Hazel."

Hazel nudges me with her shoulder. "At least I'm not the only single one left, am I right?"

"Um, yeah…" I don't dare correct her. That is not a conversation we need to have tonight, when I'm going to be shopping for sex toys for me and her older brother.

Willow shoots me a knowing look, but luckily the doorbell rings before she can call my bluff.

In a matter of twenty minutes, my house is full of over thirty women of varying ages. It's the Saturday after Thanksgiving, so I wasn't sure what to expect in terms of the turnout, but it seems a lot of women in Carrington Cove are in need of sex toys.

Huh. Something I didn't need to know about my neighbors.

Shaking off my convoluted thoughts, I slip into hostess mode and make as much room for people to sit in the living room as I can.

"Hey, beautiful ladies!" Hazel's friend Adeline exclaims from the center of the room, gathering everyone's attention. She's the rep selling the products, and judging by her pink hair, breasts on display, and banging pre-baby body, I'm guessing she is probably quite confident in bed, which means we're all in good hands. "Is everyone ready to go shopping for pleasure?" A few women hoot and holler, but most of us giggle under our breath. "No need to be shy. We're all gal pals in here, and we all have a pussy, right?" Another round of laughter and agreement fills the room. "So tonight it's about finding the right tools to make your pussy purr." She claws at the air, and I glance over at Willow who is barely holding herself together behind her hand.

"How the hell did I get into this again?" I mutter beside her.

She stifles her laughter. "I honestly don't know, but hey, at least we get free entertainment for the evening." Adeline starts dancing with two vibrating dildos in her hands, spinning them around like batons. "Oh God. I can't buy one of those now. This is all I'll be able to see!"

I snort and then lower my voice. "Dear Jesus. This is what I get for sleeping with Penn, isn't it? Is this karma?"

Willow places her hand on my shoulder. "Hardly. Tonight you'd better buy something for you two to enjoy together."

I think back on the sex I've had with Penn thus far. Honestly, I don't feel like we need anything to increase our chemistry, but I'm trying to be open. I don't even know if he'd want to use toys in the bedroom, but if he's willing, it might actually be fun. Brandon didn't want toys in the bedroom—even when he was gone. He didn't want me to "replace him." So this could be a brand-new experience that Penn and I share. And I think we might need that—something that's just ours.

Adeline spends the next thirty minutes explaining the products to us, passing them around so we can see how they look and feel and decide if it's something we might want to try. It feels like we're playing hot potato with dildos, and yet again, I don't think I'll ever be able to look at some of these women the same way again. Pam has been analyzing an anal plug so long, I know that image is never leaving my mind.

Once Adeline has shown off her gadgets and gizmos with the same enthusiasm as Ariel, we start the ordering process. I've set her up in my bedroom, and we're taking turns so everyone can make their picks in private. Before I know it, it's my turn.

"So, do you have any questions for me? Or do you already know what you'd like?" she asks as I take a seat next to her on the floor.

"Um, well...I'm kind of in a new relationship and we haven't talked about what we're comfortable with in terms of toys, so I'm not sure," I explain, feeling confident about my vague answer.

Adeline's eyes light up. "Oh, that's so exciting. Congratulations."

"Thank you."

"Do you have any toys of your own?"

"Just one of those bullet vibrators," I answer, slightly embarrassed. But it was the only thing I could convince myself to order and could hide from Brandon.

"Oh girl, I'm about to change your life."

Adeline starts suggesting various things to me, and I'm so enraptured in what she's saying that I almost miss the masculine voice that breaks through the conversation in the living room.

"Uh, hi ladies."

I feel my eyes bug out of my head. "Oh no." Scrambling from the ground, I rip my bedroom door open and race down the hallway to find Penn standing in full view of my living room and all the women holding sex toys—lots and lots of sex toys.

"Penn! What are you doing here?" I ask, and his head whips over to me.

"I, uh..." He scratches the back of his neck while trying to think of what to say. But then his eyes land on Hazel stroking a purple dildo with far too much focus. "Oh, fuck."

Hazel lifts her eyes to meet her brother's and then she smiles from ear to ear, waving her fingers in the air at him. "Hi, big brother."

Penn grimaces. "I just walked in on your sex toy party, huh?"

Hazel nods and I feel my stomach twist. First, I can only imagine how horrifying it is for him to see his sister in this light. But second, I'm sure every woman in this room is wondering what the hell he's doing showing up at my house on a Saturday night around nine o'clock. It's late enough for a booty call—well, at least a booty call for someone in their thirties.

Hazel stands from the couch and starts slapping the dildo against her palm. "That's right. And no boys allowed."

Penn rears his head back and his eyes go wide. "Believe me, the last thing I wanted to do was walk in on this."

"Why would you be walking in Astrid's house at this hour anyway?" Hazel asks, her brow lifting.

Willow meets my gaze, her eyes widening.

"Uh, he needed to drop something off," I interject, finally finding my voice.

"Like what?"

"Something for the bakery."

"Why wouldn't he just drop it off there?"

Think, Astrid. Think.

But before I can spit out an excuse, Hazel chimes in again. "You know what? It doesn't matter. What does matter is that you're not supposed to be here." She grins wickedly and then flings the purple dildo across the room, hitting Penn square in the forehead.

Chaos descends as the entire room erupts into laughter.

"Oh my God! Hazel!" Willow shouts, and Penn starts to retreat toward the door, rubbing his forehead where he was just slapped with a fake dick.

And that's when all reason goes out the window.

Hazel picks up a cock ring and slingshots it at him.

"What the fuck, Hazel?" Penn exclaims, shielding his face this time, prepared to dodge whatever she finds to launch at him next.

"Get out! No boys allowed!" she yells through her laughter as she sends a pair of edible underwear flying.

"Fine! I'm going!" Penn shouts back, walking toward the door.

"You'd better! Before I get my hands on a flogger!"

"Jesus Christ! You're deranged!"

She sticks her tongue out at him as he opens the door and I follow after him. "Don't intrude on girls' night again!"

"Hazel," I grit through my teeth as I follow Penn through the door and shut it behind us.

Penn is standing near the edge of the street, rubbing the spot on his forehead where Hazel hit him. "I think I'm going to have a bruise."

I cover my mouth, stifling my laugh. "I'm so sorry. I don't know what got into her."

"She's obviously hopped up on female empowerment." We share a laugh and then his eyes soften as he looks at me, staring at me so intensely that my heart starts to flutter. "God, you're beautiful." His words come out of left field, but I appreciate the sentiment nonetheless.

"You're not so bad yourself."

"I wish I could fucking kiss you right now," he says, his voice low and husky. "But I know there are far too many witnesses."

"Yeah. Which leads me to my question—what the hell are you doing here?"

"You weren't answering your phone and I—" He blows out a breath. "I needed to talk to you."

"Well, as you can see, I've been rather busy."

"I honestly forgot all about this party."

I take a step closer to him, wishing I could curl up into his chest and inhale him, drown in his scent and embrace that make me feel content. "So, what did you want to talk to me about?"

He clears his throat and then straightens his spine. "Don't make any plans for next weekend."

"Okay..." I draw out. "It happens to be the only weekend I have free in December. But what's happening?"

"You and I are going to the mountains."

My mouth falls open. "I'm sorry. What?"

"You heard me. We're going away, just the two of us. Far away from Carrington Cove and everyone we know."

"Penn, I can't just up and leave. I have the bakery and the kids..."

He holds a hand up. "I've already talked to Tanya. She said that between her, Anthony, and Vanessa, they can handle Friday and Saturday. And Sunday the shop is closed."

"And the kids?"

"My mom and your mom are going to trade off watching them all weekend."

I raise a hand to the center of my chest, right over my pounding heart. "I'm sorry. Did you say *both* of our mothers?"

He nods, smirking. "Yes."

"Does that mean..."

"They know about us." He tips his chin once. "Yup."

I'm speechless. Stunned. Both irritated and giddy. This man might have told both of our mothers that we're doing...whatever it is that we're doing, but he orchestrated an entire weekend away for us so we can be alone.

"Is there a reason we need to go out of town?" I ask, now nervous there may be an ulterior motive here.

Penn takes a few steps closer so there's barely any space between us. My back is to the house so I can't see if anyone is watching us, but we're just talking. Very closely.

"Yes. We need time alone, Astrid. We need to talk. And I'm fairly certain that the only way that's going to happen is if we're far away from our distractions. Plus, I don't know about you, but I'm fucking exhausted," he huffs out through a laugh. "The past few months have been insane and I need a break. I'm sure you could use one too."

"This is a big step, Penn."

"No it's not. Not to me. Our timeline is a little different, babe." He reaches up and tucks a strand of hair behind my ear. "The usual rules don't apply here because our situation is unique. So, who gives a shit how big of a step this is? All I know is that the idea of having you all to myself, naked and riding me as much as you want..." He shakes his head and a low growl climbs up his throat. "I'm practically salivating at the thought of it."

As if I wasn't already turned on shopping for sex toys, this man comes over and talks about me riding him.

God help me.

"Fine," I say, feigning irritation. "I guess I'll go away with you next weekend."

The corner of his mouth lifts slightly. "That's what I thought."

"I need to get back inside." I jerk my thumb over my shoulder.

"Yeah, I know. I'll let you go, but I don't know when I'll see you next. I have a lot of work to get done before we leave, and we might have to forego game night this week."

"The kids will survive. Bentley has a book report that he needs to work on anyway. And Lilly has dance class three times this week in preparation for her recital."

"Then I guess I'll see you Friday morning?"

"I guess so."

Penn walks backward toward his truck, keeping his eyes locked on mine. "Goodnight, babe."

"Good night, Penn."

I watch him hop in his truck and drive away as I let out a wistful sigh. For a moment, I wish I could have left with him and let Willow handle the house full of women I'm about to step back into. But now I have something to look forward to—a weekend alone with him where we can be naked twenty-four seven.

But he also wanted to talk, Astrid. Did you not catch that tidbit?

Knowing that I can ruminate on that later, I step back into my living room where the women are acting like Penn was never here.

Thank God.

I find Willow and Hazel in the kitchen, snacking on sausages. Yes—sausages.

"Hazel Grace!" I admonish when she locks eyes with me. "What the hell was that about?"

Willow tosses her head back in laughter. "Oh my God! I can't wait to go home and tell Dallas about that."

Hazel simply shrugs, a pleased grin on her lips. "He deserved it."

"Seriously?"

Her happy gaze turns into a glare aimed right in my direction. "Um, yes…he did. You have no idea what it was like growing up with three brothers, Astrid." She has a point. "Hell, even now they make my dating life a living hell."

"You have a dating life?" I ask, teasing her.

"Ha-ha. But honestly, Penn can handle it. He's a big boy. Plus, it's just so fun to remind my brothers that I have a sex life." She giggles. "It makes them crazy."

I nod in agreement. "I've done that a time or two to Grady as well, but I've never flung a dildo at his head."

"You should try it. It felt really good."

"I'm just impressed that you hit him square between the eyes," Willow interjects.

Hazel blows on her fingers and rubs them on her arm. "What can I say, girls? I know my way around a dildo."

***

"Well, good morning," my mother greets me as I walk through the front door of her house. It's the morning after the passion party and I stayed up way too late playing dildo ring toss and drinking vodka and cranberry juice.

The next time I see Hazel, I might just chuck a dildo at *her* forehead.

"Did you have a nice time?"

"It was…an experience," I say, following her deeper into the house.

"Mommy!" Lilly exclaims, jumping up from the couch and running over to me. "I missed you, but Grandma made us waffles with strawberries and whipped cream for breakfast and we stayed up late watching movies!"

"Well, Grandma sounds like a lot more fun than your mom, huh?"

She looks up at me, her arms curled around my waist. "You're still fun, Mommy."

I huff out a laugh. "Good to know." When I pop my head up, I see Bentley exiting the kitchen with a glass of orange juice in his hands. "Good morning, Bentley."

"Hey, Mom." He comes over to me, lets me pull him into a hug, and then moves away from me again just as fast.

"Why don't you two go gather your things while I talk to your mom for a minute?" my mother suggests. My kids head down the hall, and as soon as they're out of sight, she turns her gaze back on me.

And here it comes.

"Is there something you want to tell me, Astrid June?"

I bite my bottom lip. "That depends. What do you know?"

"I know that Katherine called me Friday, asking if I was free this coming weekend to help with Bentley and Lilly."

"Did she say why?"

"Yes, but I'd rather hear it from you."

Sighing, I close my eyes and say, "Penn and I are going away together."

"Because..." she draws out, enjoying dragging this out longer than necessary.

"Because we're seeing each other."

The smile that spreads across her lips is one of pure joy. "There. Now was that so hard to tell your mother?"

"Mom..."

"Astrid," she counters. "You and Penn...God, I couldn't ask for a better man for you. Honestly, I figured you two were already more than friends."

"Not until a few weeks ago," I admit on a whisper, staring down at the ground now.

My mother's brows draw together. "What's wrong?"

"Can't you see how messed up this is?" I ask.

"How? All I know is that my daughter deserves love. She deserves a man that knows her worth. And as far as I'm concerned, that's the only thing that matters."

"It's just a lot. My life is complicated enough..."

She shakes her head, making me stumble on my words. "No, honey. It's not." She lets out a loud sigh. "Maybe I raised you to be too independent because that's all I knew. Maybe losing Brandon has forced you to put up some walls. But you have to find the balance between vulnerability and strength, Astrid. It's okay to be strong, to know that you can stand on your own two feet if need be. But it's also okay to want someone in your life again. And Penn allows you to do that, sweetie—to be both of those people. You're always softer around him."

"He makes me feel things I never did with Brandon," I admit.

"And that's okay too. You shouldn't compare them, honey."

"But how can I not?"

"I guess in a way it's natural because Brandon is the only other man you've been with." She tilts her head in thought. "But you and I both know that your relationship with him was over long before he died. Give yourself a chance to get it right this time with Penn. Take that weekend, build a foundation for a relationship, and jump in with both feet."

"You're pretty good with the dating advice, Mom," I tease her. "Why have you never tried putting yourself out there again after Dad left, then?"

"I did, but I never found someone good enough to introduce you and Grady to. That was my concern."

I instantly think of the relationship Penn has with my children. "The kids love Penn."

She winks at me. "I know. I guess the question is then…do you love him too?"

Do I love Penn? I guess in a way I always have, but this type of love is different. The type of love she's referring to is the kind that could end in heartbreak.

"Now, I hate to push this further, but I have one more question," my mother continues.

"Okay…"

"Does Grady know about you two?"

Oh God. My brother. How could I have not considered his feelings on the matter? I've been so consumed with my turmoil over Penn's relationship with Brandon that I forgot about his friendship with my overprotective brother.

My mind is just a mess.

"He does not, but Penn and I should talk about when and how to tell him."

She nods. "I agree. I think him hearing it from the two of you will be best, although I honestly don't see him having a problem with it."

"I hope not."

Once my kids return with their things, they say their final goodbyes to my mom and then we head home to relax, do laundry and get ready for the week ahead. I can only hope that it goes by quickly because my time away with Penn has me excited for what we can explore together, but also nervous that what we have to discuss could end our relationship before it ever gets started.

Chapter Fifteen

Penn

"Please tell me my lunch is ready," I say as I walk into Catch & Release, wiping the dirt from my face with my forearm. It's Thursday, and once I'm done with lunch I'll only have a few more hours until I'm free for my weekend with Astrid.

Dallas grabs a burger from under the heat lamps and sits it in front of my usual stool at the bar. "Just finished up." He assesses me with his eyes. "You need a shower."

"Yeah, I know. The grout gets fucking everywhere, but I'm finally done with the tiles in both of the showers on my rental."

"Making progress then?" Dallas asks, leaning up against the bar. It's just him and me right now, but Grady and Parker will be here any minute.

"Slow progress, but I guess that's better than nothing." I pick up my burger and take the biggest bite I can muster, needing food before my stomach eats itself.

"So quit working for me then. Give me your two weeks' notice right now."

"I'm not ready," I mumble around my food.

"Does that have to do with Dad?" he asks, catching me off guard but striking a chord nonetheless.

"What's that supposed to mean?"

He sighs and brushes a hand through his hair. "I know you and I had a different relationship with Dad, but I envied how you were always with him—helping around the Veteran's Center, checking on families of Marines that were on deployment, and fixing up things around the house. He taught you to fix what's broken and help out your neighbors, and it's noble, Penn. Really fucking noble, and makes me proud to call you my brother. But, I also feel like he projected this sense of obligation on you where you feel like you can't say no now." Shrugging, he moves to the soda fountain and fills up a glass of Coke for me and slides it across the bar. "I guess I'm just trying to tell you that it's okay to be selfish, Penn. I mean hell, you did that with Astrid, right?"

"Yeah, but look at how long that fucking took," I huff out.

"But you got what you wanted, right?"

"Almost."

"Is that why you two are going away this weekend?" I stare at him, wondering how he knows that, but he answers for me. "Astrid told Willow."

I nod in understanding. "Yeah, I just hope we can get on the same page."

"You will. I believe in that. I've watched the two of you dance around each other for years, and if you don't, then all of this would have been for nothing," he says. "Make her see that she's the one you can't live without."

"There you go with the relationship advice again."

A pleased grin stretches across his lips. "I'm getting pretty wise since Willow came into my life."

"Thank God because I was wondering if you were adopted there for a while."

He tosses a dry dish towel at me just as Parker and Grady walk in through the front doors of the restaurant. "Is it Friday, yet?" Grady grumbles as he takes his stool next to me and Parker sits on the other side of him.

"I echo that sentiment," I mumble around another bite of my burger, although I can't tell Grady why I'm chomping at the bit for the weekend to be here. Wanting to defile his sister all over the cabin I rented is not something he needs to know.

"I hate Christmastime," Parker says, popping a fry into his mouth.

"Isn't it supposed to be the most wonderful time of the year?" Dallas asks sarcastically.

"Sure, but people are also irresponsible pet owners during the holidays. Do you know how many emergency surgeries we have to perform because dogs and cats ingest decorations?" Parker shakes his head. "I had a dog come in today that has a strand of garland coming out of its ass. The poor guy."

"Did you save him?" Grady asks.

"Yeah, but it will take some time for him to fully recover." He picks up his tuna melt and takes a huge bite out of it. "I need a fucking vacation."

"Same," Grady echoes.

"You're preaching to the choir," I say, finishing off my burger.

"You are taking the weekend off, aren't you?" Dallas asks as I flick my eyes to him and flash him a glare of epic proportions.

"You? Taking a break?" Parker snaps his fingers. "It's because of the comment about the bags under your eyes Hazel made at Thanksgiving, isn't it?"

"Fuck you," I spit back. "And no. I just...want some time away."

"Then good for you. I have the week off between Christmas and New Year's, and I can't fucking wait," Parker adds.

"So where are you headed?" Grady asks, turning his attention to me.

I don't want to come up with some elaborate lie that I'll have to remember later, but until Astrid and I discuss when and how to tell him, I'm going to be as vague as possible. "Up to the mountains."

"Damn, that's far."

"I know, but I just want to get out of Carrington Cove for a bit. I've been working too fucking hard, and if I stay in town, I'm just going to be tempted to work on something instead of relaxing.

"Makes sense. Maybe we need to plan a guys' weekend sometime soon then? Just a bunch of boys in the woods, drinking beer, going fishing..." Grady suggests.

"Fuck, I'm down," Dallas says. "I'd have to run it by Willow first, of course."

Parker laughs. "You're not even married and you're already whipped?"

Dallas arches a brow at him. "Are you telling me that if you'd married Savannah, you wouldn't put her before everything else?"

I tense up at the mention of Parker's ex-fiancé, wary of his reaction. "I've asked you not to bring her up," Parker says through clenched teeth.

"Well, if you're going to pass judgment on my relationship with Willow, then Savannah is fair game."

Grady looks back and forth between the two of them. "Uh, did I miss something? Parker was engaged?" he asks.

"Unfortunately," Parker says swiftly. "And we're not talking about it anymore. Got it?"

"Okay then," Grady draws out. Silence descends on us, but Grady offers up a distraction. "Penn got hit in the face with a dildo this weekend," he says. Parker starts choking on his food, Dallas throws his head back in laughter, and I shove Grady off his stool.

"What the fuck is wrong with you?"

"What? I needed to lighten the mood," Grady replies.

"And that's what you went with?"

Dallas has tears streaming down his face. "I'm just mad that Grady beat me to the punch."

"How the fuck does everyone know about that?" I ask, fucking pissed that I have to relive this embarrassment again.

Grady clears his throat. "Dude, did you forget that half the women in town were at that party?"

"The best part is, it was Hazel that threw it at him," Dallas manages to say through his laughter, and the other two morons lose their shit.

Standing from my stool, I head for the door. "You know what? That's fine. Everyone have a good laugh at my expense, but I've got work to do so I can fucking enjoy myself this weekend."

Dallas calls out to me as I get closer to the door. "Hope you have a good *fucking* time," he says, hinting at my true intentions this weekend.

And with that, I flip him off and exit the restaurant, eager to complete what I need to so I can relax this weekend. But Dallas's comment about our dad eats at me all night.

So that's when I decide that before I pick up Astrid tomorrow, I'm going to put in my two weeks' notice with him and Mrs. Hansen at the hardware store.

I can't keep living my life for someone else. I have to make the changes I set out to when I took on this venture and when I pursued Astrid. I need to full commit.

Let's just hope that all these changes I'm making don't come back to bite me in the ass.

***

"Well, that was kind of stressful," Astrid says from the passenger seat of my truck as we head toward the highway that will take us to the Blue Ridge Mountains in the western part of the state.

"You mean sneaking out of your house before the sun rises?"

"Yeah. I made sure to kiss the kids goodbye last night and they knew my mom would be there in the morning when they woke, but I mean look at me." She gestures to her body. "I even wore all black so I'd blend in."

"You act like you were robbing a bank," I say, holding in my laugh.

"I just didn't want to get delayed by the kids." She bounces in her seat. "Honestly, this whole thing kind of reminds me of Monica and Chandler in Friends when they were sneaking around so no one would find out about them. It's kind of fun, right?" she asks with a lilt in her voice. But the secrecy is less than fun for me.

Gripping the steering wheel harder, I clench my teeth. "No, Astrid. I don't think hiding how I feel about you is fun. It's stressful and it limits our time together."

She sighs and I can tell my response made her excitement fizzle. "I know." Fiddling with her hands, she twists them in her lap. "It's not fair to you, Penn. But..."

I hold a hand up to stop her. Now is not the time to have this conversation. "We'll talk about it later, okay? Not now." I grab her hand and bring it to my mouth, kissing the back of it, and then sucking her index finger between my lips.

A small moan leaves her lips. "Okay."

"Now, open up that bag beneath your seat," I say, directing her attention to the paper bag full of our breakfast and road snacks. I got up even earlier than I normally do so I could make breakfast burritos and pack snacks for our trip. I didn't want to stop since we have a five-and-a-half-hour trip ahead of us. Every moment that we get alone together is going to be spent wisely, and once we arrive, I have other activities planned for us to do—mostly of the naked variety.

"You made all this?" Astrid pulls out the burritos wrapped in foil, single serving orange juice bottles, and then peeks through the rest of the snacks in pre-portioned bags.

"I did."

She sits there, stunned. "Wow."

"What?"

"I mean, you took the initiative to plan this trip, pack food for us..." Sighing, she says, "Those are things that I usually have to worry about."

I kiss the back of her hand again. "I don't want you to worry about anything this weekend, okay? We both need this time away, and you deserve to have someone take care of the little things, Astrid. I want to be that someone for you."

She grows silent and for a second, I wonder if I said something wrong. But then she leans over the middle seat and kisses my cheek. "Thank you, Penn."

"No thanks necessary."

She drags her nose up the side of my neck. "I still plan on thanking you, that's for sure. I have some ideas I know you'll be a fan of."

Groaning, I feel my dick grow hard against my zipper. "Astrid...I'm gonna fuck you all over that fucking cabin."

"Promise?" she whispers as she nibbles on my earlobe.

"I promise. And I never break a fucking promise."

* * *

"I can't believe this is our view for the weekend."

"The drive was worth it just for this to be our backyard, huh?"

Miles of open fields roll before us, small hills covered in patches of snow and brown grass, leading to the base of the Blue Ridge Mountains in the distance, indigo peaks dusted with white. I can only imagine what this place must look like in the summer when everything is green. But for now, for us—it's offering just what we need—peace.

The drive went by ina blur once I gave Astrid control of the music and she started playing songs from when we were in high school. We laughed, she danced, and then we talked a lot about our memories. But every time she mentioned Brandon, I could tell she felt uncomfortable. And I wish there was something I could say or do about that. Hopefully by the end of the weekend she'll feel differently.

I cage Astrid in against the railing she's leaning over on the deck. The house I rented is two stories with the bottom level reserved for the garage and den. But the top level is the entire living area—a quaint kitchen with granite counter tops, two large sofas you can sink into positioned around a giant television, three bedrooms and two bathrooms, which is way more than we need. But it was the view that sold me on this place, and now I'm glad I went with my gut.

The sound of silence fills the air around us. We're the only house for miles and the main hub of the little town we're in is about a seven-minute drive from here.

We're alone. Away. Distanced from our lives back home.

And that's exactly what we needed.

Astrid pulls her beanie down further over her ears as I press her back to my chest and circle my arms around her. "I can't wait to watch the sunrise out here," she says almost breathlessly.

"You plan on being up that early?"

"I mean, I'd love to be able to sleep in, but my internal clock probably won't let me."

I drag my cold nose against her neck. "Then I'll just have to tire you out so you don't have a choice."

Giggling, she turns in my arms, her smile blinding and her eyes shining in the midday sun. She's so fucking stunning, natural and pure, strong and gentle all at the same time. She's the woman I crave every minute, the company I want at the end of each day, and the person I'm meant to be with for the rest of my life.

I love her.

I think on some level I always have.

And I'm terrified that she may never be able to open herself up to me completely because she loved my best friend first.

"Thank you again for planning this, for forcing me to take time away."

"Believe me, it was a struggle for me too." I pull a strand of her hair away from her face that the breeze blew across her lips. "But now we're here and we're going to make the most of it." I take her by the hand and lead her back through the double French doors, closing them behind us. "I'm gonna start a fire in the wood burning stove. Why don't you go unpack and then we can go grab some lunch?"

"Sounds good."

After I get the fire going and the heat starts to warm up the space, I head to the master bedroom where Astrid's unpacking. I intend to take her into town to grab some lunch and groceries, but when I enter the room, I decide the first thing I need to eat is *her*—every fucking inch of her.

Astrid is taking her toiletries out of her suitcase, walking to the master bathroom when she sees me standing in the doorway, my body rigid and about to snap. And she stops. "Penn?"

"Take your pants off."

Her eyes go wide, her lips part, and the small bag that she's holding falls to the floor. "Oh..."

I strip off my flannel, rip my beanie from my head, and reach behind my neck to bring my shirt up over my head. Astrid's eyes darken right before me. "I've waited all week to taste you again, and I'm not waiting any longer."

"But I thought we were going to lunch?"

"I'm going to eat my appetizer right now." She smirks at me. "What part of me wanting to fuck you all over this cabin did you not understand?"

She starts to laugh, but I race toward her, pick her up and toss her over my shoulder before throwing her on the bed, her giggles ringing out around us. She starts stripping off her shirt as I pull down her black leggings, finding her pussy covered in black lace that hints at the prize hiding underneath.

I drag my nose over her slit, pushing her thighs open to make room for my shoulders.

"Fuck, I can smell you. You like the idea of me licking your pussy, don't you, Astrid?"

"Yes..." she mewls, burying her hands in my hair.

I hook my thumbs under the string on her hip and pull the fabric down her legs, kissing up her calves and knees, the inside of her thighs, before I make my way back to her core, dragging the entire length of my tongue through her wetness.

"Penn..."

Fueled by the desire in her voice, I take my time building her up—worshiping her the way she deserves, reminding her of our insane chemistry, proving to her the way we want each other can't be wrong when it's this fucking good.

I'm tired of feeling guilty. I'm tired of wondering "what if?"

I just want to be here, in the present, drowning in this woman and proving to her that us together is right.

It has to be.

Flicking her clit softly, I look up at her from between her legs, watching her come undone as my fingers and tongue bring her over the edge. And when she's spent, when her breaths return to normal, she sighs contently, and I wonder if she'd rather just order in. I'm not sure if we have that option given our remote location.

But when her head pops up and our eyes meet, she licks her lips and pounces on me. "Now it's my turn."

***

"This town is amazing." Astrid takes a sip of her beer and looks around the pub we stumbled in after we were done exploring for the day. We bought food for tomorrow that we stored in a small cooler in my truck, she bought herself a new hat and some chocolates from a local shop, and we ate soup and sandwiches at the one café that served lunch. We were able to catch the sunset from one of the main streets in town, and then decided to get some drinks and dinner before heading back to the cabin for the night and probably all of tomorrow, if I have my way.

"I've spent so much time in Carrington Cove that I forget there are other little towns like this, ones even smaller than ours."

"Carrington Cove isn't as small as it used to be," I say as I take another drink of the IPA I ordered.

"True. Tourism has been good to us."

"It has."

"Is that why you want to tap into that new venture?" she asks, broaching the first of many topics we need to discuss.

"Yeah," I admit. "The contracting part is just so I have steady cash flow, but investing in real estate is something I've been interested in for a while." I draw a finger through the condensation on my glass. "I'm ready to make my plans a reality."

When I look up, I'm met with Astrid's understanding smile. "You deserve that, Penn."

Staring at her intently, I say, "Thank you. Honestly, if it weren't for you, I probably wouldn't have done it."

"Then why did you hide it from me?" she asks, reaching out for my hand and covering it with her own. "That day at the bakery, when I found out…" She shakes her head. "I was hurt."

Be honest with her, Penn. No secrets. No lies. That's not how you want to start things with her.

I take in a deep breath and then admit, "Because I'm scared of failing, Astrid. And the last thing I want is for you to see me that way. As a failure."

Her brows draw together. "I could never, Penn. With your work ethic, your strength, your heart? You could never be a failure in my eyes."

I scoot closer to her and our foreheads meet. "Thank you. I needed to hear that."

She presses her lips to mine and then leans back. "Tell me more about your plans. What do you see for your business long term?"

As I lean back in my chair and take a sip of my beer, I imagine where I could be in five years if I took the risks I need to. "I want to establish a name for myself in town and the surrounding towns as a high-end contractor. Adding more rentals to my portfolio is a must, obviously. I'm just not sure if it's realistic given the market and the fact that not many people leave Carrington Cove."

"Yeah, I get that. Have you thought about branding? Business cards? A website?"

I run my hand through my hair. "Fuck. I mean, yeah, but I'm not actively pursuing that. Should I be?"

She tilts her head at me and smiles. "Eventually, yes, especially if you want to bring in high profile clients. But I can help you with a lot of that, you know…"

I lean toward her. "You'd do that?"

"Penn, of course I would. If you would have just told me about your idea in the first place, I could have been supporting you and helping you all along."

Reaching for her hand, I bring it to my lips, pressing a soft kiss against her skin, something I just can't seem to stop doing. "I know, but it's taken a long time for me to get to this point, Astrid. I just didn't want to burden anyone else. I feel selfish enough branching out on my own."

Astrid huffs out a laugh and leans back in her chair again. "You're preaching to the choir here. You think I didn't have the exact same struggle when I bought the bakery? You think I don't feel guilty every time I'm getting home late at night, missing time with my kids? Worrying if they'll grow up feeling like I'm more concerned about my business than them?"

"Are you kidding? If anything, you're showing them how important it is to chase your dreams." I tell her. "You're teaching them that it's okay to go after something you want, to pour your heart and soul into it. I'm so fucking proud of you for taking that risk."

She shakes her head at me. "So how is it that you can say those things about me, but you can't tell yourself the same thing, Penn?"

Her question stuns me for a second, because she's right.

Why is it so easy for us to see the good in someone else, but not in ourselves? To support other people, but hold doubt inside?

Why can't I accept that I am worthy of Astrid, and that it's ok to show up for myself instead of everyone else for once?

Her words slam straight into my chest and give me so much clarity, it's as if I'm seeing the world through a new lens.

"I—I don't know." Shaking my head, I say, "But I'm working on it. I actually put in my two weeks' notice this morning. Dropped off a letter at the restaurant and the hardware store before I picked you up. I haven't heard from Dallas or Mrs. Hansen, so I don't know if they're mad or they were expecting it, but I'm ready to start this next chapter of my life." I bring her hand to my lips. "And that includes you and the kids, Astrid."

She grows visibly uncomfortable for just a second, but then I watch her brush it off. "I would love to take the kids here one day." She looks around the pub. "Not here, obviously. But this little town, to a mountain getaway."

"They would love that."

"I mean, I guess I can now. I'm my own boss. The bakery is doing really well, so I can finally afford it."

I squeeze her hand. "*We* will make it happen. You're not on your own anymore, Astrid. Okay?"

Her eyes bounce back and forth between mine. "Penn, I've never been completely on my own." For a second, I'm not sure what she's saying, but she continues. "You've always been there for me, but I'm talking about independence. Even after Brandon died, my mother was helping me survive financially."

"I didn't know that. I would have fucking helped you, Astrid. I have plenty of money in the bank…"

"You and I both know that I wouldn't have taken it." She's right. "But you were there for me in other ways, ways that no other man ever has."

Fuck. Is this where we're going to discuss Brandon? In a pub with people milling around us?

"You two aren't from around here, are you?" An old woman comes up to the table, dropping off my burger and fries and Astrid's fried chicken dinner on our table.

"How'd you know?" I ask her, slightly irritated that our conversation was interrupted, but grateful for the distraction at the same time. That discussion needs to wait until we are back in the privacy of the cabin.

"Just a hunch." She brushes her gray hair over her shoulder and extends her hand to me. "I'm Dolores."

"Nice to meet you, Dolores." I shake her hand and then Astrid does the same.

"And I'm Donald." An older gentleman steps up beside her, placing two fresh beers on the table. "Dolores's old man."

She swats at him, but he leans in and presses a kiss to her cheek.

"Do you two own this bar?" Astrid asks, popping one of my fries in her mouth.

"We do," Dolores says. "I'd always wanted to run a little place like this, and when we retired up here, the old owners sold it about a year later. Donald turned to me and said, you wanna knock that item off your bucket list?"

"And she thought I was crazy." We all share a laugh. "We'd just retired, you know? But honestly, it was one of the best things that could have happened to us."

Astrid and I share a look. Yeah, I'm sure she's feeling the same way about her decision to buy the bakery. The jury's still out on my venture, but I have faith I'll feel the same way one day.

"Astrid just opened up her own bakery," I say, bragging about her accomplishment since I know she won't.

Dolores's eyes light up and she pulls out a chair at our table, taking a seat. "That's incredible. Congratulations."

"Honey, let these two eat in peace," Donald tells her, but Astrid insists she's free to join us, so I let it happen.

Almost an hour later, the four of us have shared another round of beers, we learn that Donald was a truck driver for forty years, Dolores worked at the post office for thirty, and they've been married for almost forty-five years.

"You two aren't married?" Dolores asks, waving a finger between the two of us.

Our eyes meet and I decide to answer the question for us. "Not yet."

Astrid's eyes bug out and then she picks up her beer, drinking instead of remarking on my answer. Dolores picks up on the shift in her demeanor. "Something tells me there's a story here."

"There is, but it's complicated," I reply.

She leans in closer to Astrid. "If you don't snatch up this man, someone else will, honey. The way he looks at you? Most people never see a love like that in their entire lives." Her eyes shift to her husband. "Luckily, I'm not one of them."

Donald blows her a kiss. "I still can't stop staring at you, baby. That'll never change."

Astrid clears her throat. "You two are very lucky."

"Luck is only a sliver of what it takes, you two," Dolores adds. "It takes a lot of work, but when you have someone who supports you through thick and thin, it doesn't feel like work."

Astrid smiles at her. "Then you deserve all of your happiness." I watch her stand, smoothing her shirt down before she announces, "Excuse me. I'm going to the restroom."

The three of us watch her walk away and then Dolores stands from her chair. "I'm going to go check on things." She pats Donald's arm and walks away, leaving the two of us alone.

"It's complicated, huh?" He echoes my words from earlier with a grin on his lips.

"You have no idea."

"Lay it on me." He leans back in his chair and rests his arm along the back of it.

I don't know this man, but hell—the advice from a man that's been married for longer than I've been alive might just be worth something. "She was married before…to my best friend. He died four years ago."

Understanding flashes across Donald's face. "Ah. Yes…that is complicated."

"Told ya. And they had two kids together. They were high school sweethearts and I've been in their lives for so long that it feels like…"

"Betraying him," he finishes for me.

I nod. "He used to brag to me all the time about their marriage. I was envious…"

Donald scratches his chin through his thick, gray beard. "You know, my father asked me something when I was debating what I wanted to do about Dolores. We were teenagers when we met, too, but I knew she was it for me. I didn't want to wait to start my life with her, but I was worried about what people might think."

"Yeah, I understand that too, more than you know."

Donald taps his fingers on the table. "But my father said, ask yourself this: if you were in a room full of every person you've ever met in your entire life, who would you look for first? If the answer is her, then you know what to do."

For a moment, I picture walking into a room full of every person I've ever met—friends, family, people that live in our town. But the only face I'd want to see is Astrid's.

"It doesn't matter if she was his first. What matters is that she's the one you were supposed to find now." Donald smirks at me once again. "And that means that she never really belonged with him forever in the first place." Donald stands and I watch him move, his body unfolding as he lengthens his spine.

"Thank you, Donald—for your hospitality and your advice."

"My pleasure, Penn. Good luck. Any woman that's worth fighting for won't make it easy, just remember that too." With a wink, he walks off to check on another table and within minutes, Astrid returns.

"You okay?" I ask her, noticing her cheeks are flushed.

"Yes. The heat in that bathroom was unreal." Fanning her face with her hands, she blows out a breath.

"You ready to start heading back?"

"Yeah. I'm beat and full." Her hand rubs circles around her stomach.

"Well, I hope you're not too full." I stand and offer her my hand. "We still have to fit in dessert."

Taking my hand, she stands from her seat, reaching behind her to grab her jacket from the back of the chair. "Is that an inuendo, or do you actually expect us to eat more tonight?"

"It's both, Astrid. Just always assume it's both."

***

When we walk into the cabin, I head straight for the wood burning stove and load a few more logs in to keep the heat going. Astrid was quiet during the entire ride home, and I knew the conversation with Dolores and Donald must have gotten to her.

I find Astrid standing in the kitchen, filling up a glass of water from the fridge. I wait for her to finish drinking until I come up behind her and grab her hand.

"What the..."

"Come with me."

Leading her into our bedroom, I head straight for the bathroom and make her stand in front of the mirror over the counter with me behind her.

"Penn? What are we doing?"

I don't say anything as I reach up to pull her beanie off her head and toss it to the floor. My fingers make slow work of popping each button on the flannel jacket she's wearing, and then I motion for her to reach down and untie her boots. I take the opportunity to do the same and when we both stand upright again, I slowly peel her jacket from her arms, leaving her standing there with wild hair in nothing but a simple white tank top and her blue jeans.

"You are so god damn beautiful, Astrid." I dip my mouth to her neck and begin to kiss her so gently that the touch shocks me. Her skin pebbles right before my eyes, so I keep going, trying to keep our eyes locked on one another. "The fact that I controlled myself around you for so long still boggles my mind." She hums and sighs simultaneously. "But tonight, we're going to talk before I show you just how out of control you make me, how much you fucking own me, body and soul." Her mouth parts on a gasp. "I need you in my life Astrid, more than I need to breathe, and before the weekend is up, you're going to fully understand that." I spin her around to face me so our eyes can meet. "I'm all in, Astrid."

Her mouth drops open slightly. "Okay..."

Cupping her face, I continue, "You have ruled my thoughts for so long, I can barely remember a time before you. Your soul, your friendship, your smile—they keep me going. I've been at war with myself for so long about how I feel about you, but I'm done fighting that battle. I want you. I want us. I know we have things to discuss and to work through, but I'm in. I'm signing on for all of it. And I want you to know that before anything else happens this weekend."

She reaches up and brushes my hair from my forehead. "It scares me, Penn..."

"What does?"

"How strongly I feel for you," she whispers.

I take her hand and place it over my heart that is thrashing wildly in my chest. "You're not the only one, babe. But this is right. Us together...is *right,* Astrid. I know it with every fiber of my body, and I don't care if the timing isn't right or how hectic are lives are, I want to be with you. Really be with you. I'm tired of fighting it."

"I don't want to fight it anymore either."

Needing to show her how I feel, I push up her tank top and help her take it off, leaving her in a white cotton bra. Popping the clasp on the back, I pull it from her body and toss it to the floor. Cupping her breasts, I massage them, tweaking her nipples and twisting them, watching and feeling them tightening before my eyes before I spin her around to face the mirror again.

"I love the way you touch me," she says, reaching behind my head and wrapping her arm around my neck as I continue to play with her breasts.

"I can't stop touching you, Astrid. I won't ever fucking stop. It's you and me now, babe. This is it."

I release her breasts and pop the button on her jeans, pushing them and her underwear down her legs, helping her step out of them and delighting in the full view of her naked body standing before me reflected in the mirror.

I can see her face scrunch up with uncertainty, her body that has made two humans, and I hate that she can't see what I see.

"Stop it. Right now." I grab her chin as we lock eyes in the mirror.

"Stop what?"

"The negative thoughts in your head. The criticism you're playing on a loop over and over again." I press my erection into her back. "Don't ever question how sexy you are, Astrid. This body..." Still staring into her eyes, I smooth my hands down her soft stomach covered in stretch marks, her hips that have meat on them to grab onto. "This body brought two incredible people into the world. It keeps you alive and healthy. Your body is a miracle. And I can't get enough of worshiping every inch of it."

Quickly spinning to face me, she wraps her arms around my neck and lightly brushes her lips against mine. "Fuck me, Penn," she breathes.

She smashes her lips to mine as I reach between us to unbutton my jeans, shoving them down my legs and kicking them to the side. I quickly remove my shirt and then I give myself over to this woman, gripping and clawing at her like I can't get close enough. Our hands seek skin and warmth, my dick presses into her stomach, she rubs herself against me, and our mouths feast on each other hungrily.

Insane pleasure builds in my groin, my need to be inside of her cresting the edge of explosion.

I twist her around again and meet her eyes in the mirror. "Are you wet for me?"

"Yes."

I snake my hand around her waist and dip my fingers between her legs, finding her dripping. Fuck, I need to feel that around my cock.

But first, I want to push her a bit.

"Put your foot on the counter, Astrid."

She looks at me for clarification. "Just one?"

"Yes. Show me your pussy. Show me what I do to you."

Swallowing roughly, she slowly raises her right leg and plants her foot on the counter, giving me the perfect view of her soaking, pink cunt.

"Fuck, baby. Fucking perfection." I reach from behind her this time, moving my hand to her pussy and playing with her so we both can watch. I circle her clit with my index finger, spreading her wetness all around, and just when she's about to come, I slide two fingers inside her, and we both watch as I fuck her with my hand.

"Oh my God," she moans, her eyes locked on the sight between her legs.

"Such a greedy girl," I grate out in her ear, holding her to my chest, supporting her from behind and loving how responsive she is, how her hips move with each push and pull of my fingers.

"Penn, I want your cock."

"Yeah? You want to watch me fuck you like this?"

She nods rapidly. "Please."

I withdraw my fingers and bend my knees, lining myself up to her core and then slowly sliding inside. Astrid's eyes roll into the back of her head as I grip her hip tighter, holding her in place as I start to move.

"Oh fuck. God, yes…"

"That's it, Astrid. Look at you take me, beautiful. Look at your pussy stretched around me." She moans as I keep up my pace. "You make me so fucking hard," I grate out, watching my cock slide in and out of her knowing that it can't get better than this.

This intimacy? This closeness? This trust?

I could never have this with anyone else.

I have to make this woman mine. She needs to accept that wholly, without question.

"Oh fuck, I'm close." Astrid reaches between her legs and starts rubbing her clit.

"Come on my cock, Astrid. I wanna feel you dripping down my balls."

Her fingers move faster until she's panting and breathless. "Penn...Penn!" She tenses and then detonates, screaming as her orgasm slams into her. I keep thrusting and pulsing inside of her as wetness slides all the way down my cock and between my legs.

I slide out of her, pick her up in my arms, and carry her to the bed, laying her down gently and then hovering over her, kissing her cheek. "I'm not done with you, but I have a question."

Her eyes stare up at me lazily. "What?"

"Did you buy anything at that passion party?"

She bites her bottom lip. "Maybe?"

"Did you bring it?"

"Maybe."

I bite her nipple and she squeals. "Where is it?"

"In my toiletry bag."

I head back to the bathroom and open the bag she spoke of, more than impressed with what I see. A few vibrators, an anal plug, and something else I've never used and definitely want to try with her.

With the item in my hand, I return to the bed and lie down beside her, scooting up until my head is on the pillow. When Astrid sees what I grabbed, she huffs out a laugh. "Not what I thought you'd grab."

"Don't worry. We'll play with the other stuff another time, but I've always been curious about this thing." I stretch the silicone ring over my cock and position the vibration piece on the top of my shaft so it can rub right against Astrid's clit as she rides me.

She straddles my lap and starts stroking my cock that's still soaked in her arousal. "It doesn't hurt you?"

"No. It just feels like a tight squeeze. I feel harder, which I didn't know was possible."

With a mischievous gleam in her eyes, she moves up my body, positions me at her entrance, and slides onto my cock, making my eyes roll in the back of my head. "Oh fuck. Yeah, that's a little different."

"Good different?" she asks as she starts to move.

I gently trace my hands up and down her ribs and hips. "Fucking amazing, baby."

Astrid groans and closes her eyes as she finds her rhythm. "God, I love your cock, Penn."

"Ride me, baby. Fucking use me. Come all over me again."

Astrid circles her hips, rubs back and forth, and bounces up and down, taking her time building her body back up. And I don't complain one bit. The sight in front of me is so fucking perfect that if this was the last thing I saw, I would die the happiest man on earth.

"Turn it on, Penn," she commands breathlessly, moving faster now.

I push the button on the side of the vibration piece of the cock ring and we both moan when the sensation hits us.

"Oh fuck."

"God, yes." Astrid leans forward, her hair covering both our faces as she rubs and rides me, racing toward the crescendo that we both know is coming.

The vibrations are travelling all the way down my dick. I know that when I come, it's going to be intense. It's going to be life-changing. And the main reason why is the woman that's currently on top of me, right where she fucking belongs.

Chapter Sixteen

Astrid

"Oh God. I'm close," I whisper in Penn's ear as he tightens his grip on me and his hips slam into me so hard that I feel like he might break me in half. But fuck, it feels so fucking good, like he knows exactly how much I can take.

This man knows what I need before I can even figure that out myself.

I let his fingertips take control of me in the dark, I let him guide me up and down his cock, hitting the vibrator right where I need him, and when my orgasm crests, he finds his release too.

We're so loud that I'm grateful we don't have neighbors. And it feels good to not have to worry about that—about waking up kids, about alerting people around us, about worrying what someone might think.

In this moment, it's just him and me.

But the reality is, it will never be just the two of us.

And that's where I'm still struggling.

Penn brushes my hair from my face when I push myself up from his chest. "Fuck, Astrid. Are you all right?"

Smiling down at him, I say, "I'm perfect. So perfect."

He leans up and presses a kiss to my lips. "Let's get cleaned up."

Once we both take care of necessary business, Penn summons me back to the bed, naked still, of course. He cups the side of my face and stares down at me, reverence in his eyes. "Hey."

"Hey, yourself."

"We're alone."

"I know."

He lets out a sigh. "It's time to talk some more, baby."

I close my eyes. "I know."

"I need to know where your head is at, Astrid."

"My head is spinning right now from the orgasm you just gave me," I say, opening one eye to look at him.

A sexy grin spreads across his lips. "You mean orgasms."

I roll my eyes. "Sorry. Orgasms."

"Tell me about this benefit," he says, surprising me. I thought for sure he'd dive right in to talking about the elephant in the room we've yet to address. But honestly, I'm grateful he hasn't yet.

"You mean…"

"The one you never told me about." He bops me on the nose. "Remember, we both kept things from each other before this happened." He gestures between the two of us with his hand.

Yeah, but I'm keeping the worst secrets, Penn.

"Well, it's all Willow's fault, honestly."

Penn laughs. "When the woman gets an idea, she goes all in."

"That she does." I spend the next few minutes explaining the details of the event to Penn.

He trails his fingers up and down my arm, leaving tingles in their wake. It never ceases to amaze me how his touch makes me feel, how this shift in our friendship feels so natural that even my guilt is dwindling the more we're together. Lying here with him feels so right. "So, what's on the menu?"

"Two types of cupcakes and custom cookies with the Morgan logo on them."

"You know..." he says thoughtfully, continuing to trace gentle patterns on my skin. "I've been wondering why you haven't made a Ferrero Rocher cupcake yet, considering they're your favorite chocolates."

The question makes me hesitate. Honestly, after years of Brandon's dismissive attitude toward my baking, I never got too adventurous with my recipes. But I can't explain that to Penn without getting into everything with Brandon. So, I just shrug and say, "I guess I never really thought about it."

"Maybe you should for the benefit. A specialty cupcake like that would really make an impression."

"But some people are allergic to hazelnuts. And that many chocolates would be expensive."

He nods and goes quiet, clearly trying to devise a solution. Then, his eyes light up and he says, "You put your own spin on it, incorporating similar flavors without the actual candy. And you can make the other cupcake an allergy-free option." He smiles broadly, visibly excited on my behalf. I reach up and cup his jaw, moved that he takes interest in things that matter to me.

I take a moment to consider his suggestion. The flavor profile wouldn't be hard to recreate with simple ingredients. All I'd really need is chocolate, hazelnuts, and a *lot* of Nutella. "Okay," I say simply, returning his smile.

"I assume Willow is going to be there, right?"

"At the benefit?"

He nods.

"Yeah, she'll be there."

"Anyone else coming?"

I narrow my eyes at him. "What are you asking, Penn?"

He leans in and presses a chaste kiss to my lips. "I want to be there, Astrid. I want to support you in such a pivotal moment in your career."

God, this man. Brandon would never have wanted to do that. Even if I asked him to, it would have been unlikely. And here Penn is begging to be able to stand by my side.

"Are you sure you want to go all that way? I'll have help."

"I have a job that morning and some supplies being delivered to my rental, but I'll be there. You know I'll fucking be there for you, Astrid. I wouldn't miss this for anything."

"I know. I would love to have you there, Penn." I kiss him again, this time letting my lips linger.

"But I want to be there for you as more than your friend. I want people to know that you're mine, Astrid," he says, his voice low and his eyes penetrating mine when he lifts his head.

My heart starts to race. Our eyes are moving back and forth between each other's, and suddenly the topic I've been dreading is unavoidable.

"Penn..."

"I don't want to hide anymore, babe," he says, pushing my hair away from my face as he stares down at me. "I understood why we needed to for a bit, but life is too short to keep denying ourselves."

"But what about Brandon?" I whisper, tears forming in my eyes. It's the main reason why we've both been in denial and maybe if I know how he's feeling first, it will help me decide if I should come clean to him about our marriage.

I know that Willow said I should be honest with him, tell him about my marriage and what I want in a relationship moving forward. But the circumstances are also fragile, and if I get a fresh start with Penn, I think I want it to be just that—fresh. No reminders of the past and no chance of destroying a life-long friendship between two men when one is now gone.

Sighing, he pulls me closer to him, wrapping his arm around my ribs. "Brandon was my best friend, but he's gone, Astrid. We can't keep living our lives in the shadow of his ghost."

"I know. But…"

"I've felt guilty, babe. For the years I wanted you, for weeks after I gave in…" He inhales deeply. "Not just about Brandon, but about my dad too."

"Your dad?"

He nods. "My entire life he preached to me about helping others, honoring your friends and staying loyal to your brothers. He instilled in me that brotherhood extends beyond blood ties, so Brandon and I were as good as brothers in his eyes. Knowing what he would say to me, how he would react if he knew I gave in to my feelings for you?" A sigh leaves his lips. "It's kept me up at night."

"Penn…" My heart aches for him, for the guilt that he's carrying around too. But it makes me even more afraid that the remorse will never fully go away for either of us.

"But my mom said something last week that finally put things into perspective for me."

"What did she say?" I ask timidly, not sure if Katherine's words could make me feel better or worse about the situation.

"She said that my father was a closet romantic," he says with a small smile on his lips. "I never knew that, but she assured me that he could never be disappointed in me for going after what I want, especially if it's for love." He pulls down my bottom lip with his thumb. "And I can't keep living my life based on what my father and Brandon might have thought about it, Astrid. I refuse."

"Easier said than done though, right?"

Penn nods. "Yeah, but I think if we both adopted that mentality it would be easier." He reaches for my hand and intertwines our fingers. "I want to romanticize every little thing about my life with you, Astrid. I want to keep you forever, show you that you can have it all. That you fucking deserve that, and that I can be the someone that you need in your life."

"You are someone that I need," I tell him honestly. "I need you so much that I'm terrified of losing you, Penn." A tear streams down my cheek, but he brushes it away.

"You could never lose me."

"You don't know that. I never thought I'd bury my husband..."

Pain etches itself into his features. "I know, and I hate that you've had to experience that pain, but the only thing we can do is focus on now." He brings our clasped hands to his lips and presses a kiss to my skin. "When you went to the bathroom earlier, Donald said something to me that I don't think I'll ever forget."

"What did he say?" I ask through a sniffle.

"He said, if you were in a room full of every person you've ever met, who is the person you'd look for first?" My mouth falls open and my heart squeezes. With his eyes locked on mine, he continues. "The answer is you, Astrid. You're the person I would look for in a crowded room over and over. It'll only ever be you. You're *my* person."

My entire body is overwhelmed by his words, by the love pouring out of him. His strength, his determination, his protectiveness and vulnerability have me in a chokehold. But his next words stun me even more.

"I'm in love with you, Astrid." But before I can say anything, he presses a finger to my lips. "You don't have to say anything back, okay? In fact, I don't want you to. I just want you to know that *this*?" He waves his hand between our chests. "This is it for me. This is what I want. You and the kids. A life of the two of us chasing our dreams together, lots of naked times, and late-night talks. I want to build a future with you because you are the woman that was meant for me. Brandon may have been your first love, but I want to be your last." He rests his forehead on mine. "I just need you to let me."

And that's when I know that it's time to move on. It's time to start fresh. It's time to live my life knowing what it feels like to be loved and cherished and the most important person in someone else's life.

Penn doesn't need to know everything about my past. He doesn't need to think differently about his best friend. All he needs to know is that I want the same things he does.

"I want that too," I whisper as his head lifts from mine. "I want everything with you."

The smile that overtakes his face is pure joy, contentment, and relief. "Astrid..."

But I don't say anything else. Instead, I bring his lips to mine, seal our promise with a kiss, and vow to keep moving forward.

***

"I can't believe this weekend has come to an end," I mutter as I stare out the passenger window in Penn's truck, our hands laced together on the center seat.

The coast is to our left as we head back into town and back to reality.

"I know, but I kind of miss the kids," Penn says, making me smile.

"Sure, you say that now. Just wait until they start fighting."

He shakes his head. "Can't you just threaten them with Santa Claus? I mean, isn't that the cardinal rule of parenting during the month of December? Everything goes back to the promise of no presents if they misbehave?"

"For Lilly, yes. But not for Bentley. He already knows the truth about Santa."

Penn casts me a look. "When did that happen?"

"In the spring actually. He caught me filling Easter baskets. He told me he kind of figured that the Easter bunny wasn't real and promised to keep pretending for Lilly, though. So, while we were on the topic, I just gave him the truth about Santa, the tooth fairy, and the Leprechaun too."

Penn starts laughing. "I guess that's smart."

I shrug. "It made sense to me at the time. And it's not like I had anyone to consult with on the matter."

Penn squeezes my hand. "Well, in the future, I'd love to be the one you consult." He winks at me and my stomach does a little flip.

After Penn's confession Friday night, we spent a few more hours exhausting ourselves physically, so much so that I was able to sleep in for the first time in years. But this morning I made Penn promise to wake me so we could watch the sunrise together. We did, and then he woke me up even more with his head between my legs.

The man is insatiable and it just confirms everything I've been missing in my life—the passion, the support, the acceptance from a man for who I am and what I want. For the first time in a long time, I don't feel like just a single mom, a widow, a woman who's about to fall apart. I feel like a woman. I feel like me.

We spent all day yesterday cooking together, talking about future trips we could take with or without the kids, and fucking. My God, there was so much sex. I sincerely hope that no one comments on my just-fucked glow. Although, it's not just the idea that someone would know that we have sex that makes me anxious—it's the fact that soon, everyone will know that we're together and I'm still trying to mentally prepare myself for that.

"Are you sure you don't mind staying for dinner?" Penn asks as we get closer to his mom's house.

"Not at all. The kids are there and then I don't have to cook." My answer seems simple, but my stomach knows this is just one more step to making this all real.

"You have no idea how many times I wished you could be at these dinners with me, Astrid," he says.

"Really?"

"Yeah. You've always felt like part of my family, but now you get to be for real." He leans over at a red light and kisses my cheek. "You're mine and everyone gets to know that now."

I can feel myself blush. Every time Penn tells me I'm his, the feminism threatens to leave my body completely. Normally the idea of being referred to as someone else's property would make me scream. But with him? I want him to own me, to claim me, to take pride in being with me. And I know that he does.

When we enter Katherine's house, chaos descends upon us. "Mommy!" Lilly shouts, rushing toward me and slamming into my legs, wrapping her arms around me.

"Hey, sweet girl. How was your weekend?"

"It was so much fun! Grandma and Katherine took us to the park, for ice cream, to the movies, shopping, and now we're going to blow up a volcano before dinner!" She runs away from me just as quickly as she came.

Penn and I share a look. "And you were worried about her missing you?"

Laughing, I find Bentley on the couch, glued to his gaming system. "Hey, Bentley."

"Hey, Mom. Did you have a fun trip away?"

"Uh, yeah. I did."

"Cool." His eyes never leave the screen, so I guess he didn't notice that Penn and I arrived together. I didn't tell the kids Penn would be on the trip too because we decided to wait a little bit longer to tell them about us. Next week is going to be chaos with the benefit and I can't deal with heavy emotional conversations on top of preparing for one of the biggest nights of my career.

"Oh my God! You're back!" Willow exclaims, appearing from the hallway to greet us in the entryway. She immediately grabs me by the arm and pulls me back down the hallway, giving me no choice but to follow her. We duck inside a spare bedroom and then she shuts the door, smiling at me creepily. "So, how was it?"

I fight to hide my smile. "It was amazing. So romantic."

"And you're walking funny, so I assume Penn kept you on your back most of the time?"

My mouth drops open. "Willow!"

She shrugs. "I'm sorry, but if he didn't fuck you within an inch of your life, then the trip was a waste in my opinion."

Laughing, I shake my head at her. "You have issues."

She pushes off the door and sits down on the bed beside me. "No, I'm just happy for you." Taking my hand in hers, she squeezes it tightly. "Did you two talk?"

"We did."

"And?"

"He told me he's in love with me, Willow," I whisper, still trying to believe how much my life has changed in a matter of weeks.

"Well, duh," she replies sarcastically. "Did you talk about Brandon?"

"Yes, but..."

"But what?" She stares at me intently. "You didn't tell him everything, did you?"

"No, and I'm not going to." I take a deep breath and say, "I don't think it matters, Willow. He's gone and our marriage is over. I don't want Penn to resent him or feel like he has shoes to fill at all. I just want a fresh start."

She nods, but I can tell she's still not sold on the idea. "Well, if that's what you think is best."

"I do, but he wants to tell everyone right away, having a coming out of sorts, and I didn't necessarily agree or disagree."

"Why would you want to wait? I thought you were in this?"

"I am," I assure her. "But this week is going to be crazy leading up to the Morgan event. I think I'd feel less stressed if I could just focus on that."

She hums out loud. "Okay, I think that's reasonable. Does he know this?"

"Not entirely. I'm going to tell him when he drops us off."

She reaches out to hug me. "Well, I just want to say that I'm so happy for you. And him. And part of me feels like I had a hand in making this match, so I'm pleased with the results."

I laugh at her. "It was all you, huh?" I ask when we part.

"Totally. And call me selfish, but now this means that when you two get married, we'll be sisters-in-law."

I reach out and grab her hand this time. "I don't need a title to feel that close to you, Willow. Meeting you and earning your friendship has been life-changing for me too. I'm so grateful to call you my friend."

"Don't make me cry, Astrid," she says as her bottom lip trembles. "I hate crying."

"Yeah, I know. That's why it's so fun to do."

Chapter Seventeen

Penn

"So, how'd it go?" Dallas asks me as we stand side-by-side on the deck, surveying the backyard at my mom's house while Lilly goes crazy jumping up and down every time my mom makes the volcano explode.

"Good. I told her everything I needed to. We agreed to move forward and just be happy."

Dallas pats me on the shoulder. "Good for you. So, what happens now?"

"She has the benefit next weekend, so I know her focus is on that. But once that's behind her, I'm going to talk to her about moving in together. I want to marry her, Dallas. I want a fucking life with her that I never thought I'd ever have."

"See? Love makes you realize what's important really fucking quick."

I nod. "Yeah, I get it now. And I'm sorry I gave you shit about that."

He shoves me playfully. "It's okay. I knew you'd get there eventually."

"No thanks to your nagging."

"Hey, I think my nagging helped, actually." I arch a brow at him. "If I hadn't kept bugging you about it, do you think you would have actually made a move?"

I don't want to give him the complete satisfaction of knowing that his pep talk at the restaurant when Dick came in is what forced me to make a fucking decision. But I have to at least throw him a bone.

"It may have helped."

His smile is smug. "That's what I thought." He wraps an arm around my neck and pulls me into a chokehold against his chest. "Just don't forget that your older brother will always be smarter than you, all right?"

Struggling to break free, I push against him, finally managing to escape his grip. "Fuck you."

"Oh! Uncle Penn said a bad word!" Lilly calls from the grass below us.

"Uncle Penn, you'd better watch your mouth now," Dallas chides beside me. "Especially if you plan on taking on a fatherly role with those kids."

His comment should make me sweat, but all it does is renew the purpose I feel in my veins—the purpose I have to love those kids like my own and love Astrid the way I've been wanting to for years.

***

By the time we finished dinner and finally left, I could tell the kids were exhausted and Astrid was spent too. I drove them all back home since we came together in my truck.

My siblings now know that Astrid and I are together. My mother looked up at me with tears in her eyes several times, pleased that I'm making choices in my life that make me happy.

And the woman beside me has been smiling all night, even though I haven't been able to show her the affection that I wanted to because of the kids.

All in due time.

I help her and the kids take their things inside, but don't plan on staying. Tomorrow's a school day, the kids need to get to sleep, and I know Astrid needs to as well.

I'm standing by the front door, waiting for her to get Bentley and Lilly settled and ready for showers before I head out.

"You're still here?" she asks when she sees me standing with my hands tucked into my jean pockets.

"Yeah. I wasn't going to leave without saying goodbye properly." Reaching out for her, I pull her into my chest by her waist and plant a kiss on her lips. "It's going to be weird not sleeping next to you."

"Well, you can come by tomorrow and cuddle me for a while." She smiles up at me.

"What if I stopped by the bakery and gave you an orgasm in the middle of the day?" Her smile drops and suddenly the confidence I felt earlier dissipates. "What? You don't like that idea?"

"No, I do. I was just thinking..." Fuck. Astrid thinking is not necessarily a good thing. "I know you said you wanted to tell everyone, but could we please wait until after the benefit?"

"Okay..."

She brushes her hair back. "I just know that this week is going to be insane, and we haven't even talked to the kids yet." She drops her voice. "I don't want them to find out from someone else with the way people talk in this town, you know?"

Fuck. I didn't think about that.

But I want to kiss her, hold her, let it be known that this woman owns me.

You can, Penn. Hell, you've waited this long, what's a few more days?

"Makes sense," I say as convincingly as I can. Disappointment rests in my gut and I'm trying to hide it, but I don't think I'm doing a very good job.

"Are you sure you're okay with it?" She cups the side of my face, staring up at me.

"Yeah, babe. It's fine. But you best believe that at that benefit, my hands will be all over you so everyone in that room knows who you belong to."

Her lips spread in a smile that makes me feel slightly less irritated. "That I am totally on board with." She looks over her shoulder to make sure we're still alone, and then kisses me deeply before I open the front door and leave a piece of my heart behind.

Everything is falling into place. I'm happier than I ever thought I could be.

I should have known that something was bound to fuck it all up.

***

"Oh, look. It's Mr. Well-Rested," Parker greets me as I walk into Catch & Release on Thursday for lunch. He and Grady look over their shoulders as I find my stool and Dallas slides me my burger.

"Yeah, those bags under your eyes are a lot smaller. It must have been your mini-vacation." Grady grins as he pops a fry in his mouth.

I cup my hand around my ear. "Do I detect a hint of jealousy from both of you?" I nod my head. "Yup, I think I do."

Dallas scoffs behind the bar as he crosses his arms and his legs, leaning against the counter behind him. "I think I hear it too."

Parker rolls his eyes and Grady goes back to eating. "So, you had a good trip then?" Grady asks. Parker already knows my trip was worthwhile because he was at my mom's house Sunday night. But he's playing it off in front of Grady, which I appreciate. Astrid insisted that we would tell him together after the benefit. I figured he'd be there too, but he has other plans, I guess.

"I did. The mountains are gorgeous in the winter, but fucking cold."

"I can imagine. I'm just ready for the warmer weather," Grady adds. "I got a rather interesting phone call yesterday, by the way."

"From whom?" I ask before taking a bite of my burger.

"The new baseball coach at Carrington Cove High School." Grady wipes his mouth with a napkin. "Coach Larson retired and this new guy thought that by reaching out to me directly, he'd get a different answer than the one I gave Larson."

Parker shakes his head. "I don't get it. Why don't you want to help coach the team? You could help shape the next prodigy."

Grady grumbles, "I'm busy. I don't have time for that."

"Yes, you fucking do," Dallas counters. "I mean, hello? You're sitting in my restaurant on a Thursday taking an hour-long lunch. You'll go back to your garage, finish out a few jobs, and then what?"

"Running a business takes a ton of time," he fires back. "You of all people should know that, Dallas."

"I do, but I also know that we make time for things that are important to us, like having a life outside of work. You already have a guy that can run the place for you for a couple of hours, so why not take advantage of it?"

"Because I don't want to fucking coach, all right?" he snaps, his voice booming through the empty restaurant.

Parker and I share a look, but Dallas continues to push. "Because it reminds you of what you lost?"

Grady stands from his stool and tosses his napkin on his plate, his meal only half-eaten. "I gotta go. I forgot I told Astrid I'd stop by to see her today since she was gone this weekend." He turns to walk away, but only moves three steps before he freezes. Slowly, he turns back around and his eyes drill into mine.

Oh, fuck. Here we go.

"Uh, Dallas? Didn't you want to show me that thing about the stuff?" Parker asks as Grady and I remain in a standoff.

"Sure. Yeah, we can do that." Dallas heads to the back of the restaurant, Parker scurrying after him. And then it's just me and Grady, the brother of the woman I'm in love with.

"Is there something you need to tell me?" he asks, walking back over to the bar where I'm still seated.

"Is there something you want to ask?"

He rubs his jaw, dragging his nails through the thick scruff he's been growing lately. "Why were you and my sister away on the exact same weekend?"

"Because we were together, Grady," I say, not shying away from the truth. Grady doesn't deserve that and neither does Astrid. I'm not going to act like us being together is wrong. I've done that enough in my head, but that's the last fucking thing that's going to come out of my mouth.

He glares at me harder. "*Together?*"

I stand now so we can see eye to eye, even though I have a few inches on him. I have a few inches on everybody. "Yes. Together. I'm in love with her and I took her away to tell her that."

Grady's face softens almost instantly. "Holy shit."

"I'm not going to lie to you. She and I have been torn up about it, but I'm not going to stop living my life because of what other people might think. I've been in love with her for a while."

"So when did things change?"

"About a month ago."

He thinks for a minute and sighs. "Well, I know what I think about it doesn't really matter because you're grown-ass adults, but if there's anyone I would pick for her, it would be you." He reaches out his hand to me, and just like that, everything is good again. That's how men handle our issues—cut and dry. "But don't fucking take her for granted, Penn," he says, our hands still clasped. "She doesn't need to deal with that again."

"Again?" I ask, wondering what he's referring to.

"Yeah. I mean how Brandon never appreciated her. Their marriage was long over, but I'm sure you already know that," he says and my expression must reveal my shock because just as quickly, he continues, "Wait...you *didn't* know that?"

My pulse starts hammering in my ears, my mind starts to race, and within seconds so many things start spiraling in my mind like a montage of memories.

"Uh, no. What do you mean?"

I think back to the conversations that Brandon and I had, how much he boasted about his life, about his marriage and kids, that he felt like he had it all.

Was it all a bunch of bullshit?

No. It can't be. Astrid would have told me.

"Fuck." Grady releases my hand and blows out a breath. "Dude, she doesn't even know that I know, okay? My mom told me. She was the only one that knew the truth. They were going to get a divorce when he returned from his last deployment, but then..."

"Shit," I mutter turning away from him as I take in this information. She's been keeping this secret all this time? No one knew they were having issues? I mean, hell—I was his best friend and he sure as shit didn't say anything to me. Everything he said was always the complete opposite.

Jesus. Was he lying to me? Or was he really that clueless?

Is this why she's been so hesitant to tell people? Because everyone thought they were so in love, the perfect little family and she's the grieving widow who can't possibly move on?

My head spins but Grady pulls me out of it. "Look, I thought you would have known. Don't be mad at her."

"I'm not mad at her. I just..." I tilt my head at him. "I just...I need to fucking talk to her."

"Yeah, and I know that when you do, it's going to be my neck on the chopping block, so why don't you let me talk to her first?"

I nod. "Yeah, probably a good idea." Especially because I don't even know how to form words right now.

"And Brandon never said anything to you either?" he asks.

"Never, Grady. In fact, he told me the opposite." I grab my Coke and drain the rest of the glass.

Grady scoffs. "Sounds about right. He always was about keeping up appearances."

Jesus. Did I even know the man I considered my best friend? "I need to get back to work."

"Yeah, okay. I'll text you when I've talked to her." Grady heads for the exit and then Dallas and Parker peek their heads out from the swinging kitchen door.

"Well, I don't see a black eye, Dallas. That's a good sign," Parker says as he steps through and Dallas shoves him forward.

"Why would there be, dumbass?" He glares at our younger brother and then turns to me. "Everything okay?"

"Yes and no. Uh, Grady doesn't have a problem with us being together, but I just found out that Astrid's been keeping a pretty big secret from me," I say, grinding my teeth together harder now.

"Shit," Dallas mumbles. "Is it that bad?"

"It's pretty big."

"Relationship ending?" Parker asks. "Because you know we'll take your side over Astrid's."

The desire to punch my little brother comes out way too strong. "Just because you got fucked over by a woman, doesn't mean all women are the enemy. And for the record, Sasha was a bitch. There, I said it."

He stares at me and then nods. "I agree. Thank you. I'm just saying..."

"We'll be fine. I've got to go," I say, heading for the door, not sure if I believe myself or not. But until Grady talks to Astrid, there's only one thing I can do—distract myself by working on my rental, wishing I had something to tear apart instead of putting the finishing touches on little things.

But those little things matter, just as much as the big stuff. The past ten minutes have made that abundantly clear.

Chapter Eighteen

Astrid

"Those aren't cool enough yet for frosting," I tell Tanya before she pipes the hazelnut frosting on top of the vanilla cupcakes.

"Sorry."

"It's okay. Move on to the strawberry cheesecake ones. They need the dusting of graham crackers on top."

I watch her walk away from me and then I move back to the mixer, checking on the next batch of cream cheese frosting.

I haven't left my bakery in two days, except to eat and sleep. My mom has been taking care of my kids, my brother took Lilly to her dance class last night, my employees are going to be earning insurmountable overtime after this week, which I'll hopefully be able to afford, and I haven't seen Penn since he came over Monday night.

But this is temporary, I keep reminding myself. I'm almost done. The stress could have been worse and I'm grateful that, for the most part, everything has been running smoothly.

"Hey, sis." I twist around to find my brother standing beside me, his hands shoved into the pockets of his jeans.

"Well, hello. Do I know you? Are you from the outside world where the other people are?"

He laughs. "I think you're starting to go a little stir crazy."

"What gave you that idea?" I fire back, trying to deflect with humor so I don't cry or pass out. Adrenaline is keeping me running right now. That and caffeine.

"It smells amazing in here." He peers into the giant mixing bowl that's spinning around. "Cream cheese frosting?"

"Yup."

"You know that's my favorite."

I eye him suspiciously, wondering why he looks so nervous. My brother doesn't hide his confidence or masculinity. Blame it on years of walking onto a baseball field in front of thousands of fans, feigning confidence even if he didn't feel it, but right now? He looks borderline afraid. "What's going on?"

"What do you mean?"

"I mean you look like Bentley right now about to tell me that he broke something or lost something." I arch a brow at him. "What did you do?"

"Why do you automatically assume that I did something?" He pretends to be offended, but I'm a mom. I know bullshit when I see it.

"Grady..."

"Maybe we could talk in your office?"

I shut the mixer off, instruct Vanessa on what to do next, and then lead my brother back to my office so I can berate him in private. Once I shut the door behind us, he starts to pace the small room.

"What is going on, Grady? Why are you so worked up?"

"Well, first, I know about you two." Transforming before my eyes, he stands up straight and crosses his arms over his chest. "Why didn't you tell me?"

"We were going to tell you. We're going to tell everyone after this weekend, but…"

He reaches out to me and grabs my hand. "You deserve to be fucking happy, Astrid."

Tears well in my eyes. "I know."

"Does he make you happy?"

I nod as a tear slips free. "He does. He's so good to me, Grady."

"I know he is. He says he's in love with you…"

I smile, remembering his confession that stole my breath. "He told me on our trip."

"And do you feel that way about him?"

"I do, but I haven't told him as much."

"Why not?"

"Because I'm scared to let someone in all the way again."

My brother pulls me into his chest. "Penn is not Brandon, Astrid."

"I know," I sniffle against his chest. "He isn't and that's why I'm so scared, because I don't ever want to feel like that again or lose someone again." I lean up and wipe under my eyes. "Losing Brandon was hard. It was painful. But losing Penn? I don't think I'd survive it."

"Love always comes with risks and there are no guarantees. But you can't let fear keep you from living your life."

"Easier said than done."

He grimaces, and I'm reminded that there's another reason he's here. "Okay, so you can't be mad at me because I didn't know that Penn didn't know…"

"Jesus, what did you do, Grady?" I wave my hand toward the door. "In case you haven't realized, I'm kind of busy at the moment and don't need more stress."

"I kind of told Penn about you and Brandon."

The urge to throw up overwhelms me. "No. You didn't!"

"I thought you would have told him by now, Astrid."

He reaches out for me, but I swat his hand away. "What did you say exactly?"

"I told him that he'd better not hurt you because you've already been through enough with Brandon and deserve better, or something like that."

"That's it?"

He winces. "I may have mentioned that you two were on the verge of a divorce when he died."

I place my hand over my heart and move to my desk chair, desperately fighting to get control of my breathing. "Oh my God! I could kill you right now!" I glare up at him, wondering how the hell everything went so wrong so quickly.

He holds both hands above his head. "I'm sorry! I didn't know that he didn't know."

Breathing in through my nose and out through my mouth, I try to ward off the panic attack that I feel coming on. I haven't had one since Brandon died, but this just might be the catalyst. "What did Penn say?"

"He honestly didn't say much. I told him that I would talk to you first. Now you two need to talk."

I slap a hand to my forehead. "I didn't want him to know, Grady. I didn't want him to think of his best friend differently."

"I'm sorry, but I also think he deserves to know. He deserves to know that you were hurt in your last relationship, and you want more for yourself."

"Penn *is* more, Grady. He's so much more than I ever thought I could have and you might have just ruined it."

He shakes his head. "No way. You should have heard the way he talked about you, Astrid. He's fucking gone for you. I've never felt that way about a woman."

"You deserve that too, you know."

He rolls his eyes. "I don't think the wife and kids thing is in the cards for me, sis. The peak of my life has already happened."

"Don't say that, Grady. You're only thirty-five."

"Then why most days do I feel ancient?"

I stand from my chair and rest my hand on his chest. "Because most days you act like a grumpy old man."

We share a laugh and then he groans. "I'm sorry, Astrid. Truly."

"It's okay. It's not like you meant to share my secret, but now I'm sure Penn is going to be pissed at me for keeping this from him."

"You two will work it out. Your friendship is so solid, something like this won't change that."

"That's what makes this scary though. He's been my friend for so long that it feels like there's more pressure on us now. And there's definitely more at risk now that we've crossed that line."

Grady wrinkles his nose. "I don't need you to remind me that the two of you have seen each other naked, okay?"

I shove at his chest playfully. "Well, spill my secrets again and I'm going to scar you for life."

He points a finger at me. "That's fair. Threat made and point taken. I shall keep my lips sealed for the rest of time."

***

I wish I could say things got better after Grady left, but I'd be lying. As soon as I returned to the floor, chaos erupted. One of the mixers stopped working, which halted our frosting production. It was too late to call a repair service, so we finished cooking the cookies and cupcakes we could and I sent everyone home. I stayed and finished some paperwork, convincing myself that I wouldn't have time for it tomorrow. But let's be honest, I was avoiding going home—because going back to reality meant having to face Penn.

By the time I get home, my mother has fallen asleep on the couch.

She startles as I shut the front door. "Sorry," I say quietly as she gets her bearings.

She glances back at the clock. "You're late tonight."

"Well, tonight was a dumpster fire of epic proportions."

She stands from the couch, folding the blanket she was using before walking up to me. "Grady called me and told me that he messed up and told Penn about Brandon."

"Yeah." My eyelids feel heavy, I can feel my body wanting to give out, but a light knock on the door tells me my night isn't over yet. "Shit."

"Let me guess who that is..." Mom moves toward the door, and sure enough, on the other side is the man I know has plenty to say to me tonight. "Hi, Penn."

"Hey, Melissa." Penn nods at her and then his eyes meet mine. "Hey."

"Hi."

My mother reaches for her purse and swings it over her shoulder. "I'll leave you two alone. See you in the morning, sweetie."

"Thanks, Mom." She shuts the door behind her, leaving the two of us in the living room with nothing but silence and regrets.

I know he wants to talk and I know that he deserves my honesty, but I'm so spent that my body drops to the couch, I close my eyes, and heave out a sigh. "It's been a day, Penn."

"Yeah, you're telling me." I hear his voice grow closer to me and then the couch dips.

"I know you have questions, but I can't do this with you right now."

"Seems to be a theme with you," he says, spite in his tone.

I open my eyes, turn my head to the side to see him, and the hurt reflected back at me almost makes me want to cry again. But I have no more tears left to give. "What's that supposed to mean?"

"If not now, then when, Astrid? When is it ever going to be the right time?"

I drop my head back on the couch, the weight of the day bearing down on me. "Penn, I spent all day prepping for one of the most important events of my career, one of my mixer broke right in the middle of that prep, then my brother came in telling me he has a big fat mouth, and now you're here asking me for answers I just don't have it in me to give tonight."

"I don't know. I feel like you're keeping one foot out of whatever it is we're doing here and there's always an excuse."

"Can you blame me? Do you not understand how crazy my life is and that this added stress isn't helping?"

"But *I* could help you if you'd just let me in. If you'd let me take some of that stress off your shoulders. But you're keeping me at a distance and I'm trying to fucking understand why." I shake my head. "There are things I can't tell you."

"That's bullshit, and you know it, Astrid. If we are going to have any shot at a life together, you should be able to tell me anything, even if I might not like it. And you're going to start right now. Tell me…what was really going on with Brandon before he died?"

"You don't want to know that, Penn," I whisper as the tears start to form. I thought I had none left, but I guess I was wrong.

He takes my hand and squeezes it gently. "I want to know everything when it comes to you. I thought that's what last weekend was about, but apparently you were holding back on me. I want to understand why."

He goes blurry as the tears threaten to spill over. "I thought it'd be better if I just left all that in the past. And I didn't want you to think differently of Brandon."

He cups my face, gently brushing away a tear with his thumb. "*You are my priority.*"

I take a deep breath and send up a silent prayer that Brandon will forgive me for what I'm about to reveal, but knowing that, ultimately, it's the right thing to do.

"Brandon wasn't a good husband, Penn. You may not have seen it and I have no idea if he ever talked to you about our marriage, but I asked him for a divorce before he left on his last deployment. He wanted me to wait until he got back, hoping I'd change my mind, but I was done." I stare across the room now, giving myself permission to tell him everything. "He belittled my passion for baking, he was never present when he was home, and I never felt like I had a partner. I can't imagine what his job was like, but all I wanted when he was here was a husband, a friend, someone I could count on and he wasn't that man for me." Turning back to Penn, I see the anguish in his eyes. "I don't want you to feel guilty because you think you're disrespecting his memory or breaking some code—because our relationship was over long before he died. I just didn't find the courage to leave him until it was too late." I barely get the last word out before the tears begin to fall in earnest.

"Astrid..." He pulls me into his lap, leaning back into the cushions as I sob.

"I know he was your best friend, and I'm sorry."

"You have nothing to apologize for. I just wish you would have fucking told me this sooner."

"I didn't want to keep living in the past. What you and I have is different and I just wanted to move on."

He kisses the top of my head. "I get that now."

"I've spent so much time feeling guilty, Penn—for wanting you, for wanting to leave him, for my children losing their father, and for feeling relief that at least I get to pursue my dreams when he told me I never would. People don't talk about feeling even a sliver of relief after their spouse dies. They don't discuss how life can feel lighter knowing you don't have to deal with the whiplash of emotions your relationship held. For years, I've mourned a man I didn't even want in my life anymore, Penn. It's been horrible."

He grips me tighter and I can hear his teeth grinding. "That's fucked up, Astrid. If I would have known, I would have said or done something."

"I didn't want to ruin your memories of the boy you grew up with, the man you supported and loved. But he was a different person for me."

"I'm so sorry," he whispers in my ear before resting his lips on my temple. "I'm so fucking sorry. You didn't deserve that."

Emotion overtakes me and I stay silent for a while, just letting Penn hold me while I think about how Brandon never would have consoled me while I was this emotional. He didn't want to be bothered by me trying to communicate with him. He just didn't understand why I couldn't be happy with the life we had.

Because I was always meant to have more.

And now I do. With Penn.

I sit up and stare into Penn's eyes. "Please forgive me for not telling you."

He shakes his head, closing his eyes. "There's nothing to forgive, Astrid. I spent all afternoon trying to see it from your perspective so I wouldn't be pissed, and I get it now. I needed to hear this from you. It makes a lot of things make more sense."

"I still should have told you."

His eyes pop open again. "Yes, you should have."

"I promise that I won't ever keep anything from you again."

"I appreciate that."

Sighing, I rest my head on his chest and close my eyes. The exhaustion and stress from the day hits me all at once as the warmth of Penn's body relaxes me. I don't know how fast I fall asleep, but when I wake up, I'm covered by a blanket on the couch and Penn is gone.

Chapter Nineteen

Penn

"I can't believe you're leaving me," Mrs. Hansen says for the hundredth time since I gave her my two weeks' notice last week. After we talked, we agreed today would be my last shift as long as I helped her hire someone to replace me.

"You act like you won't still see me."

"It's hard to find good help, Penn, to find people you can rely on."

"I know, but it's time for me to go out on my own."

She huffs. "Yeah, I knew this day would come sooner or later. You sure I can't persuade you to stay through the holidays?"

The fact that I still have two more hours left is already making me itchy. "I'm sorry. I have plans and things I need to take care of."

"You're still going to help me sit in on interviews for your replacement, right?"

I stare at the pile of applications. "You act like you don't know every person in that stack, Mrs. Hansen."

"Not the young ones, and I think that's what I need. Some teenager that has the energy to do what you did for us."

How I've managed to keep up everything I do for two jobs and my own obligations is beyond me because my age is starting to catch up to me now, especially when I get shitty sleep because my mind won't turn off.

"Yes, Elizabeth. That is what we agreed to."

She claps her hands together once. "Just wanted to make sure."

Once she walks away, I go back to restocking the shelves before moving to the lumber yard out back to unload the delivery we got this morning. As of two hours from now, I'll only be here to purchase the lumber, never to stack it again. And I can't fucking wait.

But my life took a turn yesterday I wasn't expecting, and now the confidence I felt about Astrid and me has been shaken.

She and Brandon were going to get a divorce.

I still can't fucking believe it, even though last night I spent hours going over memories, trying to pick up on clues as I held Astrid while she slept on me on her couch. She cried herself to sleep in my arms and when she finally settled, I didn't have the heart to move her. Honestly, I didn't want to. I can't imagine the weight she felt lifted by finally telling me the truth, the truth I wish she would have had enough confidence in me to confide in me the first place.

Astrid must have been an actress in another life because she was phenomenal at putting on the face of a happily married woman. And Brandon? Well, he was dedicated to his country, to his title as a Marine, and that part of his identity always took precedence, I guess.

She sacrificed for him. She gave him two beautiful kids. And when she wanted something for herself, he didn't support it. He *acted* like everything was perfect, though.

If he were here right now, I'd probably punch him in the face.

Which is exactly what Astrid was trying to avoid by not telling me the truth. She didn't want my memory of him ruined because of the choices he made when he was alive.

Now the question is, what do I do with this information? Because no matter how busy I try to make myself, my mind keeps ruminating over the revelation on repeat.

"Didn't you hear? The widow moved on with his best friend." Chatter in one of the aisles catches my attention. I take a few steps from behind the counter to try to hear the conversation better.

"No she didn't!"

"Well, if I had the chance to be with a man who looked like that, I'd probably take it too," one of the women says as she and her friend huddle close in front of the painting supplies.

My pulse starts to pick up because if I didn't know any better, I'd say that the topic of their conversation is Astrid and me. But I might just be assuming.

"Still. She was married to the man, and to pursue his best friend?" Woman number one shakes her head. "That's just scandalous."

"I always wondered about them, though. The two of them were always together, and word on the street is they were spotted kissing at the grand reopening of her bakery. I honestly wonder if they've been fooling around for years."

Fury races through me now that I'm certain Astrid and I are their source of entertainment. Clearing my throat, I head down the aisle toward them. "Hello, ladies. Can I help you with anything?"

Woman number two drops the paint sample cards she was holding as woman number one's eyes go wide, watching me close in on them. "Oh, uh. No. We're fine."

"Are you sure? I can answer *any* questions you may have. You know, I have a lot of knowledge about...paint." I gesture toward the color selections in front of them, even though I'm sure all three of us know I'm not here to talk about paint.

"No, no. We're good." Woman number one grabs her friend by the hand and they head toward the door. "Have a good day, Penn."

"Yeah, you two," I mutter as they leave, and then wonder how the hell they knew about the kiss at the bakery and who else might be talking about it. If those two women had the gall to come into the hardware store and gossip about me while I'm within earshot, that means word around town has already spread, fueling one of Astrid's biggest concerns about our relationship

—the fear that the kids could find out before we've had a chance to talk to them.

I pull out my phone, looking at her text from this morning for the tenth time.

> **Astrid:** Hey. Sorry I fell asleep on you last night. I hope you're not mad at me. I'm so sorry, Penn. I don't want this to ruin us. Please come by tonight so we can talk more...

I hadn't texted her back yet because my mind is a fucking mess. But now, it seems there are other messes brewing so I contemplate whether I should text her to warn her about the gossip or wait until we have a chance to talk. The last thing that Astrid needs is more stress added to her plate. If I can find the source of the rumors before she hears about them, maybe I can put a stop to them.

My phone dings with a text before I can figure out my next move.

> **Astrid:** Oh my God, Penn. Some customers came into the bakery just now asking about us! Apparently, someone's spreading rumors.

Fuck. Gossip spreads faster than wildfire, I guess.

> **Me:** *I know. I just heard two women talking about it in the hardware store.*

> **Astrid:** *And I've had two calls this morning from people cancelling orders saying they didn't want to support a scandal.*

Fuck. This escalated rather quickly.

I type out another response.

> **Me:** *It sounds like someone saw us kissing at the reopening.*

The dots jump on the screen as I wait for her reply.

> **Astrid:** *That son of a bitch!*

Fury races through me.

> **Me:** *Who, baby?*

> **Astrid:** *Dick! He saw us, Penn. I saw him looking through the kitchen door, and he said some stuff to me afterward…*

My teeth grind together. That fucking twat-waffle. I knew he was a fucking slimeball. He never had a chance with Astrid in the first place, but apparently his ego can't stand the fact that she chose me instead of him.

> **Me:** *I'll take care of it.*

> **Astrid:** *What are you going to do?*

But I don't have time to text her back before Elizabeth reminds me of the lumber delivery that needs to be unloaded.

My phone dings a few more times while I'm working, but by the time I've seen Astrid's messages pleading with me to leave it alone, my mind is already made up.

That Dick is going to get a piece of my mind once and for all. And he'd better pray he still has use of his dick by the time I'm through with him.

***

"You know, you should pay more attention to where you're walking."

Dick shrieks as his phone jumps from his hands, landing on the ground with a thud.

Good. I hope his screen is fucking cracked. *Asshole deserves it.*

"What the hell are you doing here, Penn?" His eyes dart around the empty parking lot, quickly realizing that we're all alone.

"You honestly don't know?" I ask, pushing off the car, uncrossing my arms, and walking up to him, watching his head crane back on his neck as he stares up at me.

His throat bobs as he swallows hard. "No."

"I didn't take you for an idiot, Dick."

I watch his eyes narrow and then his jaw clench. "Don't call me that."

"I'll call you what I see fit, asshole."

"There are cameras everywhere, Penn." He smirks. "You'd be a fool to try something you might regret."

My control snaps as I grip him by the collar of his shirt and press him up against his car, his eyes full of fear as I hover over him. "I don't give a shit who sees what I'm about to do to you." He grimaces as I slam him into the car again. "Lucky for you, I don't have time to get locked up today. I'll just tell you this one time, Dick. Keep Astrid's name out of your fucking mouth for the rest of your existence."

He turns his head away from me. "I don't know what you're talking about."

I slam him into the car again. "Don't play dumb, Dick. You know exactly what I mean. This is a small town and gossip spreads like herpes—once it starts, it just keeps burning and everyone ends up catching it."

"Sounds like you have some experience with herpes. Does Astrid know that?"

This time I rear back and punch him in the face. "I said don't fucking talk about her!"

He stumbles backward and, when he lifts his head again, blood is streaming from his nose. "I swear, I don't know what she sees in you," he mutters.

"And that's just it. You don't have to understand it. But you do have to accept that *I'm* the one she chose. And if you can't, and you keep running your mouth about us, this won't be the last time my fist meets your face." He glares at me, hunched over. "Have I made myself clear?"

He nods. "Crystal."

"Good. And in case you're an even bigger idiot than I thought, stay the fuck out of the bakery too. I don't give a shit what you say about me, but when you start fucking with Astrid's livelihood, that's where I draw the line. Astrid doesn't need your money and I don't need the temptation to punch you again."

I turn on my heel and walk back to my truck, vibrating with anger and wishing I could have done more damage to his face than I did. I didn't plan on hitting him, but the second he started running his mouth about Astrid, I gave in to the instinct.

Still, there's no telling if he'll take my warning seriously, and confronting him doesn't stop the gossip from flowing. It also doesn't stop the churning feeling in my stomach that's come on in the last twenty-four hours, so I head to the one place and one person that can help me come to grips with my new reality better than anyone.

***

"Mom?" I shut the front door behind me and call out for her, not sure where she'd be at this hour. It's late on Friday night and I have an early morning, but if there's one person who can help me clear the fog from my brain, it's her.

"In the kitchen!" she calls out to me. I find her standing at the stove, pouring hot water into a cup of tea. "Penn, what are you doing here? Shouldn't you have fun plans with Astrid?" she teases before turning to me and taking in my face. And as soon as she reads my expression, her motherly instinct kicks in. "What's wrong, Penn?"

I reach up and pull on my hair. "There's just a lot on my mind, Mom."

She motions for me to sit at the counter on one of the stools. "Do you want some tea?"

My mother drinks tea every night. She and my father used to drink it together. And even though I'm more of a coffee guy, I oblige her and hope she appreciates the company. "Sure."

Once our cups are full and steaming, she motions for me to join her on the couch. She blows on her mug, takes a sip, and then says, "Talk to me, son."

"That's why I'm here."

She grins at me softly. "I have to say that as a mother, I'm honored I'm the person you all go to for things like this."

"That's because you always give the best advice."

She nods. "Most of the time, but I'm human too, Penn. Lord knows I've made my share of mistakes and needed other people to knock some sense into me a time or two."

"Well, I didn't make a mistake this time, Mom. At least not yet." I stare down into my mug, knowing damn well it's too fucking hot to drink yet. Hitting Dick wasn't a mistake, but moving past this rock in my gut could be one if I can't wrap my head around everything I know now about my best friend and his marriage.

"Talk to me, Penn."

I glance over at her and let out a long breath. "Astrid and Brandon were going to get a divorce before he died."

She swallows hard, pausing for a moment before saying, "I know."

Her admission has me straightening in my seat. "What?"

Nodding, she inhales deeply. "Yes. He told your father, and naturally, your father told me after Brandon died."

Holy shit. All this time Astrid thought that no one else knew but her mom and brother. But it looks like Brandon told my dad. He confided in my father, but not in me.

"Why would he tell Dad and not me?"

"You can imagine why, Penn," she says tilting her head at me.

"I was his best friend…"

"Exactly. Don't you think he was carrying around shame about his marriage being in trouble and didn't want you to look at him that way? Like a man who couldn't keep his relationship together?"

"Fuck." I pinch the bridge of my nose as anger burns up my chest. "Do you know how guilty I've felt for the past four years?"

"Yes, but like I already told you, you shouldn't. What happened has happened, and there's no changing that. And it wasn't my place to bring that up."

"Astrid wasn't ever going to tell me, Mom. I found out from Grady, who found out from their mom."

"Is that why you're torn up in knots? Because you feel like she betrayed you?"

Staring down into my tea again, I shake my head. "No. I'm not angry with her. I actually felt remorse when she broke apart in my arms last night. She carried that secret for years but didn't want it to affect our relationship so she just kept it to herself."

"That's what she felt was best."

"But it feels like she couldn't trust me with the truth about her past, and now I find out that my best friend didn't trust me either." I look up at her again. "He always told me things were good between them, perfect even."

"A lot of people lie to cover up the truth that they don't want to face."

"But he should have trusted *me* with the truth, right?"

Her brows draw together. "I don't think it was about trust, Penn. I think it was more about shame and disappointment in themselves, especially because Brandon was a Marine. Being a military spouse comes with certain expectations, sacrifices that you sign up to make when you take your vows, and to want out of that, there's a stigma attached to it." She reaches out for my hand. "You have to remember that when people are going through something, it's usually more about them than it is about you. They were navigating a life-altering change and did what they felt was best. Your friendship with both of them stood to be changed if you took sides. Did you ever think about that?"

"Fuck. No. But I fucking feel like my best friend wasn't the person I thought he was."

"That's understandable, but not everyone shows us every side of them, Penn. I wouldn't take this personally, honey. And if Astrid finally confided in you, I would take that as a compliment—that she felt safe enough to let you see the darkest parts of her, the parts that she didn't want to share with anyone."

"Yeah, only because Grady forced her hand."

She takes my hand in hers. "Don't you think that's a good sign too? That Grady assumed she would have disclosed that detail of her life with you? Doesn't that speak to the level of friendship and comfort you two share?"

"Yeah, I guess."

"You have to remember, Penn. What we find easy as friends becomes a burden as lovers. It's difficult to cross that line and not have it affect your relationship." She squeezes my hand and then goes back to holding her mug with two hands. "Let me ask you this. Did she tell you what was wrong in their marriage? Why she felt like she wanted out?"

"Yes," I say through clenched teeth, still irritated that a man I respected so much couldn't be bothered to invest energy into his marriage and the woman he chose to build a life with.

"And how did that make you feel?"

"Like I want to prove to her that I can be the man that she needs."

Her lips spread into a slow smile. "Then you've learned everything you needed to in this situation. The only thing to do now is move forward and love her the way she deserves."

***

The wind whips around me, but I keep trekking along in the grass, getting closer to the grave that I need to confront.

My mother may have said that the only thing I needed to do now is move forward, but in order for me to do that fully, there are a few things I need to get off my chest.

I don't know if I believe in life after death, spiritual connection and the ability to send messages beyond the grave. But tonight, before I prove to the woman that I love that she's the brightest star in my sky, I need to make my peace with the man who dulled her shine.

When the headstone comes into view, emotion builds in my throat. I've only been out here one other time, just a few months after he passed. I was pissed at him for leaving his wife and kids alone, for not coming home to all of us—and yet proud that he made the ultimate sacrifice for his country, something I never signed up to do because I didn't want to be faced with that harsh reality someday.

No matter how I feel about his treatment of Astrid, I will always hold the utmost respect for the soldier that he was, the friend that stood by me when times were tough, the man who asked me to be the godfather to his children, and the boy who offered his friendship when I was just a lonely kid on the playground.

"Hey, man." I stand above the headstone, staring down at his name and the dates he entered and left this life. "It's been a crazy month or so, and if you've been watching over us, you probably know why I'm here." My throat grows tighter as I talk, and the wind picks up. The December air is frigid and part of me wishes I wouldn't have left my big coat in my truck. This suit jacket just isn't thick enough to fight off the cold.

Pulling my jacket tighter around my body, I continue. "I honestly don't know what to say, don't know if you're even listening, don't know if this shit even works—talking to those that aren't here anymore. But for me to move forward, I need you to know that I never planned this. Hell, when Astrid and the kids lost you, I felt grief for myself *and* for them. I thought my friend had lost the love of her life, and for a moment in time, you were that person for her. But now?" I shake my head. "Now *I* want the chance to be that person for her."

The frustration that's been resting in my chest starts to come out. "All this time, all of this guilt I've been carrying around, and for what? You two were done. She was ready to move on and when I finally felt like we could, the truth slammed into me out of nowhere." I sigh and wipe under my nose that is growing colder with each minute. "I can't ever know what you may think of this. And hell, if you were still alive, I don't know if I would have felt this way about her or not. But this is where we're at now—desperate for one another and needing each other for the support it takes to keep living while chasing our dreams. And even though I know you'll always be her first, the man who gave her children, I want to be her last, her fucking everything—the man she needs and deserves for this next phase of her life." I pound my fist on my chest as my eyes go blurry from the building tears.

I stare off in the distance, letting the breeze whip around me again for a moment. "I'm sorry you can't be here, that you don't get a second chance, man. The kids deserve to have their dad, but Astrid is worthy of happiness too. And I hope you can accept that, accept that living after losing someone is one of the bravest things you can do. It takes courage and the permission to be selfish because the only person that can keep living for you is yourself."

I swipe under my eye as one tear falls. "I'm going to her event tonight, the one she's catering by herself, the one where she gets to showcase her talent and I'm going to support her, cheer for her, and kiss her in front of everyone because I want her to know how proud I am of her. I only hope you can be proud of her now, too." I nod and then take a step back. "Until we meet again, brother." I give him a salute and then turn on my heels as I blink away the tears that have yet to fall. And just before I get to my truck, something flies through the air and hits me in the eye.

"What the?" I take the thin piece of paper off my face and stare down at it as goosebumps break out on my arms. "Holy shit."

The tag from a Hershey's kiss sits right in my palm, the thin white strip with blue letters clear as day and unmistakable. I look over my shoulder, back at the graveyard behind me and swallow—unsure if this was just a coincidence or if this was the sign I needed—the reassurance that the past cannot be undone, but the future still remains bright.

And there's only one woman that I want in mine.

***

Lights flash beside me on the other side of the highway, blinding me slightly as I keep speeding toward Raleigh. I'm already behind schedule because of traffic. I don't know what the holdup was, but the irritation in my body multiplied the later the time on my app kept telling me that I was going to arrive.

I let Astrid know last night that I had some matters to take care of so I couldn't swing by her house, but also I needed some time to get my head on straight. And now that I have, I can't wait to tell her everything that she needs to hear, and I sure as fuck wasn't going to do that in a damn text message.

Brake lights flash in front of me, warning me that traffic is about to slow down again.

"Mother fucker! Are you kidding me?" I pound my palm into my steering wheel, running my hand through my hair again. This can't be happening. It's one of the most important nights of Astrid's life and I'm going to fucking miss it.

Please God, don't let me miss this.

If I don't make it, she'll never forget it. I have to be there, to support her, to be proud of her, to encourage her in everything that she's already accomplished and still has yet to.

A car slides in front of me. I slam on the brakes.

And when I hear the screech of tires and crunch of metal, I brace for the impact that I know is coming.

Chapter Twenty

Astrid

"Oh my God, this is a lot of people," I whisper to Willow as she helps me put the finishing touches on the display table for my cupcakes and cookies. The last twenty-four hours have been a blur, but what really has me on edge is the fact that I haven't spoken to Penn all day and I have no idea if he's still going to be here tonight like he said he would.

"I assure you, there are just a few under five hundred. You should have more than enough baked goods."

"Well, I made extra just in case. It wasn't easy with one mixer, but we managed."

The technician couldn't fix my mixer quickly, so I called everyone that I knew to bring in their hand mixers for me, and between me and my three employees, we managed to finish on schedule with just enough time to go home and get changed before leaving for the two-hour drive to Raleigh. I was a nervous wreck the entire trip, praying that I packed everything tightly enough in the back of my SUV and the other cars so that nothing would get ruined on the way here. And by some miracle, even through the rain, it all worked out.

"You're a rockstar, Astrid." Willow grips my shoulders. "You pulled this off and I had no doubt that you would."

"At least someone believed that because it sure wasn't me." My eyes bounce around the room again, but I still don't see the face I'm looking for. And at six foot five, Penn would be hard to miss.

"He'll be here," she whispers, squeezing my upper arms before releasing me.

"I don't know, Willow. We haven't talked since last night, and even that was a short text exchange. I have no idea what happened with him and Dick." I shake my head. "What if it was too much for him?" I say, bringing my nail to my mouth to chew on.

Willow slaps my hand from my mouth. "None of that. Penn wouldn't change his mind, Astrid. I'm sure there's a reason why he's late. He wouldn't miss this. He wouldn't let anyone down, especially you."

"Yeah, I used to think so too before we became a couple and our entire relationship changed. I mean, he won't text or call me back." I stare down at my phone again, looking at the unanswered messages from the past few hours.

"Seriously? We are talking about the same Penn, right?" Willow rolls her eyes at me. "I'm going to let your momentary lapse in sanity slide since you've had a rough few days, but if you don't chill out, I might just have to slap you around a bit."

"I'm sorry. I hope we're not interrupting something." A deep voice I don't recognize says from behind us, and as we both turn to the man standing before us in a completely black tuxedo, my eyes nearly pop out of my head at the sight of him.

"Just pretend like you didn't hear me threatening one of my best friends, and everything will be fine," Willow says through a grin, reaching out to shake the man's hand. I'm still in awe over how mesmerizing he looks—his dirty blonde hair slicked back into place, the light green of his eyes, and then I see the stunning woman with jet black hair standing right beside him, her arm woven through his. "It's good to see you, Wes."

"Likewise, Willow. You look like small-town life has been treating you well."

Willow beams and nods her head. "It has. And it looks like the Raleigh location has been treating you well."

His grin is lethal. "Thanks to your help, of course."

She winks at him. "Don't forget it. And Shayla, you look just as gorgeous as ever." Willow leans forward to kiss the woman on the cheek.

"Same to you, Willow." Her eyes veer around the room. "And the event is already bringing in more donations than we could have dreamed of."

"Well, that's what we like to hear, isn't it?" Willow pulls me forward now. "Wesley and Shayla Morgan, this is Astrid Cooper, the baker who is responsible for your dessert table this evening."

Wes reaches out his hand to shake mine. "Pleasure to meet you. And thank you for venturing all this way to help us out this evening. Willow spoke very highly of your talent."

For a moment, I forget how to form words. "Thank you. It's an honor, truly."

"These cupcakes look so beautiful that I'm almost afraid to eat them," Shayla says through a laugh. "But don't worry, I will. I never turn down sweets.?

I take them both closer to the table and gesture to the display. "Well, the ones on the right are the Ferrero Rocher inspired cupcake we discussed—vanilla cake, hazelnut filling, chocolate ganache, and chopped hazelnuts on the top. And the ones on the left are a strawberry cheesecake flavor—vanilla cake, strawberry filling, cream cheese frosting, and graham cracker dust on top. There's also a layer of graham cracker crust on the bottom."

"My mouth is literally watering right now," Shayla says, wiping at the corners of her lips.

"And the cookies," I continue, holding one up for them to see. "I wanted to bring attention to your hotel, of course. So I replicated your logo on a buttery shortbread cookie that is to die for, in my opinion."

Wes nods his head, a pleased grin on his lips. "Looks just as amazing as you said they would. This set up is incredible and I'm sure it will be a talking point all evening." Someone calls out to him from the other end of the room. He holds a finger up to them, and then turns back to me and Willow. "I hate to end our conversation, but duty calls."

"No problem. We'll be here all night," Willow answers.

"Thank you again, Astrid, for taking the time to contribute to this evening. I hope you find the time and energy worth it."

"My pleasure, Mr. Morgan. Thank you for the opportunity to contribute to such an important event."

With a nod of his head, he leads his wife away and I let go of the breath I had been holding. "Holy shit. They are two of the most beautiful people I've ever seen in real life."

"I know, right? But honestly, they're some of the most down to earth billionaires I've ever met. This benefit is very important to them personally."

"How so?"

Willow motions for me to follow her as we slide up to one of the open bars and she grabs us each a glass of champagne. "Every year the money they raise from this event goes to building another Wings & Wheels facility, like the one Wes built for his younger brother back in their hometown of Santa Barbara."

"What does the facility do?"

"Offers care and assistance to family with children with disabilities. Wes's half-brother is paralyzed from the waist down."

"Oh God. I can't imagine."

"I know, but what they do through these facilities, Astrid..." She shakes her head, tears in her eyes. "It's incredible."

"Well, that makes me even happier to be a part of this event."

She pulls me in for a hug. "And I'm so happy that you're here." When she releases me, she looks around the room. "I lost Dallas. Have you seen him?"

"No." I start searching with her. "But there are so many people in here, I'm not sure how you'll begin to find him."

"Maybe I'll just wait for him to find me." With a wink, she says, "Will you be okay if I go mingle for a bit?"

I push her away. "Of course. Go. I'll catch up with you later."

"You did good, friend," she tells me, blowing me a kiss. "I'm so damn proud of you."

Watching her walk away gives me a moment to breathe, but then my anxiety builds again as I navigate back to my display table. Luckily, there are two servers guarding my cupcakes, making sure no one samples the desserts until after dinner is served. In a matter of minutes, Wes takes the stage at the front of the ballroom, giving his opening speech. The entire room is transfixed on him at the stage, speaking so poignantly about the families that the Wings & Wheels facilities have been able to help this year. But as he holds everyone else captive, my attention is everywhere else.

I'm looking at every entrance, every hallway, every window, looking to see the man I'm waiting for. With each passing minute, I grow more disappointed, wondering how I could have read the situation so wrong.

I thought opening up to him was the right thing to do. He wanted to know the truth, so I gave it to him. But what if it was too much?

Or, what if it was too little too late and I should have been honest from the start?

What if he thought I was too critical of Brandon and he doesn't want to be on the receiving end of that?

What if he decided that I come with too much baggage?

What if all the gossip around town made him question if a relationship with me is worth the headache?

By the time dinner is served and people are starting to mill around again, the servers tell me that it's time to serve dessert. Nodding in agreement, I stand back and watch elegantly dressed people moan and devour my creations. Within minutes, I'm bombarded with questions, business cards go flying out of my hands, and I have events booked for the next few months.

But as excited as I am with how the night has gone and how promising the future looks, I can't stop looking for the one person I want to celebrate with.

And he's not here.

In a room full of people, he's the only one I want to see.

He's my person, and he's...

"Sorry I'm late, baby." Cold hands cradle my face as I'm pulled from a conversation and Penn smashes his lips to mine, claiming me in front of all these people. His tongue dives into my mouth, swirling with my own and part of me should care. Part of me should question if this is professional.

But in this moment, I don't have it in me to care. All I feel is overwhelming relief as his lips take control of mine, slowing down our kiss so that when we part, I'm only slightly breathless.

"Hi," I squeak out as his hands still frame my face.

"Astrid, I'm sorry I wasn't here sooner. I'm so fucking sorry. I just..."

"Dude, you just mauled her in front of all of these people," Dallas says from beside us and Willow grins with glee.

"Yes he did!" she squeals. "It's about time you showed up!"

When Penn releases my face, he stands back and that's when I see the turmoil in his eyes. "Is everything okay?"

"It is now. I had a day, Astrid—one that reminded me that life is messy. And then on the way here, an accident happened right in front of me. I almost was involved but managed to stop in time. But when I saw what happened, I had to stop and I'm glad that I did. It was a mom and her two kids, and I..." His hands tremble as he releases my jaw and pulls me into him.

"Hey, it's okay." I squeeze my arms around him as tightly as I can. "It's okay."

"Were they all right?" Willow asks.

Penn nods. "Yes. They got damn lucky. But I waited with them until the paramedics arrived. Then I got here as fast as I could because I didn't want to miss this. I would have called but I lost my phone in my truck and didn't want to waste time looking for it." He turns back to me. "I couldn't miss your night."

This man. His heart knows no bounds. His desire to be there for others has no limit.

I love him.

I pull him back down to me and kiss him again. I hear murmurs beside us, but I don't let up until I feel like I've told him everything he needs to know with that kiss. And then when we part, he looks to the side and notices our audience. Straightening his spine, he stands tall with his arm around my waist, and asks, "Is everyone enjoying the cupcakes?"

Laughter rings out and more guests come up to talk to us. But I barely have to say a word now. Penn answers for me. He brags about my talent. He makes suggestions on what someone should order if they visit the bakery. He also drops Dallas's restaurant in the mix, bragging about our small town that they should visit when the weather gets warmer.

"And Penn will have a few beautiful rentals available for your stay should you choose," I add in. He glances at me with a lift of his brow. "I've seen the work he's done and they're stunning." A lie, but I don't have to see the house with my own eyes to know what kind of time and care Penn puts into his projects.

"There's only one house right now," he mutters in my ear.

"There may just be two sooner rather than later," I mumble back.

As the conversation dies down and I give out my last business card, Penn grabs my hand and pulls me into a small alcove just outside the ballroom, granting us some privacy.

"You are so incredible," he says, dipping his lips down to mine again, kissing me like he needs me like oxygen.

"I wasn't sure if you were going to show up tonight," I admit on a shaky breath.

He rears back and looks at me confused. "What?"

Fidgeting with the lapels of his jacket, I stare at where my hands are and not into his eyes. "I don't know. I thought maybe the other night was too much for you, that you didn't want…"

He stops me with a press of his finger to my lips. "Don't you dare fucking finish that sentence." Trailing a finger down the side of my face, the corner of his mouth lifts as he speaks again. "I made the mistake of not telling what I was thinking after your revelation, but I'm not going to make that mistake again. And honestly, I needed some time to process." He takes a deep breath and says, "I'm sorry that

Brandon was not the husband you deserve. I'm sorry that I have been making myself sick with guilt for wanting you when you weren't really his anymore to begin with. And I'm sorry that I couldn't tell you this that night, but I'm telling you now." He bends his knees so our eyes are in line. "I promise to be the man you fucking deserve, Astrid. I love you, and I want a life with you, and that means a life that we both want. I want us to be a team because that's what we both need—a person we can count on to be there through the highs and lows, a person that will fight for us until the end of time."

Emotion overwhelms me. "I need you in my life so much that it scares me, Penn. You're the only person who has ever really seen me and values who I am." Shaking my head, I continue. "When you marry someone, people fail to realize you're vowing to love every version of that person—who they were before you, who they are when you say your vows, and who they will become. Brandon and I grew apart, plain and simple. We grew into two different people, and he wasn't the person I wanted a future with anymore. But now, I want that chance with you." His smile grows. "I want to love the friend you were before, the man you are right now, and the partner you will become. I'm in love with you, Penn, and I'm all in. I want to tell and show the world that you're mine."

"It's about fucking time," he grates out, and our smiles mirror one another's.

"I'm sorry that it took me so long to get here."

"I'd wait ten lifetimes if they led me to you, Astrid. You are my person, and I wouldn't trade how we ended up here for anything."

A tear slips from my eye. "I love you," I whisper.

"I love you more," he says before our mouths connect again.

And in the alcove of a hotel, Penn and I find ourselves on the very same page at the very same time, ready to write the rest of our story together.

Chapter Twenty-One

Penn

"Why am I so nervous?" Astrid wrings her hands together, fidgeting as she sits in the passenger seat of my truck. It's Sunday afternoon and we're headed back to her house after spending the night in Raleigh after the benefit.

My chest feels lighter than it has in years, and in its place is something I haven't felt in just as long—*hope*.

Hope for our future. Hope that we get this right. Hope that everyone can just accept that she and I belong together—including Bentley and Lilly.

"Do you honestly think they're going to have a problem with it?" I ask because in my mind, the discussion we're about to have with them should go swimmingly. I'm already a constant in their lives and Astrid and I being together isn't going to change that.

"I don't know. I'm not concerned about Lilly. More about Bentley." She bites on her bottom lip. "I guess my fear in us being together was always in him feeling like you are trying to replace Brandon."

"Believe me, Astrid. That's the last fucking thing that I want to do. Brandon will always be their father, but I want to love them enough for the both of us."

She rests her head on the back of her seat as she stares at me. "You already do, and I love you that much more for it."

"And I love hearing you say that you love me."

When we pull up to her house, Lilly comes barreling out of the front door. "Mommy! Uncle Penn!" She slams into Astrid's legs before she can get fully out of the truck.

"Hi, baby."

"How was your party?" Lilly asks, peering up at her mom.

"It was amazing."

"And did everyone like your cupcakes?"

"They did!"

"That's 'cause they're delicious." She releases her and then rounds the front of the truck to hug me. "Hi, Uncle Penn."

"Hey, Lilly Bear." I lean down and press a kiss to the top of her head. "How was your night?"

"It was so much fun! Grandma and I painted our nails and watched movies and ate popcorn. Bentley even let me put toenail polish on his big toe."

"He did?" Astrid asks.

"Yeah, but then I had to take it right back off. I told him he should leave it. That way his feet wouldn't look so gross, but he said heck no."

Astrid and I share a chuckle as we follow Lilly back into the house.

"Mom?" Astrid calls out when we enter.

Melissa comes into the living room from the hallway. "You're back! How was it?"

"Let's just say that the next six months are going to be extremely busy, but I couldn't have asked for a better outcome. The guests went wild for the cupcakes. People asked me about custom cake orders, and Penn bragged about my muffins to anyone who could listen. I think he used the phrase, 'best on the East Coast.'"

I shrug. "It's easy to brag when it's the truth."

"Well, it sounds like a success then." Melissa grabs her purse and slings it over her shoulder. "I hate to run when you just got here, but I'm meeting the girls at the movie theater."

"Is your phone on vibrate?" Astrid asks her.

She rolls her eyes. "Yes, Mom. I learned my lesson, okay?" With a parting kiss on her cheek and a wave to me, Melissa leaves and then Astrid looks in my direction.

"No time like the present, right?"

"Bentley?" I call out, nodding at her.

"What's up?" he yells back at me from his room.

"Can you come out here really quick, please? Your mom and I want to talk to you about something."

Lilly bounces into the room. "Oh! Is Bentley in trouble?"

"No, Lilly," Astrid admonishes. "You need to be a part of this conversation as well."

Bentley strides into the living room, brushing his hair back from his face. The kid looks more and more like Brandon every day. "What's going on?"

Astrid and I take a seat on the couch next to each other, and Lilly and Bentley sit on the loveseat beside us. I turn to her and prompt her to start, like we discussed.

"So, Penn and I wanted to talk to you about something," she starts, nervousness in her voice.

"Are we in trouble?" Lilly asks.

"No, baby."

"Did someone die?" Bentley asks and the look on his face almost breaks my heart in two. I imagine the last time Astrid sat him down with something to talk about, it was probably to tell him that his father was never going to come home.

Astrid's bottom lip trembles, but she holds it together. "No, Bentley. No one died."

Bentley visibly relaxes. "Okay, then what's going on?"

I squeeze her hand and take the reins. "Your mom and I are in love," I say, waiting for a reaction from either one of them. "And we wanted to let you know."

Wide eyes stare back at me before Lilly exclaims, "Like Anna and Kristoff!"

I search Astrid's face for help. "Frozen," she explains simply.

"Uh, yeah. Exactly like that," I reply, scratching the back of my neck.

Bentley crosses his arms over his chest. "So, are you two like boyfriend and girlfriend now?"

Astrid nods. "We are...Even though those titles sound so juvenile." She wrinkles her nose as she turns to me. "Am I supposed to call you my *boyfriend* now?"

"I guess. Although, I'm not a boy anymore."

She laughs. "Oh believe me, I know."

"Are you guys gonna get married?" Lilly asks, leaning forward in her seat. "And is Uncle Penn going to be our new daddy?"

And just like that, reality slams right back into us. "Well..."

Astrid puts her hand on my thigh, letting me know she's got this one. She turns to her kids and takes in a deep breath. "Look, I know that you both have a lot of questions, but here's what I want you to know. Uncle Penn will never replace your father, okay?" Bentley nods but Lilly still has hearts in her eyes. "And we want you to know that this wasn't something that just happened. Penn and I care about each other a lot. We've been friends for so long, but now we want to be together as more than friends. And we want the four of us to be a family."

Lilly jumps from the couch and claps her hands. "Then you have to get married!"

"One day, Lilly Bear." I wink at her and find Astrid staring at me. "What? You act like that's not where we're headed."

She draws in a shaky breath. "I know, but I thought we could discuss you moving in here first before we talked about marriage," she says, her voice low.

"We can hear you," Bentley says, alerting us to his presence again. I can't get a good read on him, and I wish that I could because I'm sure his mind is racing with all sorts of feelings and questions.

Astrid grimaces and turns back to the kids. "Well, we just wanted to know how you two feel about this," she says as I reach for her hand, waiting on pins and needles. Now that we're actually talking about this, my confidence in their reaction has diminished.

If Bentley's not okay with this, will she want to press pause again? Wait until he can accept the truth? Or will his feelings on the matter prevent us from ever moving forward?

"I'm so happy that Uncle Penn is gonna live with us! Then we can have game night every night!" Lilly yells and then races over to her box of art supplies in the corner of the room before we can correct her. "But that means we have to fix something now." She runs over to the vase sitting by the front door, rips off the sign and scribbles something on it, then tapes it back on. "There."

As soon as she stands back, I can see the addition she made to the Kisses from Daddy jar—"And Uncle Penn."

Fuck. I think there's something in my eye.

Astrid's bottom lip trembles again. "I think that's a great idea, Lilly."

Lilly turns around and runs over to me, throwing herself into my arms. "I love you, Uncle Penn. And if you love Mommy, then I think that's awesome." She stays in my arms as Bentley stands from the couch and walks over to us.

He reaches out his hand to me, waiting for me to shake it. And I do. "I know that you make my mom happy, and you're already here all the time, so I guess it's not horrible if you become a part of our family too."

My lips lift. "Thanks, Bentley."

"But if you two kiss in front of me, I will leave the room."

Astrid laughs. "We'll try to keep the kissing to a minimum."

"I don't agree to that," I say. "I've waited a long time to kiss you."

"Kissing is gross," Lilly says, lifting her head from my shoulder.

"But Anna and Kristoff do it," I argue.

"Yeah, but..." Lilly contemplates her reply, but Bentley cuts her off before she can speak, his voice low.

"I miss my dad. I always will. But I'm glad that we have you, Uncle Penn." The emotion in his voice almost makes me break, but I manage to hold it together.

With Lilly still wrapped around me, I stand and pull him into my chest. "I miss him too. But I think he'd be happy knowing that we're all together."

Bentley nods his head against my stomach. "Yeah, I think so too."

***

"Woo! Go Lilly!" Bentley shouts beside me and Astrid, cheering for his sister as she takes her final bow after her dance recital. Grady and Melissa are in the row beside us. We've been watching young girls twirl around in tutus for almost two hours, so my cheers are mostly for the fact that this event is finally over—although of course I reveled in watching my Lilly Bear dance around.

Fuck, I love that little girl.

As the crowd disperses, Astrid heads behind the stage to collect Lilly and her things, so Bentley, Grady, Melissa, and I make our way through the auditorium to meet them outside.

When Lilly sees me, she runs up to me just like any other time and I pull her into my arms enthusiastically. "You did such a good job, Lilly Bear."

"Thank you. I tried really hard."

I lean back and stare into her dark green eyes, the same ones her mother has. One day, she's going to break so many hearts, and I can't wait to be the one to chase off any boys who don't understand how a woman like her is supposed to be treated. "I could tell. You were amazing."

Bentley comes up to us and hands her the bouquet of flowers we purchased before the show. "You rocked it, Lilly."

"Thanks, B." She hugs him now as Astrid snaps pictures of them, and then she asks an innocent bystander to take a picture of all six of us.

It's moments like these that will still take some time getting used to—not because I don't have pictures with the three of them already—but now these pictures have a new meaning.

They're pictures of the four of us as a family, Astrid and I as a team, two people who love each other and are creating a life together.

I'm moving into her house this week before Christmas. I would have done it sooner, but as of yesterday I'm no longer an employee of Catch & Release or Carrington Cove Hardware Store, so now I finally have the time to do it.

As soon as I'm done with my rental house, my old house will be next. Astrid was right. There will be two homes to rent out next year, and if things work out well, I'll be adding a third by the spring. Pam at Cove Reality has been keeping me in the loop of small places that would work well for tourists.

In the meantime, Sheppard Contracting Services is officially up and running. My business cards just came in the mail yesterday, and my licensing is complete. I'm purchasing a new truck with better equipment to aid me in jobs, and my phone has already been blowing up with people needing items taken care of before the holidays.

But today was not about work—for once in my life.

Today was about my family—showing up for the little girl who danced with as much heart as she possesses. And tonight, we're going to celebrate her accomplishments as a family.

"Is it time for ice cream yet?" Lilly asks, staring up at me.

"Dinner first. Then ice cream," Astrid answers.

"Do we have to eat dinner first?" she continues, ignoring her mother.

"You heard what your mom said, Lilly." Being stern with this kid isn't going to get any easier, but Astrid assured me that if I'm going to slip into the role of dad instead of fun uncle, I have to be rule enforcer sometimes.

It's still a work in progress.

"Fine." With a pout on her lips, she begins marching toward Astrid's car and the three of us follow. "Can we at least go to Perky's Pizza then so we can play games?"

Astrid glances over at me. "Whatever you want, Lilly."

I arch a brow at her. "And you say I'm the pushover."

She laughs and shakes her head at me, biting that bottom lip of hers. "I never said that."

"Can you blame me though? I mean, one flash of that pout and those big green eyes, and she's hard to say no to."

"You've got to be strong, Penn."

I pull her into me as we arrive at the car. "I can't, babe. It's like staring at a smaller version of you. And you know damn well that I'm powerless when it comes to the women in this family."

Peering up at me, she says, "I guess there are worse problems to have then."

"Yeah. I could not have you in my life at all."

***

"This place is packed tonight." Astrid looks around us as we sit in our booth at Catch & Release. For two people who used to work here, being customers instead of behind the bar is making us both on edge.

Astrid bites her bottom lip. "I know. I want to go refill drinks and start bussing tables so bad."

Reaching across the table, I chuckle as I take her hand in mine and squeeze. "That's not our job anymore, babe."

"I know," she sighs. "But it's instinct. Old habits die hard."

"Believe me. I get it. But let's just focus on our date tonight, okay?"

"I would love to, but I can't help but feel like everyone is staring at us."

Yeah, that's been happening a lot lately. We didn't make an official announcement because who the fuck does that anyway, but I sure as hell haven't been shy about showing public displays of affection in the last week or so. Hell, half the town knew about us already because of Dick's fat mouth, but he took my threat to heart and hasn't shown his face around the bakery since then. Ultimately, I don't give a shit about what people think, but it's clear as day that we're a topic of conversation still. Christmas is in two days, and even though Astrid and I have been together for far longer than the past week, people around town are still getting used to the development.

My eyes dart around the room. "It must be my new flannel. Everyone is probably wondering where I got it."

She swats at me across the table. "Don't be sassy, Penn."

"Well, I think we both know why they're looking over here, baby." I lean in closer to her. "But I thought that we agreed to ignore the gossip?"

She stares down at our intertwined hands. "I know. It's just...uncomfortable still, I guess."

Hating seeing her retreat into herself, especially because I know how hard she fought to be okay with this thing between us, I decide to put a stop to the stares and whispers once and for all.

I stand from my side of the booth, put my fingers between my lips, and whistle loud enough to bring the entire restaurant to a dead silence.

"Penn! What are you doing?" she whispers up at me, trying to pull me by the hand back down into my seat.

"Good evening, everyone," I say, ignoring her and removing my hand from hers. "I hope you're all having a nice night." Murmurs fill the air. "My night is shaping up to be a fantastic one, but before I get on with it, I think it's time to set the record straight about something." I pull her up to stand next to me and spin her around so she can see everyone as well. "You might be wondering if something is going on between the two of us." Astrid covers her face with her hands, but I pull them away and spin her around so she's facing me now. With my hand on her cheek, I look into her eyes as I say, "The truth is, I've been in love with this woman for far too long. And just recently, she finally decided to give me the chance to prove that I am the man that she deserves. Life is short, true love is rare, and there's nothing wrong with going after what your heart desires. So, even though everyone might have their opinions about our relationship, I'd just like to ask you to keep them to yourself—because the only thing that matters is that I love her, and she loves me, and one day this woman will be my wife."

"It's about damn time, Penn!" someone calls out from the back of the restaurant, making everyone laugh and cheer.

"Kiss her then!" another voice shouts.

"What do you think, Astrid? Think we can seal the deal in front of everyone and leave no doubt at all that this is real?" I whisper against her lips.

Her smile is blinding as I tip her back, holding her to my chest. "I think after a speech like that, a kiss is required."

***

"I'm kind of surprised that blindfolds are one of your kinks, but I really wanted to do this to you first before you did it to me."

Astrid laughs as she guides me by the hand. The black fabric covering my eyes is so dark that no sliver of light can peek through. "Well, maybe we can turn the tables later after your surprise."

"I already had plans to devour you, but this will just heighten the entire experience."

The squeak of a door tells me we have to be close to our destination, and the longer I can't see where I'm at, the more anxious I feel.

"I'm gonna hold you to that promise, Penn."

"You won't have to. It's happening."

Astrid takes in a deep breath and then blows it out as she stands next to me. I'm aware of every noise she makes right now, especially since I've lost one of my senses. "Okay. So, we're here and now that I'm seeing your surprise, I'm not sure how I feel about this anymore."

Squeezing her hand in mine, I reply, "Baby, I'm sure I'm going to love it."

"I hope so." She reaches up and unties the sash from my eyes. Blinking away the fuzziness in my sight, I wait for things to clear up before trying to process what I'm seeing.

Lined out in front of me, in my rental home that is still a work in progress, are several frames of pictures developed in sepia tones. The images look familiar, most are outside around Carrington Cove it looks like, but I can't quite place them. "You got me pictures?" I ask, turning to find Astrid standing next to me, biting her lip.

"I did."

"Oh. Well...thank you." I'm not sure what else to say, but Astrid luckily chimes in.

"When we were talking about your business during our getaway and how you wanted to think about branding and other stuff, I had an idea." She steps closer to the frames and holds one up in front of me. "Do you recognize this?"

Staring at the image before me, it takes a minute before it clicks. "Is that the Hansen's deck that I built?"

She nods. "Yup." Placing the picture back down on the ground, she grabs the next one. "And this?"

"Mr. Hobb's carport?"

Another nod. "Right again." My eyes move through the pictures now, recalling each of these projects that I completed with my own two hands, landing on one of Willow's house that I renovated over the summer, and then the last picture that Astrid holds out in front of me. "But this one is my favorite."

I reach out and touch the frame of the ramp at the Veteran's Center that I built with my father all those years ago. "Damn, Astrid." Memories flood my mind, and the sting of tears comes on, but I hold it together. "What are all of these for, baby?"

"I thought they'd be beautiful artwork to display in your rental houses, Penn," she says, placing the last frame on the ground before staring back up at me. "Images of all you've accomplished before this venture, so you never forget where you came from and where you're at now."

Fuck. If I didn't love this woman already, this would have sealed the deal.

"I—I don't know what to say."

"I think guests will love them too." She stares back at the photos with admiration. "Your sister is quite the photographer, so they showcase her talent too."

"You had Hazel take these?"

"Obviously. I can't capture a picture like that. Hell, I still end up with my finger in pictures on my phone sometimes."

Laughing, I pull her into my chest. "Fuck, I'm in awe." Nuzzling her neck, I say, "Thank you."

"You're welcome. You deserve a reminder that who you were is part of who you are now, and I will be here supporting you and cheering you on just like you've done for me."

"I love you," I whisper against her lips.

"I love you more." Our mouths meet in an intense kiss that makes me feel like I'm living in a fucking dream—because that's what this is—my dream job, my dream girl, and my dream life.

Over the past three years, I've wondered if I'd ever get here or if these feelings and desires were just meant to be ideas that died by my own fear and stubbornness. But Astrid has helped me see that it's okay to be selfish, it's courageous to chase what I want out of my life, and the thing I wanted most of all—was her.

"Just let me know when it's time to decorate because I have some ideas for that too," she says, smiling up at me.

"I don't deserve you," I tell her, waiting for someone to pinch me.

But she cups my face and says, "Yes, you do, Penn. We deserve each other. And now we get to love each other for the rest of our lives."

Chapter Twenty-Two

Astrid

Three Months Later

"Happy birthday, dear Lilly! Happy birthday to you!" My eight-year-old girl blows the candles out on her cake as our family and friends clap and cheer.

Eight. How on earth is my daughter eight already?

"Is it time for presents now?" she turns to me, the impatience in her body amplifying the longer I make her wait.

"Yes, baby. You can open presents now."

"Yay!" She hops off her chair at the table and all the other kids in attendance follow her to the living room.

"Mom, can you make sure to take pictures of her, please? I'm going to slice up this cake."

"Sure, Astrid. Although it's a shame you're about to cut into that beautiful cake." My mom steps into the living room, her phone poised up, ready to take pictures as Lilly reads the card on the first present.

"How long did that cake take you to make?" Penn comes up behind me, wrapping his arms around my waist from behind. And I don't think I'll ever get tired of this feeling—safety, warmth, and lust. All he has to do is touch me and my body wants him.

"About four hours."

"And now everyone is going to eat it?"

"Yup."

"How does that not make you irrationally angry?" he asks, a teasing lilt to his voice.

"Because the best part of making something like this is watching people taste it and enjoy it." I pick up the knife from the counter and cut into the Frozen themed cake that my daughter requested for her birthday. Elsa's castle stands tall on the top layer, with all the characters positioned in front of it. The icing is sky blue to mimic ice, and the crystal details make it shimmer when the light hits it.

It truly is beautiful, but I know that it tastes amazing too.

Penn's lips find my neck. "Funny. I was just thinking about how *I* want to taste *you*."

"Penn…" I groan as my eyes close, which probably isn't smart considering I'm holding a knife.

"Hey. No hanky panky around the cake." Willow enters the kitchen, interrupting our moment.

Penn lifts his head. "Who the hell calls it hanky panky?"

Willow shrugs. "I don't know. That's just the word that came to my mind."

"That's fair," I say, pointing the knife in her direction before I go back to slicing the cake. Laughter and screams filter out from the living room as Lilly holds up her latest present and tissue paper goes flying everywhere.

"Penn, could you…"

"I'm on it, babe." He kisses me on the cheek, heads to the pantry to grab a trash bag, and then moves into the living room to start picking up the mess that Lilly is making with wrapping paper and bags.

"Look at you. You speak and he moves."

I roll my eyes at Willow. "No, we're a team. He helps. I help." I sigh wistfully. "It's amazing."

"And how's it been living together? You still think all of his weird quirks are cute?"

Laughing, I reply, "There's been a few bumps here and there, a little tiff or two. But the make-up sex is worth it."

Willow grins. "Can't argue with you there. When Dallas and I fight, it actually makes me horny now."

"Uh, did I walk in on a conversation that I shouldn't be a part of?"

When I look to my left, my brother is standing there, his hair standing up on all ends like he's been yanking on it all morning. "Dear lord, did you poke your finger in a light socket?" I ask him.

"What?" He tries to glance up, but quickly realizes that you can't see the top of your own head. He moves to pat down his hair and then lets out a breath so strong he might blow over Elsa's ice castle. "No. It's just been a long weekend."

"What happened?" I ask, moving to serve slices of cake onto the plates.

"The garage got broken into Friday night."

"Oh my God, Grady! Is it bad?"

Penn comes rushing over, concerned by my outburst. "What? Is everything okay?"

"Yes. No." I turn back to my brother. "The garage was broken into? Is everything okay?"

Dallas steps up next to Willow. "Dude, I fucking heard someone talking about that at the post office this morning. Did you catch them?"

Grady rubs the back of his neck. "Uh, yeah. I caught one of them. It was some kids. Three teenagers. Two of them escaped, but we got their names from the kid I caught."

I shake my head. "Damn. I swear, if Bentley ever did something like that, I'd make sure he didn't see daylight for a very long time."

"Yeah, well I think his mom had the same idea."

"You met his mom?" Penn asks.

"The alarm triggered a call to the cops, I kept the kid contained until they got there, but because he was a minor, they called his mom to come pick him up since I hadn't decided if I'm going to press charges or not."

"Why wouldn't you? He smashed in the hood of the Nova," Dallas says. "At least that's what I heard."

Penn winces. "Shit. The Nova?"

"I don't give a fuck about the car right now," Grady grumbles, his head hanging low.

I put my arm on his back, rubbing in circles. "Grady, what's going on? I feel like you're not just upset because of the car."

When his head lifts, I see the uncertainty in his eyes, the anguish on his face, and then he says something I never saw coming.

"The kid's mom is a woman I slept with a few months ago, right around Christmas. And when she came to talk to me yesterday about how to make this right, she also dropped a bomb on me that I wasn't expecting." He looks around at me, Penn, Dallas, and Willow. "It looks like I'm about to be a dad."

THE END

***

Not ready to say goodbye to Penn and Astrid? Download a special bonus epilogue here and get a glimpse at their future!

***

Curious about Grady's story? Don't worry! He will make you fall hard in Sometimes You Fall, coming January of 2025!

And are you curious about Wesley Morgan, the hotel owner, and his wife, Shayla? They have a story as well in My Unexpected Serenity.

Also By Harlow James

Carrington Cove Series
Somewhere You Belong (Dallas and Willow)
Someone You Deserve (Penn and Astrid)
Sometimes You Fall (Grady and Scottie)
Someday You Learn (Parker and Cashlynn)
Somehow You Knew (Gage and Hazel)

***

The Ladies Who Brunch (rom-coms with a ton of spice)
Never Say Never (Charlotte and Damien)
No One Else (Amelia and Ethan)
Now's The Time (Penelope and Maddox)
Not As Planned (Noelle and Grant)
Nice Guys Still Finish (Jeffrey and Ariel)

***

The Newberry Springs (Gibson Brothers) Series
Everything to Lose (Wyatt & Kelsea)
Everything He Couldn't (Walker & Evelyn)
Everything But You (Forrest & Shauna)

***

The California Billionaires Series (rom coms with heart and heat)
My Unexpected Serenity (Wes and Shayla)
My Unexpected Vow (Hayes and Waverly)
My Unexpected Family (Silas and Chloe)

***

The Emerson Falls Series (smalltown romance with a found family friend group)
Tangled (Kane & Olivia)
Enticed (Cooper & Clara)
Captivated (Cash and Piper)
Revived (Luke and Rachel)
Devoted (Brooks and Jess)

Lost and Found in Copper Ridge
A holiday romance in which two people book a stay in a cabin for the same amount of time thanks to a serendipitous $5 bill.

Guilty as Charged
An intense opposites attract standalone that will melt your kindle. He's an ex-con construction worker. She's a lawyer looking for passion.

McKenzie's Turn to Fall
A holiday romance where a romance author falls for her neighborhood butcher.

Acknowledgements

The amount of messages I got after people finished Somewhere You Belong, begging for Penn and Astrid's story, was unreal! BUT it made me even more excited for you to get their book, and I hope it didn't disappoint.

The topics in their story were difficult to navigate—a widow who wasn't utterly in love with her husband when he died, but I knew that Penn was the man that she deserved, so I gave Astrid what she needed. These two had been in fictional limbo for about three years, so it felt amazing to finally give them their story. AND while I was plotting out the series, I felt in my bones that Grady, Astrid's brother, needed a book too, so his is next!

It's been a minute since I've written a surprise pregnancy book, and TRUST ME, Grady does NOT disappoint! In fact, when I finished his book, I told my betas that he might give Walker Gibson a run for his money. Don't say I didn't warn you.

To my husband: Thank you for believing in me and cheering me on every step of the way. Thank you for traveling with me, investing in my success, and being my person, my best friend, and the man that inspires all of my book boyfriends, and my official Book Bitch. I love you.

To my beta readers: Keely, Emily, Kelly, and Carolina: you four are the best voices I have in my corner. Each of you gives me the advice, feedback, and support that I need in your own way. I'm so grateful to have the four of you on my team still after all this time. I love you all and appreciate you more than you'll ever know.

To Kait, my P.A.: Hiring you has been one of the best decisions I've ever made. Your friendship and professional support have helped me so much this year. Thank you for being my newest cheerleader!

To Jess, my social media manager: You have single-handedly made my life better! I have so much more time to focus on writing and other aspects of my business thanks to you. Your time and creativity is appreciated SO much. Thank you from the bottom of my heart for doing what you do for me.

And to my readers: thank you for supporting me, whether you've been here since the beginning, or you're brand new. I LOVE this hobby turned business of mine. It's an amazing feeling to be able to create art for someone to enjoy and forming a relationship from that. I never take my readers for granted and know that there would be no Harlow James without you.

So thank you for supporting a wife and mom who found a hobby that she loves.

Connect with Harlow James

Follow me on Amazon

Follow me on Instagram

Follow me on Facebook

Join my Facebook Group: https://www.facebook.com/groups/494991441142710/

Follow me on Goodreads

Follow me on Book Bub

Subscribe to my Newsletter for Updates on New Releases and Giveaways

Website

Printed in Great Britain
by Amazon